ROSE ISLAND

ROSE ISLAND

A TEAM Novel

ZANDER HATCH

IZZARD INK
PUBLISHING®

IZZARD INK PUBLISHING
www.izzardink.com

Library of Congress Cataloging-in-Publication Data

Names: Hatch, Zander, author.
Title: Rose Island : a Team novel / Zander Hatch.
Description: First edition. | Salt Lake City : Izzard Ink Publishing, 2024.
Identifiers: LCCN 2024029924 (print) | LCCN 2024029925 (ebook) |
ISBN 9781642281101 (hardback) | ISBN 9781642281118 (paperback) |
ISBN 9781642281095 (ebook) | ISBN 9781642281217
Subjects: LCGFT: Novels. | Action and adventure fiction.
Classification: LCC PS3608.A78948 2024 (print) |
LCC PS3608.A78948 2024 (ebook) |
DDC 813/.6–dc23/eng/20240716
LC record available at https://lccn.loc.gov/2024029924
LC ebook record available at https://lccn.loc.gov/2024029925

Designed by Daniel Lagin
Cover Design by Andrea Ho
Cover Images by Andea Ho

First Edition
Contact the author at info@izzardink.com

Hardback ISBN: 978-1-64228-110-1
Paperback ISBN: 978-1-64228-111-8
eBook ISBN: 978-1-64228-109-5
Audiobook: 978-1-64228-121-7

For Jerry

Luke Skywalker speaking to Emperor Palpatine.
"Your overconfidence is your weakness."

Emperor Palpatine responds with,
"Your faith in your friends is yours."

—*STAR WARS: EPISODE VI RETURN OF THE JEDI* (1983)

There lies within the American government an organization dedicated to making the world a better place.

Its origins: no one can say for certain.

They report only to the president; the only elected government official to know of their existence.

Its budget and resources; pooled from across the nation in secrecy. Recruiting men and women from all military branches and most three-letter agencies, they carry out overt and covert operations; domestically and overseas.

They operate in the shadows and are shrouded in secrecy.

In short, they fight the unseen battles to ensure life as we know it goes on.

They are known as . . .

The Team.

ROSE ISLAND

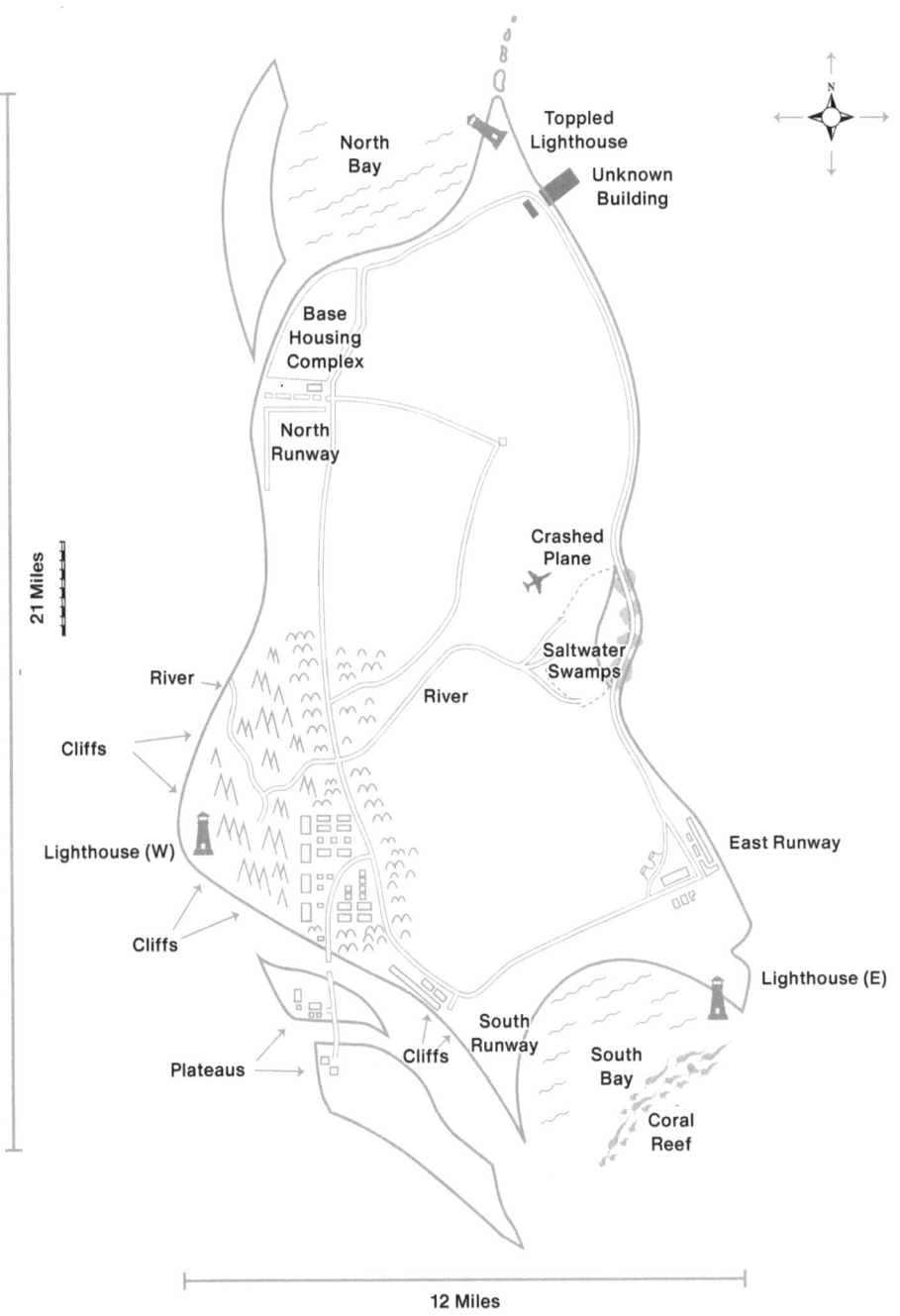

THE METAL FLOOR BENEATH HER TILTED AND SHE COULD FEEL HERSELF being sucked deeper into her seat as the V-22 Osprey banked to the left.

Madison Oakley was shrouded in darkness and the smell of diesel fuel was mildly nauseating. The communication headset clamped down over her ears only reduced the deafening sound of the rotors.

She glanced down the troop compartment of the Osprey. Fourteen United States Marines sat in silence, a few of them even sleeping. They were dressed in woodland camouflage fatigues, wore flak vests and ballistic helmets with dual tube night vision optics, and were armed with suppressed Colt M4 rifles.

Madi exhaled deeply and leaned her head back against the wall, thinking back to how she came to be in an Osprey flying out over the Atlantic Ocean to an island that didn't officially exist.

She had arrived in Washington, D.C., on the red-eye flight from London, having spent the last eight months there on assignment. After sleeping in, she now sipped coffee in her Georgetown apartment, staring at her cell phone laying on the counter.

Standing at five feet, seven inches, Madi was slim and petite with a body that caused men to turn their heads. Her blonde hair almost touched her shoulders and along with her black roots and a small stud nose piercing, she gave off a punk girl look. With bright-blue eyes, strong eyebrows, and a button nose, Madi hardly looked like a Marine or a clandestine operative.

Before she was recruited as an operative for the secret government agency known as The Team, Madi had been a captain in the Marine Corps specializing in counterintelligence operations. Running missions throughout the Middle East, going after Al-Qaeda and the Taliban, she had been instrumental in establishing positive relationships with the locals—both Iraqis and Afghanis—and preventing further loss of life. When the opportunity came to take her skillset to the next level, she lunged at it with enthusiasm. With her military career and clandestine lifestyle, Madi hadn't had much time for a personal life and even less time to put into a romantic relationship.

There was, however, one man. They had known each other for years and had gone on a few dates, but their jobs always came first and seemed to pull them apart. It was now why she stared at her phone, contemplating if she should call or if their jobs would—once again—come between them.

Lost deep in thought, she was startled when it began to ring.

She answered before the second ring. "Oakley."

A female voice said, "We'd like to speak to you about your car's extended warranty."

"Now isn't the best time," Madi responded coolly.

"Would Thursday work?"

"Sunday would be better."

"The twenty-second?"

"The eighteenth."

A pause. "Go secure."

Madi went to her phone screen, opened an encryption app and waited for the line to be encrypted.

"I'm secure."

"Stand by."

A few seconds passed before another female voice said, "Madi Oakley, I know you just got back, but we have a situation."

She recognized the voice as Lisa Warner's, The Team's North American Regional Commander.

"Over the last twenty-four hours, our analysts have picked up highly encrypted military-grade radio chatter coming out of somewhere strange."

As Lisa spoke, Madi downed the rest of her coffee, got up, and put the mug in the sink.

"Strange? How so, ma'am?"

"It seems to be originating from an island in the Atlantic. Thing is, this island doesn't exist on any maps and we can't find any record of it on our databases."

"Nothing at all?"

"Our search revealed that there's hard copy files of this island located at the Pentagon; I have an operative there now, as we speak."

"What do you need from me?"

"I need you at Andrews Air Force base within the hour, you're gonna catch a flight to the USS *Iwo Jima* and take a squad of Marines to investigate."

Goddamnit.

Madi was momentarily shocked, but ultimately not surprised. She had just gotten home and was looking forward to having a few days off before going back to work. Still, *orders are orders.*

"Roger that."

"Prep for a covert insert and expect the worst. If you need any gear, let me know and I'll have it delivered to Andrews for you."

"Will do, ma'am. I'll be on the road shortly."

"One more thing. There's a Category 1 hurricane brewing in the Atlantic. It's forecast to increase in size and strength before making landfall on this island in about forty-eight hours, so don't take too long."

Madi nodded to herself and thought, *great.* "Oakley out."

Madi's stomach lurched as the Osprey shook and she sat up straight, slightly alarmed.

Hurricane Taylor, as it was called, was now a Category 2 storm and was steadily making its way west. It was a few hundred miles away; however, some mild winds and squalls of rain preceded it.

A Marine sitting across from Madi had seen her startled and gave her a thumbs up, *okay?*

Shaking her head yes, Madi returned the thumbs up.

Staff Sergeant Kyle Cunningham nodded.

The platoon sergeant of the Special Mission Platoon, Cunningham still wasn't sure what to make of this whole ordeal.

His unit, 1st Battalion, 6th Marine Regiment, had just deployed on the 26th Marine Expeditionary Unit two weeks ago, and was destined for the Mediterranean Sea to support combat operations in Syria and Libya. Earlier that day, his battalion commander had approached him directly about this mission. He was to select his most trusted squad and be prepared to leave later that day, destination unknown.

Cunningham had spoken very little with the woman sitting across from her. She had shown him satellite imagery of an island they were to fly over and talked about a few landing zones should the need arise. When he asked her what to expect, she simply said, "Be ready for anything."

Madi's voice was in Cunningham's ear, "Special Mission Platoon, what is that?"

Cunningham keyed the push-to-talk device on his flak and spoke loudly into the microphone that hung down from his headset and rested in front of his mouth. "Pretty much whatever the rest of the battalion can't do."

A new voice spoke over the net. "I'm pretty sure any other platoon can run this fuck off taxi service."

Cunningham smiled and gave the bird to other Marines sitting around him, eliciting a string of laughter. "Stow it, Michaels."

Corporal Michaels was the loudmouth of the platoon. Cunningham liked the young Marine who was smart and eager, a quality Cunningham appreciated.

"Anyways," Cunningham continued, "we're essentially the jack-of-all-trades platoon. We can do TRAP missions, VBSS ops, and conduct SSE, things of that nature."

"Seems like I'm in good hands then," Madi responded.

"You are," Cunningham assured her.

With fourteen years of experience and multiple deployments to Iraq and Afghanistan, Cunningham had worked with mysterious individuals a handful of times. His best guess was that she was CIA, but he knew he would never learn the truth.

Never married, Cunningham was two inches shy of six feet and kept his blonde hair cut in the typical Marine fade fashion. His right eye was a shade of light blue, while his left eye was affected by heterochromia, a variation in eye color and very rare. The iris surrounding his pupil was an orange-brown color before shifting into a light blue for the rest of his iris.

He was one of the senior staff sergeants of his battalion and regarded in high esteem by all who worked with him. The young Marines of his platoon looked up to him.

"Ma'am, we have the target location in sight," the voice of the pilot said over their headset. "Six clicks out at our one o'clock."

"Copy," Madi responded as she got out of her seat and made her way to the starboard side hatch.

Flipping her night vision device down over her eyes and powering them on, Madi's world became awash in light blues and whites. She could make out the vague silhouette of the island on the horizon with the help of the ambient light of a half moon.

"I want a full sweep of the island starting in the north and working our way clockwise," Madi commanded.

"You got it."

"Keep it as low as you can."

"Sure thing."

Madi stepped to the side to allow the crew chief to man the .50 caliber heavy machine gun mounted in the doorway.

She leaned in close to the crew chief and yelled, "Condition one!"

The crew chief smiled nervously and nodded. He grabbed the charging handle on the side and cycled the weapon twice, now all he had to do to fire was press the trigger.

Madi made her way to the rear of the Osprey and Cunningham followed her down. They came to the rear where the rear-door gunner stood on the swing-mounted .50 caliber machine gun. He handed them a safety line to clip into their belts and she again told the gunner to go condition one.

With the rear lamp lowered to a 180-degree plane, Madi and Cunningham slowly stepped out and took a knee.

"What exactly are we looking for here?" Cunningham asked.

"Any sign of activity."

Madi felt a slight pit in her stomach as the pilot dropped the Osprey toward the water below and she instinctively reached for a hold on her safety line for comfort.

"Coming up on the island," the pilot announced.

Madi leaned out and looked to her left. They approached from the north and passed the island on its eastern side. Through her night vision device, she spotted a large concrete structure located on the northeastern corner of the island. It protruded into the ocean, and she figured it was some sort of covered dock for boats. They continued south and parallel to a paved two-lane road that ran against the coastline. The interior of the island, as far as Madi observed, was covered in thick forest foliage.

They followed the road south as the coastline began to rise and another structure came into view. A concrete runway adjoined by a few aircraft hangars sat in the dark by the coast, but what lay further to the west made Madi's jaw drop.

"Are those nuclear reactor towers?" Cunningham asked.

Two massive concrete nuclear reactor towers stretched six hundred feet into the sky.

Madi was awestruck. "I think so, yeah."

"What the hell is this place?"

Madi didn't answer and remained silent.

The Osprey turned to the west around the southern end of the island and Madi spotted a lighthouse situated high up on a cliff face. She peered at it closely, but it looked vacant.

As the sound of the helicopter's rotors dissipated, two men covered under a thermal tarp stood up inside their lighthouse perch. They had detected the Osprey twelve kilometers out on their radar and had a view of it through their thermal scope as it dropped in low off to the north.

One of the men said quietly into a radio, "Ospreys coming in low, straight to you."

Madi looked down below at the half-moon-shaped bay with its white sand beach and then the terrain began to rise dramatically to a height of over a hundred feet.

"Got another runway coming up on our northside," the pilot called out.

Madi leaned forward and craned her neck to the side, the wind battering against her. She spotted the runway ahead, this one also adjoined by a couple of hangars. On the roof of one of the hangars, she saw a flash of light that illuminated the entire rooftop.

Before she knew what was happening, the Osprey was in a rapid climb and banking hard to the left.

The sudden turn threw Madi and Cunningham flat on their backs where they grabbed each other for support.

"Fuck!" Cunningham cursed.

Bright flashes caught Madi's attention, and she looked out of the rear of the Osprey to see flares exploding. The pilots had deployed the aircraft's countermeasures.

She hit her push-to-talk. "What's going on?"

The panic-stricken voice of the pilot came back with, "Someone just fired a surface to air missile at us!"

Fear struck Madi.

A lone Osprey in the sky against a weapon system that nearly had a one hundred percent hit ratio.

They were sitting ducks.

The Osprey continued its rapid climb and bank to the left while Madi stared out to the rear. A sudden flash of light washed out her night vision device and she squinted her eyes shut as she felt a wave of heat wash over her.

The aircraft shook violently and suddenly dropped in altitude. Zero gravity took effect and Madi found herself floating in the air, suspended a few feet off the deck next to Cunningham.

The wind was knocked out of them as they slammed into the floor, the Osprey managing to level out. Cunningham had barely managed to take a breath when he felt his weight shift to his side and a knot tightened in his stomach; he had come down on the edge of the ramp and was about to roll out of the bird!

Madi reached out and grabbed his plate carrier, arresting his fall.

Looking toward the cockpit, Madi saw that the rear-door gunner was lying face-down on the floor, his face a mess of bloody cuts.

Madi realized what had happened.

The surface to air missile had detonated close with one of the flares, throwing its shrapnel forward where it had struck the Marine. As she felt the Osprey drop in altitude and shake violently, she knew the bird had also caught some shrapnel.

They were going to crash.

Madi moved fast.

Pulling Cunningham up, she yelled into his ear, "Door gunner is hit, help him!"

Cunningham responded with a thumps up while Madi unclipped herself from her safety line and made her way to the cockpit.

Bracing herself on the bulkhead, Madi leaned into the cockpit to see the pilots struggling with the controls.

"Can we make it back to the ship?"

The pilot shook his head. "Not a chance in hell! Port engine is gone and I'm losing the starboard!"

The co-pilot spoke up. "Managed to radio the *Iwo Jima*, let them know we were fired upon!"

"Where you going to try and set us down?"

"As far from that hangar as possible!" the pilot yelled. "We're gonna aim for that first runway we saw, if we don't fall out of the sky first!"

The pilot turned and looked at Madi. "Tell them to brace for impact!"

Madi nodded and turned around to see Cunningham approach her. He leaned in close. "Door gunner is dead!"

Madi had seen people die before and she was sure Cunningham had too, it was part of the job. Still.

"We're going down!" she yelled back. "Brace for impact!"

Cunningham nodded and the two made for their seats, quickly buckling in.

"Gents, listen up!" Cunningham called over his headset. "We took a bad hit, we're going down . . . Brace for impact!"

Half the Marines around Madi let loose a string of obscenities while the other half went pale, blood draining from their faces.

"We're gonna crash, Staff Sergeant?" Corporal Michaels asked, dumbfounded.

Madi looked over at the young Marine, no older than twenty, she guessed, and the first time he or the others had truly faced a life or death situation.

"I'm afraid so, Michaels," Cunningham responded solemnly.

Madi locked eyes with him, and keyed her push-to-talk. "Pilot managed to get a distress signal out. Someone will be coming for us shortly."

Madi paused, knowing The Team would send a search and rescue party for her from their rescue operations branch. She had a pretty good idea of who they would choose to head up the mission.

The Osprey dropped into the tree line and Madi's world went black.

FRANK HENDERSON MOVED FAST, HIS FOOTFALLS ECHOING DOWN THE hallway.

Of average height with salt and pepper hair and matching facial hair, Henderson had a fierce work ethic, little patience for bullshit, and a commanding presence whenever he entered a room.

Formerly a general in the Marine Corps, he was barely one month into his new job as Rescue Operations Branch Commander for the Americas. He was far from inexperienced, however; Henderson had served in the Marine Corps for nearly thirty years and seen combat in Grenada, Somalia, Iraq (both Desert Storm and Iraqi Freedom), and Afghanistan. Previously he had been the region commander of Australia and Oceania. He was already missing the slow operational tempo of the region and the pristine beaches of Sydney.

He walked through a pair of glass doors and threw on a light jacket as he approached a bank of elevators.

The rescue operations branch had been set up because of the time-sensitive nature of such operations; almost every region had its own section. They needed to be able to move fast and focus solely on the mission at hand without having to still run an entire region spread across thousands of miles. They worked with the support of the region commander whose region they were operating in. And when any branch had an active mission on its hands, all requests, such as Team personnel and US military support, were granted immediately without question.

Taking out the ID card that also acted as an entry card, Henderson held it up to the scanner for the elevator. The light blinked red.

"Damn!"

"Hold it, Frank."

Henderson turned to see The Team's North America Region Commander. A few years shy of fifty with her hair tied back into a neat ponytail, Lisa Warner had been a colonel in the Air Force and before that an F-16 fighter pilot with ample combat experience flying missions over Iraq and Kosovo in the 90s.

"Sorry, what?" Henderson asked and pointed at his left ear. Due to injuries sustained in Iraq, he was nearly deaf in his left ear.

Lisa understood and came around to the other side. "You gotta hold the card still for a second."

Henderson held his ID card back an inch from the scanner and the light blinked green. He looked at Lisa and gestured to the technology around them. "We're about one more damned microchip away from Skynet taking over."

Lisa laughed and joined him in the elevator. Henderson hit the button and the elevator zoomed up.

"Have everything you need?" Lisa asked.

"Yeah," Henderson answered. "All assets are being notified as we speak."

Lisa nodded. "All arrangements have been made with the 2nd Fleet Commander and the 26th MEU has been re-tasked, now under your charge."

She paused.

"I just got off the phone with the president."

When Lisa received word that the reconnaissance flight she had sent to the island had taken fire and was going down, she immediately made a call to Henderson, activating the rescue mission. It was only after they had received the hard copy files from the Pentagon that they realized what they had stumbled onto.

Her next call had been to the president.

Lisa continued. "Given the circumstances, she's concerned."

Henderson sniffed a laugh. "With what part? Us or this secret island that doesn't exist?"

"Both," Lisa answered. "She's worried with whatever this island is, clandestine secrets will become exposed and back her and her administration into an awkward corner."

"This ain't my first rodeo, Lisa," Henderson said as he turned and locked eyes with her. "Now tell the president that I didn't make this mess, but I am here to clean it up and I have the best people on it so tell her not to worry her pretty little head."

Lisa grinned. "That's what I told her you'd say."

The elevator came to a stop and the doors opened to an underground parking garage.

"Good luck," Lisa offered.

Henderson nodded. "You too."

He made to leave when Lisa called out to him, "You know the man you picked to run this operation, some consider him to be a loose cannon."

Henderson turned and smiled. "And yet others consider him to be pretty fucking good."

2

ALL IN ALL, JAKE HARPER FELT GOOD. HIS LUNGS BURNED AND HIS CALVES ached as he ran down the sidewalk, but the cool air and light drizzle felt refreshing. He made his way over a low bridge that spanned over a marshy channel, a popular viewpoint to the island's herd of wild ponies.

But the ponies weren't out today, and neither was anyone else as far as Harper had seen. The little vacation town had boarded-up windows and sandbagged doors, preparing for the incoming storm.

Harper stood tall at six feet and kept in great physical shape with a regiment of cardio and weightlifting, his body lean and muscular. His taper-faded dark-brown hair could hang down to his eyes, but was currently tucked under an old Yankees baseball hat. Most women found him attractive with his prominent jawline, tan skin, and deep, piercing green eyes.

Born in a coastal Virginian town to a single mother, Harper had a younger twin sister, Jocelyn. Their mother had been a cardiothoracic surgeon and Jocelyn followed suit, becoming a nurse and working at Walter Reed while still managing to volunteer to non-profits around the world, offering medical care to impoverished countries.

Now in his mid-thirties, Harper had enlisted into the United States Marine Corps upon graduating from high school and been deployed numerous times to combat zones around the world while climbing the enlisted ranks. Seeking more challenging work, he joined the elite United States Marine Forces Special Operations Command, MARSOC. Commonly referred to as Marine Raiders, they were their branch's component to SOCOM (United States Special Operation's Command) and conducted classified missions around the world.

That was before he had been recruited as an operative by the unheard of government entity, The Team.

A Dodge Ram truck pulled up beside Harper and slowed to a stop as the passenger-side window rolled down. Harper glanced over to the woman behind the wheel. She was maybe ten years older, pretty with long brunette hair and big chestnut-colored eyes with a small mole just beside her right eye.

One thing Harper had learned since joining The Team was to never let your guard down, no matter where you were.

He brushed the side of his rain jacket, ready to grab the compact-sized Sig Sauer P365 pistol tucked in his waistband.

"Jake Harper?" the woman asked.

"Depends on who's asking," Harper replied coldly.

The woman didn't answer and held out a phone for him.

Harper waited a few seconds, glancing up and down the road, before stepping forward and grabbing it. "Go for Harper."

"ID code India six one two, yeah, I got it."

Harper dropped his guard and opened the door. "I almost shot you, you know?"

"Your phone was off," the woman said.

"Yeah, I didn't want to be bothered," Harper said as he took a seat and shut the door.

"Some good that did you," the woman said with a smile and turned the truck around. "Kate Wellington."

"What'd we got?" Harper asked.

"Over the last couple of days we've intercepted military-grade encryptions coming out of the Atlantic, from a previously unknown island," Kate began. "Yesterday we sent an operative, along with a squad of Marines from the 26th MEU, to investigate it. At approximately 2300 hours last night, they flew over the island and were fired upon with a surface to air missile."

"Jesus."

"Last radio transmission we got was they were going down somewhere over the east side of the island, since then we haven't heard anything. Our SIGNIT guys suspect a jamming frequency was thrown over the island to prevent any calls from going out."

"You said *previously* unknown island?"

Kate continued as she picked up a tablet. "The only hit we got on this location was that whatever files documented this place were locked deep in the Pentagon; we sent an operative to retrieve them and had them digitized."

Harper took the tablet and read the scanned document.

CHRONOLOGY OF DESIGNATED ZONE, AREA 19

U.S. Navy Outpost Rose Island, Lighthouse Station
Years Active: 1929-1937
U.S. Navy Base Rose Island, Submarine Dry Docks,
Refueling and Repair
Years Active: 1937-1948
U.S. Navy Base (Restricted) Area 19, Research and Weapons
Training Grounds
Codename: Rose Island
Years Active: 1948-1986
U.S. Navy Designated Zone (Restricted, No Access) Area 19,
CBRN Contaminated Zone
Clearance Level: 1-A (EED)
Years Active: 1986-Present

It was a short history of a place called Area 19, in the hands of the Navy since the 1920s and the site of weapons testing during the Cold War. Since then, it appeared to be closed, a site contaminated by a CBRN (Chemical, Biological, Radiological, Nuclear) element. Harper's first thought was that it was an island subjected to nuclear weapons testing.

He also noticed the Clearance Level it held since the 80s; '1-A (EEO)'.
Executive Eyes Only.

It was the highest security clearance in the country, a sitting president was the only person authorized to grant such a classification.

Kate explained: "We didn't know the risk posed at the time when we sent those guys in to investigate."

"What's so secret about this place?"

"No one knows."

"What about the other files?" Harper asked incredulously.

Kate shrugged her shoulders. "All other files were so heavily redacted—blotted lines and charts—they're virtually useless. It's short history and the fact the US government did everything they could at the time to bury it and forget it is all we know."

"Great."

"The Navy is holding a hundred and fifty miles to the northeast and scanning the seas and air for any enemy contacts, as of. . . " Kate checked her watch. ". . . forty-five minutes ago, nothing. So, whoever attacked them was already on that island. A satellite is being re-tasked as we speak and will be over the island in three hours."

"You're the senior operative in charge of this mission, reporting directly to the Head of Rescue Operations who's already en route to the USS *Iwo Jima*. There's a roster of the members that have been assigned to this mission. Plan is to insert tonight via HALO jump."

A high altitude, low opening jump was a common military deployment method to avoid enemy radar and ground fire.

Harper swiped to the right and read the list of names.

TEAM PERSONNEL, MISSION HZ-23
CLASSIFIED (CLEARANCE LEVEL: 6B)

Team Leader: Harper, Jake

Bexley, Jon

Catipon, Tyler

Chambers, Travis

Rider, Derek

Stevens, Nick

Washington, Warren

Wellington, Catherine

Harper knew most of the members listed and had worked with them extensively. Kate, Jon Bexley and Nick Stevens were the only ones he hadn't worked with.

"We got an Osprey waiting for us at Wallops. From there, we'll fly directly to the 26th MEU and meet the rest of the team," Kate added.

Wallops Flight Facility, located just west of Chincoteague Island, was frequently used by NASA as a rocket launch site, but also supported science missions for the US Navy and NOAA.

"The operative that was sent in with the Marines, who was it?" Harper asked.

"Madison Oakley."

Harper's heart skipped a beat and he swallowed hard, hoping Kate hadn't noticed.

"You know her?"

The two had yet to work together on a mission for The Team, but they had run into each other during briefings and training exercises.

"Yeah, I've seen her around."

The truth was they had known each other for years, meeting for the first time while still in the Marines. Once they had discovered they had both been recruited into The Team around the same time, they went on a few meaningless dates until they began to mean something.

Harper set the tablet down and looked over at Kate, "So, is that all?"

"Hurricane Taylor is slated to hit Rose Island dead-on in less than sixteen hours."

"Great," Harper said, deadpan.

Harper ran down the situation one more time in his head.

A time-sensitive mission in a hurricane to a classified island that was occupied by an unknown hostile force to rescue the woman he had feelings for.

"Another day, another dollar," Harper said aloud to himself when things got tough.

And it was *certainly* going to get tough.

3

A LONE OSPREY TOUCHED DOWN ON THE EIGHT-HUNDRED-FOOT-LONG flight deck of the USS *Iwo Jima*. The pilots powered down and Harper and Kate exited via the rear-loading ramp, each carrying a duffel bag. They had stopped at his residence shortly after concluding their brief of the mission. There, Harper grabbed a change of clothes and the gear he would need for the upcoming mission.

On the ride over the Atlantic, Harper found out that Kate had been a lieutenant commander in the Navy as a Human Intelligence Officer for fifteen years and was recruited into The Team five years ago. She had served throughout the Middle East, often operating independently for weeks at time, gathering actionable intelligence through a series of trusted locals that led to multiple wanted terrorists captured or killed.

A Wasp-class landing helicopter dock ship, the *Iwo Jima* was a helicopter carrier. AH-1 Super Cobras, CH-53E Super Stallions, Bell UH-1Y Venoms, AV-8B Harrier jets and a dozen Ospreys were all lined up in neat rows around the flight deck and chained down. She was named after the infamous World War Two battle and the largest ship in the MEU was run by a Navy crew of one thousand sailors and carried sixteen hundred Marines.

Harper took in a deep breath of salty air as he stepped onto the deck and slipped on a pair of Oakleys. With the sway of ship in the waters beneath his feet, it felt good to be back at sea. He had spent ample time at sea aboard Navy ships and had always enjoyed it.

A Marine Expeditionary Unit consisted of a Ground Combat Element, an Aviation Combat Element, a Logistics Combat Element, and a Command Element; spread across three ships. Together their mission was to be ready 24/7 to respond to a wide range of crisis and usually deployed to an area of the world where conflict was likely.

Wearing a t-shirt, both of Harper's arms were covered in American traditional style tattoos down to the wrist, a time-honored tradition of Marines being tattooed. He took a glance up and down the flight deck of the *Iwo Jima* and spotted a man leaning against the bulkhead of the control tower next to the ramp that led down to the hangar bay below.

Harper grinned and strolled over.

Tyler Catipon stood with his similarly tattooed arms outstretched, a big grin on his face.

Half-Filipino, Catipon stood as tall as Harper, had about twenty-five pounds more muscle than him, and kept his hair buzzcut down to his skin. A fellow Marine who had also gone to MARSOC, Catipon had dreamt of being a Marine since he was a kid and loved what he did. Many of those who had worked with him found him to make timely and effective decisions under duress, always keeping a level head despite his sarcastic remarks.

The two bumped fists and then shook hands.

Harper stepped back. "Good to see ya, Brother."

"You too, man, it's been too long," Catipon agreed.

The two were like brothers. They had met early in their Marine Corps careers and had been best friends since.

Before serving together as Marine Raiders, the two rose to Marine Corps legend for their actions in the still highly classified Kronos Incident. Awarded the Bronze Star for their heroism, the citations were kept a secret from the public and there wasn't a Marine who hadn't heard the rumors; something about rogue submarines and countdowns to nuclear missiles being fired. As to whose submarines and nuclear missiles, no one was certain and neither Harper nor Catipon would say.

"You been getting smaller?" Catipon chirped at Harper.

Harper laughed good-naturedly. "Very funny."

Catipon was quickly introduced to Kate before leading them down the ramp. "I'll show you guys to your room. We got a brief in an hour."

The three walked down the ramp leading into a large hangar bay that housed a Super Stallion and Huey helicopter currently under repairs. To transport the aircraft to and from the flight deck, two large openings on opposite sides of the hangar bay opened onto an elevator platform. The two elevators protruded from the ship like a pair of wings. In fact, they were so large they had to be folded inward when the ship traversed through the cramped Panama Canal.

In between the two helicopters under maintenance, a group of Marines had set up a makeshift gym consisting of barbells, sandbags, and kettlebells. Several Marines, wearing only woodland camouflage pants and no shirts, were covered in sweat and purely focused on their workout. As they were led past the gym Harper noticed all the shirtless Marines had one common feature: a tattoo on their shoulder depicting a pirate's curved blade with the word "CUTTHROAT" riding the inside curve of the sword.

Catipon whispered to Harper, "Oh yeah, I forgot to mention, Cutthroat is here."

Harper glanced back at them as they walked past and said unenthusiastically, "Great."

Kate overheard them and asked, "Who's Cutthroat?"

"A Marine Reconnaissance Unit," answered Catipon.

Harper elaborated as they walked through a hatch and down a long passageway. "Recon Unit 16, out of Quantico, Virginia. They are the highest rated Recon Unit in the Corps, very hard to get into. They often work with tier one-rated special operations units from all over the world. And, given the fact they're stationed in Quantico, they get to train with the FBI, CIA, and DEV GRU, also known as Seal Team Six. Hell, they even work with the Secret Service from time to time, accompanying the president overseas as additional security or on Camp David when foreign leaders meet with POTUS there."

"We've run into them a few times before," added Catipon. "They're cruel and very exclusive, some say they're racist. You notice they only had white dudes?"

"No, I didn't," Kate said, shaking her head.

Harper continued as they entered an airlock. "They're commanded by Captain William Brookes, real grade-A dickhead. Back in '09 they were accused of massacring a whole village in Afghanistan, women and children, all to get a local IED bomb-maker to give up intel on explosive caches. The whole village was torched, so there was no evidence to prove it though."

Catipon opened the other end of the airlock and summed it up bluntly. "Highly trained operators, but some *bad* motherfuckers."

After going up two sets of ladder wells and taking a couple turns, they came to an area of the ship dubbed "officer's country" where the quarters of the commissioned officers were located. The deck was even colored a light blue to identify the area.

Catipon rapped his knuckles on a door as he passed and said to Kate, "This is you," and then to Harper as he came to an open door, "And this is us."

Harper poked his head in. The room was small and made for four occupants; two sets of narrow bunk beds on either side. There was a small sink and mirror on the far side next to a door that led to the room's shower and toilet. Resting on the deck were several long rifle cases with the lids open.

"What's up, Harper?" A man resting on one of the bottom racks said, long blonde hair tied back in a ponytail. "Good to see ya."

"You too, Rider."

Derek Rider had been a chief warrant officer in the Army who piloted fast-attack helicopters for the highly respected 160th Special Operations

Aviation Regiment. Dubbed the "Night Stalkers," the 160th specialized in flying at low altitudes and at high speeds, usually at night to insert special operations forces. Rider had flown over a hundred combat missions in Iraq, Afghanistan, Syria, and Pakistan.

Getting up from cleaning his rifle in the middle of the room, a short, stocky man with tree-trunk-sized arms covered in colorful Japanese tattoos came over and shook hands with Harper. "It's been too long, man."

"Chambers, glad you're here."

Travis Chambers held the rank of chief petty officer in the US Navy and had served as a Seal for most of his career. Rotating through several Seal teams, Chambers had seen combat in Iraq and conducted high-risk anti-piracy operations off the Horn of Africa and in the Mediterranean Sea.

Harper stepped into the room while Catipon leaned against the doorframe, staring at something down the hall. Stepping back out, Harper followed his gaze to see Kate walk into her room and talk to her roommates.

"You serious right now, dude?" Harper asked in shock.

"She single?"

Harper just laughed, shook his head, and walked away.

Catipon had a reputation of being a ladies' man and often dated for short periods before moving on, his job always getting in the way of a long-term relationship.

Rider overheard and asked, "He over there looking at the opposite sex again?"

"Oh boy, nothing good ever happens when he does that," Chambers joked.

The whole room erupted in laughter.

Catipon entered the room with his arms open in mock innocence. "I'm just admiring the female figure, no harm in that."

Harper tossed his bag on a rack. "Yeah, just like in Raqqa."

"How was I supposed to know she was an undercover Russian agent," Catipon shot back.

"The fact that she was speaking *Russian* didn't do it for ya?" Harper countered with a grin.

Catipon leaned against his rack as he picked up an expensive Garmin tactical watch from its charger and put it on. "Fuck you, guys, I'm done talking to y'all."

Again, the whole room erupted in laughter.

They spent the next forty-five minutes unloading their gear and catching up on old times before grabbing some coffee from the officers' mess and heading to the briefing room.

Harper, wearing a Carhart hat, sat with feet propped up on the desk and sipped on his coffee as he waited with the rest of his team.

Warren Washington had been attempting to kick the habit of smoking for the past year and popped in a piece of nicotine gum. An imposing figure standing at six feet four inches tall with black skin, he had originally wanted to play professional football before deciding to join the Federal Bureau of Investigation. After getting a degree in Criminal Justice, Washington became a Special Agent and spent the next decade in their Counterterrorism Division, often working overseas. He was currently engaged to be married and was planning his wedding when he had been whisked away to the *Iwo Jima*.

Nick Stevens, whom Harper had never met before, cleaned his glasses as he sat in the back. He was a little standoffish toward the group but, having read his file, Harper knew he was good at his job. Stevens had been an Air Force Special Warfare Airman with the Tactical Air Control Party; commonly abbreviated as TACP. There he directed attack guidance on air and naval strikes and maintained command and control communications, often attached with Seal Teams, Green Berets, and Marines of MARSOC in hotspots around the globe. Stevens was a trained expert in an array of satellite, VHF, and HF communication devices. Harper knew his knowledge in communications would be invaluable on the frequency jammed island.

The door opened and Henderson walked in, trailed by a second man Harper assumed to be Jon Bexley.

Wearing a Washington National's baseball t-shirt, he was of average height and kept his black hair cut short. Bexley had been a former CIA operations officer, in other words, a spy. Academically gifted, Bexley held degrees in Intelligence Analysis and Eurasia Affairs. He had worked for seven years in Eastern Europe and parts of Asia essentially, spying on arms dealers, sex traffickers, and combatting terrorism threats before being recruited into The Team. As a by-product of his profession, Bexley was very good with languages and could speak eight fluently.

"Everyone here?" Henderson asked as he made his way to the head of the table.

"We're up, sir," Harper responded with a thumbs up.

"Gentlemen and lady," Henderson began with a nod to Kate, "time is of the essence so we're going to cut the horse shit."

The group smirked at his bluntness.

"To recap, thirteen hours ago one of ours, Madison Oakley, along with a squad of Marines were fired upon from an enemy force, size unknown. They were investigating encrypted radio transmissions coming from a classified island for reasons unknown that was supposedly vacant for the last thirty years."

Henderson paused before continuing. "Your mission will be to find our people and those Marines."

His eyes surveyed the men and woman in front of him. "This is a no fail mission, understood?"

They all nodded.

"You'll be HALO jumping in, under the cover of darkness. Right now, we can't solidify an extraction plan due to the approaching hurricane, so I need you guys to keep a low profile on the island. We have no idea of the size of our enemy and what they're capable of," Henderson glanced at Harper, "so if you come in contact, beat feet, *expeditiously*."

Harper nodded and repeated, "Expeditiously, yes, sir."

"Smartass," Henderson growled.

Harper grinned.

"This hurricane will *not* be pretty," Henderson added. "I just got off the horn with the National Hurricane Center and they're predicting Taylor will be a Category 4 by the morning."

Catipon raised his hand and said sarcastically, "I don't mind getting wet, sir."

The group laughed and Henderson stepped aside, letting Bexley take the floor.

"As you are all aware, the only thing we know about this island is its short history and due to its classification level given by Reagan, any hope we had of finding anything else out, died with him."

Bexley approached the center of the room and set his phone down on the deck before tapping a button.

"Someone hit the lights, please."

The room went into blackness for a moment before a soft blue light shot up from Bexley's phone. A three-dimensional topographical map on an island seemed to float in the air, suspended a few feet above the deck. The whole thing was about six feet long, two feet wide, and a foot high. Harper noticed it was oriented to the north.

"This is Rose Island," Bexley announced. "NRO got a couple of their KH-13 Crystal spy satellites over the island and, using acoustic sound-waves to penetrate the hurricane's cloud coverage, managed to give us a pretty good picture of the island."

The National Reconnaissance Office fell under the Department of Defense and was tasked with designing and operating America's system of spy satellites. They provided accurate and real-time intelligence to an array of agencies. The KH-13 Crystal was the latest and most advanced spy satellite to date and was still classified to the public.

"Just bigger than the US territory of Guam, I've enhanced some of the key features for briefing purposes, so this isn't to scale but you'll be able to view in scale on your armguards, which are being uploaded right now," Bexley said and pointed over to the eight forearm guards on a table off to the side.

Harper noticed they were ForeTex forearm guards, a model 7, the latest model and designed by the Defense Advanced Research Projects Agency or DARPA. Made of carbon fiber and painted a dark gray, the user slipped their arm through it where it rested comfortably from their wrist to elbow. It featured a four-inch-high-definition LCD touch screen, an encrypted satellite link, and a two-way camera for video calls and taking photos. It also functioned as an open radio platform and could hold up to 128 gigabytes of storage. The forearm guard was water-proof up to a hundred feet and could even withstand 9 mm bullet fire.

They all gathered around the 3D projection and examined the features of Rose Island.

Rose Island was an awkward shape, at twenty-one miles long and at the widest point, twelve miles; it was longer than it was wide.

There were two bays on the island, located at the northern and southern ends. The three lighthouses from the twenties were still there; two to the south on either side and one in the north, although this one lay toppled over to the side; probably caused by a past storm. Located by the northern lighthouse was a huge building resting on the shoreline, its purpose unknown. There were three separate airports on the island, labeled north, east and south. Around the northern airport was a cluster of suburban houses. The southwestern side of the island ended in a hundred-foot cliff and ran up into a mountain range several hundred feet tall. Two rivers ran from the mountain range: one running north and one running east, ending in an area of saltwater swaps on the eastern side of the island. On the southern end of the mountain range, where it gradually turned to rolling hills, was a massive complex comprising of at least two dozen buildings, several large ones protruding from the mountain. To the south of that were two separate islands with sheer cliffs that sat even with the rest of the island. At some point in the past a small road had connected all three islands, but decades of neglect had caused one of the bridges to collapse. Just north of the swamps lay a large airplane with only one wing; the right one missing.

Bexley elaborated. "Looks like a 737, couldn't read the tail number so I looked up reports of 737s disappearing in the Atlantic that were never found, and I think I found it. It's an Atlantic Courier cargo plane out of Atlanta bound for London. It took off in February of `97. It was never heard of nor seen since."

"Until now," Harper murmured and returned his attention back to the map.

Kate's gaze fell upon what rested by the eastern runway. "Nuclear reactor cooling towers?"

"Yes," Bexley replied. "Whatever they were doing there required a lot of power. We don't believe the reactor was ever brought online, because we're not picking up signs of radioactivity."

Harper's eyes narrowed. "The Chernobyl Disaster happened in 86, same year Rose Island shut down."

"Possible Reagan was put off by that and shut the whole thing down."

Finishing off Rose Island was a two-lane road that ran generally around the four corners of the island: connecting all three airports and the complex of two dozen buildings. At one point on the eastern road, bypassing the saltwater swaps, a three-mile section ran across a small group of rocky islands off the mainland essentially making a short causeway. Two roads branched off from the western roadway and led to the center of the island where a single small building rested in a small clearing.

Bexley continued his brief of the island. "The island is covered in a temperate forest biodome. Expect to be wet, *obviously*, and watch for landslides and a significant storm surge along the coasts. It's expected to be pissing rain out there for the next twenty-four hours."

"Any sign of enemy activity?" Catipon asked.

Bexley shook his head. "Since we couldn't get thermal or infrared imaging, we're pretty much blind. We did manage to get a shot of what appeared to be a convoy of vehicles entering one of the hangars at the southern runway."

"What about recent intel chatter? Rose Island come up at all?"

"I reached out to several sources; all came back with zilch."

Catipon leaned in closer to Harper and whispered, "No QRF, no ISR, no intel. This thing has *fucked* written all over it."

"Yeah, no shit."

Harper took a moment to think and then found everyone was looking at him, waiting for the plan. He started pacing around the room. "Any sign of the crashed Osprey?"

"The moisture in the air interfered with the acoustic soundwaves' ability to pick up finer detail but due to their last transponder location before the jamming field went up, I think they went down in between the eastern runway and lighthouse," Bexley answered.

"Damn," Harper said.

"They couldn't have crashed in a worse spot," Chambers noted.

"Bottom of the ocean would've been worse," Catipon said sarcastically.

"Why's that?" Kate asked Chambers.

Chambers explained. "This lighthouse is more than likely where they got spotted from in the first place."

"It's the perfect watch tower; good eyes for miles in any direction. If anyone comes in, they'd be spotted instantly, which is already evident," Rider said.

Washington chimed in. "Probably got thermals, night vision, all sorts of optics up there with them. Not to mention good comms with a direct line to rest of their friends in case of any time-sensitive developments."

Catipon continued. "And we can only assume these guys sent out a team to check out the crash and the eastern runway is perfect jump-off point to do so."

"So, in between the enemy and the ocean, they're trapped," Kate summed up.

"Bottom of the ocean starting to look a lot better," Harper joked to Catipon.

Harper let out a long sigh and crossed his arms, staring at the map. *Is she okay? Where is she?*

He thought back to the last time he had seen her, almost nine months ago now. Then they had been very intimate, and he had been close to telling her how he felt about her, but something had stopped him. It was doubt, Harper realized later, and he hated that, hated having regrets.

Was she even alive still?

Harper pushed those thoughts from his head and readjusted his hat before speaking.

"Alright, here's the plan."

The group listened attentively.

"We're going to break into two teams. Team 1, myself, Catipon, Kate and Bexley. Team 2, Chambers, Rider, Washington, and Stevens. Team 1 is gonna land just northwest of the lighthouse, take it, grab any intel we can and see if we can spot the crash site. If we can't, we'll work our way north and find them. Team 2 is gonna land north of the reactors and recon the eastern runway, clear us a path cause as soon as we find them, we're coming your way. From there we'll head inland away from roads and hopefully the enemy, find a place to hole up, wait for the storm to pass and the calvary to arrive."

Harper examined the group. "Questions, comments, concerns, bitches, moans, gripes or complaints?"

"Too many to name," Catipon said flatly.

Harper smiled. "Great."

"Birds are off the deck at 1900 hours," Henderson informed the group. "Do what you gotta do and I'll see you guys on the flight deck. And try to get some rest, I have a feeling it's going to be a *long* night."

Little did they know that in the vent opening above their heads, a microphone attached to a transmitter sat poised to catch every word of their brief.

4 || ROSE ISLAND
1500 HOURS

THE BRANCHES TORE AT MADI'S CHEEKS AS SHE RAN THROUGH THE forest. She moved fast, a feeling of claustrophobia beginning to consume her.

Their enemy, well-armed and well-coordinated from what they could tell, was closing in fast.

She was surprised that after being awake all night, she wasn't tired and then realized it was nothing but pure adrenaline keeping her awake.

Behind her, Corporal Michaels hefted another Marine over his shoulder. Private Jacobs had twisted his ankle earlier while running and it was slowing them down.

Madi came to halt behind a tree and signaled for the others to stop. They could hear voices in the distance, along with the pouring rain.

"What now?" Michaels asked, panic in his voice.

Madi looked at the two Marines. They were drenched from the rain and covered in mud. Jacobs' eyes were wide with fear, and he was unable to keep his hands from shaking.

Madi assessed their options. Only she and Michaels were still armed with rifles; however, they were down to a magazine each, and Madi had two for her pistol. They were in no state for a firefight.

After crashing, only twelve of the original nineteen people on the Osprey were still alive with three severely injured to the point where they couldn't walk. Thinking fast, Madi suggested the injured be moved as far from the crash site as possible before the people who shot them down showed up. Cunningham agreed. So, Madi and Cunningham along with Michaels and Jacobs remained at the crash site while the others moved east. A squad of heavily armed men arrived later and gunfire was exchanged, forcing the small group to the south. During the mad dash, they had lost Cunningham and feared the worst.

Madi knew they needed a hiding place. She scanned the area around them.

"There," she said quietly and pointed. "Let's move."

Madi helped Jacobs and the three approached a small cliff face with a fissure running down the center. At the bottom was a small cave entrance just wide enough for a person to fit through. Michaels helped Jacobs through while Madi kept watch outside.

"Let's check over here!"

A voice above Madi made her spin and look up. Someone was coming from the top of the cliff.

"Move," Madi mouthed to the others and stepped into the fissure.

Michaels managed to drag Jacobs deeper through the fissure and it opened into a cave that was the size of a living room.

Madi peered up through the crack, drops of water hitting her cheek. She held her breath and remained still, realizing her shuffling could give her away.

She waited and didn't hear anything.

A figure stepped over the crack.

Madi's heartbeat quickened; a man was standing twenty feet above her.

"See anything over there?" the voice of another man called out.

The man above her looked around. "Nah, don't see any—" the man looked down.

Madi could hear the sound of heart beating through the blood rushing by her ears. She prayed the darkness would conceal her.

"Wait a minute!"

The man fished through his pockets for what only Madi could assume was a flashlight and slowly reached down for her Sig Sauer M-18 pistol.

Pulling out a flashlight, the man switched it on and, before he could aim it down into the fissure, it slipped from his grasp and fell straight toward Madi.

Madi pulled her pistol out quick as a whip and aimed it to the sky, drawing a bead on the man through the red dot optic mounted on top.

The flashlight bounced down through the fissure.

"Son of a bitch!" the man cursed.

Madi waited patiently; for the man to recognize her and knowing a gunshot would give away their position.

The flashlight fell to the ground beside Madi, its beam facing away from her and out of the cave entrance.

"I dropped my light!"

The other man's voice responded with, "I'll check it out from down here."

Madi realized the other man was going to approach from the cave entrance at any moment, she was trapped.

Her eyes flicked back and forth from above her to the cave entrance, not sure who would see her first and not sure what to do.

She heard shuffling approaching from outside.

Adrenaline was flooding her system faster than she could process it.

Looking up, she saw the man struggling with something behind him. She squinted and saw a man dressed in woodland fatigues putting the man in a chokehold.

Cunningham.

Madi looked back down to see a man step before her in front of the fissure. Not seeing her in the darkness, he bent down to pick up the flashlight and that's when Madi came down with her knife into the back of the man's neck, severing the spinal cord.

The man died before making a sound and Madi quickly dragged his body into the cave.

A few minutes later, Cunningham joined Madi and his Marines down in the cave proper.

They all took a few moments to catch their breath before speaking.

"Thanks," Madi said to Cunningham.

"Don't mention it."

"Any luck reaching the others?"

Cunningham shook his head and gestured to his radio in a pouch on his flak. "Not shit."

"No luck with mine either," Madi said. "We're being jammed."

"Who the fuck are these people?" Michaels asked.

"No idea," Madi admitted. "Mercenaries, maybe."

"Mercenaries," Michaels repeated, dumbstruck.

Cunningham went to the dead man Madi had drug into the cave and saw that he too wore a similar communications system. A headset was attached to his helmet and a radio with a push to talk was affixed to his flak.

Cunningham took the dead man's radio and removed the cord running to the push to talk, enabling any traffic to come out through the radio's internal speaker.

At first nothing and then a male voice.

"This is O'Neal, anybody got anything?"

The group listened attentively.

"Nothing to the west of the crash site."

"Had a trail leading east, but we lost it in this rain."

The man calling himself O'Neal came back. "Goddamn it, find them!"

A second later, O'Neal said, "Carter, you got anything in the south?"

No one responded.

Cunningham waited apprehensively, hoping the dead man on the ground before him wasn't Carter.

"Carter, you read?"

"Fuck," Cunningham whispered, and then an idea occurred.

He keyed the radio and whispered, "Th-Car," he spoke in incomplete words and paused, "g-noth-in south."

They waited for a response, hoping Cunningham's act of poor radio reception would work.

"Alright, keep looking!" O'Neal said.

Cunningham let out a deep breath and sat back.

"Good thinking, Staff Sergeant," Michaels said.

"We're not out of this yet," Cunningham reminded him and looked at Madi. "How come these guys can talk just fine on their comms?"

"Their radios have to be programmed with a code enabling them to talk," Madi concluded. "I mean what's the point of jamming your enemy's comms if you can't talk too."

"What do we do now?" Michaels asked.

"We can't keep going on as is," Madi said and looked at Cunningham. "We're no good to the rest of your Marines, dead. A rescue team should be arriving shortly; they'll start at the crash site first. We need to wait, link up with them, and then we can find the others. And maybe with a little luck, the hurricane will drive these guys to shelter."

Cunningham felt guilty for doing nothing, knowing his Marines could be getting killed right now, but knew she was right.

"How confident are you in the ability of your people?"

Madi answered truthfully. "They're the best."

A FEW MILES AWAY, WALTER O'NEAL STOOD BEFORE THE CRASHED OSPREY.

In his forties, O'Neal was a bulldozer of man standing over six feet and weighing two hundred and thirty pounds, arms the size of tree trunks, and his chest bulging. He kept the sides of his head shaved and sported a mohawk down the center, wore fingerless gloves, and carried a nickel-plated Desert Eagle chambered in .50 Action Express, the biggest pistol caliber in the world, on both hips.

Years ago, he had been a US Navy Seal before being kicked out for repeated violations of the Navy's code of conduct; having expressed unsavory views toward people of color, women, and religions other than his own. From there he, and a few others who shared the same opinion, had gone into business for themselves; guns for hire.

A man walked up to him and handed him a satellite phone. "O'Neal."

The phone call lasted all of ten seconds, and he finished by saying, "We'll take care of them. See you on the other side, Brother."

O'Neal took in a deep breath and smirked, glancing to the man by his side. "We're gonna have company soon."

"Can you take care of it?" Hunter Carlyle asked.

Known for having a short fuse, O'Neal's nostril's flared in anger and he clenched his fists. He stared daggers at Carlyle.

With brown eyes, black hair and a matching beard, Carlyle was cunning and methodical. Also former military, Carlyle had served in the Joint Special Operations Command tier one unit of Delta Force. Trained in unconventional warfare and information operations, there were rumors that 'Hunter Carlyle' was not even the man's real name.

But he was not a part of O'Neal's mercenary army.

Carlyle's mission was on the island, and he had hired O'Neal and his men to facilitate that. O'Neal didn't trust Carlyle for a second, but he claimed to need his resources and manpower.

Carlyle had twenty of his own men here while O'Neal had nearly a hundred.

"It was not an accusation," Carlyle added coolly. "I just want to ensure it doesn't interfere with our deal."

O'Neal calmed down and smiled without his eyes. "We'll take care of it, and you'll get what you came here for as long as you uphold your end of the bargain."

"The intel is solid," Carlyle assured him. "Everything is in place."

O'Neal nodded.

"They sending more Marines here?" Carlyle inquired.

"Not quite," O'Neal sneered. "But whoever they are will die shortly after they arrive."

O'Neal turned and started barking order at his men, leaving Carlyle alone watching him as he went.

HARPER STARED DOWN AT THE RUSHING WATER AS HE LEANED AGAINST the catwalk railing that wrapped around the ship and just below the flight deck. He steadied himself against the rocking of the ship, it had gradually gotten more noticeable as the storm approached. Looking to the east, he saw the dark and impenetrable storm walls of Hurricane Taylor on the horizon. She looked mean and Harper struggled to grasp the size of her.

Hurricane Taylor had just been classified as a Category 4 hurricane, earlier than predicted, and last measured at over 800 miles in diameter, the fourth largest in the Atlantic's history. After their insert into Rose Island, the entire MEU was to be moved 500 miles north to avoid the storm.

"Jake Harper," said a voice suddenly from behind him.

Harper rolled his eyes, stood up straight, and turned to face the man before him.

"Captain William Brookes," Harper slowly addressed him with annoyance. "I was wondering when you were gonna show your asshole self."

Brookes sniffed a laugh.

The commander of Recon Unit 16 was eyeing Harper up and down, sizing him up. He stood just as tall as Harper and ranged in the same weight. His eyes were almost black they were such a dark shade of brown and he had a sinister-looking scar that ran vertically across the side of his neck and over his jaw.

"Look at you," Brookes said calmly. "All big and bad now. I'm assuming you're working for the agency now."

He was referring to the Central Intelligence Agency. This was a common occurrence for Team operatives since they couldn't reveal who they were with.

Harper grinned, but didn't answer.

"I've seen your crew," Brookes continued. "Bunch of scrawny-looking pussies."

Harper remained silent, eyes narrowing.

"Some woman came aboard yesterday, she with you?" Brookes asked as he took a step closer.

Harper clenched his fists and Brookes noticed, grinning.

"Man, she was hot, the legs on her," Brookes taunted.

"I'm gonna stop you right there, Brookes," Harper said, inching closer to Brookes as he spoke. "It amazes me that you and your platoon of racist douchebags who are jacked up on steroids haven't been put in prison for all of the illegal shit you do." Harper raised his hand and pointed threateningly. "Now, you say one more *fucking* word I'll beat the shit out of you on this flight deck and throw you off this *goddamn* ship."

Brookes' face flashed in anger, his nostrils flaring, and stepped forward, coming within inches of Harper. Harper braced for a fight as he stared unwaveringly at Brookes.

"You wanna do this right here, right now?" Harper asked.

Brookes huffed and puffed, jaw tightening.

"Problem here?" asked a voice breaking the tension.

Neither man turned.

"Last time I checked, I'm still a three-star general in the United States Marine Corps!" Henderson snapped. "So, Captain Brookes, is there a problem here?"

Brookes turned and flashed a fake smile "No, sir, no problem here. Just a couple friends catching up on old times."

Brookes stepped away and made his way back across the flight deck, but not before casting Harper one last look as if to say, *this isn't over.*

Harper looked back out over the ocean as Henderson came up next to him and lit up a cigar. "The last thing we need right now is an all-out brawl on the flight deck before you guys leave."

Harper nodded. "My bad, sir, but that guy is a real dickhead. How the hell has that guy not been arrested yet?"

"You want the official answer or the real answer?"

"Real one."

"Recon Unit 16 is most likely in the back pockets of some very important people in Washington. They do some off-the-record type of dirty shit for the personal gain of corrupt politicians and in turn they're kept out of any investigation that comes their way."

"And let me guess," Harper said. "No one can prove that?"

Henderson blew a puff of smoke. "Bingo."

Harper changed the subject and asked seriously, "What do you make of Rose Island? What do you think happened there?"

Henderson thought for a minute to gather an answer while puffing away at his cigar.

"The 80s were a different time. Reagan was president and he wanted to bring down communism and topple the USSR; it was a race between us and the Russians. Had an old CO back in the day who loved telling stories, mostly to scare us junior officers. Stories about us and the Russians creating all sorts of secret projects. Weapons of mass destruction on a scale never seen before. Chemical and bioweapons with a one hundred percent fatality rate. Satellites carrying nukes that could reach any city on Earth. Experiments on human subjects, the kind of stuff Nazis did, to enhance them, make them faster and stronger. I never really put much thought into them."

He paused, the suspense building.

"But there was this one time. Back in 83, October 27, during the invasion of Grenada. I was still a second lieutenant back then and green as hell. Anyways, we were tasked to rescue a group of American students from a hospital and get them off island. We get to the hospital, it's got some fire damage from the battle, we get the students and as we're making our way out my platoon comes under fire from some Grenada troops. One of them throws a grenade in through a window right in front of me. I take cover in a stairwell that's got fire damage and the grenade goes off. The blast must've weakened some support structures cause next thing I know, the floor beneath me gives and I'm falling. I fell at least twenty feet to what I assumed was the basement level. I look around and I'm in some sort of lab. I can hear my men still engaged with the enemy, so I know I'm on my own for a bit. As I rummage around this burned-out lab in the basement looking for a way out, I find a burned body lying face up in the ash. From the smell, I could tell he's been dead for a couple days. And then I see a second body beneath, but something doesn't look right. I move some of the debris away to get a better look and what I saw still haunts me to this day. There's two bodies and they're *fused* together, back-to-back. Not just melted or stitched together, fucking *fused* together, like they were somehow inside each other. I find a way out, link up with my men and before I could tell them what I saw, we hear over the radio an unscheduled Air Force strike is due on our position in two mikes. We tried to raise them to call it off, but we didn't have time. We got the hell out of there and that hospital, and everything inside of it, disappeared off the face of the Earth in that strike. I never mentioned what I found in my report because I didn't find it relevant, that and the fact I don't think anyone would've believed me. I did do some digging as to who called in that Air Force strike, but couldn't find a record of it anywhere."

Henderson took a long drag from his cigar and exhaled. "So, whenever I hear of some spooky secret shit, I go back to that day in Grenada and imagine that's what it is."

Harper took it all in. He had known Henderson for a long time and didn't take him for one to believe in conspiracy theories and government cover-ups. He believed him.

A moment of silence between the two passed.

"Spooky shit, huh?" Harper joked.

Henderson laughed and nodded. "Spooky shit indeed."

6

THE SOUND OF FINGERS TYPING RAPIDLY ON A KEYBOARD ECHOED through the small room located deep underground. A man sat alone, humming along to music as he listened through a pair of headphones.

A TOC, or Tactical Operations Center, was used for on-going developments for real world operations. Normally manned by a few analysts and technicians who monitored satellite feeds and radio chatter, this one was empty save for one person.

Michael Fasswater took a second pause to take a swig of Red Bull and then went back to work.

With tussled long blonde hair and hazel eyes, Michael Fasswater was an analyst specializing in SIGNIT (signals intelligence) for The Team and extremely devoted to his job. With an IQ of 131 and a photogenic memory, Fasswater was considered one of the best in the trade. He had done similar work for the elusive Defense Intelligence Agency before being recruited.

The DIA is an intelligence agency that collects and analyzes political, economic, industrial, medical, and health intelligence on foreign nations and non-state actors to inform policymakers on their intentions and capabilities. Approximately one-quarter of the intelligence content in the president's daily brief is produced by the DIA.

Fasswater also considered himself a nerd of pop culture; *Star Wars*, *Star Trek*, and the Marvel Cinematic Universe, he loved it all. He wore one of his favorite shirts that read on the front in stenciled lettering, "USS ENTERPRISE NCC-1701."

Frowning, Fasswater leaned back and glanced to the screen next to him, the same document that Harper had looked at earlier detailing the brief history of Rose Island.

Rubbing his lower lip, he said to himself, "What are you?"

That morning, he had been working on verifying reports of an EMP device that had been smuggled out of Syria and into Central America before he had been re-tasked on investigating the mysterious island.

A hand touched his shoulder and he jumped in surprise.

Fasswater turned around to see The Team's North American commander standing before him.

"Ma'am," Fasswater addressed her as he removed his headphones. "Sorry, I didn't hear you."

Lisa nodded and leaned against the desk. "Any luck yet?"

Fasswater signed. "Nothing as to why the island was shut down and covered up, but I found something from when it served as a lighthouse station."

"Let's hear it."

Fasswater leaned forward and opened a tab. A digitized scan of an old newspaper popped up on screen.

"Found this in the archives of a small city library just outside Dover, Delaware," Fasswater began. "Dated October 8, 1932, it's a piece about a cursed island in the Atlantic, it was a weekly thing they did telling old sea stories, I guess. Anyways, this guy Johnathan A Jacobsen, claims to have worked as a lighthouse keeper for the Navy on Rose Island and he says that Rose Island is haunted. Claims to have seen weird occurrences across the island, random lighting storms that came out of nowhere and even ships that would come close to the island and just simply disappear. Said one time he got lost wandering in the forest for hours and when he found the others, they said he was only gone for a few minutes."

Lisa raised a skeptical eyebrow. "Is that so?"

"It's an old newspaper, which I'm surprised I even found, and nearly impossible to validate."

"Any chance this guy is still alive?"

Fasswater shook his head. "Nope, died in the 50s."

"Very well," Lisa said and got up. "Keep at it."

"Will do."

As Lisa grabbed the door handle, she turned back and said, "If you find anything besides scary old stories, let me know immediately."

And then she added, "And stay out of trouble."

Fasswater raised his Red Bull to her, "Wouldn't have it any other way, ma'am."

7

HARPER AND THE OTHERS HAD GATHERED IN THE HANGAR BAY TO stage their gear and conduct checks on their parachutes before rolling them up. The bay was bathed in red light, and they could hear the Ospreys spinning up outside, their pilots running their final checks.

He looked around at his team.

They were dressed in military-style clothing and the body armor of their choice, a perk of being in an unofficial government spy agency. The only standardization amongst them was their rifles that were all chambered in 5.56 mm NATO, their pistols chambered in 9 mm, and the PVS-31 dual tube night vision devices attached to their Kevlar helmets.

Their rifles varied; a 14.5-inch or 13.7-inch barrel, depending on their preference, and had suppressors attached to the end. A red dot or holographic optic, along with a magnifier to acquire targets at greater distance, sat along the top rail while a white light and infrared laser combo were attached further down the rail closer to the suppressor. Their pistols were a mixture of Sig Sauers, Glocks, and Smith & Wessons in different models with a red dot optic mounted on top of the slide and a white light attached forward of the trigger beneath the frame.

With their parachutes strapped to their backs, they all had a drop bag they would attach to their legs before they jumped that carried their packs with food, water, and extra ammunition.

Harper powered on his ForeTex armguard as Catipon walked up to him. "You good?"

"I'm great," Harper smiled, still looking at his armguard. "Let's do this."

"You run into Brookes?"

"Oh yeah," Harper responded and then looked up. "If I see him again, I might fight him right then and there."

Catipon laughed. "I got your back if you do."

He slapped him on the shoulder and walked away.

A knot of nervousness had balled up in Harper's stomach and he could feel the adrenaline starting to flow, a feeling he always got before a mission. He popped in a tablet of Dramamine to ease any queasiness he would feel on the Osprey ride.

A Marine from the Air Wing walked up to them and informed them it was time to go. The group grabbed their drop bags and made their way up the ramp and out to the flight deck.

It was nearly dark outside, save for the taillights of the Ospreys ahead, and they flipped down their night vision devices, powering them on. The wind blew sheets of rain across them, sending a shiver down Harper's spine.

The two Ospreys sitting on the deck before them weren't standard Ospreys. Officially called the MV-22(A), the angel variant Ospreys were specially designed for HALO jumps. With a ceiling limit of 14,000 feet, the standard Osprey couldn't climb high enough to defeat surface to air missile capabilities. The angel variant was twelve feet shorter, four hundred pounds lighter, and had upgraded engines with larger rotors to produce more lift.

Their plan was to climb to 18,000 feet or so, staying below the altitude of where oxygen becomes unbreathable, and jump from there. With a High-Altitude Low-Opening jump it meant they should be undetectable on any radar system and with them jumping during the night, reduce their chances of being spotted from enemy troops on the ground.

The two teams of four boarded their respective aircraft and took their seats. To help further reduce weight, there were no .50 Caliber machine guns mounted and only one Marine acting as the crew chief.

Harper strapped himself in and looked up to see Kate sitting across from him, struggling with her four-point harness. Catipon appeared by her side and helped her.

"Thanks!" Kate called out over the blaring noise of the rotors.

Catipon hit his push-to-talk and said with a smile. "No problem."

Harper rolled his eyes at his attempt to flirt as he took a seat next to Kate.

Harper looked over at Bexley, who already had his head leaned against the wall and his eyes closed, as he reached into the fanny pack wrapped around his waist. Flipping his PVS-31s up, Harper pulled out an old iPod Nano, plugged an aux cord and ran it directly into his push to talk device. Whenever he or someone would transmit over the net, it would override the iPod and he would never miss a transmission. It was something he had discovered as a young Marine and had used it many times since, something to calm his nerves.

Harper waved the iPod at Catipon and smiled, as if it were a luxury he didn't possess.

Catipon laughed and shook his head.

"*Firefly 1-4, you are cleared for takeoff,*" the voice from the bridge sounded over the net.

"Copy, India-Juliet, 1-4 is airborne."

Harper's stomach lurched as the helicopter lifted off the deck and played a song as it did so. The opening to "Burning Love" by Elvis Presley started to play and Harper hummed along.

The Osprey banked to the left and the pilot brought the aircraft around the stern of the *Iwo Jima*, waiting for the other Osprey to follow. Harper always loved the feeling of a helicopter turning, he compared it to a much more enjoyable roller coaster ride.

Henderson watched from the bridge as the pair of helicopters disappeared into the night. "Godspeed."

Flying abreast from one another, the Ospreys thundered a few hundred feet above the waters, rotated their nacelles forward ninety degrees, converting the helicopter into a turboprop aircraft and able to fly at much faster speeds.

Harper continued to sing along as the Osprey flew deeper into the night.

Over the next thirty minutes, they climbed higher in altitude, hitting mild turbulence along the way.

"Five mikes out," the pilots announced over the net.

Harper disconnected his iPod and had just stowed it in his fanny pack when his fingers brushed the metal plate of his seatbelt, a small spark of electricity shocking him.

"Ow," Harper murmured to himself.

The next moment, Harper was blinded as the entire troop compartment was illuminated by a bright flash of light. His body shook as the following thunderclap reverberated through the air and would've deafened him if not for his noise canceling communications headset.

His heartbeat quickened.

"Holy fuck!" Catipon yelled with annoyance.

Bexley sat upright from his slumber. "What the hell was that?"

"I think it was lighting—" Harper started to say.

Another flash illuminated the cargo hold and was quickly followed by a crack of thunder.

The Osprey started to shake violently as gusts of wind buffeted the aircraft. Suddenly, the Osprey went into a sixty-degree dive straight down.

"Shit!" Harper shouted, gripping his shoulder straps tightly and felt as if his stomach touched his throat.

The crew chief lost his footing, smashed his head off the bulkhead, and tumbled down the troop compartment until his safety line went taught.

With a jarring whip, the Osprey mercifully leveled out.

"What the fuck!" Harper cursed and checked his ForeTex. The icon on the map depicting their location was jumping around the map with no explanation.

Harper undid his seatbelt and made his way to the cockpit, checking on the fallen crewmen along the way. He keyed his PTT. "Bexley, get this guy in his seat."

"On it!"

Harper poked his head into the cockpit to see several red lights flashing on the dashboard.

"What the hell is going on!" the co-pilot exclaimed.

"This doesn't make sense!" the pilot said as he scanned the instrument panel. He especially eyed the compass; it was on the fritz and spinning in circles. "Everything has gone haywire!"

"What is it?" Harper asked over the roar of the rotors.

Another lighting strike flashed across the nose of the aircraft, and it felt like it was going to throw the Osprey out of the sky. Harper barely caught himself on the bulkhead and he spotted over a dozen lightning strikes in the distance.

The entire sky was *alive* with near continuous lightning flashes and thunderclaps.

"Nothing is fucking working!" the pilot explained. "Radar, altimeter, radio, GPS, it's like nothing I've ever seen."

He shot Harper a worried look. "It's like we just *dropped* off the fucking map!"

A finger of light shot down from the sky just ahead of them.

"Christ almighty!" the pilot yelled and banked hard to the right.

Again, Harper barely caught himself and was sure glad to have taken the Dramamine before he left.

"Ruptured fuel line!" the co-pilot announced and began flipping switches.

Catipon appeared next to Harper. "Fuck me!"

"Can we still make it to our jump spot?" Harper asked.

"Our port engine is about to go and if that lightning comes any closer it could ignite the leaking fuel and blow us out of the goddamn sky!" the pilot said.

Lightning tore across the sky in front of the bird's nose and the pilot swung hard to the left, throwing Harper into Catipon who caught him. As Harper pushed himself from the wall, his sleeve rolled up and he paused, squinting at something. He turned on his Kevlar mounted flashlight to see all of the hairs on his arm were standing straight up.

"Whoa."

"I'm going to assume that's a big fat fucking *no!*" Catipon said as he pounded the bulkhead with his fist.

Suddenly, sparks blew, and smoke stared to emit from the ceiling of the troop compartment. Bexley, having just finished strapping in the injured crew chief, grabbed a fire extinguisher and quickly sprayed the origin of the sparks.

The smoke stopped, then a deep coughing sound emitted from the Osprey followed by a high pitched shrill.

"Now what!" Harper asked.

The co-pilot turned and answered solemnly, "That's us losing the port engine!"

They all noticed a significant decrease in speed as the aircraft lost half of its power.

Without warning, the lightning strikes ceased and the instruments on the dash suddenly came back to life.

Harper looked at the altimeter on his ForeTex and saw they were at four thousand feet, also noticing the hairs on his arm were no longer standing up.

Catipon looked at him with amazement. "How the fuck is that possible! We just dropped twelve thousand feet in less than a minute.

Harper didn't have the answer right now and focused on the task at hand, switching his light off. "Can you set us down on the island?"

"It's either that or the water!" the co-pilot informed the pilot. "We should be able to glide there with our remaining engine!"

"Any location you prefer?" the pilot asked sarcastically.

"How about in the fucking McDonald's parking lot!" Catipon shot back.

"Quit it!" Harper yelled and then to the pilot, "Aim for the eastern side of the island toward two huge concrete towers!"

Catipon added, "And if you were wondering, yes, they're nuclear reactor cooling towers!"

The pilot managed a laugh. "Yeah sure, why not!"

Harper patted the pilot on the back. "If it helps, they were never operational!"

They rushed back to their seats, yanking off their parachutes in the process.

"What's going on?" Kate asked.

Catipon could see her eyes go wide with panic and her mouth agape. She seemed to notice him evaluating her and swallowed, closing her mouth.

"Well," Catipon began, "I got some good news and some bad news. Which one do you want first?"

"Are you fucking kidding me, right now!" Kate shot angrily at him.

Catipon threw himself into the seat next to Kate and began strapping himself in. "Bad news is we've lost the port side engine and we're probably going to crash!"

"What the hell is the good news!"

Catipon looked at Kate and tightened his harness. "I'll let you know if we survive!"

Harper laughed.

"Oh piss off!" Kate shot at him.

Catipon gripped Kate's hand and she looked at him. "It's going to be alright."

His gaze caught hers and for a moment Kate forgot about their dire situation, her gaze softening.

"Kate," Catipon repeated.

She broke her stare. "Yeah."

"You good?"

Kate nodded, leaned back, and gripped her seat harness tightly as she exhaled deeply. Her mind raced to think of anything else that would distract her from their current situation.

The Osprey dropped with a lurch out of the cloud layer.

"Island dead ahead!" the co-pilot announced to them over their comms.

Harper caught a glimpse through the cockpit's window of the silhouetted island along with the two nuclear reactor cooling towers and the eastern lighthouse.

"Remember that lighthouse I was worried about?" Catipon asked Harper through their headsets.

"Yeah, what of it!"

"A fucking kindergartener with a kaleidoscope could see us from there right now!"

"I know, I know!" Harper shot back.

Unknown to them a severed electrical wire in the port side engine sparked next to the ruptured fuel line and ignited. Flames exploded from the engine, sending a wave of shrapnel into the cockpit section of the aircraft. A piece of metal lodged itself into the neck of the pilot and he was dead before he slumped forward.

"Oh shit!" the co-pilot screamed.

Losing altitude dangerously fast, the Osprey shot above the shoreline, and began spinning uncontrollably in circles. Gripping the controls, the co-pilot knew it was a lost cause.

"Hold onto something!" he called back to the others.

Down on the ground below, a convoy of vehicles on a dirt trail stopped, and their occupants looked up to see a flaming Osprey shoot overhead.

Sheering off branches, the Osprey dropped into the tree line. The starboard wing was shredded from the fuselage and exploded into a tree trunk. Spinning around, the Osprey violently smacked into the ground and began sliding backwards down a muddy slope. Another tree tore off the port-side wing, rattling its occupants relentlessly.

Finally, the Osprey came to a sudden halt along an outcropping of rocks.

Groans and coughs filled the cabin.

"Holy fuck," Harper breathed.

"Are we alive?" Catipon.

Sparks exploded from the ceiling and smoke began billowing from the bulkheads.

"You guys good?" Harper asked, looking around.

"Barely," Catipon groaned.

"Good, I think," Kate said.

Bexley gave a thumbs up.

Harper undid his harness and looked out of the rear end of the bird. He looked down and swallowed hard. Looking back at the others he said flatly, "I hope no one is afraid of heights."

The tail section of the Osprey hung precariously over a sixty-foot-tall cliff face.

8

CHAMBERS GLIDED THROUGH THE AIR BENEATH HIS PARACHUTE, LOOK-
ing down at the ground through his PVS-31s and realized he was in the
wrong location.

"Goddamn it," he whispered to himself a couple hundred feet above
the ground. Jumps never went right, no matter how well you planned.

Looking at the map on his ForeTex, it looked like he was coming
down over the eastern edge of the island, right over the saltwater swamps.
As he descended, Chambers saw the trees approach quickly and aimed
for a gap, hoping for the best.

He crashed through tree branches, snapping them off, and braced
for impact with a tree trunk. Suddenly, his fall was arrested as his parachute got caught in the treetops and Chambers found himself swinging
gently from his lines five feet above the ground.

Pulling his quick release cord, Chambers fell into knee-deep water,
and he instantly brought up his rifle. Scanning the area around him, he
remained silent for a full five minutes before moving. His entrance was
sure to have made quite a noise and he wanted to ensure no one was
coming to investigate.

A single infrared flash of light off to his left caught his attention. He flashed back three short bursts of IR light from his PVS-31s and received a two light flash back.

It was a signaling code to identify friendlies in the dark at distance.

Chambers stripped his empty parachute pack off, dug in his drop bag, and threw on his small backpack. A few minutes later of trudging through the swamp water, he approached the figure.

"Took ya long enough," Washington whispered.

"Yeah, sue me," Chambers joked. "You got eyes on the others?"

"I got eyes on one."

"Let's move."

The two came into a small clearing between the trees and couldn't believe their eyes. Rider hung upside down by his parachute's chords from a tree branch thirty feet above the ground.

Through their night vision devices, they could see he had his pistol drawn on them.

"Jesus Christ," Rider hissed. "I almost shot you guys."

Chambers and Washington chuckled quietly.

"It's not funny," Rider said down to them.

"It's kinda funny," Chambers quipped.

Rider shook his head in embarrassment and looked up at the tangled parachute cords. He reached out for a tree branch, but it was just out of reach. Giving up, he relaxed and caught his breath.

Something caught his eye on a nearby branch and he did a double-take.

Looking closer, he didn't see anything else.

Rider concluded the darkness was just playing tricks on his eyes and he said to Chambers and Washington, "You guys gonna get me down or what?"

A new voice said from the side, "Crazy thunder we're having."

Chambers replied, "Not as crazy as the lightning."

It was a challenge and pass code for identifying friendlies at close range.

Stevens emerged from the darkness, panting from exertion. "This swamp sucks."

"You wanna climb this?" Chambers asked Washington.

"We should get him down, huh?"

Washington handed off his rifle to Stevens as he eyed the best route up the tree.

"Could be worse," Chambers mentioned to Stevens as they took up a security position around the base of the tree. "Alligators can't live in saltwater."

"Thanks for that little bit of info," Stevens said, deadpan and now worried about creatures lurking in the swamp.

"However," Chambers continued, "crocodiles could live here, I suppose. But they only live in Southeast Asia and Australia. So, we should be fine."

"Not helping," Stevens said flatly.

Washington began climbing up the tree toward Rider.

"You some sort of crocodile expert or something?" Stevens asked.

Chambers grinned. "Spent some time in Australia. Had a sort of a fling with a local gal who studied crocodiles."

Unseen in the shadows, a figure slowly rose from the waters behind Stevens.

Sensing a presence, Chambers turned and froze in place. The figure held a bow with an arrow drawn less than a foot from Stevens' neck.

"Woah," Chambers breathed and slowly raised his hands.

Stevens caught on, eyes widening. "What is it? Is it a crocodile?"

"Stop right there," Washington demanded from up above, with his Glock 17 pistol aimed at the mysterious newcomer.

For a few tense seconds, nobody moved.

Finally, the dark shadow spoke.

"You're not with the others," a hoarse female voice stated.

Chambers shook his head. "No, we're not. We're the good guys."

"What are you doing here?"

"We're here to rescue someone," Chambers answered and then asked, "Mind telling us who you are?"

The figure slowly withdrew her arrow and stepped forward. Washington holstered his pistol and continued climbing up toward Rider.

Chambers and Stevens observed that the woman was dressed in a homemade gilly suit.

Used in the military by long-range reconnaissance teams, a gilly suit was utilized to blend into the surrounding environment to remain unseen. It consisted of fabric with vegetation woven into it. They also saw she had a quiver full of arrows and two hatchets hanging from a belt.

The woman removed her hood. In her fifties, she had red hair and her face was covered in dirt and grime.

"Sally," the woman said and managed a grin. "Wow, that's the first time I've said that in a while."

Washington came to the branch that Rider's parachute cords were tangled in. Hanging five feet below the branch, Rider's leg was caught in the cords, which had caused him to turn upside down. Washington straddled the branch and scooted out toward Rider.

"Hang on, buddy, I'm coming," Washington said as he pulled out his knife.

"Just hurry up before I pass out," Rider replied.

Washington began cutting the lines around Rider's leg so he could flip back upright and utilize the quick release cord.

"How did you get here?" Chambers asked the woman named Sally.

Suddenly, Sally stood upright and cocked her head.

Washington heard it too and whispered down to the others, "Shhhh!"

The sound of a motor approached, and lights appeared in the distance.

"You should hide," Sally said.

Chambers and Stevens ducked behind a fallen log while Sally disappeared into the darkness. From his position up in the tree, Washington spotted two airboats slowly gliding in between the trees and weeds.

He hit the transmit button on his PTT and whispered, "Two airboats, four tangos each, hundred and fifty meters out."

Chambers and Stevens both peered over the log. Each airboat held four armed men wearing flaks and helmets and armed with AR style rifles: similar to themselves.

They watched the airboats creep toward their position. The men in the airboats waved flashlights through the darkness, casting shadows that danced over Chambers' and Stevens' hiding spot. Up above, Rider held his breath and Washington drew a bead on the lead man through the red dot sight on his pistol.

One of the voices called out to the adjacent airboat. "You guys seen anything yet?"

"No, not yet."

"They gotta be around here somewhere, I'm sure the wind blew them off course."

"This does not look like your average patrol," Chambers whispered to Stevens.

"No, it does not," Stevens agreed. "They're looking for us."

The realization that their enemy knew they had landed on the island was *not* good. Their minds whirled at the possibility of their plan being leaked to the enemy forces on the island and came to the same question, *who?*

Chambers looked around with a new sense of dread. "Where'd our new friend go?"

The airboats closed within twenty meters and puttered forward at a slow pace, the sound of their engines and blowing wind rustling the tree tops echoing across the swamp.

A tree branch snapped above Washington and Rider dropped a foot. Washington looked up and heard several more branches break.

"Shit," Rider mouthed.

"You guys hear that?" One of the mercenaries called out as the lead airboat came beneath Rider.

Rider's weight and Washington's slicing of several cords had shifted the parachute cords around.

"*Ahhh!*"

Rider fell from the sky and Washington was hit with several branches, forcing him to hunch over and hold on. The parachute caught onto another branch and jerked Rider, right side up now, to a stop five feet above the water and he started to swing directly toward the armed men on the airboat.

"Up in trees!" one of the mercenaries in the rear airboat yelled.

Rider had a second to react before he swung directly into a mercenary standing on the bow.

He slammed into the man and sent him flying back first into the swamp.

The mercenaries opened fire on Washington, bits of wood flying everywhere as Washington quickly shifted his body behind the tree's main trunk.

Chambers and Stevens popped up behind the fallen tree log and fired at the men in the closest airboat as Rider swung back and his lines snapped, falling unceremoniously into the water. The driver reversed away from their position in panic.

On the rear airboat, a mercenary had just finished reloading when an arrow came whizzing out of the darkness and lodged itself into the man's neck. He toppled face first into the water.

"Holy shit!" one of his comrades yelled.

"In the trees, fire!"

The men from both airboats forgot about The Team members and unleashed their firepower into the trees above wherever they thought the arrows were coming from. They didn't notice the figure that dropped down from a tree branch behind them and slipped quietly into the water.

Chambers said to himself, "Who the hell is this chick?"

Sally emerged silently from the swamp at the stern of the rear airboat and made her way to the port side. Hatchet in hand, she swung it violently into the leg of the man standing close to the side.

The hatchet embedded itself through skin and muscle before coming to a stop at the bone. The man let out a blood-curdling scream before Sally ripped him off the boat and he fell into the water. With a second hatchet, she struck the man in the neck, killing him instantly.

"In the water here!"

Sally disappeared beneath the boat as a barrage of bullets were fired into the water where she had just been, kicking up sprays of mist.

Silence.

After seeing the devasting and brutal attack, the mercenaries were frozen in shock as they frantically scanned the area.

"Who the fuck is out there!"

"Show yourself!"

Sally jumped from the water and onto the lead airboat. Before any of the three men could react, she had drawn an arrow across her bow and released it into the driver's neck. The closest mercenary lunged at her, and she easily sidestepped his attack, tripped him, and sent him falling into the water.

Before the last man in the boat could bring up his weapon, Sally was on him. She looped her bow around the man's head and with a yank, headbutted the man, sending blood gushing from his nose.

Splashing from the man she had knocked into the water caught her attention. The man stood up and fired a burst, but Sally was too fast.

She hit the deck as she pulled out an arrow. Shot by his own comrade, the mercenary she had just assaulted fell back and Sally released an arrow into the shooter's eye. Frozen in place, he slowly sank beneath the water line.

The entire encounter on the lead airboat lasted less than fifteen seconds.

"Holy fuck!" the mercenaries in the second airboat yelled.

They aimed their fire at the lead airboat, but Sally had already rolled into the water and disappeared.

"Let's get the fuck out of here!"

A small flame lit up in the darkness behind them. Then, at the last second, one of them turned and saw it.

"So long," Sally breathed as she released an arrow with its head on fire.

"*Nooooo!*"

The flaming arrowhead struck the airboat's gas tank.

The near-instantaneous explosion blew the airboat out of the water and sent screaming men flying across the swamp and into trees. Debris rained down as Washington jumped down next to Chambers and Stevens, a look of bewilderment across all their faces.

Rider stood up from the swamp, glanced at the carnage, and then looked at the others. "Who the hell is this chick?"

An arrow whizzed an inch past Rider's cheek and into the man he had knocked off the lead airboat, who had been getting up.

Sally appeared behind him, and she gestured at the remaining airboat. "Any of you boys know how to drive that thing?"

The four looked at her in utter amazement.

"I'm sure glad she's on our side," Washington admitted with a nervous grin.

9

SMOKE LINGERED IN THE AIR AS HARPER MOVED TOWARD THE COCKPIT, waving a hand in front of him to clear it.

"We gotta move," he told the group. "Two mikes."

Checking on the crew chief, Catipon couldn't find a pulse and realized the young man was dead. "Damn it," he breathed.

Kate felt a gash on her forehead and blood dripping down her face. She pressed her hand against the cut to stop the bleeding.

"You okay?" Catipon asked as he moved past her and searched for his drop bag.

Harper peered into the cockpit while keeping a wary eye on the forest around them through the cracked windshield. Seeing the pilot unmoving and slumped against the controls, Harper knew he was dead.

He went to check on the co-pilot when a bloodied hand suddenly grabbed him from the darkness. "Help!"

The co-pilot looked to be in bad shape with his legs pinned under the instrument dashboard and blood running down his face from under his flight helmet.

Harper froze when he heard a twig snap from somewhere outside and a millisecond later a gunshot broke the silence.

He heard the sound of glass breaking and a warm liquid spray across his face. Harper looked over at the co-pilot to see the side of his head and been blown out, blood and brain matter falling out.

"Get down!" Harper shouted as gunfire filled the air.

Harper rolled out of the cockpit as hundreds of bullets tore through the Osprey. Sparks flew as holes were punched through the thin metal fuselage. As he laid flat on the floor, he could feel the warm blood from the co-pilot drip down his face and he nearly vomited.

He wiped as much as he could off until the fire stopped, and they could hear voices outside. Harper lifted his head and whispered, "Fuck me."

"What a welcome party, uh?" Catipon said as he came crawling up and poked his head out of the starboard side door located behind the cockpit.

"Bexley," Harper called out in a whisper and looked around for his drop bag. "Set up the fast rope down the cliff."

Catipon looked up the hillside to see a half dozen individuals moving around. "Guys, we gotta go!"

"We're going to be short about ten feet of rope," Bexley informed them.

Through his NVGs Harper saw multiple IR lasers dance across the forest and into the Osprey as the shooters on the hill looked for a target.

"Just do it!" Harper hissed, finding his drop bag where he quickly grabbed his backpack.

More gunfire ripped through the air and tore the Osprey to further shreds, debris flying everywhere.

Catipon brought his weapon up and rapidly squeezed the trigger.

Two men dropped in twin fountains of blood as the rest took cover behind trees and boulders.

"Use the rocket on these assholes!"

Harper and Catipon gave each other a look, eyes wide with dread.

"Move!" Harper yelled.

A rocket soared through the air toward the Osprey.

Harper and Catipon sprinted down the troop compartment. Catipon took Kate to the deck just as the rocket slammed into the nose of the Osprey.

The front ten feet of the helicopter disappeared in an explosion of fire and flying metal shards. Bexley had just hooked up the fast rope and tossed it down the cliff face when the shockwave from the blast knocked him off his feet and out of the Osprey, barely managing to grip the rope in his hand.

As the smoke cleared, Harper could see a gaping hole facing their attackers up on the hill, their IR lasers weaving through the air. He tapped Catipon and Kate. "Go, now!"

Catipon said to Kate, "You go first."

Kate crawled over to the rope, gripped it, and started sliding down.

Moving down the hillside, the mercenaries unleashed another volley of fire. Catipon ejected a spent magazine.

"Well, if this isn't another fantastic shit show we've found ourselves in!" Catipon said sarcastically as he reloaded.

"Just go down the rope!" Harper shot back as he calmly squeezed the trigger.

Catipon began shifting through the wreckage on the floor, searching for something. "You see my bag!"

A bullet slammed into the bulkhead next to Harper. "I'm being shot at! How the fuck would I know where your bag is!"

"Got it!" Catipon exclaimed, slung the bag over his shoulder, and made his way toward the back. "Don't be too long!"

More bullets cut through the Osprey as the shooters approached with Harper's fire barely holding them at bay while Catipon slid down the rope.

Seeing Catipon had gone, Harper pulled out a TH3 incendiary grenade from his flak, pulled the pin and tossed it behind him as he grabbed the rope.

A TH3 incendiary grenade was a favorite in the US military for use in the complete destruction in whatever it encountered. Containing an improved version of thermite called thermate, it burned at 4,000 degrees and could even burn underwater due to the fact it produced its own oxygen.

Harper pinched the rope with his feet and slid down, the gloves on his hands saving him from burning himself.

The incendiary grenade went off with a loud hiss, throwing flaming hot thermate in every direction and lit up the forest in a bright flash of white light. Melting through the fuselage, the thermate set off a secondary explosion and the Osprey's fuel tanks exploded. Balls of flaming wreckage were slung into the air and knocked the enemy troops to the ground.

Harper slid to the bottom and let go just as the rope snapped from the explosion, barely managing to land on his feet.

"Nailed it," Harper remarked to Catipon.

Just then, they heard a screeching sound from above and they both looked up.

Cracked in half and hanging over the cliff face, the tail section of the Osprey slowly tipped over the cliff's edge and fell straight down.

"Shit," Harper said flatly.

The two took a few steps and jumped to the side as the tail section smashed into the ground with loud crash, toppled over, and rolled down a small incline before coming to a halt.

Harper groaned as he sat up. "That was close."

"Too close," Catipon agreed.

"You guys good?" Kate asked as she ran up with Bexley.

They nodded and then set off into the forest. Catipon took a final look up the cliff to see several men moving about with their IR lasers still on and white lights being turned on.

"So long, suckers," Catipon whispered and gave them the bird.

10

CAMP DAVID
FREDERICK COUNTY, MARYLAND
2200 HOURS

THE FORTY-FIFTH PRESIDENT OF THE UNITED STATES SAT ALONE IN the den of the presidential lodge, named Aspen. Wearing sweats, sipping tea, and sitting in front of crackling fire, Veronica Miller typed idly on her laptop.

Officially titled Naval Support Facility Thurmont, Camp David has been the presidential retreat of every US president for the last eighty years. Situated on two hundred acres of mountain forest, it was a sprawling complex of lodges for the president, their families, and guests from allied nations. A detachment from the Navy and Marine Corps had a barracks on the grounds and ran the camp, even when the president wasn't there. Pathed roads and walking trails crossed the landscape allowing for easy travel across the retreat. A helicopter pad rested on the western edge of the camp and President Eisenhower even had a golf course built next to the main lodge.

An infantry platoon of Marines, specially trained in close quarters battle and personal security detail operations, from Marine Barracks in D.C. posted at the retreat with the president. Armed with a plethora of small arms, they stood at the ready to respond to any crisis. In addition, nearly eighty Secret Service agents traveled with the president to Camp David where they carried an assortment of Glock 19 pistols,

Heckler & Koch MP5 submachine guns, and Remington 870 12-gauge shotguns.

The perimeter was surrounded by a razor-topped chain-link fence and covered by an extensive network of CCTV cameras and hidden detection measures, many of them classified to the public. A Sikorsky VH-92, painted dark green with a white strip across the top, stood poised at the helicopter landing zone in the event the president needed to leave quickly. Dubbed "Marine One" once the president was aboard, the iconic helicopter was manned by Marines of HMX-1, who were on constant standby to fly.

Serving as a US Senator from her home state of Montana before running for president, Veronica was a hard-hitter in Washington and possessed a natural skill at speaking which helped her to reach deals between both parties. Almost two years into her first term, she had already spearheaded a massive infrastructure deal through Congress and managed to open official diplomatic communications with the reclusive country of North Korea.

Widowed when her husband passed from cancer ten years ago, she currently had two children in college and never remarried.

Washington, D.C., had been evacuated in preparation for Hurricane Taylor and Congress had called a recess. The Secret Service had recommended to relocate to Camp David for the time being and Veronica agreed, using the time to get started on a recovery plan to respond to the damage the hurricane would inevitably cause.

She heard a knock at the door and turned to see a Secret Service agent open the door for her chief of staff.

An appointee of the president, the White House chief of staff had overall control of the Executive Office and wielded great political power. Handling the grunt work, the chief of staff was responsible for the structure of the White House staff, managed the flow of information the president received and who they met with in the Oval Office. Mainly, the chief of staff was the president's gatekeeper who had the authority with regard to what the president needed to know or didn't need to know.

Oliver Stokes wore an annoyed expression on his face as he walked to the president and put his hands on his hips.

Exhaling deeply, "Madam President, I highly advise I be read in on whatever is happening."

Veronica brought her glasses down over her nose. "Oliver, I appreciate your concern, but we've talked about this. If you need to know, you will."

"I'm your chief of staff, *I need* to—"

Veronica cut him off. "This is the last time we're talking about this."

Stokes clenched his jaw. "You have a call on line one, Madam President."

"Thank you, Oliver."

She waited for Stokes to leave and close the door before she picked up the phone. "Lisa, please tell me you have some good news."

Lisa sat on the couch in her office alone and spoke on speaker phone. "I'm afraid not, Madam President."

"Well, let's hear it."

"Only one of the insertion helicopters returned to the ship, the second never did."

"Do we know where it's at?"

"It appeared to have crashed on the island and then we lost its signal about twenty minutes later."

"Was it shot down?"

"We don't think so," Lisa responded. "The other helicopter didn't encounter any enemy fire, but we did receive reports of serve lightning from the NHC shortly after they departed. Apparently, one of their Hurricane Hunter flights was nearly knocked out of the sky flying through Hurricane Taylor by unusual weather activity and reported a massive lightning storm. We haven't been able to establish communications with any of the ground teams yet either."

Veronica took it all in. "Tell me something, how many situations like this have you been in?"

"A few, ma'am," Lisa answered and then she paused. "Madam President, the men and women on the ground are the best we have. And they are the best for a reason, so, rest assured, we'll get the job done."

"If you would've told me two years ago this ragtag organization is a real thing, I would've laughed. You must have a lot of trust and faith in your operatives."

"Absolutely, ma'am. I'll contact you with any developments."

"Very well," Veronica said. "And, Lisa, try to get some sleep, that's an order."

Lisa smiled. "Not a chance, ma'am."

11 ‖ ‖ ROSE ISLAND

THE AIRBOAT SPUTTERED TO A STOP AND BEACHED ITSELF ON A SMALL riverbank overgrown with trees, The Team members hopping out with caution. Figuring it wasn't wise to hang around should more enemy troops investigate the sound of gunfire; they took the airboat two miles to the north while they decided on their next course of action.

Chambers, Washington, and Rider took a knee on the riverbank while Sally remained in the airboat and Steven set up a tarp against the tree and tried to establish radio communications.

Chambers addressed Sally, "What do you know about these people?"

Before leaving the carnage behind they had searched the dead men for any identification as to who they were. No ID, they were all dressed in varying style of military style clothing, body armor, and carried American-style rifles and pistols. Their conclusion was that they were some kind of private mercenary force.

"Not much," Sally began. "They came a few days ago on a couple big old Russian military planes with flatbed trucks, some sort of dune buggies with machine guns, and a handful of Little Bird choppers."

"How do you know they were Little Birds?" Rider asked, an expert on the aircraft.

"I was a pilot," Sally explained. "Flew commercial 747s, but I have an eye for things that fly."

"That's your plane that crashed here?" Chambers said, and he remembered the crashed 747 they had seen on the map.

"Yeah," Sally said solemnly.

"Holy shit, that was over twenty years ago," Washington exclaimed. "You've managed to survive here for that long by herself?"

Sally cleared her throat. "Yeah, for the most part."

She paused and wiped a tear that was forming in the corner of her eye. "I can't believe it's been that long."

Meanwhile, Stevens worked on a PRC-117 military radio as he moved the satellite dish that was connected to it around. Standing for Portable, Radio, Communication, the radio could operate on the Very High-Frequency Band, Ultra High-Frequency Band, and on SATCOM nets.

"Goddamn it," Stevens muttered in frustration.

He couldn't defeat the enemy's jamming frequency without the key. Stevens pulled a piece of laminated paper that he had proliferated off one of the dead men called a Smartcard; military lingo for a list of radio frequencies that a unit was operating on.

RADIO FREQUENCIES:

All frequency bands in VHF unless otherwise stated

Main TAC-1: 36.8

Main TAC-2: 37.8

Lighthouse Teams: 38.8

Underground Complex: 39.8

Swamp Patrol: 40.8

Air (HF): 16.7

Off-Island (Satellite): 8.3

NOAA Weather Alert: 162.400

Most channels used were in the Very High-Frequency (VHF) band and the Air channel was used in the High-Frequency (HF) band, all standard procedure for the armed forces. Along with two main channels, Stevens saw that the lighthouse teams had their own dedicated channel as well as a group at an underground complex and a group at the saltwater swamps. The last frequency was the commonly used NOAA weather alert station which broadcasted updates on the weather.

Stevens wondered what they could be doing underground and decided to eavesdrop on it. Grabbing one of the enemy's radios they had also taken, he programmed the frequency for the underground complex and hooked it up to his headset.

As the wind continued to howl and blow sheets of rain into his face, he programmed the second enemy radio to the NOAA Weather Alert channel. Mainly used for updates about hurricanes in the Atlantic this time of year, they transmitted signals through a massive field of buoys placed off the entire Eastern Seaboard.

"I don't think we'd make it to the eastern runway before the storm slams into this island with full force," Chambers announced.

"Yeah, same," Rider agreed. "Looking at the map it's seven miles as the crow flies and who knows who else we'll run into."

"We just gonna leave the others?" Washington asked, knowing the hard question was on all their minds.

Chambers ground his teeth in thought. "I don't see how we'll be of any help given our current situation."

"So, we need to find a place to hole up," Washington concluded.

"My place isn't too far from here," Sally said, standing over them.

The three of them hadn't heard or seen her walk from the airboat. Sally was quite apt in moving unnoticeable.

"It's just up this river, tides are pretty high so we should be able to take the airboat most of the way," Sally said. "I think it's some sort of old missile silo."

"Of course," Rider said with a shake of his head and stood up.

Having taken down his tarp, Stevens walked over quickly. "Guys, you gotta listen to this."

Stevens held one of the enemy's radios in hand and they all gathered around to hear it over the wind.

"Carlyle, it's the excavation team. We finally blasted our way through tunnel three, we found it, Oralloy. I repeat, Orallory, Orallory, Orallory."

A second voice, presumably the person named Carlyle, came back with, "Good. Start loading it and bringing it to the southern runway. I want as much as possible before this hurricane hits. Carlyle out."

The transmissions stopped.

"What is Orallory?" Washington asked.

"No idea," Stevens admitted.

"Whatever it is, they're bringing it to the southern runway," Chambers said and looked at Sally. "Any idea where they could be excavating from?"

"The complex on the southwestern side of the island has a lot of tunnels that are collapsed, but that place is weird, and I don't go near it much any—" Sally cocked her head to the side, staring over Stevens' shoulder.

"What is it?" he asked, eyes wide with fear.

Sally didn't respond, only peered deeper into the darkness.

The group waited in anticipation for a firefight.

Finally, Sally said quietly and with conviction, "We should go, in the airboat, now."

They all took her seriously and swiftly made their way into the airboat with Sally bringing up the rear, arrow drawn across her bow.

Rider started the engine and took off down the river.

"What the hell was that?" Chambers asked.

Sally looked him dead in the eye and responded with one word, "Crocodiles."

12

HARPER'S WORLD WAS AWASH WITH LIGHT BLUES AND WHITES AS HE looked around the forest through his PVS-31s, dim lights shining back on his eyes from the device.

Up ahead, he saw Bexley scouting forward while Catipon and Kate walked in the center, and he brought up the rear.

Except for the patter of the rain and his quite footsteps, it was silent. He constantly scanned left, right and to the rear, on the lookout for any sign of trouble. With the narrow field of vision from his night vision device, Harper always felt like he was missing something. It was a very claustrophobic sensation, having your field of view greatly reduced.

Harper let his mind drift to thoughts of Madison Oakley.

She was too good for him, and he very well knew it.

Harper had had a few flings over the years, but nothing ever turned serious. In his line of work, it was hard to have a stable relationship. With the constant moving around the country, deployments while in the Marines, or on classified missions with The Team, he didn't have much time to invest into a serious relationship.

And if he was really honest with himself, he had never been willing to put in the time and effort.

Until he had met Madi.

He returned to that night that had been coming up all day.

It was Christmas Eve Day of the previous year. Harper was spending the holidays with his sister in New York City, and they happened to run into Madi whilst shopping, who was in between assignments at the time. Jocelyn insisted that she join them for dinner, and they spent the night drinking and telling old stories until the restaurant closed.

After saying goodnight to Jocelyn, Harper and Madi spent the rest of night together walking through the streets of Manhattan while the snow fell. It was a picturesque scene; two lovers walking the city streets holding hands and talking about their futures. They spent the night together in bed and, the next day, Madi got called into the London office for an assignment.

And that was the last time they had seen or spoken to each other.

Harper snapped back to reality and focused on the mission at hand.

She has to be alive, he thought.

Up ahead, Kate spoke with Catipon.

"Hey, thanks for earlier," Kate said in a hushed tone.

Catipon flipped his PVS-31s up. "Don't mention it."

"I've never been in a situation like that before and I kind of lost my cool," Kate admitted.

"You didn't do half bad for your first helicopter crash, I've seen *a lot* worse," Catipon said with a smile.

Kate laughed.

They ducked a tree branch and Catipon asked, "So, might be too early to ask, but what are you doing after this is done?"

Harper had been eavesdropping and sniffed a laugh at his friend's attempt at flirting, despite their current circumstance.

Kate hoped he wouldn't see her cheeks blush slightly. "I don't know, got anything in mind?"

"I do," Catipon said with a grin. "It's a date then?"

Kate nodded. "Sure, as long as you're not married or something."

"Me? Married?" Catipon asked ridiculously. "Not in this lifetime."

"I was once," Kate admitted.

Catipon raised an eyebrow. "Please, do tell."

"He was actually a Marine."

"Oh no!" Catipon teased.

"Yep," Kate continued. "Came home one day to see him fucking one of the new lieutenants of his unit, who was also married."

Catipon stopped and turned. "You've got to be kidding me? That's super cringey."

"Absolutely fucking not."

"Really doesn't give us a good reputation, does it?"

They walked around a tree.

"It was a messy divorce. He called me all the time saying he was sorry and whatever. Fucking asshole, never talked to him again. Don't even know why I agreed to marry him, guess I thought it was the normal thing to do."

"You're full of surprises, aren't you?"

Kate walked ahead and looked back at him. "I have my moments."

Harper came up to Catipon and slapped him on the shoulder.

"Good job, dude," Harper said with heavy sarcasm. "Managed to score a date in a life-or-death situation."

The two laughed.

From the front, Bexley flashed his IR light to get their attention. The group caught up and examined tire tracks in the mud.

"With this rainfall, I'd say these tracks aren't more than ten, fifteen minutes old," Bexley said confidently.

Harper nodded as he looked up from his ForeTex. "Okay, everyone look alive. We're gonna flank this trail, should take us straight to the east lighthouse. If things get froggy, shoot first and ask questions later."

They followed the trail east on its right-hand side for a few hundred meters until Bexley called for a halt.

Through their PVS-31s, they could see the top of a concrete lighthouse rising above the treetops. The group proceeded forward with caution until they came to a small clearing surrounding the base of the lighthouse. An off road type vehicle sat parked and alone by the door leading into the lighthouse.

It was an Advanced Light Strike Vehicle, or ALSV for short. Essentially, they were dune buggies and had been used during Desert Storm. They consisted of a turbo engine, a stabilizing suspension system, a titanium roll cage, a mounted M240B medium machine gun, and the capability to carry four people.

"What do you wanna do?" Bexley asked.

"We need some intel on these assholes," Harper said beside him in the prone. He pointed at Catipon. "We're gonna take the lighthouse, you two hold security down here, send us an IR flash if more guys show up."

"Got it," Bexley responded.

Rifles at the ready, Harper and Catipon walked swiftly across the clearing and up to the door. Harper placed a hand on Catipon's shoulder and squeezed; no words were spoken and seemingly that was all they needed to communicate.

Catipon pulled the door open, and Harper entered with the buttstock of his rifle firmly in his shoulder and his gaze slightly over the optic. Before them, a stone staircase spiraled upward. They moved silently, rifles held out in front of them and stepping with a light touch to avoid detection until they came to the top. Two men sat before an array of communications and optics, wires running to several dishes placed outside the wraparound windowpane.

Slowly, they let their weapons drop to the side and approached the two men. Once they were within arm's reach, they moved with frightening speed, and each placed one of the men in a chokehold. After thirty seconds of struggling, the two men passed out and were laid on the floor.

"Told ya," Catipon said, eyeing all their gear, and flipped up his night optic. "Now, what do we get here?"

He began examining their equipment as Harper picked up a pair of expensive high-powered thermal binoculars, articulated both tubes of his NVGs up so they rested above his eyes, and scanned the forest outside, his world converted to shades of black and white, signifying levels of heat.

"We got thermal and infrared optics," Catipon began as he rattled off everything he found. "Wow, what's this?"

Catipon took a moment to shine his helmet mounted flashlight on what he had found. "A *very expensive* coastal surveillance radar system."

He looked at Harper. "These guys are well funded."

Harper was looking out of the windows and the area around them. "Uh-huh, what else?"

Catipon continued. "Some standard day optics and . . . *bingo!*"

"What ya got?" Harper.

"Their Smartcard," Catipon said.

"Grab one of their radios," Harper said. "Search the bodies, see if we can figure out who these guys are."

Catipon saw the two were Caucasian with military style haircuts. They were dressed like he was and were armed with AR-15 style rifles. He went through their pockets, no phones or wallets but he did find a pack of cigarettes which he stowed in a cargo pocket. As he examined one of the men's watches, he spotted a tattoo on the man's wrist. Catipon rolled up the man's sleeve and examined it.

"Shit."

Through the thermal binoculars, Harper could see the vague silhouette of the mountains to the west through the rainy haze and the nuclear reactor cooling towers about two miles to the north. To the south, he scanned the beachline of the southern cove and then went back to scanning the forest area around them when something caught his eye.

"You done yet?"

Catipon was busy propping up the unconscious man and using a knife to cut off his shirt. "Give me a sec."

Harper looked down at Catipon. "We might not have a second, we got three vics inbound to our pos!"

Catipon shined his light across the bare man's skin, looking at his tattoos. "Fuck!"

The one that had initially caught his eye was a tattoo that read IGY6 in red ink. It was a common tattoo amongst members of the US military, and it meant "I got your six." A second one on his forearm read "USMC." The one that concerned him was on his shoulder and he snapped a picture of it and of the man's face with the camera on his ForeTex.

"Jake, look at this," Catipon said and showed him. "Not fucking good."

"Fuck," Harper said. "We gotta move, now!"

Harper flipped his NVGs down and made for the stairs. "You take pics?"

"Of course, I took pictures!" Catipon said, slightly insulted. "I'm a professional!"

"I'm just making sure!" Harper said as they hit the bottom of the stairs and he threw himself against the wall beside the door. "Ready?"

"Go."

Harper threw open the door just as three vehicles skidded to a stop in front of them.

Before Harper or Catipon could react, the gunner in the closest ALSV let loose with his M240B medium machine gun without hesitation.

The air split and cracked as 7.62-mm bullets flew at supersonic speeds of 2,800 feet per second in rapid succession.

Harper always swore it was one of the loudest weapons ever made.

The ground and lighthouse entrance around them was peppered with machine gun fire, throwing mud up in huge geysers and chips of concrete as they ducked back inside the lighthouse.

"Holy fuck!" Catipon said, his breathing rapid.

Over in the tree line, Bexley and Kate began engaging the mercenaries until they located them and started orientating their fires at them.

Harper looked at Catipon. "Time for them to meet *Adios*."

"Thought you'd never ask." Catipon grinned and slung his rifle to the side.

Catipon reached into his backpack and pulled out a strange-looking pistol-like device, extended the buttstock and announced, "Moving!"

"Move!" Harper said back to him.

The strange device was a M320 single-shot forty-millimeter grenade launcher. And written in white paint pen on the side was the word *Adios*; a final goodbye to anyone who had the bad luck of meeting her.

With Harper beside him firing at the mercenaries getting out of their vehicles, Catipon put the buttstock in his shoulder and fired a 40-mm high-explosive round at the lead vehicle.

The vehicle erupted into a ball of flames, flying high into the sky and launching its occupants with a scream to the flanks. At such close range, Harper and Catipon felt the heatwave wash over them.

Harper took the lead as Catipon took cover behind him, opened the weapon's breach, loaded a new round in, and stepped back around Harper.

The second ALSV blew apart as Catipon stepped to the side allowing Harper to pass him and then followed behind. They repeated the process until the third vehicle was a burning wreck and they had put down all the mercenaries.

Standing in the howling rain, all was quiet.

The sound of roaring engines approaching broke the brief solitude.

Bexley and Kate came running toward them out of the tree line.

"We got more enemy vics en bound!" Bexley reported.

"Shit!" Harper cursed as he assessed their options.

They were caught against the shoreline and could only go north, south, or west. The latter wasn't an option on account of the approaching enemy.

"North?" Catipon quickly asked, coming to the same conclusion.

The beams of the ALSV headlights flashed across them and the lighthouse.

"North!"

The four moved with haste into the tree line as three more dune buggies pulled into the clearing behind them.

"They're going into the trees!" one of the mercenaries shouted.

"Move out, go get them!"

Sprinting at a mad dash, dodging branches and leaping over fallen logs, the four Team members were moving fast. Their pursuers, with flashlights cutting swathes across the darkness, began firing and the trees around them were assaulted with splintered explosions.

"Feel like I'm escaping a goddamned prison!" Catipon exclaimed.

He and Harper dropped to a knee behind a log and fired a few short bursts at the mercenaries, dropping three.

"Just like Raqqa, right?" Harper shot back.

"Stop bringing that up!"

Harper grinned and they took off running after Kate and Bexley.

"We got a plan?" Catipon asked, breathing hard.

"I'm working on something!"

Kate was running behind Bexley when a swarm of bullets passed over her head and Bexley stumbled to the ground. Taking a knee beside him, Kate feared the worst.

"Bexley?"

"I'm good," Bexley groaned, holding the right side of his face.

Kate saw that he had taken a few flying splinters of wood to the cheek and blood was dripping down his face.

"We gotta move!" Catipon announced as he and Harper ran up behind them.

Kate and Bexley got to their feet and started running, Bexley keeping his right eye shut as blood poured over it.

The group moved another ten meters under a hailstorm of fire when suddenly the ground gave way beneath them.

Kate screamed as she tumbled and slammed into the Bexley, both of them rolling uncontrollable as they tried to stop. Catipon let loose a string of obscurities as the barrel of his rifle was jousted into his groin. The wind was taken out of Harper's lungs as he slammed face first into the ground and felt his NVGs get ripped off from its mount. As he tumbled head over heel, Harper caught a glimpse of the others ahead disappearing into a vast, black nothingness.

"*FUCKKKKK!*" Catipon shouted.

A second later, Harper fell back first and then felt nothing but air. The pit in his stomach clenched and he dropped, *fast*.

"Oh...SHITTTTT!" Harper's voice echoed as he plummeted off the side of a sixty-foot cliff!

Kate screamed the whole way down before unexpectedly landing in the ocean, the force driving the air from her lungs and water rushing into her nose. Instinct kicked in and she thrashed about, feeling for the surface as her natural buoyancy righted herself in the water.

She felt her head come up from beneath the water and tried to take a breath as she coughed up a fit from the saltwater in her sinuses. Managing to take a deep breath, Kate opened her eyes and could hear waves crashing nearby.

Catipon appeared beside her. "You okay?"

Kate nodded. "Yeah."

"Jake!" Catipon called out.

Harper, a short distance away, spit out a mouthful of seawater. "Here!"

He spotted Bexley nearby and then glanced up to see several flashlights near the cliff's edge.

"Down, now!"

They dived as several mercenaries up above scanned the waters below for any signs of their prey.

"Fan out and find them!" one of them shouted.

A minute later, The Team members resurfaced and swam closer to each other so they could converse without yelling.

"Don't think we're getting up that," Catipon said, gesturing at the cliffs.

"Agreed," said Harper. "I can't see shit, I lost my NVGs. Goddamn it!"

"Same," Catipon reported.

Bexley smacked his with the palm of his hand. "Mine are fucked."

Kate still had hers, they functioned fine. She started scanning the small cove they were in. "Looks like I got a cave right at the waterline."

"Better than this," Catipon said as a wave crashed into him.

"Lead the way," Harper said.

They swam across the cove and approached the cave, cautious of the waves threatening to slam them into the rocks. Kate timed her entry between waves and stepped up into the cave. The waves crashing at her ankles, she shined her light around. She found herself in a narrow tunnel that led up at a near-vertical angle for about eight feet before opening into a larger space.

"It goes up and opens into a bigger space!" Kate called out to the others above the sound of the breaking waves.

Kate planted her feet and hands on the wet rock and began shuffling up the narrow confines. The others followed and they stepped up into a cave the size of a two-car garage.

The area was cool and damp and received a cold breeze when the waves crashed below at the entrance. Stalactites hung from the ceiling and formed stalagmites below. On the far end, a fissure in the rock led deeper into the subterranean environment.

Harper and Catipon each cracked a blue Chemlight and held it out in front of them, casting shadows everywhere. They began walking forward, examining the cave, and looking around the rock formations.

Harper looked back at Kate when he saw a shadow move behind her and the quiet sound of footsteps.

The barrel of a pistol was pressed into the base of Kate's neck.

"Drop it!" a voice commanded nervously.

Harper, Catipon, and Bexley had their pistols drawn in a second and aimed the red dot optic sight at the unseen figure, Harper holding a Sig Sauer P229 pistol, Catipon a Smith & Wesson M&P 2.0 pistol, and Bexley a Glock 19 pistol, all with extended magazines.

"I wouldn't do that if I were you," Harper warned, his tone hard as steel.

An arm extended from around an alcove and a pistol was held at Catipon's temple.

"Shit," he breathed.

"Drop it!"

Harper holstered his pistol and raised his hands in surrender, the blue Chemlight illuminating his face. "Look—"

"Jake Harper?"

"Yeah?" Harper said in confusion.

The man beside Catipon lowered his pistol and stepped out, clicking on a small light affixed to the side of his Kevlar helmet.

A man dressed in Marine-style fatigues stepped forward. "Holy shit, Harper! What the fuck are you doing here?"

"Kyle Cunningham?" Harper said, not believing it. "What the hell are you doing here?"

"Hopefully getting rescued by your ass!" Cunningham said with a smile as they shook hands.

Harper had served with Cunningham in the same platoon during his first two deployments overseas and the two had been good friends. He hadn't spoken to Cunningham in years and realized he was a part of the Marine squad sent to the island with Madi.

The man beside Kate stepped out and stowed his pistol.

"Sorry about that," Michaels apologized.

"Don't worry about it," Kate said.

"I'm sure as shit glad to see you guys alive," Harper began. "How many of you are there?"

"Four here, several more survived the crash, but they headed east while we tried to lead whoever shot us down away," Cunningham answered. "We haven't seen them since."

"You were sent with a woman," Harper began. "Is she here?"

Before Cunningham could answer, a voice said from behind them, "Hey, Jake."

Harper turned to see Madi step into the blue light from around a stalagmite.

Wow.

Even with her hair a mess, a few cuts on her cheek and covered in mud from the knees down, Harper still thought she looked amazing.

He rushed over and the two embraced in a hug.

"Thank god you're okay," Harper whispered into her ear so the others couldn't hear.

Madi buried her head into his shoulder. "I had a feeling you'd come."

"Yeah?" Harper said with a smile.

He looked down at her and she looked up at him. After a few seconds they noticed the others were staring at them.

Catipon cleared his throat awkwardly.

The two stepped back from each other and faced the group. Michaels went over to another Marine propped up against the wall with his ankle in a makeshift splint. Kate had Bexley sit down on a rock and examined his wound.

"So, what's the plan?" Cunningham asked.

Harper let out a long sigh as he took off his Kevlar and ran a hand through his hair. "Good question."

Catipon took a seat against the wall. "This thing has been fucked since the beginning."

"Did you guys manage to find out more about this place?" Madi asked.

Harper shook his head and pulled up a document on his ForeTex, showing it to Madi. "That's all they found in the Pentagon, everything else was redacted."

"What the fuck?" Madi said. "What the hell is this place?"

Cunningham raised his hand. "What are you guys talking about?"

Harper contemplated telling him and then said, "This island was some sort of navy base in the 80s. It was shut down for reasons unknown and given a classified security so high, it was practically erased from existence."

"Speaking of which," Kate said, "did you guys see any odd lightning on the way in?"

"Lightning?" Cunningham repeated.

"Or anything else weird?" Harper asked.

Michaels spoke up from the back and approached the group. He held a compass out and they saw the needle was spinning wildly in circles.

"Checked mine and Jacobs' compass, they don't seem broken, been like that since we've been here."

"Weird," Harper said, pondering, and then asked. "What about this mercenary force?"

"Duked it with them at the crash site," Madi answered. "They came prepared for a fight and heavily outnumber us."

"Got one of their radios," Cunningham added. "Sounded like a guy named O'Neal was running the show."

"Still got the radio?" Catipon asked.

Cunningham pulled the radio from his back pocket and tossed it to him. "Haven't gotten any traffic since we've been down here, but it still has some juice."

Catipon powered on the radio and pulled out the Smartcard he took from the lighthouse.

Harper looked at Madi. "We found something else."

"What?"

"One of the mercenaries at the lighthouse we searched had a couple tattoos," Harper began. "One of them was of a pirate's blade with the word 'Cutthroat' above it."

"The Recon unit on the *Iwo Jima*?" Kate asked with concern.

"The very same."

"What are the chances that's just a coincidence?" Bexley asked.

Harper put his hands on his hips. "Unlikely."

Bexley nodded. "Yeah, figured as much."

Harper looked over at Cunningham. "They were on the *Iwo Jima*, know anything about them?"

"Unfortunately," Cunningham said with a nod. "They've been causing problems even before we left. Originally, they weren't supposed to deploy with us, it changed at the last minute. We had to wait an extra week off the coast of North Carolina for them to be flown aboard. Since then, they walk around like they own the place. They don't get along with our battalion commander and ignore the Navy when they're running drills, really pisses off the captain."

"Are we saying Cutthroat is working with mercenaries on the island?" Kate asked.

"It would explain how they found us so fast," Harper said. "They already had forces staged once we landed."

"And how they knew we were coming," Madi added.

"I'm gonna fucking kill Brookes," Harper spat angrily.

"That means the other team are also being looked for," Bexley said.

"But why?" Kate asked. "What's their end goal?"

"I'm not sure but we need comms with the others and warn the *Iwo Jima*," Harper said.

Catipon, meanwhile, had switched to the NOAA's channel and was listening to it through his headset. His eyes bulged at what he heard, and he brought up his map of Rose Island on his armguard's touchscreen.

"So, what do we do now?" Cunningham asked, seemingly defeated. "I still have eight Marines out there I need to find."

Harper placed a hand on his shoulder. "Don't worry, we'll find them."

"Uh, guys, we have a problem," Catipon announced as he stood up.

"That's an understatement," Harper said sarcastically.

"There's been an update on Hurricane Taylor."

He paused as they listened attentively.

"She's *a lot* worse than expected. She picked up speed and grew in intensity, now a Category 5 hurricane. She'll make landfall on this island in less than three hours. They're saying this is the strongest hurricane in the last *thirty* years, wind speeds expected to top one sixty and the storm surge as bad as thirty feet."

"Holy hell," Harper breathed.

Catipon summed it up grimly, "An almighty shit show of biblical proportions is about to rain down on us."

13

RIDER STEERED THE AIRBOAT DOWN THE RIVER BY SALLY'S DIRECTION. He had to squint through the slashing rain to see where he was going, the wind and rain had increased dramatically over the last thirty minutes. Stevens had been monitoring the NOAA frequency and informed them of the updates to Hurricane Taylor.

"What did you mean when you said, 'crocodiles' back there?" Chambers asked above the sound of the engine.

"They live here in the swamps!" Sally answered. "They're not pretty, stay away from the water's edge!"

Chambers gave an uncomforting smile. "Will do!"

Stevens tapped Chambers on the shoulder, and he turned around. "I got an idea!"

"What do you got?"

"It's a longshot but it could work," Stevens began. "I could send a message over the NOAA frequency via Morse code! If the others happen to find the same Smartcard and are listening in, they could hear it!"

Chambers nodded. "Do it! No locations until you confirm it's them, I don't want the enemy listening in!"

"Got it!"

Stevens started tapping his PTT with short and long strokes. Being a TACP, he had taken the time to learn Morse code and was glad it was finally paying off.

Sally pointed up ahead. "Right up here!"

Rider powered down the engine until the airboat glided forward and hit the bank with a soft thump. Sally jumped down and turned on a battery-powered lantern she had found in the boat.

"Stay close and keep your head on a swivel!"

The group followed Sally and set off through the forest, rifles at the ready and constantly scanning the ground around them.

After a few hundred meters, Stevens took a moment to catch his breath and bent over, stretching his lower back out. As he did so, he stepped into mud closer to the creek they had been following.

"Fuck," Washington mumbled to himself. "I need a cigarette."

Sally turned and said to them, "Not too much farther."

As she turned back, something caught her eye, and she instantly froze.

"What—" Chambers began to ask before Sally gave him a look to shut up.

He got the message and remained silent, Washington also following suit.

Sally looked at Stevens and hissed, "Don't move. Do *not* look behind you."

Setting the lantern down, Sally slowly brought up her bow and reached for an arrow from her quiver.

Rider was bringing up the rear when he stopped and looked over. He slowly raised his weapon and flicked the safety off.

Sally said to Chambers while keeping an eye on Stevens. "We're being hunted, get ready for a fight."

Chambers gripped his rifle tighter as he peered into the darkness behind Stevens through his NVGs.

"Step away from the creek," Sally instructed to Stevens. "Nice and slow."

Squinting, Chambers struggled to see anything. He articulated both tubes up and let his eyes adjust to the darkness.

"Is it what I think it is?" Stevens whispered, his eyes wide.

Chambers scanned right to left when a pair of dim lights caught his attention. Focusing as he stared at it, he made out a pair of vertical, slit-shaped pupils. "Oh, fuck."

"If you're thinking it's a man-eating saltwater crocodile, then yes," Sally quickly answered. "They've probably been stalking us since we left the airboat."

Three feet behind him and barely beneath the water's surface was an eighteen-foot-long olive drab colored crocodile.

Rider cocked his head, a look of confusion across his face, and whispered to himself, "Did she say 'they'?"

Stevens mouthed *fuck you* to Chambers, recalling their conversation from earlier. He took a deep breath and slowly lifted his right leg to step away.

Quick as lightning, the prehistoric beast roared forward and swiftly chomped down on Stevens' lower left leg. He barely had a chance to yell in pain before the animal ripped him down into the creek and started to roll with its prey. This was common practice for crocodiles and even alligators to tire out, drown, or even rip apart prey.

It was soon a frantic roll of crocodile and Stevens in four feet of water. His teammates raised their rifles but didn't have a clear shot amidst the trashing.

Sally said to Chambers, "Watch your six!"

Before he could respond, Sally dropped her bow, unsheathed a dagger, took off in a run and leaped into the water.

"Holy shit!" Washington exclaimed.

Sally landed on the spinning croc and wrapped her limbs around it.

Chambers articulated his PVS-31s back down over his eyes and said to Washington, "Check your six!"

In the thrashing waters, Sally started viciously stabbing the croc in its soft underbelly, blood pouring out while Stevens coughed and struggled for air.

"Come on, you son of a bitch!" Sally shouted.

Rider heard a quick rustling sound off to his left and spun to face it. Nothing showed up through his night vision optic. "Ah, guys . . . "

Chambers and Washington suddenly heard a guttural growl to their right followed by mud splashing that rapidly approached them. They looked down to see a twenty-foot crocodile charging them!

"What the fuck!" Washington shouted.

He and Chambers fired instantly, sending over thirty rounds until the creature slowed to a stop, the entirety of its head blown open and its tongue hanging loosely to the side.

"What the fuck!" Washington repeated.

In the creek, the crocodile that had Stevens in its jaws slowed and mercifully came to a stop, dead. Stevens surfaced and gasped in pain. Sally grabbed his arm and dragged him out of the creek.

"Get your gun up!" Sally said to Stevens. "They'll be more of 'em!"

Rider emptied a magazine into another charging crocodile. "Yo! What the fuck is going on!"

Sally ran over and grabbed her bow. "It's a pack of crocodiles!"

Washington went over to help Stevens, dragging him to sit up against a tree and checked his wound. They took up a defensive position around the tree.

"I'm pretty sure crocodiles don't hunt in packs!" Chambers shot at Sally.

She looked at him incredulously as she lit an arrowhead on fire and drew it through her bow. "You tell them that!"

Washington shone a light on Stevens' wound. He had a deep gash around his calf that bleed profusely. The flesh loosely hung off and Washington was pretty sure he could see the bone. He quickly pulled out a torniquet.

"It's not that bad," he lied.

"Yeah, right—" Stevens screamed in pain as Washington cinched the tourniquet around his upper thigh. "Motherfucker!"

"Sorry, buddy."

Sally waited until the fire moved down the length of the arrow before releasing it. It lodged itself into the muddy ground and its flame illuminated a crocodile barely a foot away. It roared and slithered away.

"They don't like fire!" Sally said as she lit another arrow.

"Right . . . " Rider said uneasily as if this all made sense.

Washington dumped some fresh water across Stevens' wound to rinse out the mud and leaves before packing it with QuikClot, containing kaolin which accelerated the body's ability to naturally clot bleeding. Next, he wrapped it with a bandage and pricked the skin with a small dose of lidocaine to numb the pain.

"You'll be fine," Washington assured him as he stood and brought up his weapon.

Rider eyed several crocodiles outside the perimeter of flaming arrows Sally had set up. "So, what the fuck do we do now?"

Chambers recalled the time he had spent, mostly in bed, with a female student by the name of Sienna who was studying at the Charles Darwin University in Australia to become a herpetologist. He remembered one time she had given a tour of the school's crocodile's habitat enclosure and how passionately she had spoken about them.

She had told him that male saltwater crocodiles could grow up to twenty feet in length, could weigh over 2,000 pounds, swim in short bursts of up to eighteen miles an hour and have been walking the Earth for nearly 240 million years, outliving the age of dinosaurs.

Chambers also knew the behavior he was seeing was not right.

"These are all males," Chambers said.

"Yeah, what of it!" Rider snapped as he scanned from crocodile to crocodile, waiting for one to breach their perimeter.

"The males are not tolerant of other males," Chambers explained. "They're very territorial, only every sharing territory with the females."

"Well, this is what *they* do," Sally said. "They'll send one in to distract their prey while the rest surround and ambush you. This hurricane is stirring them up."

"Like ringing the *goddamned* dinner bell," Rider added.

"We need more fire," Sally said. "Those arrows are only coated with a thin layer of napalm; it's not going to burn long in this rain."

"Let's just shoot these fuckers!" Washington countered.

"The noise will only provoke them and draw more of them in!" Sally shot back. "*Do not* shoot them unless you have to."

"Alright, so how do we start a fire?" Washington asked. "Everything around here is fucking soaked."

Stevens, feeling better after the lidocaine, spoke up, "Incendiary grenade."

Chambers looked at Washington. "If they can burn *under*water, they should be fine here. Stevens, you're a genius!"

Stevens gave a lazy thumbs up.

Chambers dropped to a knee, slipped his pack off, and began digging through it. "I got two, how many you guys got?"

Rider took one out of his flak. "I got one."

"Only one," Washington replied.

"Two," Stevens said as he took off his pack with a painful grunt.

"Alright," Chambers said as he stood back up. "Sally, how far until the missile silo?"

"Bout half a mile."

"Is it secure? Can these crocodiles get in?"

She shook her head. "Not a chance unless they can chew through metal."

Chambers looked around, grabbed a four-foot stick, and tossed it to Rider. "Rider, you lead. Toss the incendiary grenades, kick 'em along with that stick until it dies, then toss another, got it?"

Rider lifted his PVS-31s up in preparation for the bright flashes of light that lay ahead. "Got it!"

Chambers pointed at Washington. "You help Stevens." Next, he pointed at Sally. "We're on perimeter duty, *they* get too close, *we* drive 'em back, good?"

Sally nodded as she drew a regular arrow across her bow. "I'm ready."

Washington looped an arm around Stevens and with his other hand, drew his pistol. "Let's do this."

"Try not to look at them too much," Chambers warned of the incendiary grenades. "They can fuck up your eyes."

"Least of our worries right now, I think," Sally murmured.

Rider collected everyone's incendiary grenades, shoved them in his dump pouch, and drew his full-size Glock 17, holding it close to his chest.

Chambers took a final look around at the crocodiles. He counted almost ten surrounding them and then said to Rider, "On you."

Sally pointed in the general direction.

"Correct me as I go," Rider told her and then yanked the pin out of the first incendiary grenade. "Here we go."

He tossed it forward ten feet and shielded his eyes with his hand as the spoon flew off and the grenade hit the deck. Five seconds later, it exploded with a blinding flash of light.

"Move!" Rider yelled.

They ran forward and clustered around the burning source of light. Growling angrily at their potential prey, the pack of crocodiles slithered forward, but stayed away from the burning light. It was a surreal feeling, being hunted by a truly apex predator of another time period. They watched the crazed crocs climb over each other in anticipation of their next meal, moving with frightening speed for an animal that was so impossibly large.

Smoke filled the air as Rider, using his stick like a golf club, kicked the burning can of thermate along. Washington was directly behind him while carrying Stevens. Chambers and Sally brought up the rear and kept a wary eye on the pursuing crocodiles.

"Ah-ha!" Rider exclaimed. "Take that, fuckers!"

As the incendiary grenade's burn time approached forty seconds, Rider stopped and readied another grenade.

"Frag out!"

A second brilliant flash of light exploded, and they repeated the process, their crocodile friends following relentlessly. Sally corrected their direction slightly and they moved along with no problems.

During the third iteration, Chambers noticed the crocodiles were boldly approaching closer, snapping their jaws with hunger. "They're getting ballsy."

"Not good," Sally agreed.

As the molten mass of thermate died down, Rider stopped a bit too abruptly as he pulled out another grenade. Washington, following closely, ran into him and he dropped the grenade.

"Shit," Rider cursed and bent down to drop it.

With an uncanny swiftness, the currently burning grenade went out and plunged them into darkness.

"Shit!" Rider yelled, reaching frantically for the grenade.

Chambers quickly yanked his PVS-31s down and scanned right to left. He dumped several rounds into a charging crocodile, and it went down. "Anytime now, Rider!"

Rider gripped the grenade, pulled the pin, and tossed it.

A flash of light went off and Sally saw a crocodile heading directly toward her with his jaws wide open!

She stared at the beast's four-inch-long teeth for a second before releasing an arrow. It flew true and embedded itself through the crocodile's left eye and into its brain, stopping it dead in its tracks.

A crocodile attacked from Rider's front.

"I don't think so!" Rider said as he kicked the grenade toward it without a second thought.

Throwing a shower of burning thermate across its snout, the crocodile snarled and backed away in pain.

Stevens heard a rustling off to his right and with his good foot, stomped down on the open mouth of the crocodile charging him. He couldn't believe how small he looked compared to the creature; its head was nearly two feet long. With Stevens' weight on the beast, the crocodile grunted and bucked in an attempt to knock off the strike, its snakelike tail whipping back and forth.

"Motherfucker!" Stevens shouted in frustration as he fought to keep his grip.

Washington leaned over and dumped a whole magazine of 9 mm into the crocodile's head, bits of flesh and blood splashing up on them. The attack stopped and they remained still for a moment, catching their breath.

Rider looked back and sheepishly said, "My bad guys"

He resumed his duties of rolling the grenade along. The fourth died and he set off the fifth one. "Only one more after this one."

"We're almost there," Sally reassured them.

Washington felt Stevens slow, and his painful grunts increased. "Come on, buddy, you got this."

The 6th and final incendiary grenade started to burn, and Rider continued moving it along with his stick. "Where is this place!" he called out, his tone worrisome.

Sally glanced forward. "Another hundred feet!"

"What am I looking for!"

"A small mound with a circular metal grate!"

Shielding the bright light below with his hand, he searched ahead into the darkness. "I don't see it!"

The grenade started to flicker and die down in intensity.

"Just keep moving!"

"This ain't going to cut it!"

Sally drew a napalm-coated arrow and lit it with a Zippo lighter. "I didn't survive twenty years on this island *alone* just to die after meeting *you* guys!"

She ran forward, checked right then left, seemingly aimed into the darkness, and released her flaming arrow. The arrow shot to the front low and fast before coming to a stop, sticking out of the ground directly in front of a circular metal grate.

"I'll be damned!" Rider said and kicked the grenade faster, its light flickering dimmer and dimmer.

Sally lit and shot more flaming arrows around the grate as they moved toward it. The incendiary grenade finally died as they made it to the temporary safety of flaming arrows.

They all panted with exhaustion as Sally pulled down the top half of the circular gate. "In you guys go, watch your step, it's slippery."

Rider climbed up, straddled the grate, and helped Washington with Stevens and disappeared into the darkness. Washington slipped down and Chambers went down next as the first couple of flaming arrows went out, the crocodiles snapping closer.

Rider reached down for Sally's hand, and he pulled her up over the grate.

"Just make sure you close it," Sally reminded him before she dropped down.

Taking a final look at the snarling crocodiles before the final arrow went out, Rider said, "Yeah, no need to remind me."

Rider dropped down and pulled the grate close. Not a second later, the army of crocodiles leaped forward with their jaws snapping, *more* than aggravated that their prey had escaped their clutches.

14

A FLAME SPARKED AND THEN ILLUMINATED THE CAVE, CASTING SHADOWS behind Catipon as he lit up a cigarette and took a drag. He exhaled and passed it to Harper.

"I hate you," Harper joked as he took a drag and exhaled. The warmth around his hand felt good. "*This* would never fly back in the day."

He passed the cigarette back to Catipon. "Yeah, well, we were never sent into a Category 5 fucking hurricane before."

Harper laughed. "True."

They were standing alone in the outer cave with the fissure that opened onto the island. They had spent the last thirty minutes deciding on their next course of action while Kate removed the splinters from Bexley's face and bandaged it up.

Catipon flicked the ashes away. "So, you and Madi, what's going on there?"

Grinning, Harper just shrugged his shoulders.

"You two have been flirting forever," Catipon said. "I've known you for a long time, Jake, you've never been the one to hesitate, you always jump into everything without thinking, which is not always a good thing."

They both laughed, thinking back to when it truly hadn't.

Catipon continued. "But for some reason, when it comes to Madi, you hesitate." He paused as he took a drag. "What I'm saying is, stop pussy-footing around and jump in."

Harper nodded as he took the cigarette. "You may be right."

They could hear the others coming from the other cave. Catipon leaned in close and said, "Just walk up and kiss her, man."

"Thanks, Brother," Harper said and slapped his shoulder.

Harper stomped out the cigarette before taking a final drag and throwing his Kevlar back on.

"We're ready to roll," Kate announced while everyone else shuffled into the cave behind her.

"It's about a mile and a half to the eastern runway," Harper addressed the group. "We move together, if you see something, say something. With any luck, our mercenary pals have paused their search for us and are also taking shelter. Any questions?"

There were none.

With Harper leading the group, they stepped out into the storm. They were immediately stung with rain as it was hurled through the air at seventy miles an hour. It was so strong, it nearly blew Harper off his feet, he had to lean into it and crouch down. Leaves and branches constantly whizzed by and slammed into them.

They moved north where a shallow valley and the thick tree cover provided some relief from the wind. At the halfway point, Harper looked back at the group. Cunningham and Catipon were helping the injured Jacobs move on his sprained ankle.

In the pre-dawn light, movement up on his right caught his attention and he turned to face it.

A forty-foot tall tree was coming straight at him!

Harper turned and leaped as far as he could, bringing his knees to his chest to avoid them being crushed.

He felt the vibration of the tree slamming to the ground and rolled over to see it had missed him by mere feet.

Madi appeared over the fallen tree, yelling his name Harper presumed but couldn't hear due to the howling wind.

He gave a thumbs up, stood, and took a step when he tripped on something and fell back down. Looking down by his feet, he spotted a dark shape beneath the branches. Harper moved the branches aside only to reel back in horror, a human skull looking back at him.

Catching his breath, he moved more of the branches to see the body was wearing a pair of faded and torn US Marine-style woodland fatigues. He waved to Cunningham and motioned for him to come up.

After confirming the identity, Cunningham yelled directly into Harper's ear, "That's Martinez!"

They both looked down at the body again and it just didn't make sense. The body was in an advanced stage of decomposition, the skin was dry and colored a dark brown, the eyes and tongue were long gone, and parts of the skeleton were exposed. They could see the bones in his fingertips, his cheek bones, his nose bone, and holes across the skin connecting the jaw, revealing his teeth. The state of his clothes suggested he had been wearing them for months.

"Are you sure?" Harper shouted.

Cunningham shook his head yes.

Harper believed him, but it didn't make any sense, staring down at the body with sympathy for the Marine. His empty eye sockets seemed to be looking back at him and his open jaw looked like he was yelling in agony. An eerie feeling crept into Harper, and he looked around the forest, unsure what to make of it.

"We gotta get moving!"

Cunningham agreed and they continued their trek north.

They finally came to the end of the tree line and Harper could see a group of three buildings a hundred meters away and further to the north the faint outline of the nuclear reactor towers. He had the map of the island up on his ForeTex and studied the eastern runway complex.

On a north to south running line the facility was slightly cockeyed to the west. The pair of nuclear reactor cooling towers to the north towered over the landscape at six hundred feet tall. The runway ran parallel to the shoreline while three five story buildings sat side by side to the west. The roads that came from the north and west and split off to form a triangle in the middle of the complex, allowing easy access to all the facilities. In the middle of the triangle stood a five-story parking garage. The three buildings to the south had a pedestrian bridge on the second and fourth stories that ran over to the parking garage.

They set off for the nearest structure, the furthest west building, the wind throwing them to the ground with such force they had to practically crawl the hundred-meter distance. Catipon and Cunningham used their fixed blade knifes to get a purchase on the ground as they dragged the injured Jacobs behind them.

Harper and Bexley came up to the corner of the building and spotted an emergency fire exit. Hugging the wall tightly, they moved down to it to find it locked. Harper brought up his rifle and fired several rounds into the handle and a few inches above it. As soon as Harper pulled open the door the wind caught it and immediately ripped it from its hinges, sending it flying high into the sky and into the storm.

The two fell into the doorway, exhausted and panting from the extreme amount of physical effort it took them to move the short distance. One by one the others filtered in and caught their breath, thankful to have respite from the gale force winds.

After a short break, they ventured down the hallway, passed a few offices, and came out into a lobby on the north side of the building. The far side was a glass-walled entrance where a few of the windows had broken and the winds came rushing in. Passing an out-of-service elevator they took a staircase up to the second story. The northern section of the floor held private offices and a small lounge area by the pedestrian bridge entrance. The southern section was a field of open office cubicles.

The group settled into a few of the private offices on the side facing away from the wind. Jacobs was laid on an old leather couch while the others took a seat on the floor or in swivel office chairs.

"Thirty-minute shifts out on the office floor," Harper commanded to the group. "I'll take first watch, everyone else get some shut eye. Once the storm dies down, we're on the move."

They all agreed.

Harper rolled an office chair out onto the floor and took a seat, keeping an eye on the staircase and on the pedestrian bridge. As he sat there with his rifle at the ready, he thought of the lightning storm, the compass spinning wildly, and the body of the Marine that showed months of decomposition.

Nothing about Rose Island made sense to him.

15

THE SOUNDS OF WATER DROPLETS SPLASHING ECHOED DOWN THE DARK tunnel.

Rider blinked rapidly as spots danced around in his vision, a repercussion of glancing at the incendiary grenades. He rubbed his eyes and leaned against the wall of the underground tunnel. "Goddamnit."

"You good man?" Chambers asked.

"Yeah," Rider responded and stood back up. "Think I got a newfound fear of crocodiles though."

"You're telling me," Stevens added as he shuffled past them with Washington assisting him.

Sally had led them down from the entrance before the tunnel flattened out, flooded with a few inches of water from the storm.

After a short distance, she took them right through a doorway and went to the side, started a portable generator, and pulled a switch. A series of lights running in vertical lines up to the ceiling turned on one by one and illuminated the enormous subterranean space.

"Whoa," Washington said, looking up. "Nice."

Cylindrical in shape, the empty missile silo was over a hundred feet high and almost twenty feet wide. Catwalks ran around the inside every twenty feet in elevation and were connected by ladders.

Sally made her way across the silo and toward an oddly constructed structure.

In the shape of a half circle, it looked like a treehouse resting on stilts. She had laid down sheets of metal and wood across the first catwalk level twenty feet up from the floor and used tarps and sheets of plastic for the roof. A set of stairs in the middle of the space led up to the home and beside it was a homemade pulley system used to haul up heavier objects.

"There's eleven other silos just like this one, all empty," Sally stated, stripping off her gilly suit and tossing it on a rack by the stairs. "Probably had ICBMs if I had to guess. There was one of these places close to where I grew in Nebraska."

"You're a Cornhusker too?" Stevens winced through the pain as Washington helped him up the stairs.

"Third generation, born and raised."

"Go, Big Red," Stevens said cheerfully.

They made their way into Sally's abode and were surprised by what they saw. Several wooden crates and beach chairs were scattered about. Pots and pans sat around a firepit sunk into the floor. In the corner laid a mattress with blankets and pillows. A few pictures even hung on the walls.

Sally grabbed a bean bag chair, placed it against the wall, and gestured for Stevens to sit. "You remember how the '97 season went by chance?"

Washington helped Stevens sit down in the chair. "If I recall, we were 13-0 and won the national championship."

"Shame I missed it."

"Where'd you get all this stuff?" Rider asked.

"My plane," Sally answered. "It was a cargo plane, and most of it was intact. You'd be surprised what some people ship."

Through his headset still switched to the NOAA net, Stevens heard the thirty-minute update and then transmitted his Morse code message to which he didn't receive a response.

Sally walked over. "I can take over, just tell me what to say. You get some rest."

"You know Morse code?" Stevens asked.

"My father was a Navy pilot during Vietnam, he insisted I learn," Sally explained.

Stevens passed the radio off and shut his eyes. The others stripped off their gear and laid down on the floor, using their flaks as a pillow. Sally started a fire and boiled some water, passing the warm drink out to the others.

"It's not much," Sally said. "But it sure does warm you up."

Chambers took a sip. "It's delicious."

Sally laughed. She went about loading more arrows into her quiver and dipping a few into Napalm to be used later if needed. As she sharpened her hatchets on a piece of porous sandstone, she looked over at Chambers.

"So, what'd I miss out there in the real world?" she asked. "I see those fancy screens on your arm, what is that?"

Chambers gestured to his armguard. "It can hold maps, all sorts of other documents. Take pictures and video, it can be used has a radio."

Sally looked unconvinced. "It can do all of that?"

Realizing she had been missed the advancements in technology over the last twenty years, Chambers elaborated. "We have cellphones now that are the size of your hand and can fit in your pocket."

"And there're no buttons, you use it by touching the screen," Rider added.

"Touching the screen?" Sally repeated. "What else did I miss?"

"We invaded Iraq," Washington offered. "And Afghanistan."

"We're at war?" Sally asked.

Chambers nodded. "Since 9/11."

He immediately realized that she had no idea what that was and explained. "You remember the World Trade Center bombings in '93?"

"Yeah, I remember, it was all over the news."

"Well, on September 11, 2001, Al-Qaeda attacked again. This time they hijacked four American civilian airliners. Flew two into the Twin Towers, one into the Pentagon, and the fourth crashed in a field in Pennsylvania when the passengers tried to take it back."

Sally's jaw dropped; she was speechless.

"We've been in Iraq and Afghanistan ever since, Syria too. We got Bin Laden a few years back, killed him in a raid."

Sally set her hatchet aside, unable to comprehend.

"Did you have any family before you crashed?" Chambers asked.

"Um," Sally began as she tried to process this world-shattering information. "No, my parents had already passed, and I never married or had kids, didn't have the time."

She added, "I knew if I ever made it off this godforsaken island the world was going to be different, but . . . "

"You're going to get off this island," Chambers promised. "We all are, we'll get you home."

Sally nodded and got back to work on her hatchet. "Thank you."

16

O'NEAL CROSSED HIS ARMS AND GRINNED AT WHAT WAS BEFORE HIM while puffing on a cigar.

Standing in a massive airplane hangar at the southern runway, his men were using a forklift to unload the last of the heavy metal cases from a flatbed truck. It was the final load that had been brought before the storm had gotten too bad and he had returned to the hangar while keeping a portion of his forces on the east side of the island to resume the search once the hurricane had passed.

Along the western wall, the seven Marines they had captured sat chained to a pipe that ran horizontally above the floor.

O'Neal's forces had found them hiding in the forest and they had given up without a fight. A few of them were critically injured and didn't appear to be conscious. The other Marines had begged for medical help, but O'Neal refused.

Weak, O'Neal thought with disgust.

That was the problem with America these days, he figured. Weakness, it was a like a plague that needed to be put down. O'Neal had become enraged when politicians and the people began to welcome change; tolerating the rise of the LGBT community, advocating for more racial diversity in the workplace, defunding of police departments, and letting illegal migrants to pour across the border unfiltered. He believed politicians were to blame, that they had given in to greed, becoming filthy rich as they stayed in power for decades.

He often looked to American Revolution for inspiration, the people revolting against an unjust government.

O'Neal believed it was time for another change, a drastic change where people would listen and inspire others to stand against the filth that was poisoning his country.

Carlyle came up beside him. "What are you going to do with them?"

O'Neal turned and walked, Carlyle stepping beside him.

The interior of the hangar was massive. Two massive doors faced the runway and were currently shut to keep out the storm. On the opposite side a small administrative and workshop area took up a portion of the space. In the middle sat a Soviet-era Antonov An-124 Ruslan military transport aircraft, where the steel containers were being loaded onto. With a length of 226 feet, a wingspan of 240 feet, and a height of nearly 70 feet, it was the world's largest military transport aircraft. Along with an identical plane parked at the northern runway, they had been used to transport his army of mercenaries and their gear. The east side of the floor was taken by their fleet of ALSVs, flatbed trucks, and Little Bird helicopters. On the west side sat pallets of gear and cots where his men slept.

"They don't seem to know why they're here," O'Neal began. "I'll wait till the storm passes, I'm sure their friends will want them back." He smiled devilishly.

"How much longer will you need to load everything?"

"Four hours," Carlyle responded. "Plenty of time before they'll be able to launch reinforcements."

"Very good," O'Neal said. "And this time tomorrow, America will be changed forever."

17

MADI CAUGHT GLIMPSES OF HER AND HARPER RUNNING IN A PANIC. There was lots of gunfire and yelling echoing in the distance, the voices she couldn't recognize. Flashes of Harper's green eyes and the feeling of his lips on hers. And then images of Harper dead beside her and him yelling her name.

She awoke from her slumber with a jolt and sat upright, her heart beating out of her chest and sweat running down her temple.

Kate was across the office sitting against the wall. "You okay?"

Madi nodded, catching her breath. "Yeah, just a bad dream."

"Yeah, I used to get the worst fever dreams in country," Kate said. "You've going for so long, never knowing when someone is gonna shoot at you or drop a couple mortars on you."

"This one felt so real," Madi said and then shrugged her shoulders. "Guess all dreams do though."

Outside in the hallway, Catipon stood by the windows and looked out at the storm. It had been just over two hours since Hurricane Taylor had made landfall and he was starting to notice the wind dying down. He waited for NOAA's update to finish before consulting with the map on his ForeTex.

Harper walked up behind him.

"Check this out," Catipon said and gestured outside. "I think the eye is about to pass over us."

"Any chance we can move in it?"

Catipon was about to answer when he heard something through his headset and held up a finger.

"What is it?" Harper asked, alarmed.

"Holy shit!" Catipon exclaimed. "I think I'm picking up Morse code!"

"What? Do you know Morse code?"

"No," Catipon said evenly and rushed to the offices, pulling out his radio. "Yo, does anyone know Morse code?"

Kate turned and heard him, confused. "I do!"

Catipon barged in and handed her the radio. "Listen."

A few seconds passed before several clicks came through, barely audible. Kate's eye widened. "Paper! I need some paper and a pen!"

Madi pulled out a small notebook and a pen, handing it to her. Kate listened as she wrote down a series of dashes and dots in an apparent random order. After she finished, she translated it and read aloud, "Charlie-six-one-quebec-one, does anyone copy?"

"It's an authorization code!" Harper said. "One of ours, someone from the other team is trying to reach us."

At the commotion Cunningham came out into the hallway from an adjacent office and caught a view of outside. Curious, he walked toward it and saw the wind had nearly all but stopped. He stepped outside and looked around just as the clouds parted and he could see the blue sky above.

Harper instructed Kate: "Reply with our authorization code and ask them where they're at."

Bexley joined Cunningham out on the bridge. "It's the eye."

Cunningham watched a few palm tree fronds, now without the howling wind, drift down from the sky and land on the pavement. His ears hummed due to the abrupt silence and he was amazed that the hurricane could go from such severity to such calmness.

It was quickly broken by the sound of motors roaring in the distance.

Bexley looked in the direction of the sound. "I think we're about to have company."

"They're north of the swamps," Kate reported back. "Said they found the pilot of the crashed 747."

Cunningham ran up behind them. "They found us! They're coming our way!"

"Fuck me," Harper said and looked around in thought, spotting a few cars in the parking garage across the way.

"How the fuck did they find us so fast?" Catipon asked.

"The radios!" Madi said. "They're tracking the electronic signature from our transmissions."

"Get a couple of those cars started, we're leaving," Harper told Cunningham and then to Kate. "Let them know we have company and to meet us at the building on the northeast corner of the island, what we think is a boat dock. Tell them the Morse code is compromised."

Cunningham and Bexley were racing across the pedestrian bridge and into the parking garage while Michaels helped Jacobs to his feet. Catipon was standing by the bridge while the others threw on their gear and grabbed their rifles. From the east, Catipon saw a convoy of three ALSVs fly around the corner and head straight toward them.

"Things are about to get loud!" he announced.

No sooner had he said that than the gunner in the front vehicle pulled the trigger on his medium machine gun. Rounds impacted all around the side of the building and pedestrian bridge, throwing up bits of debris and sparks.

Catipon brought out his grenade launcher, waited for a lull in the shooting, and stepped out onto the bridge. The round flew through the air and impacted into the hood of the front ALSV, detonating immediately and throwing the vehicle flipping high into the sky on fire.

He looked at the others inside the building, "Let's go, clocks ah-ticking! That's not going to slow them down forever!"

Michaels and Kate helped Jacobs across the bridge as Bexley pulled up in an 80s era Honda sedan.

"Where's Cunningham?" Michaels asked.

"He's coming," Bexley answered and then yelled to Catipon, "We got company coming from the north, parking garage, first level!"

"Shit!" Catipon cursed and peered over the bridge.

Three more ALSVs pulled up to a screeching halt outside of the building and several armed men began rushing inside.

"Jake!" Catipon yelled. "We got bad guys on the first deck heading our way!"

As he said this, he looked at the ALSVs to the east and saw that they were stopped in the road due to the destroyed ALSV. And then he saw a man step around the wreck with something over his shoulder.

Catipon knew what it was and bolted toward the parking garage. "Rocket!"

Inside the building, Harper and Madi heard him and hit the deck. The rocket slammed into the bridge and exploded in a flash of light and fire. They felt the heat of the blast pass over them as the bridge cracked in half and fell to the ground below.

Madi looked up at the ruined bridge. "Fuck me."

Catipon looked back at them and motioned to Harper, pointing up. Harper understood and responded with a thumbs up.

"Let's go," he said to Madi as they took off running toward the stairs.

In the parking garage, Cunningham arrived in an 80s Ford Taurus and Catipon ran up to the passenger side, yelling to Kate, "You guys go! We'll catch up!"

"Got it!" Kate said and hopped in the Honda.

Bexley took off as Cunningham headed in the other direction.

Harper burst through the stairwell door and was immediately thrown into the wall by one of the mercenaries charging up the stairs. With a single headshot, Madi dropped the man and turned to face another three men coming up.

Moving fast, she jammed the suppressor of her rifle into the throat of the closest man. Eyes wide and coughing, the man stumbled back into the mercenary behind him, giving Madi precious few seconds to act. She squeezed the trigger and fired three rounds into the man she had muzzle thumped while she drew her pistol and aimed it toward the second man. Before she could fire, the man grabbed her wrist and thrusted it away. The first man fell to the ground dead as they fought for control of the pistol. Madi shifted her weight and let loose a kick at the man's foot. The man fell to the ground and Madi used her other hand to drive the man's head down, smashing his face into the ninety-degree angle of a stairstep. The man screamed before Madi placed the end of her pistol against his Kevlar helmet and pulled the trigger.

Gunshots rang out through the stairwell as the third mercenary fired in her direction from ten feet, missing her head by inches. Harper appeared from the side and fired back, the man falling backwards down the stairs, riddled with bullet holes.

Harper helped Madi to her feet as they heard more men running up the stairs. They wasted no time and took the steps up two at a time. Rushing onto the fourth floor, they saw it was the same layout as the second and made for the bridge.

Coming outside and into the sunshine, they both were momentarily awestruck as they looked around.

"Whoa," Harper breathed.

Over thirty miles wide and stretching fifty thousand feet into the sky, the eye of Hurricane Taylor was directly overhead. Its dark gray and impenetrable storm walls encircled the island and allowed them to see blue skies high above. He found it hard to fathom something so impossibly large and so fearsome. Looking at the symmetric eyewall to the west, he swallowed hard knowing it was moving toward him and they didn't have much time.

The sound of squealing tires diverted their attention and they turned to see Cunningham bringing the Ford to an abrupt halt.

"Let's go, ladies, we ain't got all day!" Catipon said from the passenger seat.

Harper and Madi got in the back seat and, without another word, Cunningham hit the gas and took off. The car leaned hard to the left and right as he maneuvered the car around tight corners and floored it down the straightaways.

Catipon, impressed with Cunningham's driving skill, reached forward and pressed Play on the cassette, not knowing if it worked or if there was a cassette currently in.

"You've got to be shitting me," Madi groaned, realizing what song started to play.

Harper looked at her and grinned. "Kinda fitting, don't ya think?"

"Rock You Like a Hurricane" by the Scorpions started to emit from the speakers.

Cunningham pulled hard on the e-brake and sent the Ford drifting around a sharp corner, its occupants trying to fight the inertia.

Catipon turned up the volume as Harper and Madi rolled down their windows and set the barrels of their guns on the windowsill. Cunningham started to hum along to the beat and Catipon slapped the dashboard, quietly mumbling the words.

Cunningham saw the exit ahead. "Here we go." He stepped hard on the gas pedal. "Hold on!"

The car flew off the ramp leading out the parking garage and they were outside heading north, the concrete cooling towers looming before them and dwarfed by the towering storm walls in the background. Further ahead they could see the Honda speeding away.

Madi looked out of the window to the right. "You guys see that!"

"Shit," Harper said. "Not good."

Traveling in a convoy on the road parallel to them, were seven ALSVs and soon, both roads would merge into one.

"Damn," Catipon said, squinting. "I *cannot* see that."

Harper sighed. "I told you, you need glasses!"

Catipon gave him a dismissive wave with his hand. "Yeah, yeah, I'll be fine."

"You need glasses!" Harper repeated.

The Honda hit the split and raced on. Next, three of the ALSVs passed the split as the Ford approached it, on a collision course with the four remaining enemy vehicles.

Catipon slapped the dash. "Can't this flying potato piece of shit car go any faster?"

"It was made for fuel economy, not speed!" Cunningham snapped, pushing the outdated Ford past its limit.

Machine gun fire tore into the ground around them, tossing showers of grass and mud into the air. Cunningham swerved to dodge the fire while Catipon fired back.

Harper knew the ALSVs would eventually rip them to shreds. "We need one of their vics."

"How?" Madi said.

"Are you crazy?" Cunningham asked.

Catipon looked at Cunningham deadpan. "He is."

Harper ripped open the middle console, which acted as an arm rest for the rear passengers and pulled open a hatch that led into the truck. "Ah-ha!"

"What are you doing?" Madi asked.

The Ford reached the split a hundred meters before the four ALSVs and they now had a good look at the road as it ran along the coastline. The turbulent waters of the ocean crashed relentlessly against the shore and a few even managed to spill out across the road. The inside eyewall of the hurricane was visible miles away, tall and dark.

Harper stripped off his flak and Kevlar and handed Madi his rifle. "Please hold onto this."

Not understanding, she took it as Harper leaned forward and turned to Cunningham. "Get us in front and be ready to pull the trunk release."

"Got it!"

Harper crawled headfirst into the truck as the lead ALSV quickly got up to the Ford and rammed into it, nearly driving it off the road. Being banged around in the truck, Harper drew his pistol in anticipation. "Let me know when I'm good!"

Releasing what his plan was, Madi watched the ALSV as it approached. "Now!"

Cunningham hit the trunk release and Harper stood up, hanging onto the truck overhead for support and pistol outstretched. Emptying the magazine with deadly accuracy onto the mercenaries, they all slumped forward.

A second later, Harper leaped from the trunk and onto the hood of the speeding ALSV.

Crawling forward, he swung into the ALSV and shoved the dead driver out and quickly took control of the vehicle.

Cunningham looked at Catipon and Madi with amazement. "Who the hell are you people?"

Harper sped up behind the Ford and got alongside of it.

Cunningham glanced in his mirrors as he noticed the other ALSVs dropping back and then spotted something that made him do a double-take. "Ah, guys, take a look behind us, what is that?"

Madi looked out of the rear windshield, flipped her magnifier up in front of her optic, and spotted two black objects flying from the south and over the road. "We may be in trouble."

They were MH-6 Little Bird helicopters. Used by special forces, they were small, mean, and fast, they were armed with a M134 Minigun and held two rocket pods on either side.

"Jake, you seeing this!" Catipon shouted out the window.

"Yeah I see it!"

Harper's mind raced; an approaching hurricane, a car chase with the mercenaries, and now attack helicopters.

"Tyler, I need you over here now!"

Throwing over Harper's kit and rifle, Catipon started to crawl out before he paused and handed Madi his M320 single shot grenade launcher. "Take care of that, would you?"

"No promises!" Madi said as she took it.

Catipon climbed out onto the windowsill, hanging one leg out and one leg in. Harper brought it in closer as Catipon judged the gap, eyeing the speeding pavement below.

"Oh, god, what am I doing?" he mumbled to himself.

Heart racing, Catipon leaped and grabbed the roll cage and planted his feet on the running boards.

Harper pointed forward and shouted over to Cunningham, "Go help them! We'll take care of these guys!"

Cunningham sped forward and Harper gave Madi a nod, locking eyes.

"Good luck," she mouthed to him.

Harper slowed down as a wave crashed over the guardrail and slammed into the ALSV. Catipon, climbing across the backseat, hadn't been expecting it and got a mouthful of seawater. "Son of a bitch!"

"Sorry!" Harper called out.

Catipon sat up and grabbed the roll cage above to steady himself. "So, what's the plan, chief! Got about three minutes before those choppers are on us!"

Harper swerved without warning to avoid the brunt of another crashing wave. Catipon was thrown to the side and almost slid out of the vehicle.

"Can you drive!" Catipon shot angrily at Harper as he sat back up.

"Would you like to drive!" Harper snapped.

Catipon leaned forward. "Yes!"

Harper pushed the dead mercenary in the passenger seat out of the vehicle and started to climb out. "It's yours then!"

Catipon lunged for the steering wheel and jumped into the driver seat. "Asshole!"

Harper laughed as he threw on his flak and Kevlar and began searching the vehicle. He opened the glove box to find several tube-shaped objects that he recognized as pyrotechnics.

A pyrotechnic, or pyro, was essentially a firework used for military applications, mainly for signaling nearby units. Encased in a foot-long silver tube, they contained a mixture of magnesium and red phosphorus, which produced a bright explosion of sparks. Harper also knew they could burn through some metals and the smoke was toxic if enough was breathed in.

"Nice," he said, closed the glove box, and looked behind over his shoulder.

The first Little Bird helicopter shot over them and the second one quickly approached.

BRRRRRRRRT!

The sound was deafening as the Little Bird's minigun simply tore up the concrete road around them, sending up a shooting cloud of dust and concrete debris. Catipon slammed on the brakes, and they dropped out of the impact zone. The helicopter shot past and started banking around to make another pass.

"That thing is gonna tear us to shreds!" Catipon exclaimed.

The ALSVs behind them sped up and opened fire. Catipon swerved left and right to dodge their impacts skipping off the road and guardrails on either side. Harper jumped into the backseat and stood up in the gunner's turret, spinning it around to face the rear.

The machine gun jarred his senses as he let loose with a long burst. One of the driver's chests violently exploded with blood and the ALSV crashed into the oceanside guardrail before it rolled and flipped spectacularly down the road. The trailing ALSV, having no care for the men inside, smashed into it and sent it flying over the guardrail and into the crashing waves.

Ears ringing even with his noise cancelling headset, Harper squeezed the trigger again when Catipon aggressively swerved to avoid another wave. His burst went harmlessly high.

"Hold it steady, would ya!

"Stop backseat driving!"

The two ALSVs dropped back, and Harper's eyes shot to the sky. "Oh, shit!"

Dropping its nose forward, the Little Bird was coming in for another attack.

A phalanx of rockets was released in rapid succession and headed straight down for Harper and Catipon.

Harper barely had time to duck before the rockets came raining down.

BOOM!-BOOM!-BOOM!-BOOM!-BOOM!-BOOM!

Massive explosions of fire and concrete impacted on either side of the ALSV, blowing away sections of guardrails off their mounts and rocking the vehicle with violent ferocity.

The ALSV shot out of the cloud of smoke as Catipon coughed and wiped the dust from his eyes. Harper, his ears ringing, eyed the turret above him. The M240B machine gun had been wrenched from its mount and was now gone.

"We lost the 240!" Harper grimly announced and then to himself as he massaged his ears, "And maybe my hearing."

Catipon watched as the Little Bird circled around back over the ocean. He also noticed the inside wall of the hurricane was getting closer. "We're not gonna last much longer against that thing!"

Harper sat up and thought, biting his lip as he looked around the ALSV.

"I got it!"

Harper reached forward, opened the glovebox, and grabbed the five pyros there. He shoved them into his flak and braced himself in the seat behind Catipon, facing backwards with one foot on the running board.

"Hold it steady as it passes!"

Harper waited patiently as the Little Bird completed its circle and headed toward them. He gripped a pyro in his hand, taking off the cap and placing it on the bottom.

"Come on, you bastard," Harper whispered, eyes narrowing.

The pilot dipped the aircraft's nose.

Harper struck the bottom of the pyro tube and a bright flash of red whizzed up into the sky.

The helicopter pilot was momentarily shocked until the pyro reached the height of its arc and exploded mere feet in front of him. Burning hot particles were shot in every direction as the pilot took evasive action.

Harper shot off another pyro charge as the Little Bird dropped in altitude, the pyro smacking into the plexiglass bubble windshield, went off, and sent a shower of fiery embers across the cockpit. The two pilots were hit in the face and neck with burning hot particles that ignited their clothes. They patted themselves in a frenzy in an attempt to put out the fires.

A third pyro rocketed in through the side door and lodged itself into the rear wall. It exploded in the cabin and now smoke started to pour heavily out of the chopper.

"You get it!" Catipon asked.

"Yeah, I got it!"

One of the pilots screamed in agony as he crawled at his face, peeling burning flesh off. Overcome with fear, he thrashed about and shoved open the door before he stepped out.

Harper watched as the man dropped and hit the ground. He grimaced.

The other pilot was in better shape but was bleeding profusely from his face and neck. He coughed from the smoke filled cabin, struggling to maintain control of the aircraft.

Harper watched as the Little Bird went widely out of control, picking up speed and pitching up and down.

Through the one eye he could still see out of, the pilot, overcome with pain and anger, launched rockets at no specific target. Rockets impacted the forest and even the ocean, exploding harmlessly.

Harper noticed the helicopter was starting to come straight toward them.

"You might wanna speed up!" he advised Catipon.

Catipon stole a glance to see the Little Bird descending rapidly toward them at a dangerous rate. The fire had spread to the outside of the chopper and flames licked their way down the fuselage. He even spotted the pilot in the smoke clogged interior.

Harper gripped the roll cage as he watched the same scene unfold. Traveling at almost seventy miles an hour, the helicopter dropped below a hundred feet and then fifty feet.

"Punch it!"

Catipon jammed the accelerator to the floor as the Little Bird shot toward them barely ten feet above the road, flames pouring out and chasing them.

The chopper's engine coughed and the rotors came to an abrupt halt. It dropped like a stone for a second before the gas tanks exploded and landed directly on top of an ALSV passing beneath it!

"Oh, yeah!" Harper cheered, thrusting a fist into the air.

The occupants of the stricken ALSV screamed as they caught fire from the cascading fuel that was pouring from the chopper. Tilting forward, the Little Bird rolled off the front end of the dune buggy and slid onto the pavement. The trailing ALSV took this moment to sped forward just as the rotors slammed into the ground and snapped off, shards of it flying into the passing vehicle's rear tire while causing the chopper to come to jarring stop.

The force of the shrapnel lifted the ALSV by its back end while simultaneously the burning ALSV blasted *straight* through the Little Bird, throwing up an explosion of fiery derbies. The front ALSV landed on its side and rolled over a dozen times down the road, ejecting mercenaries to the sides while the rear ALSV and remains of the helicopter came to a halt, crackling with fire.

"Holy shit," Catipon said, glancing back at the damage. "Good shooting, Tex!"

Harper jumped into the passenger seat and looked further down the road. Leading the pack was the Honda while the three ALSVs chased it and the Ford brought up the rear. The entire convoy was about to cross the three-mile-long causeway that ran across the ocean adjacent to the saltwater swamps.

Bexley glanced in the side-view mirror a moment before a burst of machine gun fire tore it off. He swerved to the right and a wave crashed over, hitting the windshield with a resonating thump. He hit the windshield wipers and looked in the rear-view mirror. The Ford was steadily gaining on the ALSVs, but not fast enough.

They passed onto the causeway as the closest ALSV sped up.

"Hold on!" Kate yelled.

The Honda was struck hard from the rear, throwing it up against the guardrail and casting up a shower of sparks.

"Motherfucker!" Bexley cursed, fighting to retain control of the vehicle.

Cunningham gained on the rear ALSV as Madi loaded a projectile into the breach of the grenade launcher.

"Get me nice and close," Madi said as she leaned out of the window.

A huge wave crashed over the causeway ahead of them and Cunningham's eyes went wide, slamming on the brakes. The wave smashed into the ALSV with such force, it carried it laterally across the road, through the guardrail, and into the ocean.

"Well, that solves one problem," Cunningham said with a shrug and sped back up.

Bexley swerved hard to the right as another burst of machine gun tore up the road around them. Suddenly, a few rounds ripped through the rear window and exited out of the front windshield, splintering it and obscuring their view.

"Everyone okay?" Bexley asked.

Michaels looked up and noticed Jacobs was slumped over and a huge bloodstain on the seat in front of him.

"Oh, Jesus!" Michaels cried.

He reached over and pushed Jacob's up. Blood squirted with each heartbeat out from a bullet wound in his neck, his carotid artery severed.

Michaels was frozen, he had never witnessed such a gruesome sight. The blood landed on his thigh and he was shocked to feel how warm it was.

And then the blood stopped squirting out.

Michaels looked at Jacobs, his eyes unblinking.

"Jacobs is dead," he said quietly.

"Son of a bitch," Bexley said under his breath.

Kate's nostrils flared with anger; the Marine was no older than the age of twenty. She leaned out of the window and fired her pistol at the pursuing vehicles in frustration.

One of the ALSVs exploded as a forty-millimeter grenade slammed into its rear. The vehicle lifted rear-end first into the air and tumbled in a flaming mess down the road.

Kate looked back to see that the Ford had caught up.

"Nice shot," commented Cunningham to Madi as she ejected the spent round.

They came up on the remaining ALSV as they exited the causeway and Madi pulled out a new 40 mm round. Cunningham swerved suddenly as the ALSV braked, came up alongside them, and sideswiped them.

Madi dropped the 40 mm round and it went rolling across the floorboards. "Fuck!"

Seeing a man in the rear seat bring up his rifle, Cunningham brought up his Sig Sauer M18 pistol and fired several rounds. The man's dead body slumped out of the ALSV as his slide locked to the rear, a sign it had run out of ammo.

"Shit."

The driver rammed them again and Madi noticed a man with sunglasses in the front passenger seat aiming at Cunningham with his rifle.

"Lean back now!" Madi shouted.

Cunningham hit the seat adjuster and leaned out of sight from the gunmen. His sight was replaced with Madi looking down her own sights a second before she yanked the trigger!

The man slumped forward on the dash, dead.

"Good!" Madi said with a shoulder slap to Cunningham.

Cunningham sat up just as they heard a thump come from the roof above.

They looked at each other with confusion a moment before a burst of rifle fire punctured the roof and impacted across the dashboard, one of the rounds catching Cunningham in his left pinky finger.

"Son of a bitch!" Cunningham roared in pain, blood running down his hand.

The last passenger of the ALSV had leaped onto the roof of their car.

Madi, turning in her seat, fired back at the ceiling just as a hand reached down behind her and gripped the back of her head. The attacker, with a fistful of her hair, attempted to pull her out of the speeding car!

"Motherfucker!" Madi screamed in pain as she grabbed the attacker's arm, fighting his pull.

Cunningham, now unarmed, acted fast.

"Hold on tight!"

He put the car in neutral and spun the wheel hard to the right, pulling on the e-brake. Tires squealing and sending up smoke, the car spun violently around and smashed squarely into the guardrail. The force of the impact sent the man flying across the roof of the car and sailing out into the sea.

Cunningham quickly put the car in reverse and turned around so he could see as he drove backwards. The remaining ALSV was just ahead, trailing closely behind the Honda.

"You good?" Cunningham asked Madi.

She massaged the back of her head and nodded. "Yeah."

Looking out of the front windshield as they traveled backwards, Madi yelled, "Watch out!"

Cunningham spun around, seeing the MH-6 helicopter swooping in and preparing to conduct an attack on the helpless Ford. "Fucking shit!"

Cunningham put the car in the neutral, yanked the e-brake, and spun the wheel just as the Little Bird released its payload of rockets. With the car in the middle of spinning around, rockets exploded all around them. Plumes of fire and concrete engulfed the car. The windshield shattered while Cunningham and Madi held on tight and squeezed their eyes shut.

With their spinning motion, the shockwaves from the blast tipped the Ford over onto his roof. The Ford careened, upside down, across the road, smashing into the guardrail before finally coming to a stop.

The helicopter flew forward and chased after the Honda.

A wave breaking across the Ford and blasting the interior with seawater brought Madi to her senses. She lay on the ceiling of the car. Cunningham let out a groan as he undid his seatbelt and dropped down to the ceiling.

The sound of a motor approached and an ALSV screeched to a halt next to the upturned Ford. Cunningham and Madi reached for their weapons and braced for a fight.

A figure ran toward them and crouched down.

Harper offered his hand to Madi. "Come on, lets go."

They quickly got into the ALSV and Catipon hit the gas the moment they were all inside. Cunningham pulled out a bandage and wrapped it around his bleeding hand.

"Where's my grenade launcher?" Catipon asked.

Madi winced. "I lost it, sorry."

Catipon moaned. "So not cool!"

The Little Bird ahead fired its minigun at the Honda while the lone ALSV trailed leisurely behind it, now with only its driver.

Bexley veered left then right as minigun fire strafed the ground around them. They rounded a slight bend in the road and the supposed boat dock building lay a few miles ahead. The eyewall of the hurricane was less than a mile away now.

"Almost there!" Kate said.

Catipon gained on the ALSV while keeping a wary eye on the Little Bird. "We got a plan yet!"

Harper took out his last two pyros and held them up. "Worked last time!"

Up in the chopper, the lead mercenary, formerly in charge of directing *both* aircraft, sat in the back with legs resting on the skids below while a safety harness clipped to his belt kept him secured. He wore a headset that could talk to the pilots and their man in the ALSV below. The man noticed that the eye was getting dangerously close and was about to order them back to base.

He glanced to their rear and his jaw dropped. "Down! Go down!"

A sizzling pyro shot straight toward the helicopter as the pilots descended rapidly to within twenty meters of the road. The man held on tight as the bird leveled out and looked back just in time to see a second pyro smack him in the chest.

A bright flash of burning hot particles exploded inside the bird, catching the man on fire. The man screamed and panicked, forgetting he was sitting on the edge of a helicopter. He rolled about, stepped forward, and fell fast until his safety harness jerked him to a halt five meters above the ground.

"Damn it!" Harper exclaimed after seeing his pyro attack had failed to bring down the chopper.

Then he spotted the hanging body of the man below. He yelled to Catipon, "Get me that rope!"

Catipon hit the gas.

"What are you thinking?" Madi asked warily.

Harper looked back and said with a wink, "Gonna play a little tug of war."

"You can't be serious!" Cunningham said.

Harper climbed up onto the roll cage frame of the ALSV as they sped toward the hanging and flaming corpse at almost seventy miles an hour. Balancing himself as he stood upright, Harper reached for the man's leg. He couldn't help but glance up at the eyewall, it was about to cross in front of the sun.

"Little closer!"

Catipon maneuvered the vehicle directly under the corpse.

Harper gripped the man's pant leg and yanked him down, taking a seat on the metal roll cage. Spot fires still burning, Harper unclipped the rope from the man's belt and shoved him to the side. He wrapped it around and secured it to the ALSV's frame and hopped back down.

Harper pointed at the remaining enemy vehicle ahead. "Get us closer and jump across!"

Catipon got close to the dune buggy just as a shadow passed over the road. The interior wall of the hurricane was about to cross over the island. Already a light rain fell, and the winds picked up.

"Go! Go!" Harper yelled at those in the back. "We don't have much time!"

Cunningham went first and landed in the small, recessed trunk space. He moved fast down the running board, grabbed the driver, and promptly threw him out. He took control of the vehicle as Madi jumped next, crouched down in the trunk and prepared to help the others cross over.

She waved them on. "Come on!"

Winds buffeted the Little Bird chopper above. The pilots could see they were attached to the ALSV below and yanked up to try and snap the rope. The rope held firm, and only succeeding in pulling the vehicle temporarily off the ground. Catipon struggled for control, and they grew further away from Madi and Cunningham.

"Son of bitch!" Harper cursed, the winds starting to howl and blow saltwater into his eyes.

The hurricane was closing back in around them and with the helicopter impending their control, he deduced there was no way he and Catipon could cross.

Harper waved to Madi, signaling them to leave without them. "Go!"

Madi could barely hear him but understood what he meant. She shook her head, refusing to leave them behind.

Cunningham shouted back. "We have to go! This hurricane will blow us off the road!"

"We can't leave them!" Madi said.

Harper waved at them again and then gave her a thumbs up.

She relented against her better judgment. "Damn it!"

Madi climbed into the ALSV and said to Cunningham, "Go!"

They sped forward after the Honda, leaving Harper and Catipon behind.

Visibility was cut down to ten feet as the hurricane moved in closer. Waves crashed across the road and the Little Bird was tossed around like a child's toy in a bathtub.

Catipon looked over at Harper. "I wanted to go!"

Harper laughed at his friend's cheery comment. "Move over, let me drive!"

Catipon climbed out of the driver's seat and Harper got behind the wheel. The Little Bird struggled to get free of the vehicle, but weighing less than half of the ALSV, it was a lost cause. Harper struggled to retain control as the Little Bird lifted them up a few feet at a time, smashing them into either guardrail.

"What now!" Catipon frantically asked.

"Just hold on!"

Harper gunned it forward, getting all four wheels back on the wet pavement and blasting through several waves that slipped onto the road. The Little Bird had no choice but to follow along.

"Remind me, if we survive, to never do *this* again!" Harper yelled above the storm.

Catipon looked over at him in shock. "No! Jake, this is a bad idea!"

"Just get ready to jump!" Harper shot back.

Catipon stepped out onto the running board and held on tightly to the roll cage above. Harper sped up and suddenly cut the wheel hard to the right, crashing straight through the guardrail and soaring out over the ocean!

Harper moved fast as he mirrored Catipon's position.

The rope between the ALSV and helicopter went taut and the jarring halt tossed Harper and Catipon forward out of the vehicle and flying into the open air, both of them cursing repeatedly.

The Little Bird was jerked harshly down and forward against the wind as the ALSV crashed into the water. Alarms blaring inside the cockpit, the pilots fought for control as a hundred mile an hour gust of wind caught them and sent the helicopter into an uncontrollable roll. Now stalling, the helicopter fell down from the sky as the hurricane carried it through the air and toward the ground. The helicopter exploded several times as it slammed into the road and rolled in the forest, flaming wreckage spilling across the ground.

All of the destruction that laid on the road was quickly engulfed by the ocean as the storm surge spilled over the shoreline, erasing all evidence of the chase.

There was no sign of Harper or Catipon in the water.

Hurricane Taylor had resumed its assault upon Rose Island.

18

SNAPPING AT HIS PHONE AS THE ALARM WENT OFF, FASSWATER ROLLED over with a groan. He sat up, rubbing his eyes for a few moments until he was fully aware of where he was.

Fasswater worked through the night and managed to get a few hours of sleep on a cot in the back of the TOC. And so far, he hadn't found much else besides a preliminary survey report from the US Navy Seabees to expand the island's base of operations shortly after World War II.

The report called for a complete overhaul and expansion of the infrastructure around the northern runway. The runway was extended, and a fully functional community was built to handle the families of nearly a thousand permanent personnel. A second runway was to be built to the south with a road connecting the two locations. The report ended with an analysis of the soil composition of the mountains to the northwest of the proposed southern runway. It deemed it was solid and fit for tunnel construction, however there was no mention as to what exactly was to be built there.

Fasswater stood and stretched out his arms before reaching down and touching his toes, holding the pose for a few seconds. After slipping his shoes on, he brushed his teeth in the restroom across the hall.

Feeling fresh as he left restroom, he decided he needed caffeine before he could continue his work. He made his way down the hallway and to a vending machine, where he bought a Red Bull. As he made to walk away he turned straight into someone walking behind him. Fasswater immediately reeled back as the woman tried to sidestep him.

The two regained their footing without injury.

Crisis averted, Fasswater thought to himself.

His heart fluttered as he recognized who it was; Natalie Woods, and it was safe to say he had a crush on her.

"My bad," Fasswater stammered as he glanced into her light-green eyes. "Sorry, didn't see you."

Natalie smiled sweetly. "No problem."

With fair brown skin, long curly black hair and a slim figure, Natalie Woods was undoubtedly attractive. A graduate of Oxford University and formerly employed by the Central Intelligence Agency as a foreign language interrupter focused on the intelligence gathering of Russia, she was an expert in Russian affairs and had been critical in predicting their next move on the world stage. Natalie had even spent a few years in Russia with the CIA doing low-threat operations but gaining invaluable field experience and trusted contacts in the process.

"Hey, cool shirt," Natalie said with a nod. "*Star Trek* fan, I take it?"

Fasswater was momentarily flabbergasted. "Yeah, sure am, you?"

Natalie laughed at his excitement and gave him the Vulcan salute. "Yeah, a little bit."

"Wow, that's awesome," Fasswater said with a smile.

An idea occurred to him. "Hey, are you busy right now?"

"Not at all," Natalie said as they began walking together down the hall. "I've been reading intercepted Russian intelligence reports that I've labeled between boring and *really boring*."

"I was wondering if I could get your help with something."

Natalie beamed. "Sure."

As they walked back to the TOC, Fasswater stepped forward and opened the door, allowing her to go in first.

She smiled sweetly.

Fasswater explained his assignment of researching a secret place by the name of Rose Island. He intentionally left out the part about a team of operatives being sent in to rescue one of their own.

"So, how can *I* help?" Natalie asked.

Fasswater elaborated. "Everything from our side is erased or just non-existent. Rose Island was a super classified base, and no one can find out what happened there. However, I'm hoping the USSR might've spied on what went on there."

Natalie smiled, catching on. "And that's where I come in."

"Bingo," Fasswater said. "Got any contacts that can find the information we need?"

"Let me make a few calls," she said. "What's the timetable looking like on this thing?"

Fasswater replied seriously, "Yesterday."

Two hours later, the two were walking into a strip mall coffee shop in Leesburg, Virginia. Although Hurricane Taylor had yet to make landfall, it was pouring outside and Fasswater was surprised to see the coffee shop open. He'd figured everyone would be staying home to avoid the Category 5 hurricane.

However, when he entered and noticed the teenage workers glued to their phones, completely uninterested to the storm or his presence at the counter, he understood.

They ordered a coffee and took a seat in the far corner against a window. Dressed in plain street clothes with a rain jacket, the two were unarmed. Usually intelligence analysts, like them, didn't go out into the field. For them to check out firearms for an operation they would've had to run it up the flagpole and it would've taken some time.

The way Fasswater saw it, Lisa told him to investigate Rose Island and that's exactly what he was doing.

"Is this guy reliable?" Fasswater asked as he glanced at his watch.

"I wouldn't have drugged us out here in this storm if I didn't think so," Natalie replied.

Thunder clapped close by, rattling the window.

Fasswater shrugged. "Good point."

After several calls Natalie had located a possible individual with knowledge on Rose Island. The only sort of background she got on the man was that he had connections to the KGB, Russia's infamous intelligence gathering organization.

As if on cue the door chimed and in stepped a figure whose face was concealed by a baseball cap and hood. The figure moved their way with a slight limp in the leg and took a seat in between the two while keeping an eye on the door.

"Mark?" Natalie asked.

The man removed his hood and nodded. "Da."

Mark, as the man went by these days, was completely bald and had a few extra pounds around the belt that he wasn't found of. Despite his old age, Mark's eyes were sharp and glistened with intelligence.

Looking over his shoulder and whispering in low tones, the old Russian asked, "So, what do you want to know?"

Fasswater swallowed and asked, "Have you ever heard of Rose Island?"

The color drained instantly from the man's face and several seconds passed before anyone spoke.

"Rose Island," Mark whispered, barely audible. "Is a place that never should've been."

"What do you mean?" Natalie inquired.

Mark went on to elaborate in his Russian-accented English.

"I don't know how they discovered it, some say it was Albert Einstein or Nikola Tesla, but I wasn't there. Wasn't long before your countrymen stepped in and realized there was some military application for it. The first large-scale test was conducted in '43, on a navy ship called the *Eldridge*."

Fasswater shot a wary look to Natalie. "I've heard the conspiracy theories."

"It became known as the Philadelphia Experiment, considered by most to be nothing more than a *farfetched* conspiracy theory," Mark paused as he finished the sentence to stare at Fasswater and then continued. "I'll tell you the truth, it is anything *but* a conspiracy theory. Twelve sailors lost their lives that night and from the reports, it was a terrifying sight. Men were *fused* to the ship. Whole limbs were inside bulkheads, and some men were still alive as they bled out. Others were turned to-to," he stammered as he thought for the right words.

"Best way to describe it would be human beings turned into bags of *soup*. Bones were simple not where they should be, and those men died the worst way imaginable."

Fasswater and Natalie grimaced at the thought.

"What was the Navy trying to accomplish then?" Fasswater asked.

"It's simple really," Mark said as if speaking to a child. "They wanted to get ships, troops, bombs, whatever, behind enemy lines without being seen. The tactical advantage they would've gained would've ended the war in a few months. They were trying to prefect the transportation method of . . . *teleportation*."

Natalie's brow furrowed in skepticism. "*Teleportation?*"

"That's not possible," Fasswater stated.

Mark threw up his hands in frustration. He cursed in what they assumed was Russian and then said in English, "I am not a scientist, I can't you tell how it works. I just know they were trying to make it work."

"How does this connect to Rose Island?" Fasswater said, moving the conversation along.

"The Philadelphia Experiment isn't a complete failure, and they continue to work on teleportation in secret. But they need a place to conduct this test, far from the public eye. An old Navy submarine base in the middle of the Atlantic was deemed a good place to do it and within a few short months, becomes the most closely guarded American secret of the Cold War. They do dozens of short-range tests, exploring this new field, however, they never do tests as big the Philadelphia Experiment. As the 80s approach, something strange *occurs . . .*"

"Time starts to behave like it shouldn't, either moving too slow or too fast. Gravity is also affected. Things start disappearing. All of this goes unnoticeable at first, until, you know, they're not."

"This happened on Rose Island?" Natalie asked.

"No," Mark said and thought, trying to recall the exact details. "Small island in the Caribbean, your country intervened militarily in the 80s"

"Grenada?" Fasswater asked.

Mark snapped his fingers. "Da! That's it."

He continued.

"Don't know why it started there, but it did. Anyway, the US sent scientists down there to investigate, some under the guise of medical students. Things are happening down there, and no one knows why. People are mysteriously vanishing. The US needs to control this and control this *fast*. As luck would have it, Grenada goes through some internal conflict and provides the US military with an excuse to go in and take care of this little problem. These, *anomalies*, as they're called by this point, stop. A few years later the US is *this*," he held up his thumb and pointer finger an inch away from one another, "close to a breakthrough in teleportation technology when Russia, also trying to harness the power of teleportation, have a major blunder. Chernobyl. They were using nuclear energy to power their experiments and it all went to hell. Reagan got cold feet and ordered the entire project shut down. The entire island was quarantined, and every shred of the project's existence was erased. All the personnel working there were threatened with hard prison time if they talked, and the entire thing quickly became a distant memory."

Natalie and Fasswater sat there for a few moments to let it all sink in.

Fasswater asked, "What would anyone want with Rose Island today?"

Mark leaned back and thought for a moment, going through the possibilities in his mind. "We tracked a shipment destined for Rose Island days before it was shut down. The level of security around the shipment was like nothing we had ever seen before. We believe that shipment was left on the island, because we never tracked a secure movement like that leaving."

"What kind of shipment?"

Mark smiled. "The convoy left from a small town in your state of Ohio, by the name of Piketon. I'm sure you can figure out what it was fairly easily."

Fasswater took out his phone and Googled "Piketon, Ohio."

"You said they almost had a breakthrough," Natalie recalled. "What kind of breakthrough? They almost figured out how to teleport?"

"Much more than that," Mark nodded with hesitation as he leaned forward on the table.

Fasswater looked up from his phone as the results of his search loaded.

"They almost figured out how to teleport to a—"

Crack!-whiz-splat!

The next words never left his mouth.

Instead, his head simply *exploded.*

Fasswater had once fired a shotgun at a watermelon, and it looked very much like that.

Blood and brain matter coated everything in a ten-foot radius as the glass window beside them fell to the floor in shards.

Fasswater's jaw dropped, and his eyes grew as wide as saucers as his brain processed what just happened in a manner of milliseconds. The blood that had been splattered all over himself and Natalie felt warm as it dripped off his chin. He slowly looked over at Natalie, who was frozen in a similar state of shock. She let out a petrified scream.

Spotting the broken window, Fasswater quickly realized what had happened.

Fasswater grabbed Natalie and brought her to the floor as a supersonic bullet ripped over their heads and shattered a second window. The coffee shop workers looked up idly from their phones at the commotion, failing to register the gunshots.

Fasswater couldn't believe what was happening; *they were being shot at!*

He looked bewildered at the workers, who just stood there.

"Get down!"

A third shot slammed into the table above their heads and a fourth bounced off the floor by their feet.

They realized what was happening and several screams rang out as they ducked behind the counter.

Natalie crawled over the dead body of Mark, holding back the vile building in her throat at the sight of his missing head.

The two crawled around the corner away from the window and backed up against the wall. Fasswater spotted a hallway that led toward the back of the shop. He also noticed another set of windows in between them and the hallway.

Fasswater looked Natalie in the eyes. "We can't stay here! We gotta move, okay?"

She nodded.

"On three, we're heading for that hallway!"

Again, she nodded.

Several more shots punctured the walls and floors around them, sending up bits of plaster and shards of glass flying everywhere.

"One, two, three!"

They sprinted across the coffee shop, windowpanes shattering and bags of coffee exploding on the countertop as more shots were fired.

Rushing out of a fire exit and into the rain, the two ran down an alleyway and toward the road. They came onto the road and looked around in a panic. Neither one of them had any idea what to do, they weren't field agents, they weren't trained for this!

Sirens sounded and a cop car pulled to a halt in front of them. Two uniformed police officers got out, firearms drawn, and ordered them to turn around with their hands up.

With their faces on the hood of the cop car and the rain washing away Mark's blood from their faces, the two were searched and hand-cuffed behind their backs.

"Great," Fasswater mumbled.

"Now what?" Natalie asked as she looked at him.

Thirty minutes later, they sat in the back of a cop car in the parking lot surrounded by a dozen EMS vehicles and lots of yellow tape. Following Team regulation, the two remained silent as the police took their IDs and ran it in the system. They knew a representative from The Team would arrive shortly and Fasswater was sure they would be in some sort of trouble.

"Time for you to tell what this is all about," Natalie said. "This goes way deeper than your run-of-the-mill intelligence gathering operation."

Fasswater signed and figured she was going to find out the truth eventually. "We started to detect military-grade encrypted signals coming from the island."

"Shit."

"We sent one of our operatives and a squad of Marines in to investigate, they were shot down."

"Shit."

"We sent in a second team to rescue them, and no contact has been made, so, who knows what's going on . . . "

"And this hurricane?"

"Hit the island straight on."

"*Shit.*"

"Sorry I roped you into all of this," Fasswater apologized quietly. "This is not how I intended this to go."

"It's okay, not your fault. Kind of exciting so far."

Fasswater looked over to see her smile and asked with caution, "So far?"

"Everything besides having a head explode on me," Natalie added.

The two front doors were suddenly flung open, and two police officers wearing raincoats got inside. They were dressed in the standard police officer uniforms, covers wrapped in plastic, and, oddly, wore matching Aviator sunglasses in the rain.

The hairs on the back of Fasswater's neck stood up as did Natalie's. They both gave each other a wary look.

The officer in the passenger seat slowly turned, opened the middle hatch in the gate separating them, and calmly leveled a Glock 19 pistol with an attached suppressor at them.

"Now, what did the old man tell you?" the man demanded from the two.

Across the parking lot a black Suburban eased up to the perimeter of yellow tape and the driver flashed an identification badge that got him past the police cordon. Coming to a stop, two men dressed in all black attire got out, gave a quick gaze around, and then opened the back door.

Lisa popped open an umbrella as she stepped outside. She spotted the shot-up coffee shop and shook her head.

"Find me Fasswater and Woods," Lisa told her small security detail.

Back in the cop car, Fasswater was staring at the pistol, the color draining from his face. Sure he had just been shot at for the first time but seeing a loaded gun pointed at him two feet away was terrifying. All it took for him to die was a squeeze of the trigger.

"I'll ask one more time," the man in the passenger seat threatened, "what did the old man tell you?"

Fasswater caught a glimpse of movement from his peripherals, Natalie was silently fiddling with her cuffs.

Facing a life-or-death scenario, his brain went into overdrive

Odd, what is she doing?

She's former CIA, wasn't a clandestine officer, but still in the CIA, did some field work.

They must've taught her some basic spy craft skills to operating in a foreign environment . . . like how to pick a pair of handcuffs!

Fasswater wasn't sure how that would help but they needed to do something.

He needed to stall.

Swallowing nervously and licking his lips, Fasswater said, "We have no idea who that was."

The man had no time to play games. "If one of you doesn't start talking, I'll shoot the other."

Natalie had picked her cuffs and made her move.

Sitting in the back left seat, Natalie went for man's gun arm and slammed it into the far side of the opened hatch. While at the same time with her left hand, handcuffs around it acting like a pair of brass knuckles, she connected with the man's nose and sent blood gushing.

The man in the driver's seat threw the car in reverse and hit the accelerator, intent on getting away before *actual* cops arrived. At the sound of squealing tires, Lisa and her security detail instantly turned their heads.

With their attacker seeing stars, Natalie slammed his forearm into gate to try to get him to drop the gun. The man grabbed his gushing nose and fired several shots wildly out of frustration.

Several suppressed bullets whizzed past Fasswater as he ducked in his seat and the side window shattered.

At the sound of gunfire Lisa's security detail drew their weapons. "That's them," she said with conviction.

Fasswater crouched low in the seat with his legs crammed against the seat in front of him.

The man landed a blow on Natalie's jaw, and she fell back into her seat.

"Fucking bitch!" the man spat as he leveled his gun at Natalie.

Fasswater saw what was about to happened and acted.

He shimmied lower into his seat and kicked with all his strength at the man's arm. The gun went off, busting the window by Natalie, as the man's forearm was crushed in the opened gate, snapping the bone.

The man howled in pain as Natalie pounced and slammed her makeshift brass knuckles into the man's Adam apple!

He dropped back into his seat like a sack of potatoes and the driver, seeing this, drew his own weapon, an unsuppressed Glock, just as Natalie wrapped the pair of handcuffs around his throat and yanked back with her full weight. He dropped his weapon in surprise and it landed in the cup holder next to him.

"Ahhh!" Natalie yelled in exertion, trying to choke the driver out.

Meanwhile, the driver was no longer focused on driving and the cop car smashed through a row of shopping carts.

"The gun!" Natalie yelled at Fasswater. "He's going for the gun!"

Fasswater understood. He brought up his knees to his chest and wiggled his arms out from under him and tried to get them over his feet.

The driver fumbled around and tried to locate his gun as he fought for breath.

"Hurry!" Natalie pleaded.

The cop car, still flying in reverse, hit a grassy medium and went bounding over it, throwing everyone harshly around. The movement threw the gun up into the driver's hand and he reached over his shoulder, aiming the muzzle directly at Natalie.

"Michael!"

Fasswater looped his hands over his feet and shot up through the hatch!

He grabbed the man's wrist with both hands and wrestled for control of the gun. Several shots erupted into the ceiling above them. As the empty shells were ejected, Fasswater turned his head to the side and saw what lay behind them.

"Shit!"

Fasswater elbowed the man in the nose and let go of his wrist. Next, he jumped back to his seat, grabbed Natalie by the waist, threw her flat on the floorboards, and covered her body with his.

"Hold on!"

The driver regained his senses just as the man in the passenger seat sat up.

They never saw it coming.

A big rig truck with a trailer sat straight in the path of the backwards speeding cop car. The cop car came at the trailer from its side and went directly under it.

The sound of the trailer *literally* scraping off the top part of the cop car was noise deafening inside and sent a shower of sparks cascading over Fasswater and Natalie.

It also took off the heads of their two attackers right at their shoulders. Their headless bodies crumpled over to the side.

Now driverless, the cop car came to a halt next to a row of bushes.

With the rain still pouring on them, Fasswater sat up and helped Natalie to her feet. They surveyed the damage and the two headless assassins sprawled out before them.

Tires squealed as a black Suburban stopped beside them. Natalie and Fasswater remained motionless, unsure as to what they should do.

Lisa rolled the window down. "Get in you two," she said sternly. "We need to talk."

Natalie and Fasswater both gulped nervously.

Twenty minutes later they were on the highway at eighty miles an hour heading north into Maryland under an armed escort commanded by Team assets. Domestic attacks on Team personnel were few and far between, and when they did occur, the entire region was on high alert and security was the utmost priority.

The Suburban in which Natalie and Fasswater were in was modified, the middle row of seats faced the rear row so the passengers could all face each other.

Fasswater ran a towel through his hair for the fifth time to get the blood and brain matter out. Next to him, Natalie was doing the same. They were soaked to the bone and still splattered with blood.

Before they left the parking lot of the strip mall, they had told Lisa what they had learned about Rose Island to which she responded with a short call to persons unknown.

"What's going on here, ma'am?" Fasswater asked. "Where are we going?"

Lisa began. "You two stumbled upon something that was meant to stay buried for a very long time, for forever. No one is sitting in this current administration knew of the existence of Rose Island or what occurred there. This thing has gone all the way to the top."

"What about the force on the island?" Natalie asked. "Any contact?"

Lisa cast an angry glance at Fasswater. "Our satellites caught what appeared to a running gun battle against some of our assets and the unknown hostile force as the eye of the storm passed over, but that was almost an hour ago now."

"Where are we going now?" Fasswater asked again.

"Camp David," she answered. "The president wants to talk to you two."

For the only God knew how many times today, Fasswater's and Natalie's heads snapped to the side to look at each other, mouth agape.

"Can we at least change first?" Fasswater asked.

19 | ROSE ISLAND

MADI AND BEXLEY MOVED FAST ACROSS THE SMALL PARKING LOT AND through a pair of shattered glass doors, while the others followed behind. Weapons held out in front and stepping forward heedfully, they switched on their white lights to cast away the darkness. Coming to an intersection, they nodded at each other and stepped forward in opposite directions, clearing both left and right.

Madi walked forward and came into a large cafeteria area.

On the left were kitchen serving lines and long dining tables taking up the rest of the cafeteria.

"This is good for now," Madi declared and slipped her Kevlar off.

After arriving at the unknown facility to which they assumed was some sort of covered boat dock, they consulted over the map on their ForeTex's. With a two-story parking garage on the west side and the large concrete building on the east side with a pair of pedestrian bridges connecting the two, they decided to seek refuge in the larger building.

Michaels took a seat and sat in silence. Cunningham noticed he was being more quiet than usual as he started off aimlessly. He had seen Jacobs' dead body in the Honda parked outside and remembered that Michaels had never been to combat before, this was the first time he had seen violence like this.

Cunningham sympathized with him. During his first combat tour, he had seen several of his friends killed and it took him a long time to learn how to grieve.

Taking a seat across from him, Cunningham set his Kevlar on the ground.

"Hey, Michaels."

The young Marine didn't respond.

"Corporal Michaels," Cunningham repeated with a smile. "You with me?"

Michaels finally noticed and looked at him. "Yes, Staff Sergeant. I'm good."

"I need you with me," Cunningham said seriously. "We're not out of this yet, understood?"

"I'm good, Staff Sergeant," Michaels insisted. "You can count on me."

Cunningham smiled and stood. "I know I can."

Meanwhile, Madi was counting her magazines and seeing how many rounds she had left. She counted two rounds of 9 mm ammo and two full magazines of 5.56 mm. She winced, the back of her head where the mercenary grabbed her burned like hell. She could tell it was bleeding and had even pulled out a few loose hairs.

"Shit," she said and then asked the others. "How you guys looking on ammo?"

They all reported low numbers, too low numbers to survive another gunfight. After multiple encounters at the crash sites, the lighthouse and the chase down the oceanside road, they had expended most of their ammo.

"I'll go check that ALSV out there," Cunningham offered.

"I'll come with," Bexley added.

Cunningham put his Kevlar on and called out to Michaels, "Corporal Michaels, care to join us?"

Michaels stood up, rifle ready and smiled. "Always, Staff Sergeant."

"We'll be back," Cunningham said, and the group set off to head outside.

Outside, they braced the best they could against the storm as they rifled through the ALSV, finding several magazines of 5.56 mm rounds, a few grenades, and a pair of rockets. As they grabbed the ammo, Bexley caught sight of headlights coming from the north.

He motioned to the others as several vehicles came into view and came to a stop fifty meters away.

"Into the parking garage," Cunningham said quickly.

The three shuffled into the parking garage and took cover behind a low wall that faced the road. Bexley peered around the corner and counted eight ALSVs, the mercenaries were all making their way toward the larger structure.

"Enemy reinforcements just showed up," Bexley reported to Cunningham. "Probably sent to cut us off from the north."

"Not good," Cunningham said, grinding his teeth. "No way we can take them here."

"Agreed."

"They're sitting ducks in there," Michaels said. "We gotta do something!"

"We will," Cunningham assured. "Just not here."

Bexley looked outside and spotted the pedestrian bridge. "We'll go high and flank them."

Cunningham nodded and they moved deeper into the parking garage, heading for the staircase. As they approached, a side door was thrown open and three armed men stepped out.

Bexley went to squeeze the trigger when he recognized who it was. "Jesus Christ! Where the hell did you guys come from?"

Chambers lowered his rifle. "Glad to see you, man, our friend showed us a tunnel that ran underground from her place to here."

"Stevens?"

"He's fine," Washington said and then paused. "Had a run in with some crocodiles."

"Where's everyone else?" Rider asked.

"Madi and Kate are inside," Bexley answered. "Harper and Catipon are MIA, our friends just showed up and Madi and Kate have no idea."

"Let's go then, after you," Chambers said.

They went up the stairs and Bexley asked, "Your friend tell you what this place is?"

Chambers smiled. "You wouldn't believe if I told you."

"Try me."

In the cafeteria, Madi ran her fingers through her tousled hair, exhaling loudly and deeply. Yawning, she leaned back over the table and stretched. Her mind whirled at the thought of what had happened over the last day and a half. Thoughts of Harper, the mercenaries and their unknown goal, and the weird occurrences on the island.

She was interrupted by the sounds of footsteps and hushed voices coming down the hall.

Madi locked eyes with Kate.

Trouble, they both quickly deduced.

Kate moved to a pair of swinging doors that lead deeper into the building while Madi threw her Kevlar on and quickly followed, beams of light starting to come from the hall.

"Shit—shit," she whispered to herself.

"Hurry up!" Kate urged from the swinging doors.

Madi ducked behind a concrete pillar as several mercenaries stepped out into the cafeteria.

"Fan out!" one of the mercenaries yelled out. "They couldn't have gotten far!"

Kate glanced at Madi through the faded glass window in the door and kept a wary eye on their enemy spreading out. They searched the cafeteria floor and were moving back into the kitchen. Madi peered around the corner of the pillar and spotted one of the mercenaries come to a stop, his attention on something resting on a table.

Madi saw what it was, one of her empty pistol magazines. She must've forgotten to grab it in her rush. She looked back at Kate and mouthed the word. *Shit.*

Kate brought up her rifle and cautiously pushed the door open an inch.

The mercenary turned on his rifle's mounted flashlight and picked up the magazine, examining it. "Hey, I got—"

The man dropped dead, a bullet hole in his forehead.

Kate kicked the door open and unleashed a spray of automatic rifle fire, yelling to Madi, "Move!"

A few men were caught in Kate's attack as others dived for cover, bullets exploding into the walls behind them. Madi sprinted toward the doors and reached for something on her flak as she slid over a cafeteria table.

The mercenaries began to fire back as they called in the rest of their forces into the cafeteria. Madi came to the doors and said to Kate, "Go, I'll bring up the rear!"

She pulled the pin from her M-67 fragmentation grenade and tossed it back into the cafeteria. She curled up against the door and braced for the blast.

The grenade exploded from beneath a table, splintering it in a massive shockwave of splinters and fire, lifting several men off their feet. One man, screaming terribly, flew directly toward Madi's position behind the pair of swinging doors. His body smacked into one door and threw it from its hinges, dead body and door landing beside Madi with a thud.

"Take that," she gloated.

Madi took off down the hall as the mercenaries recovered from the grenade blast. One of them said into a radio, "They're moving toward the sub pins. Cut them off from the north and we'll trap them!"

Madi caught up to Kate and she asked, "Any idea where we're going?"

"Away from the people trying to kill us!" Kate exclaimed and paused as they came to a set of short stairs leading down.

"Works for me!"

They moved down the steps and stepped into ankle deep water at the bottom. Flashing her light forward, Madi saw another set of stairs leading down into deeper water.

"Not sure we want to go this way."

The sounds of hustling men echoed down the halls behind them.

"I don't think we have a choice!" Kate said.

Madi took off in an awkward run in the thigh-high water and came to a door. With a swift kick, the door flew open, and she stepped through it. With her light she saw the water continued past her light's beam and sensed she was in a massive space. Turning her light off, Madi took out a small pin flare gun and fired several into the air.

The two were illuminated in flickering orange light and what they saw took their breath away.

"Think we know what this place is now," Madi reported.

Kate's eyes locked onto something on the far side. "Impossible."

It was an indoor submarine dry dock facility, and it was *absolutely gigantic.*

Nearly a hundred feet high, eight hundred feet long and four hundred feet wide, the space was huge. Two massive dry docks; where a submarine would pull into, be anchored down, and the surrounding water drained out, took up most of the floor space. A series of catwalks ran overhead and out across to where the submarines would be located at. Each dry dock had a massive door where a submarine could traverse through and the southern door, closest to them, was open a few feet and was allowing the hurricane's storm surge to flood the interior.

Due to the lack of light, Madi almost missed it. She squinted and spied a dark cigar-shaped object sitting in the dry dock farthest from them.

"Is that a—" Madi started to ask before the door behind them was shredded with gunfire.

"Time to go!" Kate yelled and slammed the door shut.

They sloshed their way north along the wall, Kate covering the front while Madi covered the rear. The door they had come through was thrown open and Madi fired at the first man to walk through, sending him splashing into the water under twin mists of blood spray.

At the same time, more mercenaries appeared from the front. Kate realizing they're too many and dived for cover behind a pile of crates and a derelict forklift.

"Madi, down!"

Madi turned just as the mercenaries in the front oriented their fire on her. Before she could react, she felt a massive force punch her in the chest and she fell on her side, into the water.

"Madi!" Kate screamed, fearing the worst.

Leaning over the forklift, Kate let loose a few shots toward their attackers and reached out for Madi. She gripped the back of her flak and pulled her with ease through the water and behind cover.

Madi coughed up seawater and struggled to catch her breath, a jarring pain throbbing in her chest. She went to speak and couldn't even muster a single word. Her first thought was that she had been shot and she was dying. Fear immediately gripped her, and she fought desperately to breathe.

Kate frantically swept her fingers on Madi's side and under her flak, feeling for a bullet hole. The top of her hand bumped into something on the inside of her flak and she let out a sigh of relief. She examined the front of her flak and saw a small hole in the fabric. With her fingers, she dug into the fabric and felt the SAPI plate had a significant deformation in it.

"Madi!" Kate said. "You're okay, the plate caught it!"

Relived, Madi calmed down and was finally able to take a breath.

"You good?" Kate asked, gunfire still sounding in the distance.

"No," Madi breathed and sat up. "But I'm alright."

Bullets slammed into the crates and forklift above them, cascading them in bits of wood and sparks.

Kate fired to the north and then ducked back down, reloading. "Last mag!"

"Fuck!" Madi yelled and fired a few rounds back toward the men to the south. They had moved closer to them, using the field of crates as cover.

Madi caught movement from the south behind the mercenaries and squinted at something moving beneath the water.

"Who the hell?" she asked herself.

The two men in the rear of the group moving from the south never saw two figures creep up behind them, swimming silently below the waterline.

In a coordinated strike, those figures suddenly exploded from the water and each grabbed a mercenary, clamping their mouth shut and falling backward into the water. After a short struggle, they stood, crouched over the mercenaries.

"I can't fucking believe it!" Kate said, seeing who it was.

"I can," Madi said with a smirk.

Harper, breathing hard, wiped the water from his face as he grabbed the mercenaries' rifle and threw Catipon a smile. "See, what'd I tell you? Not so bad."

Catipon cast Harper a death stare as he slipped his knife back into its sheath on his belt.. "I'm never swimming through a hurricane with you ever again!"

They quickly plundered the dead men of their magazines, Catipon also grabbing a rifle.

Harper inserted a fresh magazine. "I hope we never have to. Now, let's get to work."

They stood up from behind cover and unleashed their combined firepower on the men before them. Bodies slashed into the water as the group from the north spotted them and shifted their fire. Under a field of exploding geysers, Harper and Catipon cleared the south of mercenaries and moved to Madi and Kate.

"You guys good?" Harper asked as he ran up.

Catipon dragged a dead mercenary behind him. "I come baring gifts."

They nodded and went about proliferating the dead mercenaries' ammo. Harper dropped into the water beside Madi. She slapped him repeatedly on the shoulder.

"Hey, stop it!"

"Asshole!" Madi said angrily. "I thought you guys were fucking dead!"

"It's gonna take more than a hurricane to kill us two!" Harper joked.

Madi fired a few rounds and noticed a team of mercenaries appear on the catwalk to the north, several of them armed with M240B machine guns. She motioned to Harper, "How about that?"

"Fuck me," Harper said.

Their attackers were gaining the high ground from both directions to gain a tactical advantage over their prey. Harper glanced around for a way out. They were trapped in the open in between the two submarine dry docks with no viable escape.

And then he noticed the shadowy object resting in the northern dry dock. "Is that a—"

Madi cut him off. "A submarine? Yep."

Harper smiled. "Awesome."

She caught his mischievous gaze and sensed what he had planned. "That's not a way out! We would only be trapped inside it!"

"I'd rather be trapped in that than trapped out here!"

Madi rolled her eyes, reluctantly agreeing. "I hope you know what you're doing!"

The submarine in question was a Los Angeles-class nuclear powered attack submarine. With a length of 362 feet, a beam of 33 feet, and a draft of 31 feet, the black painted steel beast was massive. The submarine was currently resting on struts located beneath the water's surface and secured firmly. Neglected for over three decades, she was covered in a fine layer of grime and dirt, but still retained her malevolent look as one of the most feared vessels to ever roam the seas.

Two metal gangplanks led over the surrounding moat and to the two crew hatches located on top of the submarine and to the rear of its coning tower, which contained the ship's radar equipment and communication antennas.

"Yo!" Harper yelled over to Catipon.

Catipon turned his head.

"Sub, now!"

"Got it!"

Catipon laid down a burst of fire as the group bounded backwards toward the closet gangplank. The army of mercenaries were now moving with coordination across the flooded surface and elevated catwalks. Kate stopped at the bridge entrance, turned and fired, covering the other's movement across.

Harper was last, tapped her shoulder, and followed in trace. In his mad dash across, he spotted a loading platform suspended from a crane system sitting on hydraulic rollers level with the catwalk thirty feet above. The platform swayed a few feet above the sub in front of the coning tower. Sitting below was a small hatch that had fallen over but had refused to fully shut.

Harper's thoughts were quickly shifted as bullets pinged off the metal railing inches from him, casting up sparks and sending him to the ground for cover.

Reaching the crew hatch on top of the submarine, Catipon gripped the flywheel and made to spin it, but it was shut solid.

"Son of a bitch!" he cursed and slung his rifle to the side.

Catipon gripped it with both hands as Kate crouched down to assist. With a countdown, the two pulled with all their might to no avail.

Madi took a knee by the gangplank as Harper joined her.

"Great plan so far!" Madi said before she leveled her sights on a mercenary and pulled the trigger.

"Ha ha," Harper mocked sarcastically, "save the critiques for later, will you? Tyler, how we looking back there!"

Catipon's face was beat red from exertion until his hands slipped and he tumbled awkwardly backwards. "Fuck me sideways!"

Harper and Madi continued to provide covering fire for Catipon and Kate as they fought with the stubborn flywheel. After a few butt-stocks from his rifle in nothing other than pure frustration, the flywheel budged a hair and then started to spin freely.

"Ah-ha!" Catipon exclaimed as he threw open the hatch. "We're in business ladies and gentlemen!"

Catipon quickly ushered Kate down a ladder and into the darkness below.

"Go!" Harper yelled to Madi.

Madi disappeared into the hatch with Harper following behind until he stopped, looking at his friend.

"I got you!" said Catipon and gestured for him to climb down.

"No, I got you!" Harper replied.

Catipon looked over at him. "No, I got *you!*"

"*No,* I got *you!*" Harper said exasperated.

Just then several deep *thumps* echoed across the battlefield. Harper and Catipon turned their heads instantly.

The mercenaries had employed several M203 grenade launchers that were attached to the bottom of their rifles, sending multiple 40 mm grenades heading their way.

"You've gotta be fist fucking me!" Harper shouted.

"Move!" he roared as he grabbed Catipon and threw him down the hatch.

A split second later, Harper was following Catipon down, pulling the hatch close behind him. Harper landed eight feet below right on top of Catipon a millisecond before the hatch slammed shut and a multitude of muffled explosions could be heard.

"Ow," Catipon moaned as Harper rolled off him. "That hurt . . . a lot."

Harper managed a painful laugh as he flipped on his helmet mounted light. "You'll be fine."

Next to him, Madi lit up the space with another light. "What now?"

Harper noted the damp and stale air in the sub, he figured the boat had been sealed shut for over thirty years.

"The control room," he stated.

"How's that going to help us?" Madi asked incredulously.

"I'm hoping this boat's communications systems are still functional," Harper explained as they moved forward through a cramped passageway. "We need to contact the *Iwo Jima*."

"What do you know about submarines?" Kate asked.

Harper cast a knowing glance back at Catipon. "I've seen *Crimson Tide*, great movie, one of my favorites. And I've spent a fait amount of time on them."

Madi realized what they were talking about as they entered the confined control room of the submarine, this space even more stuffy with stale air. "Are you talking about the 'Kronos Incident'?"

"That was you guys?" Kate inquired.

Harper and Catipon, looking at each other with a smirk, remained silent.

Kate, shining her own light around, examined a control console and hit a few buttons. "This old boat might have enough residual power in it to power up a few basic systems."

Harper raised an eyebrow quizzingly at Kate's apparent knowledge of submarines and sarcastically asked, "*Crimson Tide* fan?"

"Stop with the submarine movie!" Madi snapped.

Kate quickly explained. "I wanted to serve on submarines until I found out that females weren't allowed for sub duty at the time."

"Real shame," Catipon commented.

Harper shifted focus and addressed Kate. "You're reading my mind; can you get a message out?"

"The antennas topside looked functional and if there's no water damage, I should be able to get a message out."

"How? I thought we were being jammed?" Madi asked.

Kate moved across the cramped space, shining her light on various switches and dials, looking for something in particular. "These boats transmit on a much lower frequency than our satellite communications. They transmit in the Very Low Frequency Band or VLF."

She wiped the grime off a panel and flipped a switch. "Reason being is cause VLF is very conductive and effective in seawater and across long distances allowing these boats to communicate when they're submerged. And I doubt these guys thought to set their jammer to that low of a frequency."

While shining his light around and listening to Kate, Harper spotted a ballcap hanging on a hook and read the faded insignia on the front.

USS *LINCOLN*
SSN-002

"The *Lincoln*," he breathed. "Umm."

Harper shrugged and grabbed the hat, pointed at Madi with it and said, "Let's go seal the hatches and cover our rear."

She nodded.

Harper looked Catipon and Kate. "Stay here and get comms with the Iwo Jima."

Kate was looking at Harper's newly acquired hat and shined her light at it.

"What is it?" he asked and held up the hat so she could get a better view.

"Your hat," Kate said confused. "The 'Lincoln'?"

"What about it?"

Kate waved her head. "Not important. We'll get comms up."

Harper nodded and preceded to leave with Madi in tow, shoving the hat in his cargo pocket.

"What do you need from me?" Catipon asked Kate.

She pointed to the far wall. "I need you to find a dial marked REBOOT SYSTEM and let me know when you find it."

Catipon nodded and made his way over there. He called out, "What about that hat threw you for a loop there?"

"My father served in the Navy," Kate began as she unscrewed a panel off the wall and pulled out a mess of wires. "He was a submarine captain actually, back in the Cold War, never home much which sucked but you know, all part of the job. He took me on a few tours of the Los Angeles and Ohio class submarines, and I was hooked. I read all about submarines and did all sorts of school projects on them. I knew just about everything about nuclear powered submarines, could even name them all."

She paused and took a glance at Catipon. "A sub by the name of the USS *Lincoln*, I've *never* heard of it."

Catipon raised an eyebrow. "How is that possible?"

Kate went back to stripping a set of wires. "It leads me to believe this sub was a part of the *Dark Boat Program*, a fleet of subs built in secrecy to participate in classified missions in which if things went sideways, could be plausibly denied."

"That would explain why they left a sub here, it never existed in the first place," Catipon concluded.

"Just like this freakin' island," Kate added.

"Found the dial," Catipon announced.

"Perfect, hold on."

Kate finished stripping the two wires and struck them together. A spark flew and she quickly tied them together. Rushing over to a control console she stared at an unlit bulb patiently.

"Come on!" Kate urged, biting her lip.

After a few more tense seconds the bulb illuminated green. "Hit the dial!"

Catipon did so.

Every light in the control center briefly flashed before going dark and then coming back on, a low humming emitting from deep within the boat.

"Ah-ha! We got power!" Kate exclaimed with a smile.

Madi dropped down from the ladder they had come down. "Hatch is secured."

"They won't try this one, they'll go for the rear one," Harper said as he moved past and down the port side passageway.

As they neared the rear crew hatch, a low hum sounded and one by one the lights overhead started to come on. Harper looked down the passageway as the lights continued to flicker on and illuminated a man standing there, rifle out in front of him and pulling the trigger.

Harper felt the adrenaline immediately rush into his bloodstream, his heartbeat quickening and pupils growing larger.

Bullets pinged and ricocheted all around Harper and Madi before he released a salvo from the hip and the man dropped to the deck. A second armed gunmen quickly took his place and Harper could see more mercenaries shuffling further down the passageway.

"Move!"

Madi retreated ten feet and rounded a corner that led to the starboard side passageway and the two took off sprinting down it toward the control room. Mercenaries filtered into the passageway behind them and sent bullets flying toward them. Harper and Madi ducked into a side room, returning fire from around the corner.

Harper shouted down the hall, "Kate, how we looking up there?"

"I'm working on it," he heard her yell back.

Kate wiped the thick layer of dust and grime from a computer screen and paused, realizing she was missing something.

Catipon stood in the doorway, rifle at the ready. "Who are you going to contact?"

Kate looked up from her station and scanned the bridge, looking for something. "Navy has a VLF radio station up in Maine."

She spotted what she was looking for, a keyboard, ran over and grabbed it. Next, she climbed under her workstation and began wiring it in. "I'm hoping they think we're legit and put us in touch with the Iwo Jima."

Finished, Kate grabbed a chair, took a seat, and started typing on the keyboard. "Seems to be working."

Grabbing a handheld transmitter, Kate began speaking. "Naval Radio Station Cutler, this is the USS *Lincoln*, do you copy?"

Seven hundred miles to the north, one of two of the US Navy's VLF radio stations sat under a gloomy sky. It was almost lunch for the young ensign assigned to the facility's constant VLF radio watch.

Suddenly the radio squawked, and the ensign sat up, confused. He slipped on a pair of headphones and turned the volume up.

"Naval Radio Station Cutler, this is the USS *Lincoln*, do you copy?"

A quizzed look crossed the ensign's face. He knew of no ship called the USS *Lincoln*.

"Naval Radio Station Cutler, we are Americans under fire, and I need to speak to the USS *Iwo Jima* located in the middle of the Atlantic immediately!"

The ensign dropped his headphones and sprinted out the door, yelling for his superior.

A M84 flashbang grenade came to a stop against Harper's foot to which received a bug-eyed stare from him.

"Grenade!" he yelled, kicked it back, and moved.

An explosion of light and sound ripped through the cramped confines of the sub and the soundwave, amplified within the metal tube, deafened anyone close by.

Recovering from the blast, Harper slapped the side of his head, as if it would dissipate the internal ringing noise and restore his hearing. "Fuck me!"

"You good?" Madi asked.

"What!" Harper screamed back, still having trouble hearing.

Madi leaned around the corner and fired a few rounds to keep the mercenaries at bay. "We can't stay here! We're gonna run out of submarine eventually!"

"I know!" Harper said as he looked down at his rifle to see he had gone empty of ammo. Tossing it to the side, he drew his pistol. "I think I have a plan, let's get to the bridge!"

"To the last calling station, using this net for a prank is a federal crime," the commanding officer of Naval Radio Station Cutler said harshly into the transmitter. "I order you to cease any further transmissions!"

"What! Motherfucker!" Kate cursed and then sternly into the transmitter. "This is not a fucking prank! Listen to me very carefully. I am an American citizen and we are under attack. Several Americans have already been killed here and more will continue to do so if you fail to act. Now, run this up the flagpole to the president and put me in contact with the USS *Iwo Jima* or I'll have the Chief of Naval Operations bust your balls so low that only job you'll get in the US Navy will be within the fucking sanitization department. Understood?"

The commanding officer's jaw dropped as he stared bug-eyed at the receiver. Swallowing nervously, he replied, "Roger, stand by."

Catipon was shocked by her harsh and demanding tone; it kind of impressed him.

"Two friendlies entering!" Harper shouted as he ran into the control room. "How we looking, guys?"

"We made contact, they're putting us in touch with the *Iwo Jima*," Kate reported.

"What kind of ordnance does this sub have?"

Kate's brow furrowed, "Why?"

"I got an idea."

Kate began typing and then walked over to a wall and examined a series of lights. "We have a torpedo loaded in tubes 1 and 2, plus a dozen Tomahawk cruise missiles."

"Holy fuck," Catipon murmured to himself. "Talk about a lack of accountability."

"Everything functional?"

"Should be."

"I saw a hatch just forward of the coning tower."

"The weapons loading hatch."

Harper smiled, "So, here's the plan."

A minute later, Kate had programmed the appropriate commands into the sub's firing computer as more men could be heard making their way down the passageways.

"Where the hell is *the Iwo Jima!*" Catipon said in frustration. "I don't know how much longer we can stand around here for."

As if on cue, the radio crackled. "This is the USS *Iwo Jima*, please identify yourself."

Kate jumped for the transmitter. "This is Oscar-Four-Whiskey, identification code zero-six-three-romeo-two-quebec. Mission number hotel-zulu-two-three."

A couple-second pause and then Henderson's voice said, "This is Six, go ahead."

Kate handed the transmitter to Harper.

"Six, this is Harper, they're jamming our comms, but we've made link up with our asset and some of the Marines. Enemy force is yet to be identified, but they are well-sized, well-funded, and *very* relentless."

Catipon ducked back around the bulkhead as gunfire clacked off from down the hall, bullets ricocheting around the doorway. "Son of a bitch!"

"This thing is more complex than we originally thought," Harper continued. "I think Cutthroat is aiding the mercenary force here on the island, why and for what, we have no idea."

"Roger, I'll handle them on my end," Henderson said. "Listen, we just got a report from the NRO, they've detected—" his voice was drowned out by the sound of Catipon firing his weapon. Harper had to shove the speaker against his ear to hear what he had said.

"Yo, we gotta go!" Catipon shouted. "Like, now!"

Harper went to speak again into the transmitter when more rifle fire sounded, bullets whizzing across the control center.

"Jake!" Madi yelled.

"Fuck!" Harper cursed. "Six, we have to move, Harper out!"

He looked over at Kate. "Start the clock!"

Kate nodded, flipped a switch and hit a button. "We got ten minutes!"

Everyone moved to the far side of the bridge and disappeared down a passageway that led to the bow of the boat. They ran down a cramped passageway and came to a ladder, hearing the echoes of their pursuers enter the control room behind them.

Catipon was the first one up and, with pistol drawn, cautiously pushed the hatch open and scanned the area. The interior was dimly lit, and the coning tower put the hatch entrance in an even darker shadow.

He saw several mercenaries standing guard by the catwalk that led to the submarine and another group moving on an elevated catwalk over by the door leading into the front of the building. One individual seemed to be directing troops while talking on a radio.

Catipon crawled out and spotted the cable operated platform swaying a foot above his head.

"Let's go," he whispered to the others below.

Kate came out and they quietly stepped onto the elevator platform. Consisting of a thin guard rail and measuring three by five feet, the elevator was used to lower heavy supplies down into the sub from the catwalk above.

Harper motioned to Madi to climb up and the two locked eyes. Wanting to say something, Madi nodded awkwardly and started climbing. She had just gotten to the top when a barrage of gunfire erupted below.

"Shit!" Harper shouted and ducked around a bulkhead.

His shoulder screamed in pain, and he peered down to see blood slicking down his arm; a ricocheting bullet had grazed him.

"Jake!" Madi called out.

Yelling from outside the sub the sentries heard this and looked over.

"Go!" Harper said and fired a few rounds back down the passageway. "Seal the hatch! I'll find a way out!"

Catipon was watching the scene outside and watched the sentries spot them and raise their weapons. "We gotta go right now!"

"Not without Jake!" Madi shot back.

"Go, goddamnit!" Harper yelled.

The gunfire increased as the mercenaries encroached on Harper.

"Shit!" Madi yelled and slammed the hatch out.

Catipon gripped the controls, "Hold on!"

Kate reached out for Madi's hand as Catipon hit the controls and the sentries opened fire on them. Bullets danced off the bottom of the elevator as they whizzed up toward the sky.

Down in the sub, Harper ejected a magazine and inserted a new one. "What now, Jake? Think, think . . . "

He looked around for an escape and his eyes came to a rest toward the bow of the boat. "Yeah, fuck it. That might work."

Taking a few deep breaths, Harper sprinted toward the bow under a hail of gunfire.

The elevator arrived at the catwalk above and the group quickly departed, sprinting for the front of the building. Catipon and Kate brought up their rifles as the mercenaries there swung around toward them when a door behind them was thrown open. A group of men rushed out guns a blazing.

"What the fuck?" Catipon said as he squinted to see who it was.

They ran up to see Chambers, Rider, Washington, and the others behind them.

"Holy shit!" Catipon exclaimed. "Damn good to see you guys!"

Harper entered the boat's torpedo room and quickly scanned the instrumental panel, keeping a wary eye on the passageway behind him.

"Come on, where is it!" he said to himself frantically and checked his watch; four minutes left.

Harper came to a button on the front bulkhead labeled: 'LAUNCH TUBE 1' and smiled. "Bingo."

He hit it and instantly heard a *swoosh* emanate from the hatch located behind the bulkhead. Outside, a Mark 48 torpedo shot from the sub's bow and headed toward the dry dock's wall barely fifty feet away. Harper had no clue if the torpedo would detonate, he just needed the torpedo tube cleared.

The torpedo did explode, quite spectacularly in fact.

A thousand pounds of high explosive tore through the concrete wall and sent a plume of water eighty feet into the air. The mercenary sentries outside were thrown backwards and everyone in the sub was thrown against the wall or to the deck.

About to enter the interior of the building and exit the dry docks, The Team members were nearly thrown off their feet and grabbed the railing for support. A mist rained down on them as they surveyed the massive explosion site.

"What the hell was that?" Chambers asked.

"We gotta go," Catipon said quickly. "This whole place is about to go up."

"What the hell was that then?" Rider asked, dumbfounded.

Kate raised her eyebrows. "*That* was nothing."

"Hol—" Harper coughed as he stood up, "—lee fuck!"

Quickly spinning the flywheel open, Harper hit the launch button again. With no torpedo loaded in the tube, water flooded in through the opened hatch and out onto the deck. Harper stripped off his flak and Kevlar, leaving on only his gun belt and fanny pack so he could fit into the cramped tube.

"This is a bad idea," he mumbled and started to climb into the torpedo tube, fighting with the current of the rushing water.

Next, he shut the hatch behind him and managed to take a final breath before being completely submerged. With the hatch now closed behind him there was no current and he easily managed to swim ahead and out of the sub's torpedo tube. Breast stroking out in front of the sub's rounded bow, Harper dwarfed in comparison to the massive vessel. He took a moment to steal a glance behind and shook his head in amazement.

The mercenaries pursuing him came to the torpedo room and were confused to find no one there.

"Where'd they go?"

"Search the sub!"

Harper surfaced in front of the destroyed concrete dock wall amid a haze of water vapor. He climbed up onto the dry dock's surface and stayed low in the rocking thigh-deep water. Glancing around, he only saw the dazed sentries over by the catwalk leading onto the sub.

SHROOOOOMMM!

The noise startled him, and he looked down at his watch. "Oh, shit!" The ten minutes was up.

Harper looked back to see fire and light shoot out from the midsection of the sub as a Tomahawk cruise missile roared into the air! Twenty feet long and weighting almost three thousand pounds, the Tomahawk cruise missile was a terrifying sight to behold launching at such a close range.

Harper's eyes widened as he turned and made a dead sprint sloshing through the water for the nearest door leading back into building. *"Fuck-fuck-fuck-fuck!"*

The Tomahawk's billowing smoke cloud nearly engulfed Harper as he lowered his shoulder into the door, flinging it open and continued sprinting. Not a second later, three thousand pounds of metal, fuel, and explosive connected with ceiling moving at nearly two hundred miles an hour!

BOOM!-BOOM!-BOOOMMM!

A two-hundred-foot radius of the concrete ceiling and the wall closest to the sub was simply pulverized and blasted outward high into the sky. The fireball reached out in every direction, engulfing the sub. With astonishing force, the concussive shockwave flattened the maze of catwalks and blew out every door and window of the building face inside the dry docks. Huge chucks of concrete and derbies rained down into the ocean outside.

Severely weakened by the gaping hole in it, the ceiling and wall started to collapse. Whole sections of the wall toppled outward into the sea and concrete slabs rained down below. The sub's coning tower was crushed like a tin can and the sub was quickly covered in a field of ruins, trapping the helpless mercenaries within.

The ragtag group were running across the pedestrian bridge through the rain when the Tomahawk exploded, and they quickly spun to watch the fireball.

Scanning the road below them, Catipon urged, "We need transpo!"

"The vehicles these assholes came in should do just fine," Michaels offered.

Cunningham slapped him on the shoulder. "Good idea."

Michaels smirked and continued trotting down the bridge.

Madi stopped to look back, waiting for Harper to appear.

"He'll meet us down there," Catipon assured her. "I'm sure of it."

Madi nodded and followed the others into the parking garage.

Taking the stairs two at a time, they quickly came onto the parking garage's first level and made to run outside when multiple mercenaries stepped out from behind pillars and parked cars, rifles drawn.

"Drop it!" one of them commanded.

Everyone had their weapons drawn on each other, staring at each other tensely. Catipon knew they were outmatched and would be gunned down in seconds. He couldn't see a way where they all lived.

He glanced over at Madi, she was thinking the same thing.

"Son of a bitch," he cursed as he lowered his weapon and shut his eyes in defeat.

The others followed suit, slowly placing their weapons on the ground and raising their hands in surrender.

A mercenary approached Catipon.

"Fuck you," Catipon spat.

He quickly received a blow to the stomach with a rifle buttstock for his remark and he doubled over to the ground wheezing for breath. Catipon looked up at the man, eyes glaring with malice.

Cunningham helped him up to his feet as they were quickly disarmed, relived of their flaks, Kevlar's, and ForeTex armguards, and had their hands tied behind their backs with a pair of zip ties.

Meanwhile, Harper was making his way through the building and came out onto the pedestrian bridge. He noticed the wind and rains were not nearly as violent as they were before, the storm was dying down.

Moving across the bridge with caution, he made his way down the stairwell and stopped when he heard unknown voices. Harper got low and with his pistol held high, moved out into the parking garage and came to a halt behind a parked car.

Peering around the rear bumper, he saw Team members and Marines being forced under gunpoint to climb into a canvas topped troop transport truck. Nearly two dozen mercenaries stood around the truck and several ALSVs.

Fuck, Harper thought and closed his eyes. He spotted Madi and wanted nothing more than to come out running and shooting, but he knew he wouldn't make it two steps before he was killed.

As Madi waited to climb into the truck, she glanced around and caught sight of Harper hiding behind the car. Her heart fluttered with hope and then she released he couldn't do anything without himself getting killed.

"Move it!" One of the mercenaries shoved her to the ground.

Harper moved before he stopped himself.

Goddamn it.

Madi looked over at Harper and gave a quick shake of her head.

She was lifted to her feet and climbed reluctantly into the troop transport truck. Once they were all loaded into the truck, Madi gave a withering death stare at the mercenary that had shoved her. "You're gonna wish you hadn't done that."

"I fucking doubt it, sweetie!" the mercenary said sourly.

A moment later, the truck and fleet of ALSVs rolled out of the parking garage and headed down a dirt road at the back of the parking garage that led into the interior of the island.

Madi stole a glance at the parking garage as they rumbled down the road, hoping to see Harper.

But he was nowhere to be seen.

"Goddamn it, Jake," she whispered to herself.

"ANY WORD?" CAPTAIN MATHESON ASKED AS HE BARGED ONTO THE bridge of the *Iwo Jima*.

An officer with his ear in a phone said, "No, sir, not yet. Their berthing was empty."

"Search the whole damn ship!"

"Aye, sir."

As soon as Henderson had gotten off the radio with Harper, he had informed Matheson of Cutthroat and he had ordered his master-at-arms to apprehend them. General quarters had been sounded, meaning everyone besides essential personnel had to return to their berthings.

In the hangar bay of the *Iwo Jima*, Marines and sailors were in the process of returning to their assigned berthings when the twenty-four members of Recon Unit 16 walked in, quickly. They were dressed in dark green fatigues, lightweight flaks, bump helmets with quad tube night-vision devices, and armed with suppressed Daniel Defense MK-18 rifles with a 10.3-inch barrel and Glock 45 pistols.

Brookes led the group as they made their way to the ramp that led outside when he spotted a pair of master-at-arms Navy sailors. They noticed them and one of them spoke into a radio. At the same time, a Navy officer dressed in blue overalls walked up to Brookes.

"Excuse me, but you can't go up there, we're in general quarters."

"Hey!" one of the master-at-arms sailors yelled across the hangar bay. "Stop them!"

Several of the Marines and sailors looked around in confusion.

The navy lieutenant seemed to realize he was talking about the group in front of him. "I think you guys should wait here."

He never noticed a recon member approach from the side with a short-bladed knife in hand. The navy officer was stabbed repeatedly in the kidney as a hand was cupped over his mouth to silence his screams. Within three seconds, the man was dead, and his body was lowered to the deck against the bulkhead and his hat was thrown over his face. The entire had been blocked from view by the platoon of rogue Marines.

The team of MAs started to run across the hangar bay, shouting.

"Move! Move!"

"Stop them!"

Walking up the ramp, Brookes said, "Seems we've been made, slow 'em down."

"Roger that."

One of the recon Marines dropped to a knee and fired a burst from his rifle, sending men and women running and screaming in every direction.

"What the hell was that?" Matheson demanded, hearing the gunshots from down below in the ship.

Two Navy sailors were shot dead as more MAs rushed into the hangar bay, alerted by the sound of gunfire.

The men of Recon Unit 16 approached an Osprey sitting on the flight deck, where they unchained it and two of the members started the engines.

"What the hell?" someone in the bridge said, raising a pair of binoculars to his eyes. "Sir! It appears we have a bird spinning up on the flight deck."

"No one has been authorized to depart!" Matheson. "Who the hell is it?"

"Looks like those recon guys!"

"Son of a bitch! Get them on the horn, they are not allowed to leave!" Matheson commanded. "Where's our response team! Anybody find out where those shots came from!"

"I have reports of casualties in the hangar bay!"

"Get a medical team down there now!"

"Firefly 2–3, you are not authorized for departure! Shut down your engines!" an ensign said into his radio.

In the Osprey's cockpit, the two pilots heard this and remained silent. Brookes was the last one to run up into the helicopter and gave them the signal to take off.

"Track that bird! I want to know where it's going!" Matheson called out, watching it climb higher above the flight deck.

They watched the Osprey's backend come level with the bridge's windows and could see a man standing up in the troop compartment. Brookes gave them a small wave and a smug grin before the Osprey applied power and shot out in front of them, climbing high into the clouds.

"Brookes, that fucking weasel!" Henderson cursed angrily, slamming his fist down on a table.

"Got any idea on what *that* was about?" Matheson asked.

"I got a feeling it's not good," Henderson said and pulled out a satellite phone. "I've got to make a call."

21

CAMP DAVID
1200 HOURS

A PAIR OF MARINES DRESSED IN FULL BATTLE RATTLE AND ARMED WITH Colt M4s slung across their chests patrolled slowly through the forest around the presidential retreat. The hooded ponchos they wore did little to stop the pouring rain from soaking them to the bone, but they took their job seriously and were focused.

"Control, this is Rover 2, radio check."

"Rover 2, Control, loud and clear."

The Marines, catching a glimpse of Aspen lodge in the distance, continued with their patrol.

Inside the president's lodge, Veronica took a moment to process what she had just been told. She stood up and slowly walked to the large floor-to-ceiling glass doors that looked out over the back porch and golf course.

Behind her, arranged on the sofas around the fire were Lisa and two junior intelligence analysts of hers that were wrapped up in this whole thing. No Secret Service Agents or aides were present; it was *way* above their security clearance.

During the three-hour drive into Maryland, Fasswater had taken some time to investigate the mysterious Russian's claims of teleportation. Other than what he had seen in science fiction movies, Fasswater knew very little on the subject.

He started with a Google search on his phone and the first result came from Wikipedia. It stated that teleportation was the hypothetical transfer of matter or energy from one point to another without traversing the physical space between them. It said there was no known physical mechanism that allowed for teleportation and the page was rather short.

At the bottom were related subjects with the Philadelphia experiment being one of them. Fasswater clicked on it and read through it. The conspiracy theory claimed that the US Navy was developing a form of stealth technology that would render an entire ship invisible to the naked eye. Apparently, they had achieved a limited success and on one test disappeared in a flash of blue lights and reappeared over 200 miles away in Norfolk, Virginia, before appearing back in Philadelphia. However, the entire allegation was considered nothing but a hoax stating the claims go against the laws of physics.

The second related subject, wormholes, was long and very in-depth. Also called an Einstein-Rosen bridge, wormholes were a speculative structure linking two points in spacetime and were consistent with the general theory of relativity, but their existence remained to be proven. He read about their visualization, terminology, and development, mentioning two- and three-dimensional spaces, cosmic strings, gravitational collapse, the event horizon, and exotic matter. Fasswater found it very complicated and hard to fully understand.

He left the article with the understanding that teleportation used wormholes that could theoretically connect distances of billions of light years or a few meters, different points in time, or even different universes.

Fasswater decided that he had read enough about conspiracy theories and theoretical physics for one day and went to close the tab when he saw something that he had forgotten about. A tab with the search results for Piketon, Ohio.

In the madness of the grisly murder and encounter with assassins disguised as cops, the mention of the town had left his mind.

He read about the small Ohio town and suddenly things started to become clearer.

"How can any of this be verified?" Veronica asked without turning from the window.

Natalie spoke up. "The very fact that highly trained assassins killed my contact and almost killed us proves that there's something worth hiding, giving this whole thing some sort of validation."

Veronica managed a laugh at her blunt answer and then turned and looked at Lisa. "Do we have any idea on who those would be assassins are?"

"No positive ID yet, ma'am," Lisa replied. "They weren't carrying any identification which is not surprising. Their uniforms were stolen from a local cop who is currently out of town, we're looking into that, but we don't think he was involved. Their weapon's serial numbers, a couple of Glocks, haven't popped up on any databases. Facial ID is proving . . . *difficult* due to the state of the bodies." She paused to glance at Fasswater and Natalie before continuing. "No tattoos were found, fingerprints came back with nothing, and we're still awaiting blood results, but I wouldn't hold my breath. Based on their accents we can safely assume they're American. These guys are good, *expensive*, and they know how to be invisible."

"Who's capable of carrying out that level of autonomy?"

Lisa thought for a moment. "If we're talking private companies, I can think of a few. Foreign governments, a couple countries in Western Europe, China perhaps, I wouldn't count Russia out . . . " she paused, "and *us*."

Veronica exhaled deeply and rubbed her temples as she walked around the desk and leaned against it. "I don't like a single part of this."

"Madam President," Fasswater said nervously. "There's one more thing that we found right before the contact was killed."

Veronica listened attentively.

"The Russians were tracking a highly secured shipment to the island shortly before the island was vacated. A shipment from Piketon, Ohio."

Just then Lisa's cellphone rang, and she quickly answered it. "Go for Warner."

"Lisa, it's Frank. Just got word from our boys."

"Wait one," she said, set the phone down, and put it on speaker. "You're on the line with POTUS and two of my analysts. We believe we found the true purpose of Rose Island. A couple of unknown assassins were willing to kill to keep it a secret."

"Oh Christ," Henderson said. "Look, our boys found our asset and some of the Marines, they were taking fire and couldn't talk long."

"By whom?" Veronica asked incredulously as she walked over and took a seat.

"An enemy force that is extremely well equipped for this situation," Henderson answered.

"What exactly is going on here?" Veronica asked no one in particular.

"I have more bad news," Henderson continued. "Just got off the line with the NRO. Satellite scans show a significantly large amount of highly enriched uranium being transported across the island."

"Weapons grade?" Veronica asked, afraid of the answer.

"Scans confirm weapons grade beyond a doubt."

The color drained from Veronica's face.

"The shipment from Piketon," Fasswater said.

"Did you say Piketon?" Henderson asked.

"Yes, sir."

"What does a small town in Ohio have to do with any of this?" Natalie asked.

"Piketon, Ohio, is the site of one of three facilities in the US that enriches uranium to be weapons grade," Henderson explained.

"And in the 80s, it was the busiest," Fasswater continued. "It's estimated over a fourth of all enriched uranium on the planet was processed there, over a million pounds."

"Why the hell would there be weapon-grade uranium on that island?" Veronica asked.

Fasswater snapped his fingers as the answer struck him. "The nuclear reactors on the island. Each reactor requires about a hundred tons of weapons-grade enriched uranium to function."

"Our reports say the two reactors were never online," Henderson protested.

"They had to been close," Fasswater said. "Make senses that they started stock piling uranium there for when it came online."

Natalie continued. "And when they shut down the base in a hurry, they probably left it stored in a lead lined bunker. Hence why our scans never saw it until now."

"If they moved enough uranium for two reactors, that's over 400,000 pounds," Lisa stated, unable to believe the impending ramifications.

"And if they manage to get that stuff off the island and into the hands of our enemies . . . " Veronica's voice trailed off.

"Iran, North Korea, and other unfriendly nations looking to start their own nuclear weapons program would pay handsomely for something like that," Natalie said.

"All that a cell of ISIS or Boko Haram would have to do is strap it to a few pounds of explosive and they'd have their own dirty bomb," Fasswater added.

Veronica shook her head in agreement. "There's no telling what kind of damage could be done."

"I'm afraid the bad news doesn't stop there," Henderson continued. "My men on the island believe that Recon Unit 16 is working with the mercenary force on the island, to what end, they couldn't say, but when we went to arrest them, they killed three sailors and stole an Osprey helicopter. We tracked them for a few miles before their transponder went offline."

Veronica looked at Lisa. "I'm afraid the situation is becoming rapidly untenable. I need to inform the joint chiefs of staff. This thing has the potential to be a full-blown international security threat and I will not let that happen."

Lisa nodded. "I understand, ma'am."

Veronica made to leave. "I'll keep you informed of any further decisions, and I'll keep the presence of your men on a strictly need-to-know basis."

"Appreciate that, ma'am."

Veronica opened the door and was immediately met by her Chief of Staff Stokes and several Secret Service Agents.

"Oliver, I need you to set up a teleconference call with the joint chiefs of staff immediately," Veronica began. "We'll take the call in the situation room downstairs."

Stoke's gaze of judgment and suspicion lingered on the three Team members before quickly following in trace of Veronica. "Yes, ma'am."

Once they were out of earshot, Fasswater asked, "What the hell is that guy's problem?"

"He's very protective of his boss," Lisa replied. "Doesn't like it when he doesn't know everything. Has a reputation for making more enemies than friends and will stop at nothing to get what he wants."

"Sounds like an asshole."

Lisa grinned. "He is." She then turned back to her phone still on the line with Henderson. "Things are about to get very complicated, Frank."

"When doesn't it?" Henderson joked. "Have your analysts look into Cutthroat, see what they can find."

"I'll get them right on it, I'll keep you updated."

"Henderson out."

Lisa put her phone away and looked at Fasswater and Natalie. "Follow me."

She walked out of the den and down the hall at a brisk pace, passing several Secret Service Agents standing diligently at their posts. They came to the lodge's foyer and Warner grabbed her raincoat from a hook, quickly throwing it on.

She leaned in close and addressed the two quietly. "Fasswater, we need to contact our forces on the island. They *need* to know about the uranium before Washington does something drastic. Natalie, I need you to look into the roster of Recon Unit 16, current and former members. Anything out of the ordinary, dig deeper."

A Secret Service Agent opened the front door for them, and they moved into an enclosed front porch, the wind blowing sheets of rain across their feet.

Lisa looked back at the two analysts. "We'll go get you guys set up in a separate lodge. Whatever you do end up finding, you report it directly to me, got it?"

Fasswater looked over at Natalie, nodding confidently. "We'll get it done, boss."

22 ⫼ ROSE ISLAND

CATIPON STUDIED THE MERCENARIES AS HE SAT IN SILENCE, WARY OF staring for too long.

Two sat in the front and two sat in the rear, pistols drawn and keeping a watchful eye on their prisoners. From his position toward the rear, he was confident he could take the two in the rear but wasn't sure about the two in front.

He decided now was not the time to try and escape.

Glancing at his watch as the vehicle drove onto sturdy ground, he figured they had driven south for the last twenty minutes on uneven terrain.

Fifteen minutes later, the vehicle slowed as they entered a large space, Catipon judged by the echoes of the engines and voices yelling. Turning, the truck finally came to a stop. The back flap of the troop transport was thrown open and a mercenary ordered them to get out.

Madi was the first one off and her feet landed on dry and polished concrete. She took in her surroundings to find she was in a massive aircraft hangar, assuming it was one of those at the southern runway.

The others jumped down on the floor behind her and they were led to the western wall, passing crates of supplies and cots. In the middle of the hangar, several mercenaries were using a forklift to transfer heavy steel containers from a flatbed truck and onto the plane.

Catipon squinted at the containers with curiosity. He nudged Kate and gestured over to them. "Is that what I think it is?"

"Yeah, I saw it," Kate said.

The steel containers being loaded onto the plane all had a black trefoil with a triangle-shaped yellow background painted on the sides.

"*Not* good."

As they approached the wall, the seven captured Marines from the squad that had accompanied Madi came into view. They were all handcuffed to a horizontal metal pipe and look defeated, bruised and dirty. A few of them remained slumped against the wall, severely injured from the crash. Madi remembered those who couldn't walk after the crash.

One Marine had a twisted knee and had his leg in a makeshift splint of tree branches. Another had an open bone fracture in his arm. Pale and shivering, she knew an infection was spreading due to the open wound. One of the pilots who had survived was unconscious. His face was swollen and bruised, Madi suspected he had internal hemorrhaging somewhere in his head.

"Goddamn it," she swore under her breathe, feeling responsible for bringing them here.

They soon joined the Marines, handcuffed to the wall as several of the mercenaries stood guard over them close by.

Catipon turned to face away from the guards and asked Kate, "Is that what this is all about? Nuclear material?"

Kate made a gesture of scratching her nose to conceal her mouth. "Has to be. If it's enriched, it could be worth a fortune on the open market. I can think of a few nations and terrorist groups that would pay *very* handsomely for stuff like that."

Chambers spoke up. "We caught one of their transmissions earlier, said they were excavating something, must've been that."

One of the previously captured Marines looked over at Cunningham. "Sorry we let you down, Staff Sergeant. We had nowhere else to go, we lost Martinez, and I'm not sure we would've made it out of there."

Sergeant Vasquez was one of Cunningham's squad leaders and the squad leader of the Marines sent to the island.

"Nothing to apologize for," Cunningham assured him, thinking back to the weird circumstances surrounding Martinez's body. "I know you did your best."

"Where's Jacobs?" Vasquez asked.

Cunningham shook his head. "He didn't make it."

Vasquez glared at the mercenaries across the hangar.

Madi was doing the same, watching them as they went about their work. She spotted one by the lowered rear ramp of the Russian plane. Carlyle stood there with his arms crossed and just stared at Madi for a few seconds. Madi tried to remember if she knew the man as a group of mercenaries cut off her view and then the mysterious man was gone.

O'Neal appeared from under the port side wing of the aircraft, starting to slowly clap as he strolled toward them. The prisoners turned their attention to him.

"Congratulations on making it this far," O'Neal said as he flashed a wicked grin to reveal a row of rotten and skewed teeth. His eyes lingered creepily on Madi and Kate. "What do we have here? Very *nice*."

"Come over here and I'll show you how nice I can be," Madi said fiercely.

O'Neal chuckled and approached her, his eyes staring too long at her features. "You must be quite a catch; get any guy you want."

Madi lurched forward, handcuffs rattling. "I'll show you something you can catch you fucking bastard!"

O'Neal leaned forward just out of her reach and inhaled deeply, as if to try and smell her. "Maybe later, dear."

"I need to know one thing and one thing only," O'Neal began as he walked slowly down the line of prisoners. "What does the government know about me?"

No one said a word.

"Before you all answer at once, I must remind you, I can make things very *unpleasant*," O'Neal threatened as his hand came to a rest atop his holstered pistol.

"Fuck you," Vasquez said firmly.

O'Neal shook his head in frustration. "How . . . unfortunate."

Quick as a whip, O'Neal drew one of his Desert Eagles and aimed it at Vasquez..

"No!" Cunningham shouted, reaching forward.

O'Neal pulled the trigger and the back of Vasquez's head exploded in a wash of red, blasting blood, brain matter, and bits of skull all over Madi!

Madi was frozen in a state of pure shock. Her face and chest were covered in dark-red blood and the warm goo slowly dripped off her chin. She slowly reached up and wiped her eyes clear of the stuff.

"You sick *fuck!*" Catipon shouted, pulling on his cuffs.

As she wiped her hands on her shirt, Madi watched Vasquez's limp body slump to the ground with his hands still handcuffed around the pipe.

She looked up through her eyebrows. "I'll kill you for that."

O'Neal's eyes blazed with fire as he yanked Madi by her hair and placed his pistol against her chin. Madi screamed and fought against his brute strength.

"I'm in fucking charge here and you *will* tell me what I want to know!" O'Neal roared, voice echoing across the hangar. "I will pull her fingers off *one* by *one* as I do unspeakable things to do her body until I get the information I want!"

Madi screamed and began elbowing him as he then ran his hand across her breasts and stomach.

Those nearest moved toward Madi when several mercenaries stepped forward and held them back or buttstroked them.

"You motherfucker!" Cunningham yelled.

"Get your goddamn hands off her!" Kate screamed.

Catipon headbutted a guard just to have another strike him in the kidney and he fell to his knees.

O'Neal laughed wickedly as he licked across Madi's blood smeared cheek and began sliding his hand up her shirt when she craned her neck to the side and swiftly chomped down on his left ear, biting down hard and quickly turning back away.

O'Neal reeled back and howled in agony, placing his hand firmly against the side of his head. "Ahhh! You fucking bitch!" he spat, pacing frantically around.

Madi calmly spit out O'Neal's ear lobe on the ground and faced him defiantly. "Too much for you to handle?"

O'Neal clenched his jaw in anger, blood running down his face and arm. He pointed his Desert Eagle at the lifeless body of Vasquez while glaring at Madi. "Anyone tries something *like that* again and they end up like your little friend here!"

Madi wiped her cheek where he had licked her and then wiped it off on her pant leg. "You're a fucking pervert."

O'Neal shoved the barrel into her face, flashing his terrible teeth again. "Why, *yes*."

He grunted in pain from his missing and profusely bleeding ear lobe and made to leave. "Next time, sweetie, you and me are gonna have a lot of *fun*."

O'Neal snickered as he walked back to the plane and the mercenary guards stepped back.

"You okay?" Kate asked softly.

Madi was bent over, running her hands through her hair to get the chunks of brain and skull out. "Yeah, I'll be fine."

She stood, wiped her lips, spit repeatedly, and fought the urge to vomit before glancing up at Kate. "I might be sick though."

Chambers said to Catipon, quietly, "We're super fucked."

"As soon as this hurricane passes, there's gonna be a whole fucking battalion of Marines storming this goddamn island," Catipon said.

"Question is, what are we supposed to do until that?"

Catipon looked around at their current predicament. "Try to stay alive."

ACROSS THE MEU, THERE WAS A FLURRY OF ACTIVITY AS THEY PLOWED through the waves at full speed to the south. Everything that could be fastened down to the deck or bulkhead, was, due to the constant swaying side to side or back and forth.

They had just received the latest report from NOAA. Due to unexpected colder waters, Hurricane Taylor was steadily starting to dissipate and swing south. The order had been given to get ready and the MEU slowly started to make their way toward the island.

The boat and helo company of 1st Battalion, 6th Marines staged their gear and weapons in the hangar bays and well decks. They loaded magazines of 5.56 mm ammunition, passed out M-67 frag grenades and loaded encrypted radio frequencies into radios, ready to load into their respective Ospreys and rubber inflatable Zodiac's at a moment's notice.

The commander of Alpha Company, callsign Apache, briefed his platoon commanders in the well deck over a map. "First and second platoon will land *here*, at the southern bay. You'll secure the beachhead for third platoon to follow and head north to this road *here*. You guys will own that road and kill anything that isn't friendly."

In the hangar bay the commander of Charlie Company, callsign Coldsteel, did the same thing. "First, second you land on the southern runway, I want that airfield under our control. Third, with your attachments from Blackfoot, you will land *here* by this structure. Last contact we had from our forces on the island came from there, they were currently engaged with the enemy."

On the bridge of the *Iwo Jima*, Henderson consulted with the ship's weather officer. "How's the hurricane coming along on the island?"

"Waves breaking at twenty feet along the proposed beachheads and winds still gusting up to seventy miles an hour," the weather officer replied. "Judging by our speed and the anticipated sea state of our launch site, I'd put us at almost two hours before we can start sending our forces ashore."

"Damn!" Henderson blurted.

He knew it wouldn't be long before he heard a new directive from the president after she had consulted with the joint chiefs of staff. And Henderson had a sneaking suspicion that it would be a knee-jerk reaction not thoroughly thought out; he had played this game many times before.

"Everything okay, Frank?" Matheson asked.

"This thing is more complicated than we originally thought, and Washington is getting involved," Henderson explained. "It's only a matter of time before they do something . . . *drastic*. And I can't do diddly fucking squat about it from here!"

"What do you need from me?"

"The moment this hurricane lets us, I want the US Navy to unleash the full fury of a thousand devil dogs onto that island like bats outta hell," Henderson with conviction. "I want your flyboys in the sky to shoot a fly off a horse's ass from 30,000 feet and I want Norfolk to send me a Spectre gunship."

"I'll get on the horn with them right now," Matheson said.

Henderson's satellite phone rang, and he answered with a curt, "Go."

"You're not going to like this," Lisa began grimly. "The president just finished with the Joint Chiefs of Staff. They've decided the uranium cannot be allowed to leave the island and are about to order an airstrike on one of the hangars at the southern runway, orders are being drafted for a pair of F-35s out of Andrews as we speak."

"Goddamn it, I have people on that island, and I have no idea where they're at!" Henderson protested. "This is not how we do things, Lisa."

"Frank, listen, I've done all I can do. Any more word from our boys there?"

"No, not yet. How's things going on your end?"

"My analyst is digging into Cutthroat and SIGNIT hasn't had any luck yet reaching our forces through the jamming field."

"Roger, give me an ETA on the airstrike once you know, Henderson out."

24 ⫼ ROSE ISLAND

HARPER PANTED FROM EXERTION AS HE RAN ALONG THE SIDE OF THE
dirt trail and was glad he had kept up on his running routine. It had
continued to rain and the only thing keeping him warm and from suc-
cumbing to hypothermia was that he had been jogging for the last hour.

After the convoy had departed the parking garage, he decided to
follow their tracks left in the mud.

So far, he hadn't seen the vehicles.

He came to a stop, bending over and placing his hands on his knees
to catch his breath. "Fuck me."

Realizing it wasn't much of a plan, he became frustrated.

Hell, it wasn't a plan at all.

With no plan, no allies, no communication with the *Iwo Jima*, and
seemingly no other options he had failed.

What now, Jake?

Frustration and anger started to creep in, his nostrils flared, and
his hands curled into fists.

When first joining the Marine Corps, Harper had had a tendency
to lose his temper and often acted first before thinking. One time, he
had punched an Army supply captain while on deployment in Iraq and
he had nearly been kicked out with a dishonorable discharge.

Getting mad is not going to help anyone.

During his time on the teams with MARSOC, he had been put through grueling training evolutions from the swamps of Mississippi to the frozen tundra of Alaska. One lesson that had been drilled into him was anger only prolonged the problem at hand and made it worse. While on deployments in Syria or Somalia, his teammates relied on one another to make timely decisions under pressure and to put their emotions aside, to find a way to win.

Madi and the rest of his team were counting on him now.

Now, let's find a way.

Harper took a deep breath and stood up straight, relaxing. He slicked his hair back and slipped on the hat he had taken from the submarine. Pacing around and throwing a fist into his other hand, Harper looked around.

"Come on, give me something."

He stopped when he spotted the top of a radio tower in the distance over the tree line, eyes narrowing.

"Bingo."

Harper ran off into the forest as he moved in closer.

Coming to small clearing, he observed a thirty-foot radio tower attached to a small communications building. A single ALSV sat parked next to the building, but he couldn't see its owners.

On the west side of the clearing, a paved road led off to the northwest and to the southwest. He recalled seeing this on the map of Rose Island before they left. The road leading to the south was covered in muddy tire tracks, presumably from the convoy carrying the rest of his team.

A twig snapped behind Harper.

His eyes widened and he whirled around, reaching for his pistol as an arrow lodged itself into the tree beside him.

Harper froze as he scanned for a threat, pistol held out in front of him. He never saw the bush to the side suddenly move and morph into a human figure with another arrow drawn across a bow.

"That gun won't help you."

"Shit," Harper cursed.

Harper holstered his pistol and stood, hands up. "Listen here, Rambo."

The figure lowered their bow and arrow. "Harper?"

"How do you know my name?" Harper asked, confused.

Sally put her hood down to reveal herself. "I met your friends earlier. In the swamps. My name is Sally, I was one of the pilots of the plane that crashed here twenty years ago. Your friend Stevens told me about you guys."

Harper lowered his hands, relived to meet an ally, and gestured to the radio tower behind him. "Do you know what they're doing here?"

Sally walked forward and ducked behind a bush. Harper took a knee and they looked out into the clearing. "I've been watching them for an hour or so. No movement, but a huge convoy came through here, headed south."

"That was my team," Harper explained. "They've been captured."

"What will you do know?" Sally asked.

"Steal that vehicle and rescue them," Harper said firmly.

"How can I help?"

Harper raised an eyebrow and eyed her bow and arrow. "How good are you with that thing?"

Sally smirked as she looked at him.

Inside the small building, two mercenaries sat at a table playing cards and chatting casually. A radio beside them squawked from time to time, but they paid no attention to it. They were on orders from Carlyle and were here to guard their biggest asset on the island.

A knock came from the door.

One of the men quickly grabbed his weapon while his comrade just laughed.

"What?" the first man asked incredulously.

"You really think someone who means us harm would knock?" the second man asked sarcastically. "Probably just our relief, did you lock the door?"

The first man peered through the window, didn't see anyone, and tried the door to find it locked. His comrade laughed as he opened the door.

"There's no one—"

The man fell backwards with an arrow sticking out of his forehead. His comrade lunged for his rifle just as Harper rushed in and launched a vicious kick at the man's head. He fell back and toppled over the table, unconscious.

Harper walked back to the door and gave a thumbs up to the tree line. He turned back around and examined the room. Along the side wall, an instrument panel was lit up like a Christmas tree with red and green bulbs, some flashing, some solid.

"Whoa."

Sally came in and shut the door behind her.

Harper pulled out a handheld light from his fanny pack, flicked it on, and studied the instrument panel.

"What is it?" Sally asked as she retrieved her arrow from the dead man's forehead.

"This whole thing has gotten a twenty-first-century upgrade," Harper explained. "Definitely not 80s technology."

He came to a silver device plugged into the panel with several wires running out of it and back into the panel at different locations.

Harper read the small display screen on the side.

FREQUENCY BAND:
VHF

BEGIN:
30.00

```
END:
300.00
```

"Fuck," Harper said, mouth agape.

He saw a second identical device to the right.

```
FREQUENCY BAND:
SHF (SATELITE)

BEGIN:
3.00

END:
30.00
```

"Fuck," he repeated. "This is how these guys have been jamming us the entire time."

The two devices were broadcasting a signal, via the radio tower, over their respective bands that overpowered any other transmissions on that band. A crypto key could be inserted into the two devices and then uploaded into radios allowing *those* radios the ability to communicate. With these devices plugged into the radio tower, they were jamming the entire VHF and SHF radio bands.

"Can you disable them?"

"I can." Harper looked at her and smiled. "But I have a better idea."

After a few minutes of working on the two devices, Harper reached into his fanny pack and pulled out an earpiece with an attached wraparound throat mike. He put it in and pressed a few buttons on his armguard.

"This is Harper, does anyone copy?"

Harper answered what he was doing before Sally could ask. "I switched the frequencies on the jammer, jamming the enemy's comms and leaving one open where I could talk."

Henderson's voice went off in the earpiece in Harper's ear. "This is Six, damn good to hear from you. What's your status?"

"The rest of my team has been caught," Harper reported. "I've managed to switch the frequencies jammed on the island; I'm going to need to get this net secured ASAP. Has Cutthroat been arrested?"

"Roger, I'll have the SIGNIT guy get on it and negative, they killed three sailors and escaped in a stolen Osprey, but I have more pressing news," Henderson said. "Satellite scans picked up large amounts of weapon-grade uranium at the southern runway. Washington has ordered an airstrike to destroy it."

Harper paused, shocked at the reports of uranium. What was more concerning was the fact it was to the south, the direction his team was taken.

"The southern runway," Harper repeated.

Sally heard him and said, "Your friends heard a transmission mentioning taking something there."

Harper connected all the dots in an instant. The mercenary force had taken the uranium to the southern runway, presumable their base of operations, and where they would take their prisoners.

He looked at Sally. "What's the fastest way there?"

"I'll show you."

Harper said to Henderson. "You have to call that airstrike off! The rest of my team have been taken there!"

He quickly commandeered a rifle and the mercenaries ammo and moved outside with Sally.

"I can't do that; they just took off and they've gone radio silent!"

"Fuck!" Harper cursed and then asked, "ETA?"

"Best guess, forty minutes. I'll have the SIGNIT guy reach you and give you real-time updates."

"Fuck!"

"I'll drive!" Sally said as she hopped into the driver seat of the ALSV.

Harper made to jump in the passenger seat when he spotted an object covered in a tarp next to the vehicle. He ripped the tarp off and let it fall to the ground.

The object before them was oval in shape, encased in a rectangular metal frame, and was about the size of a dining room table. On top was a small display screen, a number pad, and a slot for a key.

"Fuck!"

"You say 'fuck' a lot," Sally commented.

"Yeah, well, it comes in handy sometimes," Harper explained and then said to Henderson. "Stand by, Six. I think I've got something here."

He walked around the object, examining it and leaning over to read the display screen.

"What is this thing?"

Harper looked up grimly at Sally. "It's a goddamn Vacuum Bomb."

It was one of the most destructive and powerful non-nuclear weapons ever created, a thermobaric bomb.

A thermobaric bomb was unique compared to other bombs. In conventional bombs, their explosives consisted of 25% fuel and 75% oxidizer mixture. In a thermobaric bomb their explosives are almost 100% fuel, making them much more energetic. With almost 100% fuel combined with oxygen, the shockwave produced is much longer and destructive. When detonated they produce a fireball that consumes oxygen from much farther away. They were used to great success in the mountains of Afghanistan against insurgents using caves as cover.

Harper spotted the Russian markings on the bomb's casing and realized it was worse than he thought.

The Russians used nano-thermite fuel in the production of their thermobaric bombs. Nano-thermite fuels had a high energy release rate that approaches numbers normally compared to those of atomic weapons.

In short, thermobaric bombs blow fast and consumed the oxygen from miles away. So it was aptly nicknamed the "Vacuum Bomb."

"Holy Christ," Harper breathed, realizing what the enemy was planning to do.

He could see Sally was thoroughly lost and he elaborated. "Once these guys get what they want, they're gonna detonate this bomb. It'll kill every living thing in a twenty-five-mile radius."

"Can you, like, disarm it?"

"No," Harper said. "Not without the command key and deactivation codes."

Sally swallowed nervously. "How long do we have?"

Harper synced his watch to the bomb's timer. "Two hours, forty-three minutes, nineteen seconds, and counting."

"Fuck."

They made for the ALSV. "Six, we got a situation here."

Sally started the ALSV and took off down the paved road leading southwest.

"I just found a Vacuum Bomb!" Harper yelled over the sound of the engine and wind. "Set to blow in two hours and forty-two minutes, it'll kill everything on this island! How long until you can launch the calvary?"

"Our estimate puts us in between an hour and a half and two hours."

Harper thought. Forty minutes until the airstrike, two hours and forty minutes until an explosion sucked the oxygen out of every living thing, and the Ospreys able to launch in between that. He was confident he could make it.

"Six, we're gonna rescue our people, launch those Ospreys as soon as possible so we can get the hell out of here before this place becomes a wasteland!"

"Sounds good, good luck, Six out."

"Thanks, we're sure as hell gonna need it!"

Sally drove the ALSV hard, sliding around corners and sending up showers of mud, and flying over bumps in the road. Harper grabbed onto the roll cage for support.

"You know a way into that hangar?"

"There's an old tunnel system between there and the main complex!" Sally said. "We'll park about a mile and a half away; it'll lead us right into the hangar!"

"Sounds good!" Harper said. "You mind me asking how you ended up crashing here? Anything odd?"

"Everything about this island is odd!" Sally said. "We had clear skies that day, not a storm cloud in sight. All of a sudden, the sun disappears and we're flying in an almighty lightning storm like nothing I've ever seen before. We lost our starboard engine, set the wing on fire, and threatened to blow our plane out of the sky. We had to get on the ground and fast. We were goners until this uncharted island came into sight and we managed to set her down, *barely.*"

"We saw a lightning storm on our way in, same thing happened to us!"

A voice spoke in Harper's ear. "Hello? Is anyone there?"

He could tell the other person on the end of the call did not have much practice speaking over the radio. "Who the hell is this?"

"I'm looking for Jake Harper, my name is Michael Fasswater. I've managed to encrypt this frequency. We work for the same organization."

Harper was unsure. "Okay, Mr. Fasswater. How do I know you're telling the truth?"

Hundreds of miles to the west, Fasswater and Natalie sat in a separate lodge from the president's hunched over their equipment.

"Uh . . . " Fasswater said, looking at Natalie for an answer. "I don't know—"

Lisa walked up behind them and grabbed the microphone. "Harper, its Warner. Identification code zero-six-three-romeo-two-quebec. Mission number hotel-zulu-two-three. Fasswater is legit."

"Roger, Fasswater, you got an ETA for me on that airstrike?" Harper asked urgently.

Looking around, Fasswater was at a loss of words. "Uh . . . wait one."

He began typing rapidly at his computer and whispered to himself, "Just need to log into the Pentagon's servers and tap into their live feed."

"Is that legal?" Natalie asked.

"Absolutely not," Fasswater said with a nervous laugh.

"Fasswater!"

He scanned the screen. "Thirty-seven minutes!"

"Punch it!" Harper urged Sally. "We got thirty-seven minutes!"

"What ordnance are they using?" Harper asked.

Fasswater typed and scanned the screen. "They took off carrying GBU-32s JDAMs."

"Jesus Christ," Harper breathed.

A Guided Bomb Unit-32 was a thousand-pound dumb bomb with nearly half of its weight comprising a high explosive called Tritonal. With the Joint Direct Attack Munition guidance kit, it turned the dumb bomb into a precision-guided munition capable of frightening accuracy and devasting results.

"Thanks, Fasswater. Harper out!"

"Oh, okay, roger, over and out," Fasswater responded awkwardly and then looked over at Natalie.

"Good job," she said with both thumbs up.

Sally came to a T intersection and went left. As they turned something caught Harper's eye and he turned around in his seat. He saw the rear end of a flatbed truck carrying something just as it disappeared over a hill, heading north.

"What is it?" Sally asked, flooring the ALSV to eighty miles an hour.

Harper sat back down. "Nothing we have time for!"

Up ahead, a maze of buildings in varying sizes came into view set against the base of the mountains.

"My best guess is that place is where they did whatever it is the hell they did here!" Sally said to Harper. "A lot of it goes underground and into those mountains!"

"Ever been in there?"

"One time!" Sally began. "Two years after I crashed here. Myself and our navigator, Gary. We were exploring the tunnels underground when he got separated for over an hour and when I found him," she paused and searched for the right words, "he was half-inside of the wall, the concrete wall! Like the concrete had been poured around him somehow, it didn't make any sense! It had crushed him, his lungs forced out of his mouth and his eyeballs popped like goddamn balloons. It was the most terrible thing I've ever seen! Safe to say, I never went back there!"

They passed the huge complex and came to a bend in the road, in the distance Harper could see the southern runway and the two hangars through the rain. Sally pulled off the road and parked the ALSV beside a small concrete building with a rusted metal door. She led him down a narrow stairwell that led in a wide tunnel with knee-high running water down it.

Harper tossed Sally his flashlight. "Lead the way."

He glanced at his watch. Thirty minutes and counting.

They ran.

25

MADI STOOD UP STRAIGHT AS SHE COUNTED DOWN FROM FIVE, HER head turned to the side and stretching her sore neck. The events of the last couple days had put stress on her neck, a reoccurring issue for her. Madi swore it started when she was in a helicopter crash during her time in the Marines.

Thirty minutes ago, she had watched the man who had stared at her leave with one of the flatbed trucks. Now it had returned without the mysterious man and men went about unloading the cargo and loading it onto the plane.

Rolling her shoulders to loosen up her muscles, she watched O'Neal yell at his men when he failed to reach someone over their radios, and it seemed all their radios weren't working. She grinned smugly.

"Think that was Harper?" Cunningham asked quietly.

"Has to be," Madi agreed.

"Just a matter of time before he shows up with a shitload of Marines."

Madi nodded in agreement. "Hopefully they come before these guys finish getting what they want, otherwise we may not be alive for much longer."

Catipon leisurely leaned against the wall as he watched O'Neal and his mercenaries argue about their lack of communications. Beside him, Kate exhaled deeply as she placed her head against the wall, eyes shut.

"Something wrong?" Catipon asked, light-heartedly.

Opening an eye, she looked at him and smiled. "Just bored, that's all."

Catipon stood up straight. "Well, we can't have that now, can we?"

Kate turned as Catipon waved at one of their guards. "Excuse me, you guys got any boardgames or something like that? We're kinda bored over here."

"Shut the fuck up!" the guard snapped.

"Jeez," Catipon whispered and looked at Kate. "These guys are real buzzkills, uh?"

Kate giggled and looked down on her shoulder to hide her laughter from the guards.

After fifteen minutes of running down the tunnel, Harper and Sally came to a staircase and took it up two steps at a time.

"This will lead us to the hangar floor," Sally advised as they came to a landing and gestured at a shut door.

Harper nodded and put his ear against the door while he got his breathing under control. He could make out a few voices occasionally shouting across an open space.

Nodding at Sally, who drew an arrow across her bow, Harper, very slowly, inched the door open.

"What the—" he heard a nearby voice say before—*Swish!*

Sally released an arrow that pierced the unlucky mercenary's head and he dropped straight to the floor.

Harper reached out and quickly dragged his body inside and then waited with the door cracked to see if anyone would come and investigate.

No alarm was sounded, and Harper continued scanning the hangar.

A Russian Antonov plane sat in the middle of the hangar with a yellow fuel truck parked beneath the aircraft's right wing closest to Harper.

Along the eastern wall a line of ALSVs, two Little Bird helicopters, and a few flatbed trucks sat parked. The hangar's doors were open partially, allowing a gust of rain to blow in. Along the western wall Harper spotted the canvas-topped truck and the rest of his team, along with the remaining Marines. They were under guard from a few mercenaries and Harper counted another twenty milling about the hangar.

He checked his watch, fifteen minutes until the airstrike, and looked at Sally. "Here's what we're gonna do."

At 30,000 feet and approaching Rose Island at breakneck speeds, were two US navy-operated F-35 fifth generation fighter jets. The two pilots scanned their instrument panel and continued rocking through the sky.

With fourteen minutes to go, Harper and Sally calmly departed from the stairwell and split up.

Sally had ditched her gilly suit and threw on the dead mercenary's blouse, having to roll the sleeves several times and threw on Harper's hat to conceal her feminine features. She walked toward the plane and ducked under its starboard side wing. Pausing for a minute by the fuel truck's rear, she got in the driver's seat and started the truck.

Harper, with the dead mercenary's flak on and his rain jacket hood up, made his way down the eastern wall toward the fleet of vehicles.

In the hornet's nest now, Harper told himself.

He was on edge, his senses firing on all cylinders. It took all of his might to walk at a casual pace and not glance over his shoulder to see if anyone noticed his façade.

Passing a pair of armed men with a curt head nod, Harper cut right and made his way directly across the hangar. He shifted his gaze toward the floor as he walked quickly by a huge man with a mohawk arguing about radios. Next, he weaved his way past his captured friends and through a field of crates and cots, heading for the parked troop truck in the corner.

The fuel truck rumbled down the middle of the hangar, Sally keeping her head down as the forklift drove past her. She looked in the side view mirror to see if she had been spotted, so far so good.

Sally parked the truck in between the open hangar doors. She got out and quickly made her way to the corner to meet Harper at the troop truck. With only a nod to each other, they got in and Harper started the engine.

Madi watched O'Neal walk away from his men and light up a cigar, pacing around the lowered ramp of the plane. She smiled when she saw that his left ear was bandaged up.

As O'Neal puffed on his cigar, he caught the smell of something besides his tobacco smoke. Lowering the cigar, he inhaled deeply and glanced around.

Sally stood on the running boards of the troop truck, unsheathed her bow and drew a napalm-tipped arrow across it.

O'Neal crouched down around a puddle beneath the right wing of the plane, reaching down and bringing the liquid to his nose.

Sally tossed a lighter to Harper and presented the arrow to him. "Care to do the honors?"

O'Neal smelled diesel fuel and followed the trail of fuel across the hangar to the parked fuel truck.

Harper smiled and flicked the cartwheel of the lighter. "Gladly."

O'Neal stood and whirled around, eyes scanning the hangar in a hurry.

Catipon watched him and then noticed a flame off to his right, standing up straight. He nudged Kate and whispered to the others, "Get ready for something loud and a *whole* lot of shooting."

O'Neal's eyes fell upon Sally in the corner as she aimed her flaming arrow at the fuel spilling out of the fuel truck.

"So long, motherfuckers."

O'Neal pointed and screamed, "You idiots, shoot them!"

Sally let the arrow fly and it flew into the rushing stream of fuel, igniting instantly.

"Go!" Sally shouted and slammed the door shut.

The fuel truck blew apart a second later, throwing liquid fire in every direction as Harper stomped on the gas pedal. With a roaring shriek, a trail of fire shot toward the plane and the puddle of diesel Sally had let pool there.

Several mercenaries noticed the moving troop truck and began firing at it. The truck became a mess of flying bullet sparks and glass shards as Harper and Sally ducked in their seats. Not being able to see where he was driving, Harper drove through several piles of crates and cases.

The trail of fire came beneath the plane and with a *whoosh* sent flames billowing high into the air, engulfing the starboard wing in its grasp and setting it on fire.

In the panicked chaos two of the mercenaries standing guard duty rushed past, too close to their prisoners.

Madi kicked out the farthest she could and sent a guard sliding flat on his face. Catipon jumped out and wrapped his legs around the second's waist and forcefully threw him into the wall. Kate was waiting for him and quickly kneed him in the groin. The guard doubled over in pain and Kate kneed him again in the face. The first guard looked up as he came to a stop and received a swift kick to the face from Cunningham, knocking him out.

The other two guards looked back at their prisoners and brought their weapons up.

"Tyler!" Madi exclaimed, helpless to stop them.

Catipon grabbed the unconscious guard's sidearm and twisted around.

Firing awkwardly from the hip, he managed to shoot both mercenaries in the head and they fell to the ground.

Kate quickly found the keys on the guard and began undoing her cuffs when she noticed several mercenaries approach.

"Oh, shit . . . "

A troop truck came flying in from the right and slammed into the men, throwing them a short distance where they landed unconscious.

Madi looked at the driver's seat as Harper jumped down. "Jake!"

Kate finished uncuffing herself and quickly undid Catipon's. Bullets impacted the wall above them.

"Get down!" Harper yelled.

He leaned out around the bumper of the truck and began engaging the mercenaries while the others unlocked themselves from the pipe. They began to arm themselves from the unconscious guards and join Harper behind the cover of the truck.

"Good to see you, Brother!" Catipon said as he came up beside him. "What took you so long?"

Harper leaned against the truck as he reloaded. "I knew you could handle yourself for a while without me."

Catipon laughed as Cunningham came over.

"Listen," Harper began, "we gotta get out of here, there's an airstrike due on our position in," he looked at his watch, "in eleven minutes!"

"Airstrike!" Catipon repeated.

"Long story," Harper said. "Cunningham, get your Marines loaded up in the truck, we'll cover you."

"Roger."

Above them, Sally stood on the running boards and shot arrows across the hangar at anything that moved.

"Who's the bow and arrow chick?" Catipon asked.

Harper watched Madi grab a rifle off the floor and rush over to them. "Another long story, right now I'm gonna take your advice."

"Uh?"

Harper walked toward Madi, grabbed her by her hips and kissed her. Madi went wide-eyed and then kissed him back.

At the same time, the starboard wing was fully ablaze and then the massive fuel tank was ignited. A resonating boom echoed throughout the hangar as the blast set off consecutive explosions ripping through the plane, cracking it in half!

The shockwave and radiating fireball tossed men and debris flying in every direction.

Harper ignored the blast, holding Madi tight and kissing her as fiery debris rained down, casting a red and orange glow across them.

Catipon said to Kate, "I told him to do that. Just walk up and kiss her."

She looked unconvinced, however. "Yeah, sure ya did."

Harper pulled back and said simply, "I'm sorry. I should've done that earlier."

Madi smiled. "It was worth the wait."

At the rear of the truck, Bexley and Cunningham helped the injured Marines into the back while Chambers and Rider covered them, using crates nearby for cover. They saw the mercenaries were advancing on their position and would soon overwhelm them if they didn't move.

"We can't stay here all day!" Rider said.

As Cunningham helped lift the unconscious pilot into the back of the truck, Michaels stood around the corner waiting to climb aboard.

He glanced nervously around, feeling useless without a weapon.

A mercenary to their flanks caught his attention, he was bringing up his weapon to fire, Cunningham with his back to him and Chambers and Rider oriented toward the hangar proper.

He acted.

"Staff Sergeant, watch out!"

He grabbed Cunningham just as the mercenary fired.

Michaels jolted as two bullets struck him in his back.

Rider turned, saw the shooter and immediately put him down.

Michaels fell to the floor as Cunningham dropped beside him. "Oh, Christ!"

He held Michaels as blood pooled on the floor beneath him. A look of amazement crossed Michaels face, strangely he felt nothing.

"Michaels! Michaels!" Cunningham shouted. "Hang in there, we need you to hang in there!"

Deep down, Cunningham knew there was nothing he could do for the young Marine.

Michaels coughed, blood dribbling down his chin. "I tried . . . Staff Sergeant."

Cunningham's throat closed up, his eyes watering as he watched Michaels die in his arms. "You did good Michaels, you did good. You saved my life . . . you're a hero."

The corners of Michaels' mouth started to curl into a smile before his eyes rolled to the side. Cunningham felt for a pulse and found none. He wiped a tear from his eye.

Rider appeared at his side, putting a hand on his shoulder and bowing his head solemnly. "I'll help you put his body in the truck."

They lifted his body in the troop truck and Rider yelled down to Harper, "That's it, they're good to go!"

Over behind a crate, Chambers reloaded and saw something on the floor that had been in a case Harper had driven through.

He grabbed a M72 Light Anti-tank Weapon, a portable one-shot 66-mm unguided rocket, the same ones the mercenaries had been using all day, and shouted to Harper, "Yo! They're gonna need a distraction to get out of here!"

Harper saw it and agreed. "Alright, Bexley and Washington get these guys out of here! Rendezvous to the north at the end of the runway and keep your heads down, airstrike is coming in six minutes to flatten this place!"

"The rest, on me! We'll cover them and clear us a path across the hangar, I got a way out!"

Bexley and Washington climbed into the truck as Chambers and Rider prepared to fire their rockets.

"Now!" Harper shouted.

Chambers and Rider stood, aimed at the mercenaries, and pulled the triggers. Twin rockets flew forward in a cloud of smoke as the troop truck started driving and turned around. One rocket slammed into a pile of crates that the mercenaries were using as cover and detonated spectacularly, throwing torn body parts high into the air. The other skipped off the floor and sailed into one of the MH-6 Little Bird helicopters on the other side, the burning wreck slamming against the wall.

"Let's move!" Harper yelled.

The group advanced forward with their guns up and firing.

Cunningham dropped a mercenary running toward him and he went sprawling across the floor. An arrow whizzed past his face. Reeling back in surprise, he watched the arrow impale itself into the neck of a mercenary with his head exposed over a case.

Cunningham looked over at Sally as she drew another arrow. "Thanks."

"Don't mention—" Sally began to say when a mercenary appeared from around the corner of a flatbed truck.

Sally shoved the tip of the arrow into the bottom of the man's jaw and pushed it violently up into his brain. The man's eyes rolled into the back of his head as she yanked the arrow out and drew it across her bow.

Cunningham was speechless at her savage act.

As Washington gunned the truck through a line of cots, his left shoulder exploded in a burst of red. He roared in pain and Bexley leaned over to grab the wheel. "Just keep your foot on the gas!"

Bexley steered the truck toward the open hangar doors and through the field of fire from the exploded fuel truck.

On the hangar floor, they moved past the burning plane which was quickly filling up the place with a thick layer of hazy smoke. The group moved in harmony, firing left and right and covering each other as they reloaded, Sally ripping her arrows out of the bodies as she ran past.

In the rear, Harper and Madi were moving past a field of crates when they lost sight of the others in the haze.

"Shit!" Harper cursed, looking around.

A mass suddenly leaped on them from above, throwing both falling across the floor. Harper looked up to see O'Neal grab Madi by her hair and toss her to the side, coming his way.

From his position on the floor Harper brought his rifle up just to have it ripped out of his hands by O'Neal. Getting on a knee he whipped his pistol out, but O'Neal tore it from his grip and tossed it away.

"Oh, crap."

O'Neal grabbed Harper by his shirt and tossed him against a crate, rolled across it and fell to the ground beside Madi. They both stood and faced O'Neal, looking through the haze for their weapons and the heat from the burning plane on their backs.

"What's Bebop's here fucking problem?"

"Too many to name," Madi said.

O'Neal laughed and rushed them. Harper shoved Madi to the side as O'Neal kicked the crate, sending it sliding across the floor. Jumping back on a plastic case, Harper landed on the crate as it came to a stop. He launched himself knee-first at O'Neal, only to be grabbed midair!

"Holy fuck!" Harper said, marveling at the man's strength.

O'Neal just laughed. "Pathetic! I'm gonna have a real blast with your girl here!"

He slammed Harper down back first on the floor. Harper wheezed and gasped for air as O'Neal stood over him. Madi came sliding in feet first from behind him and kicked at his knee, forcing him to kneel. She then landed a brutal blow at his groin, and he howled in pain.

"Good luck having kids, motherfucker!"

O'Neal turned and reached back, grabbing Madi by her shirt and belt. He stood up, grunting as he hefted her over his head, and threw her to the side.

"Fucking bitch!"

Madi landed on a cot and rolled onto the ground.

As O'Neal turned back around, he received a roundhouse punch across his jaw that sent him stumbling back a few paces.

O'Neal glared at Harper through fiery eyes and smiled a bloody row of teeth, calmly spitting out a tooth. "That all you got, pussy?"

He came charging at Harper as he frantically looked around for a weapon. Spying a LAW rocket launcher nearby, he grabbed it, stood, and swung it like a baseball bat.

O'Neal simply grabbed it in his beefy palm.

Harper sighed. "Motherfucker."

O'Neal swung the launcher and Harper around with a roar. Harper tumbled across a crate and landed on the other side, both of them still gripping the rocket.

"I'm gonna enjoy getting to know that hot piece of blonde ass of yours!" O'Neal sneered.

"Jake, go low!" Madi yelled as she appeared from the side.

Harper did what he was told and hit the deck as Madi's hand gripped the rocket's pistol grip tightly.

O'Neal looked down in confusion.

"Lick on this, asshole!" Madi said and yanked the trigger.

O'Neal's eyes widened as he realized what was about to happen.

The rocket went off and the backblast slammed into O'Neal with tremendous force. Screaming, he was sent flying backwards and out of sight, disappearing into the thick haze. The rocket disappeared in the other direction and exploded in the distance.

Harper stood and looked at his watch, coughing in the thick smoke. "Four minutes, let's move."

The two ran across the hangar, collecting their weapons along the way, and to the door leading down to the tunnel.

Catipon stood waiting for them. "What the hell happened to you guys!"

"Later!" Harper said as he stripped off the flak he had took. "Right now, we gotta run!"

Descending the stairs rapidly, they came to the tunnel and splashed through it as they ran north.

"What's our time?" Catipon called out.

"Three minutes!"

Breathing hard from running in water, Catipon responded. "Goddamn it!"

Twenty thousand feet above them, two of the F-35's circled the island as the pilots eyed the target through their sensor pods, imputing the exact grids into the targeting system.

"Tyler, what's the MSD for a GBU-32?" Harper asked, quickly looking at the map on his ForeTex.

A Minimum Safe Distance was the distance one needed to be at to safely be outside the effects of a certain type of munition.

"Uhh . . . fourteen hundred meters!"

"Yeah, that's what I thought!" Harper said. "We need to go faster!"

The group gave everything they had, legs and arms pumping as fast as they could.

Above them with the targeting information entered, one of the pilots announced, "Savage 4-1 in."

The pilot sent the fighter jet into a dive toward the southern runway and thirty seconds later the second pilot said, "Savage 4-2 in."

At the end of the southern runway, Bexley was applying a bandage to Washington's gunshot wound when he heard jets coming in overhead. He looked outside and up at the sky. "Shit."

Coming to five thousand feet, the first jet pulled up. "Savage 4-1, one and two away."

Thirty seconds later. "Savage 4-2, one and two away."

Four one-thousand-pound bombs fell from the sky and screamed down toward Earth. Guided by GPS, they couldn't miss.

Harper's watch beeped and he looked down in horror. "Times up."

A brief screech of something tearing through the air could be heard outside before the first two bombs slammed into the roof of the hangar and detonated a millisecond later.

The roof was blown open in towering twin fingers of flames and plumes of dust. Slabs of concrete rained down from the roof as it started to collapse.

Down in the tunnel, the floor rumbled beneath their feet, and they were thrown into the water, bits of debris falling from the ceiling.

Thirty seconds later, the second two bombs came in through the destroyed roof and impacted on the hangar floor next to the burning plane. The sound was deafening and resonated for miles. Twin explosions simply blew open the walls of the hangar with awesome force and created a crater thirty feet deep, sending a plume of smoke high into the sky.

BOOOOOMMM!

Down in the tunnel, the soundwave pierced their ears, sending chunks of concrete falling from the ceiling.

Harper looked down the tunnel to see a wave of fire heading their direction. "Get down!"

Everyone dived into the water as the wall of fire passed overhead before quickly dissipating.

Rising to his knees and gasping for breath, Harper looked around. "Everyone good?"

"I wouldn't say good," Catipon said a short distance away. "But I'm alive."

Everyone else said they were okay, and Harper exhaled a sigh of relief, falling back into the water.

"You guys are fucking crazy," Cunningham said to them.

Harper laughed. "You know I've been thinking"

"That could be dangerous, you know?" Madi teased with a smile, sitting in the water beside him.

"Ha ha," Harper said mockingly. "I've been thinking that I've needed to take a piss for the last hour."

The group burst into laughter.

Twenty minutes later, they exited the tunnel and walked out of the small concrete building. The wind was only mildly gusting along with a light rain fall.

Harper keyed the radio on his ForeTex. "Six, Harper."

"Harper, go for Six."

"I've rescued my team and the Marines," Harper said. "How long—"

He stopped as the sound of an aircraft flew overhead. Heads turned and looked up to see an identical Russian aircraft flying high into the sky and heading south.

"Shit," Harper said and recalled the truck he had seen earlier heading to the northern runway. "Six, wait one. Fasswater, you still up this net?"

"I'm here, what do you need?"

"I got eyes on an enemy aircraft leaving the island and heading south, any chance those F-35s are still in the sky to follow it?"

"Negative, they already returned to base, they were low on fuel."

"Damn," Harper said and then keyed his comms. "Six, I'm sure you heard. How long until the Ospreys launch?"

"Thirty minutes and we'll be in range. Listen, we're running the math here, with the time of flight to the island and to get outside of the thermobaric's bomb radius, we're gonna have about a fifteen-minute window to get you guys outta there."

"Roger, Six. We'll be waiting."

Harper passed him their location and with Sally's help, gave him instructions to find Stevens in her hideout.

After that, he turned to the others and grimly revealed to them the impending countdown of the Vacuum Bomb to which he got dropped jaws.

26

AS THEY WAITED FOR THE *IWO JIMA* TO LAUNCH THE RESCUE CHOP-
pers, the group walked over and gathered around the troop truck at the
end of the southern runway. While some of them tended to the injuries
of the wounded Marines, Harper stared off to the south, his mind trying
to make sense of something.

"What's on your mind?" Madi asked as she walked over.

"I just can't make sense of their plan," Harper said. "It just doesn't
add up."

"How so?"

Harper turned to look at her, using his hands as he spoke. "These
guys come here to steal a bunch of uranium, sell it to some unsavory
characters and make a shit load of money. I got it, that makes sense. But
why is Cutthroat involved? They were on that MEU well before we
showed up, so they had to be there for another reason. And why the
Vacuum Bomb? To kill us? I don't think so, that's a serious piece of
hardware to acquire so it had to be a part of their plan from the beginning. And the plane we saw leave, who the hell was that?"

"Almost like these guys were being led by two different people,"
Madi realized, and she snapped her fingers. "There was a guy watching

us when we were being held, he didn't say anything, but I got a weird feeling from him, like he knew *me*."

"Was he there when the airstrike came in?"

"No, he left well before it."

"That's it!" Harper exclaimed. "He must've known about the airstrike, allowing him to get a clean getaway."

"And the Vacuum Bomb?"

"Regardless of the airstrike, he had a way to silence everyone on this island after he left."

"None of this explains Cutthroat," Madi said.

Harper went to speak and then stopped himself. "You're right, shit."

The sound of rotors thumping through the air broke the silence and they turned to see three Ospreys fly in from the east.

"We'll figure this out later," Madi said. "Right now, let's get out of here."

The Osprey landed on the runway as the other one did circles overhead, waiting for their turn to land. They saw the third Osprey head toward Sally's hideout to pick up Stevens. A squad of Marines came rushing out and set a security perimeter around the chopper. The Team members helped load the injured Marines into the Osprey as they talked to the Navy Corpsmen about their injuries. Washington, his arm in a makeshift sling, was helped up the ramp by Bexley.

The crew chief of the Osprey walked up to Harper and yelled over the rotors, "We don't have room for all of your people! I got room for two more, the rest will have to go on the second bird!"

"No problem!" Harper responded. He turned to Cunningham and Sally. "You guys should go!"

"First ones in, last ones out!" Cunningham said with a nod.

"I've been here for twenty years, what's a few more minutes?" Sally said.

"Alright!" Harper yelled over at Chambers and Rider. "You guys go ahead and get out of here!"

"I'll see you back on the *Iwo Jima!*" Chambers shouted. "I'll have the beers ready!"

Harper laughed. "Sounds good!"

With Cunningham and Sally, Harper was staying back with Catipon, Madi, and Kate. They moved away from the chopper and waited for the squad of Marines to load back up.

Two miles away, O'Neal stumbled out of the rubble of the destroyed hangar, stepping onto the road to the north. His head rang and his vision blurred. The heat of the rocket backblast had signed off his eyebrows and the front half of his mohawk. Blood dripped out of his ears and nose and several blood vessels had popped in his eyes.

Beyond all of that, he was extremely pissed.

He turned at the sound of rotor blades and could barely make out the outline of the Ospreys. O'Neal looked at the five mercenaries that had escaped with him and shouted, "I want those shot out of the fucking sky right now!"

A convoy of enemy vehicles coming from the east pulled over on the road. One of the men jumped out and asked, "What happened?"

O'Neal grabbed the man by the collar. "We're gonna kill the rest of those weak fucks once and for all!"

The man shifted uncomfortably. "You got it boss."

They watched as an Osprey lifted off from the runway and the second one lower as it hovered to land.

"Let's go!" O'Neal screamed.

Fifty feet off the ground, the Osprey's rotor wash slammed him into them, and they shielded their faces with their hands. Harper looked through his fingers and what he saw made him do a double take.

"Fuck!" Harper shouted and pointed it out to the others, a convoy of vehicles driving out onto the runway from the destroyed hangar. He then keyed his radio to speak with the pilots. "Firefly 4-3, wave off, wave off, wave off!"

"Firefly 4-3, wave off, wave off, wave off."

The pilots gave more power to the engines and the Osprey took off high into the sky.

Catipon looked down the optic of his weapon and reported, "Five ALSVs and two troop trucks!"

"Fuck!" Harper said, looking at his watch that mirrored the countdown to the Vacuum Bomb.

"We don't have time for this!" Kate said.

Harper's watch read fifty-two minutes until detonation. He thought fast. "Everyone in the truck, now!"

"I'll drive!" Cunningham called out as they ran for the truck.

Sally hopped in the passenger seat while the rest climbed into the back.

"Where we going?" Cunningham quickly asked and started the truck.

"What about the main complex over there?" Catipon asked. "There's gotta be a place deep enough for us to hide!"

"It'd take too long to navigate our way down there," Sally said with a shake of her head. "We'll get lost!"

"Are there any other tunnels we can hide in?" Madi asked.

"They wouldn't be sealed, the oxygen would still get sucked out," Harper countered. "We need a fallout shelter or something."

"The school!" Sally exclaimed. "There's a nuclear fallout shelter beneath the gym!"

After what they had been through, Harper trusted her. "Cunningham, north!"

Cunningham stepped on the gas and set out toward the road.

"Six, Harper!" he said into his comms.

"Harper, Six."

"We got enemy in bound, we're not gonna make it on the Ospreys! Hold everyone behind the thirty-mile marker, we're heading for a fallout shelter at the housing complex!"

"Roger, be advised air support is en route should you need it!"

"Appreciate it, I'll contact you afterwards, Harper out!"

Cunningham brought the truck onto the road heading north, shifting gears and picking up speed. Behind them they saw ALSVs desperately chasing after them. Madi looked nervously over at Harper.

He grabbed her hand and squeezed. "We'll make it, I know we will."

27

APPREHENSION FILLED THE GROUP.

Catipon checked the chambers of his rifle and pistol, ensuring a round was present while glancing back at the approaching ALSVs.

His words from earlier resonated in Kate's mind, *you good?* She steadied her nerves and nodded to herself, gripping her rifle tighter.

Madi watched Harper, his surprise kiss still on her mind.

God I hope we make it through this.

The sound of the roaring engine and the flapping tarp filled Harper's ears as he looked down at the map on his ForeTex, zooming in on the housing district.

Most of the complex laid to the west of the main road. Consulting with Sally, a shopping mall/grocery store and school took up roughly the northeastern portion while the maze of unorganized homes sat to the west and south. A series of cul-de-sacs took up the southwestern corner that Harper guessed to be the residences of the high-ranking officers stationed on the island. Harper spied a gas station, a park, and a flooded portion of the complex west of the school. On the other side of the main road was a football field/track and a baseball field.

If they could stay on the main road, Harper thought, they'd have a direct route to the school.

The truck crested a hill, and the northern runway and base housing district came into view. Catipon observed the road to their rear.

"I think they're gonna beat us!" he reported.

Harper looked back. "Shit, you're right."

The lead ALSV engaged them with their machine gun and rounds whizzed over the truck. Everyone hit the deck as Cunningham swerved.

Catipon and Kate brought up their rifles and fired back. When the machine gun fire ceased, they frowned and looked at each other. Then they saw three flashes of light and smoke emanate from the lead ALSV.

A trio of rockets flew toward the speeding troop truck.

"Rockets!" Catipon shouted.

Cunningham saw them in the side mirror and gripped the wheel hard. "Hold on!"

He cut the truck hard to the left twenty meters short of the first intersection of the housing district and bounded over the curb, throwing everyone in the back off their seats. The rockets missed them by feet and exploded upon impacting the complex's welcome sign, sending plumes of masonry and dirt high into the air.

"Jesus Christ!" Catipon exclaimed, having been thrown in the back like a ragdoll.

"Sorry!" Cunningham called out.

The truck sped across the grass and came back onto the road heading west toward the officer housing. Cunningham spotted a "No Outlet" sign and said, "We got a dead end ahead!"

Harper saw on his map the roundabout lead into three different cul-de-sacs.

"You guys get ready to jump out," Cunningham announced. "I'll buy you some time."

Harper hit him on the shoulder. "Thanks, Brother. See ya at the school!"

Cunningham smiled. "Can't wait!"

They entered the roundabout and Cunningham slowed down at the street leading to the right. "Now!"

Harper and the others quickly jumped off, rolling across the soft grass. Sally yelled from the passenger window, "Go, your friend is gonna need some back up!"

He nodded and turned to his team. "Let's move people, down the road!"

Cunningham took off back around the roundabout and nodded at Sally. "Appreciate the company."

Sally stared out the window at the ALSVs as they turned the corner behind them. "Thank me later, if we survive this!"

Catipon led the group with his gun up through the overgrown lawn flanked by the road and a patch of thick trees. A rocket came soaring over the road and struck the rear of the troop truck, tore apart the canvas frame and set the canvas covering ablaze.

Coughing as she looked behind them, Sally said simply, "We are now on fire."

The ALSVs entered the roundabout right on Cunningham's heels as Catipon lead the group into the cul-de-sac ahead. Three massive homes with huge yards full of overgrown vegetation lined the road.

Cunningham gripped the wheel hard as he swung onto the left most road, leading them away from Harper and his team.

"Go right!" Harper called out. "Need to cut through these houses!"

Machine gun fire peppered the dirt around them as two ALSVs sped toward them. Harper and Madi fired back as Catipon and Kate ran across the open street and in between two homes.

Harper and Madi moved toward Catipon when the ALSVs entered the cul-de-sac. A mercenary hefted another rocket on his shoulder and prepared to fire. With machine gun fire chasing them, Harper saw this.

They weren't going to make to Catipon's position.

Harper grabbed Madi's hand and changed directions. "Into the house!"

The two made a beeline straight for the nearest window as the rocket was fired. Catipon came to the alley between the two houses and turned around.

"Oh, shit!"

The rocket slammed into the corner of the house where he had just been standing. Blasting wood and plaster everywhere, the explosion threw Catipon to the ground. Inside the house, Harper and Madi had just leaped through the window when the far corner was blown inward by the explosion, sending debris crashing over them as they hit the floor.

"How many we got?" Cunningham asked.

"Three vehicles!" Sally shouted as machine gun fire slammed into the concrete around them.

The troop truck came out into the cul-de-sac and had nowhere to go.

"What now?" Sally asked.

Cunningham saw a yard that connected to the adjoining cul-de-sac and steered in that direction, bouncing over the curb and smashing through the backyard fence.

In the northern cul-de-sac, O'Neal shouted orders at his men following the rocket strike on the house when the flaming troop truck rumbled out of a yard behind him.

"Shoot them!" O'Neal demanded.

The two machine gunners on the ALSVs swiveled their weapons and opened fire.

"Holy fuck!" Cunningham shouted as he ducked behind the dashboard.

He realized they had nowhere to go except keep moving forward. The only problem, Cunningham saw, was that there was no yard in front of him; only a narrow strip of grass between the two homes.

"It's about to get really rough!"

Sally looked at him and said with heavy sarcasm, "Oh, joy! I was waiting for the fun to start!"

In between the two houses in front of the troop truck, Catipon was getting up on his feet when Kate shouted and pointed, "We gotta move now!"

Catipon turned and eyed the speeding truck.

The two dashed away as the truck crashed into both houses and continued at breakneck speeds behind them. The truck simply tore away the weakly rotted walls and ripped them to shreds.

Harper and Madi had just exited the back of the house when Catipon and Kate came running around the corner and jumped to the side. The truck was a second behind them and continued onward, down a slope that was covered in trees.

Harper looked at Catipon and Kate. "Let's move."

The three ALSVs that had been pursuing the troop truck came to a stop around O'Neal.

"Smith, take your guys and chase them down by foot!" O'Neal snapped. "Robins, take the vics and cut them off from the north. I want these fuckers dead!"

The troop truck crashed through the low-lying branches as Cunningham swerved left and right, desperately trying to miss the wide tree trunks. "Oh fuck! Shit! Fucking shit!"

Going fast down the incline, the truck burst out of the tree line and straight into a row of houses built on a short steep slope. With the aid of a wooden deck, the second story sat flush with the ground while the on the other side, it was truly a second story with the first story built into the hill.

Cunningham knew he couldn't slow down in time or swerve away without rolling the truck.

The truck's right-hand side crashed through the house and his world went sideways as the vehicle corkscrewed. Cunningham gripped the steering wheel as Sally was thrown into his lap. The truck soared out over the street amid a raining field of debris. With a jarring halt the truck crashed into the street on its left-hand side, sliding to a stop against the curb.

A few moments later, Cunningham pushed open the passenger side door and climbed out. He could hear vehicles approaching in the distance.

"Anything broken?" Cunningham called down to Sally as he reached down to offer a hand.

He pulled her out and for a moment the two sat on the side of the overturned truck. Sally brushed her hair to the side and caught her breath. "I don't think so."

Harper shuffled down the wooded hillside, following the trail of destruction left by Cunningham in the troop truck.

"We don't have a fuck's chance in hell of making it to the school if this keeps up!" Catipon called out.

Harper chuckled. Even against the overwhelming odds and a very real chance of death, he was still in good spirits. "Another day, another dollar!"

Catipon rolled his eyes and continued down the hillside.

They came down into the street to see Cunningham and Sally jump down from the wrecked truck.

"You guys good?" Cunningham asked.

Harper responded with a thumbs up as soon as gunfire erupted from the trees behind them. He immediately took a knee and fired back. "Go! Get across the street!"

Cunningham and Sally moved fast and kicked down the door of the nearest house. Catipon took cover by the truck's bumper and covered Harper's movement to him as the gunmen appeared from the tree line and took up positions around the homes, firing down at them. Three ALSVs appeared down the road and raced toward them.

Harper tapped Catipon. "Time to go!"

The two ran into the house just as machine gun fire ripped through the walls. They hit the deck and Harper kicked the door closed as bits of wood and plaster rained down. Cunningham, Madi, and Kate fired back from the living room windows using several couches and end tables as cover. Harper and Catipon crawled around the corner to join them.

"Any station, this is Gypsy-Zero-One checking in. Radio check?"

Harper heard the voice through his earpiece and leaned up against a corner wall. "About fucking time!" And then into his radio. "Gypsy-Zero-One got ya loud and clear. Sure as shit glad to hear from you. What's your playtime and ordnance?"

"As long as you need, this is a Specter gunship, fully loaded."

"Holy fuck!" Harper exclaimed and yelled to his team. "They sent us whole fucking *gunship*!"

The AC-130 gunship was a modified version of a C-130 transport aircraft designed to attack ground targets with a variety of munitions. In service since the Vietnam war, it had undergone several re-designs over the years and could provide long duration fire support due to its lengthy flight time.

Outside, the ALSVs pulled up and unleashed their full firepower on the house in coordination with their comrades coming down the hill. Volleys of bullets slammed into the house and rockets and grenades exploded every other second, throwing fireballs and mounds of dirt every which way.

"We better get that thing in the fight, *like right fucking now!*" Madi yelled over.

"Right!" Harper said and consulted with his map. "Gypsy-Zero-One stand by for fire mission!"

He briefly wondered what the pilots and crew were thinking as they heard him yelling over the sound of intense gunfire.

"Standing by."

"This will be *danger close* fire mission! Call contact on several enemy vics and troops surrounding an overturned troop truck in the south-western section of the housing complex!"

In the air above them, the AC-130 descended to 7,000 feet as its fire control officer looked through the plane's optics pod mounted on the outside. Through it, his world was awash in thermal signatures, identi-fied as black and white shapes. He spotted the heat signature of running vehicles and several armed men moving around a crashed truck. "Con-tact!"

"That's your target! Requesting 25-mm HE rounds, engage at will! Be advised friendlies are in the house immediately to the north, bring the rain!"

"Roger that, sixty seconds to rounds on target."

Harper shouted to the others, "Sixty seconds!"

In the gunship, the fire control officer announced to the pilots via his headset. "Target ID'd and locked on, commence pylon."

"Roger, target locked on, commencing pylon."

A pylon, or pylon turn, was when an aircraft flew in circles around a fixed location as if an imaginary line connected the two. It was standard procedure for a gunship during an attack run. The huge aircraft banked to the left so it's port-side mounted guns faced Rose Island below.

The fire control officer said to one of the plane's four gunners, "Load gun one, thirty rounds HE. Stand by for firing."

"Load gun one, thirty rounds HE, standing by!"

"Pylon is a go, commence gun run on your command," the pilots called out.

"Roger, starting attack."

Harper and the others waited patiently as they fired a few rounds to keep the mercenaries from advancing any further.

"Where the fuck are these—"

WHIZ-THUD! WHIZ-THUD! WHIZ-THUD!

The sound pierced the air as 25-mm high-explosive rounds rained down from the sky in consecutive burst of three that rapidly picked up in pace, the glass windows above Madi and Catipon shattering.

Men screamed and scattered as huge plumes of concrete and dirt were thrown high into the air!

WHIZ-THUD! WHIZ-THUD! WHIZ-THUD!

Several rounds hit the ALSVs and troop truck and simply turned it into plumes of fire, sending wreckage flying twenty feet into the sky!

WHIZ-THUD! WHIZ-THUD! WHIZ-THUD!

A dozen men had their limbs torn from their bodies or were merely pulverized into pink mist by the fire power raining down from the heavens.

In the house, Catipon felt something land on his leg and looked down. An arm from the elbow down rested on his shin, a bloody stump remained where it had been previously connected to a body.

"Jesus!" he screamed and kicked it away.

WHIZ-THUD! WHIZ-THUD! WHIZ-THUD!

The rain continued as The Team members bunkered down and braced themselves from the shockwaves and overwhelming sound.

A few seconds passed after the firing had ceased and they cautiously peered over the windowsill to see the street empty of enemy fighters and bathed in a thick layer of haze. The acidic smell of explosives and fire drifted in and assaulted their nostrils.

"Gypsy-Zero-One rounds complete. All targets prosecuted."

"Tango, Gypsy-Zero-One, ground force out."

Over in the trio of cul-de-sacs, O'Neal and a few of his men took cover and watched the AC-130 gunship climb into the sky after completing its attack.

Harper and Cation moved through backyards and came to a knee behind a car parked on the street, guns up and scanning in either direction. A few cars sat rusting among the debris covered pavement along with a bus sitting to Harper's left, blocking the road.

Harper eyed the bus closely. "We need some wheels."

A minute later, they were in the bus while Catipon laid under the steering wheel and worked on hotwiring the controls. Kate stood at the rear of the bus, watching through the grime covered windows for any signs of the enemy.

"How long until the device goes off?" Cunningham asked.

Harper checked his watch. "Twenty-eight minutes."

"This is a fucking nightmare," Cunningham complained.

"Yeah," Catipon said. "You should've been with us in Raqqa."

Down the street, figures moved around cars and through yards looking for them.

"I think they found us!" Kate yelled in a whisper.

"You got it or what?" Harper whispered to Catipon.

"I'm working on it!" Catipon hissed back.

"Twenty meters and closing!" Kate announced.

The group prepared for a fire fight, bringing up their weapons to engage.

Catipon finished tying two wires together, got a spark, and then the bus sputtered to life. "We're in business ladies and gentlemen!"

Immediately shots rang out and the windows of the bus shattered, throwing glass everywhere. The Team members fired back, dropping several men standing out in the open.

"Tyler, get us out of here!" Harper shouted.

Catipon jumped into the driver's seat and threw the bus in drive. "Roger that!"

The bus rumbled off down the street and smashed into several parked cars, pushing them away with ease. Called in by their comrades, two ALSVs quickly gained on them from the rear and opened fire with their machine guns. Cutting left and right over the street and yards, Catipon attempted to avoid their fire with little success. In the back, The Team members tried to steady themselves and fire back only to get tossed around uncontrollably.

"Will somebody shoot back!" Catipon shouted.

Madi shot him an annoyed look and Catipon realized that they couldn't. "Sorry, that's my bad!"

As they came up to an intersection, a troop truck appeared from the left and two men jumped out, hefting rockets onto their shoulders.

"Fuck!" Catipon said and glanced right.

The right corner of the block was occupied by a front yard. He cut the bus hard to the right just as two rockets came straight for them and sailed past, missing the bus by inches.

One of them connected with a trailing ALSV and turned it into a flying heap of metal. The second one skipped off the road, went high, and exploded into the second story of a house.

"Ah-ha!" Catipon exclaimed, happy to see the mercenaries take out each other.

The bus came back onto the road only to find that up ahead a grouping of cars blocked any further traffic. Harper came up to the driver's seat and saw what lay ahead. "Go left!"

Catipon had no choice but to continue diagonally and straight into a park. Surrounding the crescent shaped park was a series of mounds topped off with trees. Harper gripped onto the bus's handrails as the bus hit the low hills at nearly fifty miles an hour.

The bus flew ten feet into the air and crashed back down hard on the ground. Harper was thrown back first against the front windshield, cracking it, while the others were thrown over seats and were sent sprawling across the floor. Catipon slowed down as he regained control of the bus.

Behind them, the ALSV also hit the hill at much faster speeds and launched itself into the air, heading straight for the bus!

Facing backwards, Harper saw the ALSV go airborne.

With a resounding thud the enemy vehicle slammed into the roof of the bus, caving the roof in a few feet and breaking the windows, sending shards of glass flying. The ALSV bounced off to the right and hit the ground at an angle. The dune buggy cartwheeled across the park spectacularly, flinging mercenaries and tires into the side of the speeding bus.

Harper looked at Catipon incredulously, just shrugging his shoulders.

Bullets slammed into the side of the bus.

Harper looked to the rear to see the troop truck chasing after them through the park. The canvas covering on the side was rolled up, allowing several shooters to engage them.

"Get us outta here!" he said to Catipon.

Catipon stepped on the gas as he steered for the north side of the park.

Harper took up a position in a bus seat beside Madi, set his rifle on the windowsill and began engaging the enemy.

As the two sides shot at each other and more bullets whizzed past them, Harper took a moment to look over at Madi. Her hair fluttered in the wind as she stared down her optic, calmly pulling the trigger

She seemed to notice and turned, smiling. "Hey."

Damn, that smile.

"Hey."

Several rounds punctured the right-hand side tires and the bus started to shake and slow.

"Fuck," Catipon cursed, white knuckling the steering wheel. "I think this bus has about had it people!"

Looking away from Madi, Harper looked down the optic of his rifle and set his sights on the driver of the troop truck. Pulling the trigger several times, he watched the windshield shatter and red spray across the inside of it.

"Good shooting," Madi complimented.

They watched the bus veer to side before it tipped over and rolled over several times, crushing the men in the back.

Catipon drove the bus through the mounds on the northern side, sputtering to a stop. He looked at the others in the back. "End of the line!"

They quickly exited the pass and onto the street. Harper studied the adjacent streets, looking for movement and noticed how quiet it was.

Cunningham looked at him, noting the same. "Yeah, that can't be good."

Kate looked down the optic of her rifle. "Pretty sure I got eyes on the school, end of this road."

"Awesome," Harper said and drew his pistol, out of ammo for his rifle. "Let's go."

Kate and Cunningham took off at a run down the road using parked cars as cover while the others followed behind.

Harper noticed the block of houses to his left were still under construction. Most were just wooden frames with walls and half-finished roofs resting on a concrete foundation. Window fixtures, doors, and siding had yet to be installed. He could see the school ahead, signified by its large sidewalk awning.

Halfway to the school they came to an intersection with a road branching to the south. The sound of roaring engines broke the silence.

Kate turned to the others. "Down!"

The group ducked behind several cars.

Three ALSVs and a troop truck braked to a stop in front of the school, cutting them off. Men began to dismount and spread out, walking down the road.

O'Neal leered as he watched his men move down the street. He stepped onto the hood of a car and walked onto the roof, eyes searching.

"Come out, come out wherever you are!" he hollered.

"These guys don't fucking give up, do they," Cunningham whispered.

Catipon looked at Harper and pointed up at the sky. "Think it's time to call our friends."

He nodded and sat against a tire, keying his mike in a whisper. "Gypsy-Zero-One, stand by for immediate fire mission."

"Standing by."

O'Neal waved his Desert Eagle around as he spoke. "You can't hide forever; I will find you!"

"Gypsy-Zero-One, this will be danger close fire mission," Harper continued while looking at his ForeTex. "Call contact on the football field in the housing district."

"You hear me bitch! I want my fucking ear back!"

Harper glanced at Madi; eyebrow raised. She shrugged, suppressing a grin.

"Contact."

"To the west is a large parking lot, directly west of that are multiple enemy vehicles, that's your target. Friendlies two hundred meters to the west, fire when ready."

O'Neal turned as he heard the sound of the AC-130 descending through the clouds.

"Roger, rounds on target in sixty seconds."

O'Neal grinned. "You're mine! No one is gonna help you now!"

Harper looked at the others as he said this, confused.

The gunship reached an altitude of 7,000 feet and began its pylon turn around their target. The crew loaded shells into the breech while the fire control officer readied to fire.

What the hell does he mean? Harper thought to himself.

He locked eyes with Madi.

Madi.

How did she get here?

She flew in on an Osprey.

It crashed.

Harper's eyes bulged as he realized.

It was shot down.

"Gypsy-zero-one, abort, abort, abort."

O'Neal said to the man beside him with a Stinger missile hefted over his shoulder, "Now."

They all heard the Stinger missile launch and watched it zoom into the air.

In the cockpit, urgent alarms sounded, and the pilots reacted immediately.

"Holy shit! We have missile launch!" the co-pilot yelled.

"Evasive maneuvers!" the pilot shouted! "Launch countermeasures now!"

The pilot hit the throttle, banked out of its turn, and started climbing back high into the sky.

"Launching counter measures!" the navigation officer responded, sitting behind the pilots.

A series of flares were emitted from either side of the aircraft, trailing out and behind like a pair of wings as a Stinger missile ascended from down below.

A FIM-92 Stinger, a man portable air-defense system, fired infrared homing surface-to-air missiles that were highly effective against low flying aircraft. The missile system had downed hundreds of aircraft across the world across several conflicts. It was what O'Neal had used to down the first Osprey to fly over the island.

The missile detonated dangerously close to the plane, thanks to its distracting flares, and threw a barrage of shrapnel into the fuselage and starboard wing. Climbing higher into the sky and out of sight from the island, the gunship headed west out over the ocean.

"Gypsy-Zero-One, you guys okay?" Harper asked.

"Fucking bastards," Catipon growled.

"Suffered some fuselage damage and our number three engine is out of the fight, but we're okay," came the reply. "Sorry, but we gotta check off station."

"Roger that, tango."

"Good luck, Gypsy-Zero-One out."

Getting by on the skin of their teeth, Harper knew they were going to need all the luck that they could get.

"What do we do know?" Sally asked.

"Time?" Madi said.

Harper checked his watch and grimaced. "Seventeen minutes."

With over a dozen mercenaries closing in on their position and with dwindling ammo, they were as good as dead.

Harper got up on a knee and said to the others, "I got an idea." He paused. "I'll draw their fire, head north. You guys go around to the south and get to that bunker."

"That's suicide, man," Catipon argued.

Madi reached over and grabbed his hand. "Jake, no."

"I don't see another way."

He brushed the side of her face; he could see her eyes watering. "I'll be okay."

"You meet us at the school, right?" Catipon asked, his demeanor serious.

"Yeah."

"Alright," Catipon said and reached into his cargo pockets, pulling out two smoke grenades. "Snagged this from those guys in the hangar, you'll need 'em to make it across the yard."

Harper nodded.

Madi wrapped her arms around him, running her hands through his hair. "Jake . . . "

"Yeah?"

Cunningham interrupted. "Seventy-five meters and closing."

"Now or never," Catipon urged.

Harper pulled back, staring into Madi's bright blue eyes. "Tell me later."

He moved to the rear bumper of the car, judging the distance to the nearest house to be thirty meters.

"Ready?" Catipon asked, smoke grenades in hand.

Harper inhaled deep and fast. "Now."

Catipon pulled the pin and tossed the smoke grenade over the car.

O'Neal's men turned and a second later thick violet smoke started to billow out over the road. Madi looked at Harper and then back at the others, thinking.

"They're close, get 'em!" O'Neal yelled.

Catipon threw the second smoke grenade as purple smoke wharfed over their position. Harper knew the smoke wouldn't last long.

Madi made her decision.

Harper took off in a sprint, heading for the front door of the nearest house.

O'Neal spotted movement through the haze. "To the right, there's that bitch!"

Harper looked to the rear to see Madi running behind him.

"What--,"

He was cutoff as gunshots split the air.

Rounds skipped off the ground around them as they hurdled the front porch steps and jumped inside the house, sliding to the ground.

"Move out!" O'Neal ordered as he jumped off the car. "I want *her* alive!"

On the smooth concrete floor, Harper looked at Madi with bewilderment. "What the fuck are you doing here!"

"You needed help!" Madi shot back.

She wiggled her way around the corner with her pistol held out in front. Firing a few shots, a mercenary dropped to the ground dead.

"You needed to go to the school!" Harper countered.

Catipon observed the mercenary army pivot to the north. He shook his head, feeling guilty for leaving Harper and Madi behind.

But he had a job to do.

"Let's go," he whispered to the others.

Harper stole a glance over a windowsill and spied a man preparing to fire a rocket right at his location. "I'm so tired of these guys and their goddamn rockets."

He tapped Madi. "Move!"

The two got up and sprinted for the rear of the house. Just as they exited the rocket slammed into the doorway, blasting sheetrock and splinters out of the back door.

They stumbled out of the haze and into the backyard. Before them, the housing block was flooded from the storm.

"Which way?" Madi asked.

Bullets whizzed by from behind.

Harper grabbed Madi's hand. "Forward!"

The two sloshed into the water, making their way across the flooded backyard and to the next row of homes; also under construction. Several armed men emerged from the house behind, guns firing.

Harper and Madi hit the deck behind a portable cement mixer, bullets sending up geysers around them.

"I got half a mag of 5.56 and two pistol mags," Madi reported.

Harper ejected his magazine and looked at the round indicator. "Mag and a half for my pistol."

Bullets pinged off the cement mixer and ricocheted off into the water. Harper spotted an open garage door of a complete house to the north and sitting on dry ground.

"There," Harper said, pointed, and kissed Madi on the lips. "Run like hell."

Harper emptied his pistol as Madi took off, running awkwardly through the knee-deep water. Once he ran out of ammo, Madi dropped to a knee and fired. Harper ran past her, ejected the mag and inserted his last one.

Madi fired the last of her rifle ammo, ditched it, and took off toward Harper. The two made it out of the water, slipped under the garage door, and Harper slammed it shut just as their pursuers rounded the corner.

28

HARPER LET HIS EYES ADJUST TO THE DARKNESS OF THE GARAGE while he caught his breath.

Ejecting the magazine from his pistol, he pushed the rounds out into his hand, counting them. "I got one in the chamber, three in the mag. You?"

"Eight," she reported grimly.

Outside they could hear men close by, communicating with one another as they searched.

Moving quietly, Harper and Madi entered the house and came into the kitchen/dining room. The front door and a huge grimy window adored the dining room's wall that looked out into the street. Staying low they crept through the dining room when a shadow passed by the window.

The two laid flat on the floor, watching the man walk by until he passed. They continued to wait, staying still and listening.

The window shattered as a man crashed headfirst into it, rolled across the dining room table and landed at their feet.

O'Neal smiled. "Got *you*."

Harper sprang into action.

He pushed Madi to the side and seeing O'Neal about to stomp on him with his boot, rolled backward and came up to a knee. Harper dodged a blow from O'Neal's fist and then tucked his arm under and around his neck. Next, he shifted his weight back and fell to the floor, taking O'Neal down with him.

Harper squeezed his forearm against O'Neal's jugular vein in a classic chokehold technique. O'Neal reached down and drew one of his massive Desert Eagle pistols.

"Fuck me!"

Harper swung his legs to the side and wrapped them around O'Neal's gun hand, straightening it out so he couldn't bring it up to shoot Harper.

O'Neal, in frustration, squeezed off several rounds in Madi's direction.

"Watch out!" Harper yelled.

Madi threw herself over the kitchen's centrally located island countertop, bullets exploding everywhere. O'Neal's gun ran out of ammo, and he tossed it away.

O'Neal, outmatching Harper in strength, used his other arm to slowly pry away his grip around his neck. Harper knew he was fighting a losing battle and let go, scrambled away and quickly got on his feet.

Harper took up a fighting stance as O'Neal jumped up, saw him, let out an animalistic roar and rushed him.

"Ah, shit."

O'Neal crashed headfirst into Harper and picked him up off his feet. Harper went flying across the living room and into the sheetrock wall, cracking it.

"Motherfucker!" Harper yelled as he elbowed O'Neal in the back.

Grunting, O'Neal threw a punch at Harper's head. He ducked and O'Neal's fist went through the wall. Harper kneed O'Neal in the gut and then went to move around him.

His movement was halted when O'Neal grabbed him by the collar.

"Where do you think you're going!"

O'Neal swung him around and tossed Harper straight into the damaged wall, cracking it more. He then punched Harper hard in the face and took Harper's pistol from the holster on his belt, levelling it at him.

Harper froze, he had nowhere to go.

O'Neal pulled the trigger consecutively, giving Harper just enough time to throw his arms up in defense and launching himself backwards through the sheetrock wall, vanishing in a haze.

Satisfied Harper was dead, O'Neal discarded Harper's pistol and drew his second Desert Eagle and looked back at the kitchen. "It's just you and me now, sweetheart!"

Madi crouched down on the other side of the island, gun in hand and keeping her mouth open to silence her breathing.

"Come on out," O'Neal taunted as he stepped into the kitchen. "Let's play."

Spotting a kitchen knife on the floor, Madi held it up around the corner to get a better look in the reflection.

She saw O'Neal a split second before he shot the knife from her hand.

"Playing hard to get, I like that."

O'Neal popped around the island's corner, expecting to see Madi, but found nothing.

Madi jumped up from the other side, rapidly bringing her gun to fire. O'Neal lunged toward her and caught her wrist, knocking her gun from her hand in the process.

"Nice try."

Madi landed a blow straight into O'Neal's nose, breaking it and sending blood pouring onto the countertop. O'Neal screamed and let go of Madi's wrist, bringing his Desert Eagle around in a sweeping arc. Bullets chased Madi to the deck as she dived to the floor, and O'Neal emptied the clip.

"You little bitch!" O'Neal spat, wiping the blood from his mouth.

O'Neal reloaded and then jumped onto the island countertop, peering over both sides. The only place he couldn't see over was the far end, ten feet away.

"There're no more places to hide," O'Neal said as he stalked across the island countertop. "No one else to save you, nowhere else to go."

Madi thought through her options. There weren't any good ones. She was trapped and O'Neal would be one her in seconds.

"You and me are gonna have so," O'Neal stepped closer, "*much*," and closer, "*fun.*"

O'Neal had her dead to rights.

"Madi, go high!" Harper yelled from behind.

Harper came sprinting into the kitchen and went flying across the countertop, crashing into O'Neal's legs. He fell onto the countertop as Madi took a leap forward, kicked off the counter in front of her, propelled herself into the air, and spun around.

O'Neal had landed with his head hanging over the countertop's ledge and briefly watched Madi bring both her feet together.

Madi landed on O'Neal's head and with a sickening—*snap!*—broke his neck.

O'Neal's head slumped lifelessly downward, only skin and muscle holding it to his neck.

Madi leaned against the counter, breathing hard as Harper got up on the other side of the island.

"Told ya I'd kill you," Madi said without remorse.

"Guy talked *way* too much," Harper added through clenched teeth and she noticed he was holding his hip.

"What happened?" Madi asked as she rushed over.

Harper took his hand away from his hip to reveal it was slicked in dark red blood. A bullet had passed through the side of his abdomen just above his right hip. "Got shot."

"Jesus," Madi exclaimed as she examined the wound and pulled out a pack of Quikclot-coated gauze. "Guess he wasn't a good shot."

"I wouldn't say that," Harper said and held up his arm to show that a round had impacted his ForeTex armguard. "Good to know these things are actually bulletproof."

Harper let the destroyed armguard fall to the floor as Madi finished dressing his wound. They could hear the mercenaries yelling outside as they approached.

Madi retrieved her pistol. "We gotta move."

Harper walked over to O'Neal and quickly went through his pockets. Pulling out a satellite phone, he shoved it in his cargo pocket. The two moved into the adjacent house through the broken wall, Harper grabbing his pistol off the floor, and took a seat against the counter in the kitchen. Shadows moved across the windows outside.

"They got us surrounded," Harper said.

Madi gripped his hand and squeezed. "Is this it?"

"We still got . . . " Harper looked at his watch, "just under five minutes. A lot can happen in five minutes."

She sniffed a laugh. "Always the optimist, uh?"

Harper smiled and went to say something, hesitating. "Look, Madi . . . "

She looked into his eyes, waiting patiently.

"Fuck it, I'm just gonna say it," Harper said, frustrated with himself. "Madison Oakley, I-I want you in my life, I want a life with you."

Tears rushed into Madi's eyes.

"I've known since that night in New York," Harper continued. "I should've said it a lot sooner—"

Madi cut him off when she leaned in and kissed him.

"I want a life with you too, Jake Harper."

Harper laughed. "Only took being chased around by a bunch of mercenaries and a countdown to imminent death for us to get that cleared up."

"Better late than never," Madi said with a wink.

"Yeah . . . " Something caught Harper's eye hanging on the wall by the fridge, a set of keys.

"Please be here," he said to himself as he grabbed them and went to the garage.

In the dim light he saw a car resting in the closed garage.

"Oh, this is gonna be fun," Harper said with a smile as Madi came over.

"You think it'll run?" she asked.

"It has to."

Harper jumped in the driver seat and started the car to hear a deep throaty purr of the engine echo in the garage. Madi hopped in the passenger seat, pistol tight in her grip.

"How far do you think it is?" Harper asked as he spied a cassette resting on the dash and picked it up.

"Less than a mile."

Harper slipped the cassette into the cassette player and hit play. The intro of Led Zeppelin's "Rock and Roll" began emitting from the car's speakers as he revved the engine. Outside, the mercenaries heard the car start and quickly closed in with coordinated movements.

"Get ready."

Madi looked over at Harper, smiling "Punch it, *babe.*"

Harper floored it and shot off the mark with a squeal of the tires. The black 1968 Ford Mustang tore through the garage doors and flew out onto the street.

A mercenary standing out in the middle of the street immediately opened fire. Bullets pinged off the car as Harper sent the back-end skidding to the side and smacked directly into the mercenary, sending him flying straight into a parked car!

Gunfire raked the ground them.

"Go! Go!" Madi yelled, eyeing the team of mercenaries converging on them.

Harper punched it just as a mercenary leaped onto the hood and brought his rifle around.

"Shit!" Harper yelled, seeing the road in front of him was flooded.

Madi shot through the windshield, hitting the mercenary, just as Harper slammed on the brakes and sent the dead man flying into the flooded street. Harper threw the car in reverse just as—*crash!*—a mercenary came up and shattered the window with his rifle beside Madi.

Harper reached over and grabbed the barrel, thrusting it against the ceiling.

Bullets ripped through the car roof as the man squeezed the trigger, wresting for control of the weapon. The barrel was burning in Harper's hand as hot empty cartridges landed on Madi and fell down her shirt.

"Motherfucker!" she yelled and drew her pistol.

The man's head exploded in a burst of red, splattering the inside of the windshield, and he fell to the street, dead.

Harper sent the Mustang flying down the street in reverse. He saw a mercenary in his side view mirror preparing to fire his underslung M203 grenade launcher.

"I don't think so!"

Harper kicked his door open, and it crashed into the attacker, shattering the glass and tossing the man over the door and to the ground.

Yanking the e-brake and spinning the wheel, Harper threw the Mustang around, threw it in drive and raced down the street.

"They're heading for the next street over!" one of the mercenaries said. "Go cut 'em off!"

The Mustang drifted right around the corner and while turning around the next corner, Harper saw a mercenary standing in the street hefting a rocket over his shoulder.

Bug-eyed, Harper yelled, "Shit!"

Harper kept the Mustang drifting around in a wide circle as the rocket zoomed toward them. The projectile shot over the hood with inches to spare and slammed into a parked car behind them. The explosion engulfed two cars and sent wreckage flying out onto the street, blocking the road behind them.

The Mustang spun out and came to a stop as Harper and Madi watched more mercenaries filter out onto the street, scanning for a way out.

"Straight!" Madi yelled and pointed. "Between the houses!"

Harper stepped on the gas and brought the Mustang across a front yard and through a wooden fence separating the two homes.

"How we looking on time!" Madi asked.

Harper checked his watch. "Minute, forty-two!"

"Right! Go right!" Madi said quickly. "Through the backyards!"

Harper spun the wheel to the right, grimacing as they crashed through another wooden fence and tossing aside a grill. "Really ruining a really nice car."

Up ahead they spotted several mercenaries rush into the backyards laying in front of them.

Harper dodged a swing set as a rocket zoomed through it and detonated into a pool behind. Gunfire erupted all around them, throwing up plumes of dirt all over the car. Madi spotted a mercenary on the back porch deck preparing to fire a rocket and leaned out of the window with her pistol.

The mercenary dropped dead just as he pulled the trigger.

Shooting high over the Mustang, the rocket slammed into the second story of a house and blasted derbies of wood and siding all over the speeding car.

"I see the school!" Madi exclaimed. "Up ahead on the left!"

Harper pounded the steering wheel in triumph. "Ah-ha! That's what I'm talking about! And with," he checked his watch, "forty seconds left!"

The Mustang bounced over a few curbs and into the school parking lot to see Catipon waving them on over by the entrance.

Braking to a stop, Harper and Madi jumped out.

"You find the bunker?" Madi asked.

"Yeah, follow me!"

"Cutting it a *bit* close!" Catipon called out as he took off running. "Less than a minute!"

They followed him through a small courtyard in between the school's buildings, sprinting at full speed.

"We stopped for coffee!" Harper sarcastically quipped.

The three hit a set of double doors leading into a large indoor basketball court, feet pounding on the hardwood floor as they raced across it.

"You get me some?" Catipon asked with equal sarcasm as he held open another door for them.

"Yeah, it's back in the car!"

The three descended a staircase for thirty feet before coming to huge bunker door still cracked open. They rushed inside to see the others waiting tensely in a space as large as the basketball court above. Cheap metal bunk beds sat in neat rows and dim lights illuminated the space.

"Help me close this!" Catipon said urgently.

The three of them grabbed the door's handle and pulled with all their strength on the two-thousand-pound door. Harper nervously watched the timer on his watch tick down past five seconds.

They pulled the door shut and Catipon slammed the latch down to seal it.

The timer on Harper's watch beeped and they held their breath, looking up.

Nothing happened.

Less than a mile away, O'Neal lay still on the island countertop, his head hanging unnaturally over the edge. He blinked and gurgled incoherently, trying to speak. He was just barely alive.

Harper frowned.

"Maybe you didn't synch to it exactly?" Catipon offered.

"I don't think—" Harper was saying when the ground shook.

The five-hundred-pound thermobaric device detonated.

Big.

The surrounding half mile of forest around the bomb was simply pulverized in a fast-moving fireball that reached a mile high in the sky, rapidly consuming oxygen from twenty-five miles away to fuel the deadly fire. The near-instantaneous force of air being sucked in at breakneck speeds ripped trees out of the ground, collapsed the damaged hangar at the southern airport, and tore houses apart in the housing district. Vehicles were pulled through the air and a landslide of mud slid down the mountains in the southwest, partially concealing the buildings there. It even knocked the eastern lighthouse over and sent it crashing off the cliffs.

In the house where O'Neal was dying the doors were torn from their hinges and windows shattered. Before O'Neal knew what was happening, his lungs were grotesquely *pulled* through his body and out of his mouth in the blink of an eye. The bloody sacks of disfigured lungs were splattered against the walls and ceiling with a gross *smack!*

Five miles away from the blast, the room shook, and dust fell from the ceiling as the group in the bunker braced themselves against the rumbling.

The fireball grew higher and larger as it consumed oxygen, reaching its zenith of two miles high in the sky before it came to a stop. From the thirty-mile marker out at sea, the men and women of the 26th MEU stared at the spectacle in wonder, drawing similarities to that of a nuclear bomb's mushroom cloud.

Mercifully, the thermobaric detonation ran its course and subsided. Debris and water droplets rained down across the island and a brisk wind rushed in to fill in the void caused by the explosion. A few fires burned in the burnt-out patch of forest but quickly died.

The battleground of Rose Island was now, finally, silent.

FASSWATER AND NATALIE WERE SEPARATELY OCCUPIED WITH THEIR own tasks in the Birch lodge, him trying to re-establish comms with any of their forces after the line went dead and her with looking into the background of Cutthroat.

Sheets of rain continued to patter against the windows. Hurricane Taylor had dissipated into a tropical storm, but still managed to force several road closures in the area due to flooding.

Sharing a desk in the lodge's bedroom, they both typed on their laptops, clicking and swiping every few seconds as they squinted at the screen.

Taking a sip of her third cup of black coffee with an espresso shot, Natalie scanned the current roster of those assigned to Recon Unit 16.

First, she read the dossier of their commander, Captain William Brookes. He had been their leader for ten years, something very unusual for people in the military considering they often moved units every couple of years. She had read the report of accused war crimes committed in Afghanistan in 2009, but the charges were later dropped due to a lack of evidence. After checking his bank accounts to find nothing out of the ordinary, Natalie moved on.

She went through every current member of Cutthroat to find nothing spectacular. All were single, didn't have social media accounts, and held no debt with clean banking accounts.

Next, she moved to former members, those had exited the military or had switched units. She came across two men who had both left the unit and exited the military at the same time three months ago, a Sergeant Williams and a Sergeant Bell.

They were both discharged honorably and didn't seem to have jobs currently.

Interesting, Natalie thought. *The beginning of a pattern.*

A thought occurred to her, and she opened a new tab. Natalie searched Instagram for accounts belonging to Williams and Bell and found they both had a private account. The two appeared to be friends, both tagging each other in posts showing them hunting deer.

One geo-tagged location in several photos posted by both stuck out to her. Independence Firearms, a gun range and store in rural Virginia an hour's drive from the Capitol.

Strolling through Independence Firearm's Instagram page, Natalie saw they were heavily invested in 2nd Amendment rights and supported the military and police forces. They featured posts with soldiers and Marines stationed in the DC area and police departments from Virginia and Maryland. Williams and Bell were even featured in several pictures standing with police officers in uniform. One account seemed to like and comment the page's content regularly, a page by the name of Diehard_Patriots.

Diehard_Patriots seemed to be a loose collection of far-right ideals with most posts declaring the left as a detriment to American freedom. They cited politicians as corrupt and greedy, demanding change and resentment toward the current federal government. Natalie saw that Williams and Bell had both liked and shared their posts.

There was a link to a Reddit forum, and she went to it. In it there was a lot of talk about taking violent action against people of color, homosexuals, and pillars of the federal government. The last post she read made her jaw drop.

"Oh, fuck," Natalie breathed.

Fasswater suddenly sat up at his computer beside her. "What the hell?"

"What do you got?" Natalie asked.

Fasswater rapidly threw on a pair of headphones. "I'm getting an encrypted satellite call."

"From where?"

"I'll have to backtrack the origin, but it's calling someone on Rose Island."

"Is it one of our people?"

He shook his head. "Nope, if it was, I could listen in but they're running a different encryption than ours."

A few seconds passed and he took off his headphones. "I'm in."

They listened attentively, waiting. Finally, a voice said, "Where the hell have you been? I've been trying to reach you for hours."

They both recognized the voice but couldn't remember where they had heard it.

A second voice asked, *"Who is this?"*

Fasswater and Natalie both recognized that voice and looked at each other.

The call was immediately disconnected.

"That was Harper," Fasswater said confidently.

He had tried to reach him through the frequency they had established for the last hour to no avail.

Natalie turned her screen to him. "Look at this."

"Fuck," he said. "Go let Warner know, I'll stay here and track the origin of the call and get in contact with Harper."

"Hurry," Natalie said and made to leave. "We may not have enough time."

30   ROSE ISLAND

A NAVY CORPSMAN WAS FINISHING STITCHING UP HARPER'S BULLET wound as he thought about the call he had just received on the satellite phone he had taken off O'Neal.

They were gathered on the football field across from the school as several Ospreys landed and Marines disembarked en masse. They had been launched shortly after the thermobaric explosion went off and they had flagged them down as they buzzed the island, looking for Harper and his team.

"What is it?" Madi asked.

"Someone called O'Neal and then hung up," Harper explained.

Cunningham walked past as he made his way to a waiting Osprey, his hand wrapped in bandages. "Damn good to see you, appreciate everything you did."

Harper shook his hand. "I'll see you around brother, take care."

Sally followed behind and just gave Harper a nod. He gave a small salute and watched the Osprey take off, heading east toward the *Iwo Jima*.

A Marine officer walked up to Harper, holding a satellite phone. "You Jake Harper?"

"Sure am."

He handed him the phone. "It's for you."

"Go for Harper."

"Harper, it's Henderson you're on with Fasswater, he's got something to share with you."

"Send it, Fasswater."

"Hey, I just heard you answer a satellite phone call," Fasswater started. "I'm still working on pinpointing the location and I've got it narrowed down to the DC metro area."

"Cutthroat?" Harper asked seriously.

"That's my guess," Fasswater said. "Looks like they were working with the mercenary force on the island, and we think we know why. Seems their former teammates are some far right extremists that have a burning hatred for the federal government; we suspect they're going to try and assassinate the preside—"

The line went silent.

"Fasswater? You there?"

No response.

"Six, you caught that?"

"Yeah, I heard, I'm trying to reach Camp David right now. Listen, if Fasswater is right . . . "

Fuck.

Harper was exhausted and his body ached over, his hip sending waves of pain through his body with every step. He wanted nothing more than to get out of his wet clothes, crawl into bed, and sleep for three days.

But people were counting on him, innocent people who were in harm's way.

Harper spied an Osprey that had just touched down and started walking toward it. "I'm on it, sir."

Madi followed him and he waved over to Catipon and Kate. "Six, I need you to put the captain of the ship on the phone."

"What's going on?" Catipon asked them as they ran up.

Madi just shrugged her shoulders as Harper ran into the troop compartment of the chopper and up to the cockpit, to speak with the pilots. A few moments later, Harper came back and shouted, "This isn't over! Camp David just went dark, and Cutthroat is making a move on the president!"

"What are we waiting for then?" Catipon said.

Harper grinned and they quickly boarded the Osprey. Taking a seat, Harper donned a pair of headphones and asked the pilots, "How fast can you get us to Camp David?"

The pilots looked at each other dumbfounded and then responded. "With this tailwind, forty minutes!"

"Good, punch it! The president's life is in danger!"

The Osprey lifted off the field and headed due west over the housing district. Catipon waved over to the crew chief and asked, "Got any weapons on board?"

The crew chief nodded and dragged over a small case. Inside were several Colt M4 carbines and Berretta M9 pistols. After they had armed themselves, Harper put the satellite phone back to his ear.

"Any luck?"

"No dice with Camp David, at all!" Henderson reported. "No one can establish comms with anyone there! It's like no one's there!"

"They must've planned this thing since the beginning. Contact Secret Service headquarters and get some local police to Camp David!"

"Already did!" Henderson said. "But flooding from the storm has closed all of the viable routes. They're spinning up some air assets, but it's gonna take some time!"

"Roger, Six! Keep me updated, Harper out!"

Harper turned and looked at his battered and beat team. "Looks like it's just us!"

"Fan-fucking-tastic!" Catipon shouted. "Another day, another dollar right?"

Harper smiled. "Absolutely!"

31 CAMP DAVID

NATALIE HAD JUST RETURNED TO THE LODGE WHEN EVERY LIGHT ON the compound went dark. She froze mid-step. As she waited for her eyes to adjust, she could hear the blood running past her ears, it was so quiet.

"Michael?" she nervously called out.

"I'm here."

Fasswater felt along the wall, tried the light switch to find it did nothing, and pulled out his phone.

"Power outage?" Natalie asked, walking slowly through the darkness toward him.

"More than your average power outage," Fasswater said and showed her his phone; it was completely dead. "Phone's dead."

"What the hell is going on?"

Fasswater walked toward the lodge's living room, hearing people running outside. "I don't—" He stopped and whirled around. "EMP!"

"EMP?" Natalie repeated.

"Electromagnetic pulse," Fasswater explained. "I was tracking reports of a stolen EMP smuggled in through Central America."

EMP devices could discharge a massive surge of electromagnetic energy with very little physical damage, shutting down whole power grids and anything with an electrical charge.

The two walked into the living room and saw several panicked armed Secret Service agents and Marines running around and shouting orders. In the distance at the front gate, they saw two pairs of flashing red and blue lights belonging to two police cruisers that had pulled up.

I thought the roads were closed? Natalie thought to herself.

Lisa entered the lodge with her two-man detail, soaking wet and wearing rain ponchos. Both of her security men had their pistols drawn.

"What's happening?" Natalie asked.

"Everything has gone to shit," Lisa responded. "They're saying we've been nuked! Comms are fired, and everyone is losing their goddamn minds. The vehicles won't start so they're moving POTUS to Marine One, which is EMP resistant."

"Not a nuclear blast, ma'am, just an EMP one," Fasswater corrected.

"What are you talking about, Fasswater?"

"Before you pulled me for this assignment, I was tracking unconfirmed reports of a stolen EMP, this has to be it!"

"That means Camp David has been *deliberately* and *specifically* attacked," Lisa realized.

"Ma'am, I think its Cutthroat," Natalie said. "I was looking into them, and they have amassed a group of followers who I believe want to strike hard at the federal government, I think they want to kill the president, *here*."

"That would explain why they stole an Osprey from the *Iwo Jima*."

"Ma'am, haven't the roads around here been closed due to flooding?" Natalie asked.

"Last report I got, yeah."

She pointed at the flashing cop cars. "Then how'd *they* get here so fast?"

Lisa and her security detail looked at her, suddenly confused as well.

Natalie jumped where she stood, mind racing back to Instagram posts made with police officers. "Shit!"

"What is it?" Fasswater asked.

"That's gotta be accomplices of Cutthroat!" Natalie gasped. "I saw a few posts of former Cutthroat guys with cops!" She pointed again. "They must've been lying in wait for the EMP to go off!"

Lisa drew her Glock 19 pistol and chambered a round just as—
thump.

The ground shook and the windows rattled. Just then the door was ripped open and another of Lisa's men came rushing inside.

"Explosion at the barracks and Secret Service are saying an Osprey is landing at the helo pad," the man reported.

Before Lisa could respond, gunshots rang out in the distance and everyone's head spun to look out of the windows. They spotted the cop cars speeding onto the compound a moment before a massive fireball ripped through the front gate, illuminated the forest in glows of brilliant orange.

Lisa talked quickly to her men. "Sullivan, find SIAC Weathers tell him those police officers and men in that Osprey are *not* to be trusted, its Cutthroat!"

Sullivan nodded and took off.

"Cutler, Arnett, go to the truck and get the rifles. I'll meet you there in a second."

Lisa turned to looked at Fasswater and Natalie. "Can you two find some way to establish comms with anyone on the outside? We need reinforcements, now."

"We'll figure something out, ma'am," Fasswater said instantly.

Natalie shot him a baffled look.

"Figure it out fast," Lisa said and promptly left.

32

LISA WAS MOVING TOWARD HER SUV WHEN GUNSHOTS AND FLASHES of light went off ahead of her. She dived behind a tree and peered around the trunk. In the flashing cop car lights, Lisa saw several armed men dressed in dark fatigues and wearing flaks and Kevlars with quad-tube night vision devices search her vehicles and them move out. Her two security men lay dead on the ground.

"Shit," she breathed.

Lisa figured it was the rogue unit of Cutthroat and they were killing anyone on the compound who opposed them.

Rushing forward, Lisa grabbed a Heckler & Koch MP5 submachine gun along with a few magazines from her trunk and moved quietly toward the two police cruisers parked just to the north over a low hill. Taking cover behind a tree, she spied four men milling about dressed in sheriff police uniforms. They all had their guns drawn and looked nervously around.

She stepped around the tree with her MP5 and Glock held out in front of her. "Nobody move!"

The cops whirled around; pistols held down by their sides.

"Miss!" one of the cops began. "We're not here to harm anyone, we're here to help!"

"Sure ya are," Lisa said, unconvinced. "I'm going to need all of you to slowly drop your weapons."

None of the cops moved.

"Now!" she shouted. "Or I start shooting."

The cops looked at each other and nodded. Two of them went to place their guns on the ground while a third threw his at Lisa's feet. She blinked and the fourth cop made his move.

Bullets slammed into the tree behind Lisa, and she squeezed the MP5's trigger. The cop went flying backward as his chest exploded with blood and landed on the cruiser's hood. In the process of placing their weapons on the deck, the cops rolled to the side and brought thier guns up toward Lisa.

Lisa moved faster, bringing her Glock around, and the pair fell went down to the ground, dead.

The final cop, who had thrown his weapon at her feet, ducked behind the cop car as she unleashed a burst from her MP5. The cruiser's lights were shot off and exploded in glass shards. Lisa moved around the front of the car as the last cop grabbed his comrade's sidearm from the hood. Both parties aimed at each other.

The entire engagement had lasted a few seconds, Lisa didn't even have to think before she pulled the trigger at the same time the cop did.

A bullet hole appeared in the man's forehead, and he slumped forward.

Lisa gasped and dropped her weapons, clutching her stomach. She looked down to see blood pouring out from in between her fingers. "Shit."

In Birch, Fasswater and Natalie spent ten minutes examining their equipment, before inferring that they couldn't fix their communications.

"Damn it!" Fasswater exclaimed.

"So, we need a power source," Natalie began talking to herself. "But the power is out so we need a battery of some sort."

An idea came to mind, and she looked at Fasswater. "What about a car battery?"

Fasswater thought. "That could work since the car was off, the battery should be fine. I can easily rewire to power our basic comm systems."

They both realized the nearest vehicle was fifty meters to the west parked alongside the road. Gunfire constantly rang out in intermediate bursts and fires blazed in the distance, casting uncertain shadows across the forest. It was a battlefield out there.

"It's too dangerous out there," Natalie warned. "Don't go."

"Someone has to," Fasswater replied. "I'll be right back."

He went for the door when Natalie grabbed his arm. Fasswater turned and she gave him a quick kiss on the cheek. "For good luck."

Fasswater blushed.

Exiting the lodge in a crouched run, Fasswater took cover behind a tree and looked toward the road. His hands shook as adrenaline coursed through his veins, sending his heart beating rapidly.

How the hell did I end up here? Fasswater asked himself.

Sprinting from tree to tree, Fasswater came to the two SUVs The Team personnel had driven to the compound. He froze once he saw Cutler and Arnett dead on the ground. Fasswater checked for a pulse and found none.

Lifting the hood, Fasswater strained to locate the battery in the darkness, using his hands to aid in the process. He disconnected it and, with a final glance around him, took off back toward the lodge.

Fasswater was twenty feet away from the door when a figure tackled him from the side. Dropping the battery, the air was driven from his lungs as he slammed back first onto the ground and a knee shoved into his chest, Glock pistol pressed against his forehead. Fasswater was frozen with fear and before he could speak the man pressed a hand over his mouth.

A voice whispered nearby, "Stand down, Russel. I recognize him."

The man got off Fasswater and he saw a team of Secret Service agents appear from the darkness. In the middle of their defensive posture stood the president, wearing sweats and soaked to the bone.

"Ma'am," Fasswater said with a nod.

"What are you doing?" the agent demanded.

"Trying to re-establish communications," Fasswater explained.

"Everything is dead."

"I think I can fix it," Fasswater said confidently. "With that car battery."

The president said to the agent in charge. "I trust him, Weathers."

Weathers nodded at a nearby agent and then said to Fasswater, "Let's go."

An agent scooped up the battery and they entered the lodge, a team of agents staying outside to set up a security perimeter.

Elsewhere in the country, things were happening *fast*.

The moment communications between Camp David and Secret Service headquarters in Washington, D.C. went dead and the backup frequencies were silent, alerts started going off. A reinforcement team of Secret Service agents began to be pooled together and local authorities in the area were notified. Once they had gotten word from the USS *Iwo Jima*, a hostile force was bent on attacking Camp David, Ospreys had been scrambled from Joint Base Andrews in Maryland to ferry the Secret Service response team to Camp David, as well a second infantry platoon from the Marine Barracks.

In the event this was a coordinated strike, the vice president, having been in Oklahoma City, was awoken in his hotel room and quickly flown to a secret bunker in Nebraska. The speaker of the house and president pro tempore of the Senate, number three and four in the order of presidential succession, were also whisked away to separate bunkers located in the Appalachian Mountains.

All non-essential staff were evacuated from the White House and DC police set units to guard the Capitol building. The Secretary of Defense, the Secretary of Homeland Security, and the Joint Chiefs of Staff were rushed to a bunker deep below the Pentagon.

After a quick teleconference call with the vice president as he sat aboard Air Force Two, it was decided the alert status of the armed forces be elevated to DEFCON 3, the highest it had been since 9/11. They notified the FAA to ground all flights along the Eastern Seaboard and prepare to ground all flights across the country.

"Seven minutes and we'll be in visual range!" the pilot of the Osprey called out over their comms.

Harper glanced at his watch; they would get to Camp David just thirty-eight minutes after taking off from Rose Island.

The Osprey rocketed over the state of Maryland at speeds of over 300 miles an hour in the driving rain. Beginning to descend, the pilots slowed down and rotated the nacelles into the vertical position, allowing the bird to fly like a helicopter.

Catipon announced bleakly to the ragtag group of reinforcements, "These guys are gonna have the homefield advantage!"

"What do you mean?" Madi asked, confused.

"These guys have trained and worked with the Secret Service," Harper explained. "They know Camp David and the Secret Service's SOPs."

"This is pretty fucking bold of them, even for Cutthroat!" Catipon said. "To attack Camp David and kill the president!"

"They wouldn't pull something like this unless they were sure they could succeed" Harper countered. "So, keep your eyes peeled and get ready to hit the ground running. We find the president and stop them!"

"Semper fucking Fi," Catipon shouted, quoting the Marine Corps motto.

In Birch, the Secret Service stood guard at all the lodge's entrances and windows, submachine guns at the ready. In the back room, Fasswater and Natalie worked on attaching their equipment to the car battery. The president sat on the floor leaning against the bed and surrounded by three agents.

"What's going on out there?" Fasswater asked Weathers as he paced around.

"As soon as the power went out, we were moving POTUS to Marine One," he began. "They detonated explosives at the front gate and the barracks and were landing a bird at the LZ when one of your men warned us of them. Enemy came out of the fucking woodworks, and we fought our way back to Aspen, only to find it occupied."

"That's when we found you guys," Veronica finished.

"Any sign of Warner?" Fasswater asked.

She solemnly shook her head.

Natalie asked, "Don't you guys have backup in place for something like this?"

Veronica managed to crack a smile, despite their dire circumstances. Her face covered in dirt, her hair in a mess, and her ruined clothes, the president of the United States looked more like a refugee than the leader of the free world. Natalie couldn't believe she was barefoot, having been practically carried by her protective detail and not having time to grab a pair of shoes.

"They're in route," Weathers said, his expression emotionless. He checked his watch. "How much longer? We can't stay in one spot for too long."

Fasswater finished splicing two wires together and looked up. "Should be good."

Natalie switched the computer on and the screen came to life. "Got it! Who we contacting?"

"Patch me into the Secret Service's headquarters in D.C. and make sure it's encrypted," Weathers instructed, walking over and leaning over her.

Natalie typed a few keystrokes. "You're in, press the button to transmit."

"Handshake, this is SAIC Weathers," Weathers began urgently. "Evergreen is secure, I repeat Evergreen is secure. Buckeye is severely compromised by a coordinated strike by multiple attackers using military small arms. Marine One and Aspen is a no go, Orange One cannot be accessed. We are trapped. ETA on backup?"

"Reinforcement element Tabletop is fifteen mikes out and are accompanied by a Marine infantry platoon. Local police have been notified but all the roads are closed due to flooding."

"Roger. Currently located in Birch, will signal with flare when the rescue units get here."

"Copy all. Be advised of an additional rescue asset en route from the USS *Iwo Jima* via Osprey. Three mikes out."

Weathers frowned at that.

"Our forces from the island?" Natalie asked Fasswater.

"It's gotta be," Fasswater said, excited as he grabbed a headset and contacted the *Iwo Jima*.

After thirty seconds, he was patched into Harper's satellite phone and said to Weathers, "I'm contacting that force right now."

The Osprey approached Camp David from the southeast a hundred feet above the treetops. Harper unstrapped himself and leaned into the cockpit, looking through the windows down below.

"Jesus Christ," the pilot breathed.

Camp David now resembled a warzone.

Marine One was being consumed by a raging fire on the helo pad. Several Secret Service vehicles and the front gate house had been hit with explosives. The barracks building on the north side also burned as he watched sections of it collapse.

His satellite phone rang. "Go for Harper!"

"It's Fasswater!" he said and put it on speaker for the room to hear. "Where you at?"

"On approach to Camp David, I have eyes on. What's going on down there?"

Weathers took over. "This is SAIC Weathers, POTUS is secure for now, we're in the center of the compound, can you land anywhere near us?"

Harper asked the pilots as they swung in a circle above Camp David. He spotted the Aspen lodge, easily the largest on the compound, with a skylight located on its roof next to a chimney. "They can land on the golf course."

"Negative!" Weathers said. "Enemy has control of Aspen!"

He pounded his fist in frustration on the table.

As the pilots passed over the LZ they spotted the Osprey Recon Unit 16 had stolen sitting there with its rotors spinning in wait. They pointed it out to Harper.

"Roger," Harper said over the phone and walked out of the cockpit. "Look, we're gonna fast rope down and secure that golf course!"

Upon hearing this Catipon went to the rear ramp and began setting up the fast rope.

"Copy all," Weathers responded with no other choice but to wait.

"Harper out!" he said, hung up, and then to the pilots, "Get us over the golf course and keep an eye for enemy targets in that nearest lodge!"

The pilots obeyed and positioned the bird over the golf course, lowering to an altitude of fifty feet, rotor wash buffering the nearby trees less than twenty feet from the rotors.

Catipon gave Harper a thumbs up, "We're good to go!"

"Once you get down, guns up and find cover!" Harper instructed his team as they readied to fast rope down. "We need to secure the nearest lodge so we can land the bird!"

Madi and Kate zipped down the rope. As Catipon grabbed the rope the pilots squinted through their night vision devices across the treetops.

The enemy Osprey was rising from the helipad.

"Fuck!" the co-pilot said.

"You guys gotta go right now!" the pilot screamed. "Enemy air inbound!"

"Move!" Harper shouted and pushed Catipon down the rope.

The enemy Osprey pilots opened up with their belly mounted minigun and at this range they couldn't miss.

Catipon fell on his ass below and looked up. Rounds slammed into the fuselage and worked their way down toward Harper.

"Oh, *fuck meee!*"

Harper took a step off the rear ramp, grabbed onto the rope as he fell and immediately started sliding down it, the rotor wash throwing him around him a ragdoll. Another burst of fire tore through the cockpit, killing the pilots and sent the helicopter falling from the sky to the left.

The fuel lines ignited, and the Osprey's starboard engine exploded midair just thirty feet above Harper's head. He was dragged away as the bird fell on a diagonal path, heading toward the forest surrounding the golf course. The Osprey's port side wing crashed into a tree and was torn off with a—*Shriek!*

"Jake!" Madi screamed, staring skyward at the falling helicopter.

Harper let go of the rope ten feet off the ground, hit the wet grass, and slid into a sand trap. The Osprey continued to descend into the trees, twisting apart and breaking trees in half until a second explosion occurred. It illuminated the forest and threw shrapnel in a sweeping arc across the gold course.

Catipon went to move toward the sand trap when the ground around him was strafed with machine gun fire, throwing up clumps of grass and dirt.

"Shit!"

He followed the others as they sprinted and slid to cover behind a low stone wall wrapping around the back porch of the Aspen lodge. Perched on a low hill, an extensive stone patio faced the golf course along with a pool and grilling area. A small pool house rested adjacent to the pool.

The Team members crouched down behind the patio as machine gun fire tore through the stone above them, throwing bits of it flying.

Catipon wiped the water from his face and said with frustration, "I'm so *over* being shot at."

No sooner had he said that when a grenade rolled off the patio and landed at his feet!

Kate looked up at Catipon like a deer in headlights.

Catipon grabbed the grenade and hurled it back over the patio. "Down!"

The grenade bounced against the pool house exploded, tearing apart the structure and slinging wooden siding in every direction.

In Birch, the Secret Service agents had observed the Osprey crash and the ensuing gun battle that had followed. Weathers was quickly informed.

"Fuck," he breathed.

Rifle fire emanated from outside as the agents engaged with the approaching enemy from the east.

Weathers grabbed Veronica and made for the door. "Madam President, we need to leave!"

Natalie followed and Fasswater went to grab his communications equipment when—

The far wall was rocked by an explosion, blowing the entire wall inward in a shower of smoke and splinters. The Secret Service agents immediately threw Veronica to the ground and shielded her. A second explosion detonated in the living room, ripping furniture apart and tossing several agents into walls and out of windows. The enemy had just hit them with several M203 fired 40 mm grenades.

The firefight raged outside as the Secret Service agents retreated into the lodge under the onslaught of gunfire. Dead agents littered the ground as the rogue Recon team ascended on the cabin.

Weathers groggily got up, calling for more agents as he helped Veronica stand. "You okay, ma'am?"

She nodded feebly, her face a wash of anger and pain.

An agent ran into the living room from outside and shouted, "They got us surrounded!"

He was torn to shreds by rifle fire from a nearby window and he dropped to the ground dead. Weathers guided Veronica out of the destroyed bedroom and to the narrow hallway that led to the living room. He counted four agents behind cover and shooting at the enemy outside.

Back in the bedroom, two enemy troops slowly approached the hole in the wall. Natalie was getting up when she heard them approach. She spotted a Remington 12 Gauge shotgun lying beside a downed agent and reached for it. One of the Recon men entered the lodge just as Natalie swung the barrel around and pulled the trigger.

Six feet away, the man was struck by a massive blow that tore his body apart and launched him back outside.

"Holy shit," Natalie breathed, looking down in awe at the shotgun.

Weathers saw they were slowly tightening the noose on their location and made his decision. He pushed open a nearby bathroom door with a small window that faced to the west, away from the encroaching enemy.

"Michael, get up!" Natalie shouted. "We gotta go!"

Fasswater crawled out of the bedroom, grabbed an agent's MP5 on the way and followed Natalie into the hallway.

"Madam President, time for you to leave," Weathers said grimly and gestured to the window.

The look he gave her said it all, he was going to stay.

"You two!" Weathers yelled to Fasswater and Natalie. "Come here!"

They crawled over while keeping an eye behind them for intruders. Weather handed Fasswater several magazines of MP5 ammunition. "I need you two get the president out of here, whatever it takes!"

Fasswater's mind whirled. How could two *analysts* be put in charge of the president's safety!

He nodded weakly. "Okay."

Weathers shoved them in the bathroom after Veronica and then thrust a flare gun into Fasswater's palm. "You see help, signal them. Now, go!"

He slammed the door shut and joined in the battle raging all around them. Natalie knocked the window out and shimmered her way through. She helped Veronica down and Fasswater leaped out, gun up and scanning around.

"Where to?" Natalie asked.

"The road!" Fasswater blurted.

Running from tree to tree away from the gunfire, the Recon members quickly entered the lodge after another minute of fighting and dispatched of the remaining Secret Service agents

"They're getting away!" a voice suddenly echoed out.

"Shit!" Fasswater cursed.

Gunfire followed a second later, tearing up the ground and trees around them.

"We can't stop!" Natalie yelled over from behind a tree with Veronica. "I'll cover you!"

Fasswater stepped around the tree and sprayed his submachine gun across the landscape. Natalie and the president moved behind him.

Fasswater heard a hollow *thump* whiz through the air. "Get down!"

But it was too late.

The grenade slammed into the side of a tree in front of Natalie and Veronica and detonated. Hit with the shockwave, Natalie yelped as she was thrown to the side and into a tree while Veronica was tossed backwards.

Gunfire chased Fasswater as he scrambled behind a tree and saw Veronica lying on the ground. "Fuck!"

He went out to get to her when overwhelming fire drove him further away. The Recon members quickly approached the president and dragged her away.

"No, no, no!" Fasswater whispered helplessly to himself. "Goddamnit!"

The Recon members retreated to the east, heading toward Aspen lodge, leaving Fasswater and Natalie behind.

Harper got up from the sand trap and surveyed the area around him. He spied a large group of individuals moving past the helicopter crash site toward the president's lodge. Getting up, Harper ran around the wreck and into the forest, approaching the group quietly and using the trees as cover. In the dim light of the burning fire behind him, Harper could see they were dragging a woman clearly against her will.

Cutthroat had the president.

They quickly entered the lodge from the front and disappeared from his view.

"Fucking hell."

Harper needed to do something and do something fast, before Cutthroat could kill her.

A branch snapped nearby.

Harper turned and raised his weapon to see a man raising his hands in surrender. "Whoa, don't shoot!"

Harper studied the man. Soaked and dressed in plain civilian clothes, the man was covered in dirt and had a MP5 slung to the side. He looked out of his element and not like a Secret Service agent or member of Cutthroat.

"Who are you?" Harper demanded.

"Michael Fasswater," he stammered nervously.

"Fasswater!" Harper said relived and lowered his weapon.

"Jake Harper?" Fasswater.

"The one and only, good to finally meet ya. Wish it was under better circumstances, but I need your help, they have the president."

"I know," Fasswater said and came over.

Fasswater had found Natalie on the ground passed out after the grenade strike and decided to leave her until he could bring back help. He had followed Cutthroat from a distance until he had come across Harper.

"What do you want me to do?"

Harper thought as he looked around. They couldn't wait for help to arrive and the rest of his team was pinned down on the golf course. His eyes caught sight of the two police cruisers parked a distance away with their lights still flashing.

Harper took Fasswater's MP5 and then noticed a flare gun in his waistband and took that too. "You a good driver?"

Veronica was roughly shoved through the lodge as she heard gunfire erupting from the den.

"What the hell do you people want!" she demanded as she struggled against the men's grasp.

They led her down a stairwell and into the basement. Rushing into a large room with a few steps leading down to a field of cubicles on one side and a glass walled conference room that acted as a Situation Room on the other side. Since the power was out, a few glowsticks were cracked and tossed on the ground to provide light.

Brookes stood before the conference table that was shoved to the side and smiled. "Ah, Madam President how nice of you to join us."

Remaining silent, Veronica was not easily intimidated and stood confidently as the members of Cutthroat surrounded her.

I'll cut right to it," Brookes continued and took out a satellite phone. "I need you to call off the reinforcements that are en route."

"Or what?" Veronica asked rhetorically. "You'll kill me?"

"Quite the opposite."

He snapped his fingers and several Recon men brought in a group of hostages who were thrown to their knees against the side wall. The president saw two Secret Service agents and a Marine covered in cuts and dirt, looking defeated, along with two civilian maintenance contractors who had been posted to the camp.

The last hostage to be brought in was the president's chief of staff, Stokes.

"Oliver!" the president gasped. She had last seen him moving with her to the helo pad before Cutthroat had attacked.

"Madam President," Stokes said and stopped.

The Cutthroat member buttstroked him in the kidney and he fell to the ground. Stokes shot an angry glance at Brookes.

"That's enough," Brookes said as Stokes was brought over and shoved to the floor with the other hostages.

Brookes stepped forward to within a foot of Veronica. "Make the call or I'll start shooting them."

A few tense seconds passed. Veronica looked over and one of her Secret Service men slowly shook his head.

"The United States does *not* negotiate with terrorists."

Brookes immediately drew his pistol and shot one of the civilian contractors in the head.

Veronica slapped Brookes. "You son of a bitch!"

Brookes waved off his men that stepped toward her, feeling the blood on his lip. "Pretty good for a politician."

He then backhanded her, hard, across the face and she stumbled backwards to the ground. "Don't make things difficult!"

Out on the golf course, The Team members managed to get a few bursts off, but were otherwise stuck in place. Cutthroat resisted from tossing more grenades, knowing now one could be thrown back at them.

"We can't stay here forever!" Kate urged.

"I know, I know!" Catipon responded and then looked around. "Where the fuck did Harper go!"

Harper, meanwhile, came to the side of the Aspen lodge, slung his rifle behind him and tucked the MP5 into his belt.

The edge of the patio extended past the lodge and formed a corner that now Harper looked up at. Stepping onto a small electrical box, he reached up for the patio's surface and pulled himself up. Standing on the edge of the patio, he reached higher for a windowsill. Hanging ten feet above the ground, he pushed off the patio and lunged for the lodge's roof. His foot slipped on the west stone surface, and he hung precariously by one hand.

"Shit!"

Muscles straining, Harper grabbed the roof's edge with his other hand and hauled himself up. Getting his upper body on the roof and breathing hard, Harper rolled his eyes and mumbled sarcastically to himself. "I had no idea Maryland could be this much fun."

Harper swung his legs over and laid still on the roof, glancing into the woods he had just came from. "Come on, Fasswater."

Fasswater ran up to the two police cruisers to find several dead sheriffs strewn about, laying in their own blood.

"What the—."

He was cut off by a shallow voice off to his left. "Fasswater . . . "

Lisa leaned against a tree clutching a bullet wound in her abdomen. Her skin was pale, and blood trickled out of her mouth.

Fasswater rushed over. "Ah, shit!"

He took off his jacket and pressed it against her wound. "Here, hold this! I'll be back."

Lisa smiled weakly. "You do what you gotta do. And Fasswater . . . "

"Yeah?"

"Pretty damn good for an analyst."

Fasswater jumped in a police cruiser and threw it in drive, tires spinning as he hit the gas and went off into the forest.

"Anybody got any bright ideas?" Madi called out as she ducked back behind cover.

Catipon eyed the patio. "I'll make a run for it, just cover me!"

"They'll shoot you in a second!" Kate interjected.

Catipon shrugged. "Maybe, maybe not!"

Police sirens suddenly sounded nearby, and they were getting closer. Red and blue spinning lights came around and out of the forest.

"Who the hell?" Catipon asked.

A police cruiser came speeding over a low mound and went soaring onto the gold course, sirens and lights blaring. Fasswater nearly lost control of the car as the vehicle went sliding across the slick surface. He turned the wheel back and gained a measure of control.

The Cutthroat men shifted their fire to the cruiser and lit it up with dozens of bullet sparks that cracked the bullet proof windows.

"Whoever it is, they're giving us an opportunity!" Madi yelled. "Let's move!"

The Team members moved to the right under the stonewall intent on flanking the Cutthroat unit.

Upon sight of the police car, the Recon members called for their helicopter support to come and take care of it. Turning on its nose mounted spotlight, the Osprey rolled forward over the treetops.

Harper got up and ran across the roof, looking for the skylight he saw earlier. Down below, he saw the rest of his team moving to the side of the patio and gave them a quick wave.

"What the hell is he doing up there!" Madi said to no one in particular.

Harper took out his MP5 and prepared to jump down through the glass when he was illuminated bright as day by the Osprey's spotlight as it hovered above. Raising his hand to shield his eyes, Harper glanced at the helicopter and then back down at the skylight.

"Enemy on the roof! Enemy on the roof by the skylight!" the pilot announced into his radio and to his fellow Cutthroat comrades.

Several men inside aimed their weapons to the ceiling by the skylight and fired.

"No fair!" Harper shouted and dived away as bullets shattered the glass and penetrated the roof beneath his feet. He rolled behind the cover of a chimney and glanced skyward. "Son of a bitch!"

The Osprey turned its attention to the police cruiser and unleashed it's minigun. Fasswater nearly missed the deadly burst that tore up large amounts of the golf course, throwing clumps of dirt and grass over the cracked windshield, obscuring his view.

Fasswater spun the wheel as the fire relentlessly chased him across the green and hastily searched for the car's windshield wipers.

"Got it!" he yelled and hit the wipers.

He brought the vehicle around and headed west, intending on driving into the forest for cover.

Harper watched the scene unfold from above and knew Fasswater had no chance of reaching cover before the minigun's fire found him. He glanced at his two weapons, no way he could cause any significant damage to the bird. Then he spotted the engine intakes on either side of the helicopter's wings.

A line of minigun fire forced Fasswater to turn the vehicle wide to the right, heading straight for the lodge. The fire finally found it's mark and tore a devasting series of holes in the engine and right side of the vehicle.

Harper appeared from behind the chimney with his flare gun outstretched before him. He took careful aim for the starboard side engine and fired.

At the same time, Fasswater had ducked to avoid the minigun's burst and lost control of the car. The cruiser barreled through the remains of the pool house at forty miles an hour and flew into the air.

The flare zoomed from the rooftop through the slashing rain.

Harper held his breath.

The projectile got caught in the engine intake and was sucked in.

Down below, the cruiser traveled diagonally across the pool and crashed into lodge's wide sliding glass doors.

The flare's charge went off in the engine, causing it to seize and came to a flaming stop. Alarms started going off in the cockpit as the pilots fought for control. A fire burned in the engine and ignited the fuel lines.

The starboard engine exploded and took half the wing with it. Completely out of control now, the Osprey started to rapidly descend into spinning circles.

Harper saw that it seemed to be coming straight for the lodge and said deadpan, "Of course."

Fasswater's foot remained on the gas as the cruiser tore into the lodge and tossed furniture and armed men aside. The cruiser ran into the stone fireplace and came to a jarring stop, directly below the skylight.

Harper took off in dead sprint for the skylight as the Osprey headed his way. He gripped both of his weapons in each hand. The Osprey was twenty feet away, the rotor wash smacking into Harper with a distinct-*whump-whump-whump.*

Harper took a bounding leap and fell through the skylight.

The Osprey impacted with the roof and traveled horizontally across it, missing Harper's head by a foot.

Harper landed firmly on top of the police cruiser as the Osprey scraped laterally along the roof, tearing off sheets of shingles and digging into the frame. The roof finally gave way to the Osprey's weight and collapsed.

Crashing through with speed, the Osprey fell through the roof at an angle and continued ripping apart the walls as it made its way to the front of the lodge. The Osprey, slowing down, got snagged by a support beam and flipped upside down, its port side rotors slashing their way down to the floor and slinging debris every which way. With a *bang!* — the port side wing punched a hole through the floor and drove down toward the basement, the rotors snapping and flying off!

A massive hole was torn in the ceiling of the conference room below as the destroyed Osprey wing came swinging in causing several glass panes to shatter behind Veronica lying on the floor. Brookes dived away as the broken and still spinning rotors blades came at him. Veronica screamed and frantically crawled backwards as the rotors spun toward her. She backed up to an intact glass pane and had nowhere else to go.

The rotors finally slowed and came to a stop at her feet.

She let out a sigh of relief.

Harper stood on the police car while in the crashed Osprey, fuel leaked and connected with several sparking wires.

The helicopter exploded, ripping through the destroyed lodge with flames and a field of debris. The entire front section of the lodge was blasted outward in a destructive shockwave and caused more of the roof to collapse. The force of the blast carried into the den and threw Harper from the cop car's roof and into a couch, knocking the couch over and spilling him across the floor.

In the basement, flaming debris split out across the floor.

Groaning in pain, Harper climbed over the couch in a daze and looked around for his weapons. Spotting his MP5, he grabbed it and stumbled toward the cop car. Smoke began to filter into the room from the fire at the front of the house, burning his eyes and clogging his nostrils.

Harper opened the driver side door and then fell to the floor, feeling the stiches in his hip rip apart and the warm blood drip down his leg.

Regaining his composure he said, "Fasswater, you good?"

"I think I broke my fucking arm." Fasswater coughed.

Harper managed to laugh as he reloaded his MP5. "You did good."

Gunfire broke the cop car windows above Harper and sent glass falling on him, one shard cutting a gash down his temple. Fasswater threw himself out onto the floor as bullets pinged all around him.

Harper shut one eye as blood flowed over it and poked his head around the corner, spotting men appearing from a hallway and moving toward the crashed car.

He wiped the blood from his eye and wiped it on his pant leg. "Just fucking great."

A few gunshots rang out and one of the Cutthroat men dropped to the floor

Harper whirled around to see Catipon moving into the lodge and take cover behind a desk. Madi and Kate were right behind him and took up similar positions, engaging with the Cutthroat unit. Gunfire went rampant and bits of couch stuffing went flying, gun smoke joining the smoke-filled air.

Harper yelled over to Catipon, "You got this? I gotta find the president!"

"Go!" Catipon shouted back and yanked the trigger. "We got this!"

Harper turned to Fasswater. "Where would they take the president?"

Fasswater thought as he clutched his throbbing arm. "The basement, maybe? The entrance to the bunker is there, but there's no power to open it!"

"I'll start there!" Harper said. "Stay here!"

Harper ran crouched over around the fireplace and out of the den, heading into the burning inferno slowly consuming the lodge.

Catipon dropped the nearest man standing by the hall entrance and moved cautiously toward it, Madi and Kate following closely behind.

"Where's Jake?" Madi asked.

Catipon poked his head into a side room and quickly cleared it. "Said he had to go find the president."

A burst of M240B machine gun fire suddenly tore down the hallway and the three split up, Catipon and Kate going right and Madi going left.

Sprinting, Catipon and Kate were chased by the line of fire as the shooter moved into the same room from further down the hall. The machine gun fire simply ripped through the wall over their heads as they ran for cover into the living room.

Catipon leaped over a couch as it was torn to shreds, stuffing shooting off into the air. Kate slid under a table and turned it over, bullets slicing through it a second later. Kate curled up into a ball as splinters rained down upon her.

Kate looked over at Catipon and shouted, "What the fuck do we do now!"

Catipon's mind raced through options and quickly deduced none of them were good. Suddenly the fire stopped, and they heard the man cursing.

The man's machine gun had a misfire, a common malfunction with the weapon.

Catipon looked up, a beaming smile across his face. "Ah-ha! Finally!"

He jumped to his feet and took aim, firing a single shot. The man, now with a hole in his forehead, fell to the floor.

Madi found herself in a dining room with a long table taking up the center. Half of the far wall had been blown out while the other half burned, giving Madi a look into the fire consuming the lodge.

She came to her feet only to come face to face with one of the men of Cutthroat.

Madi went to raise her rifle only for the man to grab it and wrench it from her grasp. She punched the man, hard, across the jaw. Before he could recover, Madi grabbed his weapon and brought it around his back, tightening the sling tight across his neck. The man gasped for air as Madi yanked back and fell onto the dining table.

"Ahhhhh!" Madi grunted in frustration.

The man slowly reached up and unclipped the sling, causing the weapon to fall and Madi to lose tension on the sling, falling back. "Shit!"

The man turned around and wrapped his hands around Madi's neck.

Gasping for air, Madi brought her legs up and quickly put him in a guillotine choke, enclosing one of his arms and putting pressure against his jugular vein. Madi reached for her foot and pulled down, adding significantly more pressure to the choke. In the orange glow, she caught a quick glimpse of several objects dangling from the man's vest in front of her face.

Face turning a shade of purple, the man drew his pistol and brought it down on Madi. A round went off just as Madi craned her head to the side and missed the bullet by an inch. She grabbed his wrist and pushed it to the side.

The man fired off more rounds in desperation that struck nothing but the wooden table. Madi squeezed harder when another member of the Recon unit entered the room from behind.

Madi's eyes widened.

She reached for the man's flak, released him from her choke, and kicked him away and into the wall. The newcomer shot at Madi as she rolled backwards and off the table, crashing into a pair of chairs and falling to the floor.

The man that Madi was choking fell to his knees and caught his breath. His comrade glanced down at him and noticed something amiss.

Madi hugged the floor, around her finger she held the pin to a M-67 fragmentation grenade.

The grenade on the man's chest exploded, tearing his head from his neck, and sending the second man flying into the wall, hit by a load of deadly shrapnel.

Madi looked up at the bloody carnage, wincing at the sight of the headless man. "Ouch."

33

FIRE RAGED ABOVE AND FIERY EMBERS DRIFTED DOWN AS BROOKES stormed toward Veronica, shoving aside the helicopter's rotor blade and dragged her by her hair in front of the hostages.

Tossing the satellite phone into her lap as she touched her red and bruised cheek, Brookes shoved the barrel of his Glock 45 against the head of one of the Secret Service Agents.

"Call off the reinforcement teams!" he spat. "Or I shoot him!"

Veronica repeated herself. "The United States does *not* negotiate with terrorists."

Brookes smiled. "Do you know what the definition of insanity is?"

She remained silent.

"Doing the same thing over and over again and expecting different results," Brookes chastised. "So, time to try something else."

Without so much as a second thought, Brookes aimed down at Veronica's leg and fired.

She screamed horribly.

"Motherfucker!" the Secret Service agent said and went to strike Brookes.

Brookes hit him over the head with his pistol and he was dragged back over to the wall.

Veronica started to hyperventilate as she clutched her calf, blood oozing all over her hands and her leg screaming in pain.

Brookes crouched down. "How about now?"

"You know," Veronica said through clenched teeth, "I've never been a huge fan on the death penalty, but for you, I'd make an exception."

He laughed. "I have a lot more bullets, but not so much when it comes to my patience."

Harper used his sleeve to wipe the blood running down his face as he moved down the hallway, firing consuming the far end and stretching to the ceiling above.

"Stairs, stairs, come on, where are you," Harper said to himself as he checked doorways.

A flaming piece of wood fell from above and he sidestepped it. His eyes fell upon a doorway with stairs leading down into darkness and he smiled. "Got ya."

Creeping down the stairs with his MP5 held out in front of him, he saw the ceiling was alive with fire.

A section of ceiling and wall suddenly collapsed on Harper, and he stumbled down the stairs in a panic, frantically patting the spot fires that burned on his clothes. Coming to a heap at the bottom of the stairs, Harper waved his sleeve around and snuffed the last fire out.

"Jesus Christ," he breathed as he got up and leaned against the wall for support, MP5 out in front. "Can't get a break, can I?"

Down the corridor in the conference room, the men of Cutthroat looked up at the sound caused by Harper tumbling down the stairs.

Brookes said to one of his men, "Go check that out."

Hugging the wall as he moved down the hallway toward unknown voices, Harper saw a large field of cubicles ahead on the left and the bright glow of fire on the right through a glass wall where several of the panes had shattered. He also spotted a sideways Osprey engine with broken rotors sticking out from a hole in the ceiling.

Without warning, a man stepped out six feet in front of him. Harper instantly fired his MP5, and the man's head and neck were torn to bloody shreds.

At the sound of gunfire, a second Cutthroat man jumped out of the conference room from further down, bringing up his rifle.

"Oh, shit!"

Harper rushed forward and grabbed the man he had just shot, dropping the MP5 for it to be caught by its sling.

Using the man has a shield, the body took the brunt of the rounds as Harper pushed him forward in front of the conference room by the front of his flak. He reached down and pulled the dead's man Glock 45 pistol from his holster and fired over his shoulder.

The man was struck fatally, and he fell backwards as Harper spotted two more Cutthroat members standing in the conference room through his peripherals who were rapidly orienting their weapons on him.

"Fuck!"

Harper dropped the human shield, pointed both MP5 and pistol toward the conference room and fired in their direction. Glass panes shattered as the two Cutthroat men fired back and Harper took off running past the Osprey wing, bullets chasing him.

With a yell, Harper leaped from the top of the steps and launched himself toward the nearest cubicle. A round grazed the back of his thigh as he turned upside midair. Bits of corkboard and sheets of papers exploded around Harper, and he rolled off a desk, landing roughly on the floor.

Brookes' remaining man standing over the hostages ceased firing and looked over at him. Pulling Veronica to her feet, Brookes stood behind her and placed his pistol against her cheek.

Harper sat up against the desk's filing cabinet, grimacing in pain as the bullet graze across his hamstring stung, blood seeping through his pants.

"Is that you buddy?" Brookes called out, taunting Harper. "Where you been? I had a feeling you might show up!"

Harper ejected the magazine from his MP5 to find it empty. Rolling his eyes, he called out, "Didn't know you were throwing a party!"

"Sorry, I would've invited you!" Brookes said. "But I didn't think you were into this sort of thing!"

Harper looked at two rounds in the Glock 45's magazine he had acquired. Along with the round in the chamber, he had three rounds left. "Damn, just my fucking luck."

He shouted back to Brookes, "You mean killing dirtbags like you? Like I killed your pal O'Neal? Invite must've gotten lost in the mail!"

Brookes grinned. "O'Neal was always a little blunt for my liking, but alas we did share the same end goal!"

Harper looked around the cubicle. "And what's that? Going down in history as a bunch of traitors?"

A computer and telephone along with an assortment of office supplies lined the desk, nothing of value stuck out to him.

"Harper!" Brookes said. "Do you even realize what is happening to this country?"

Harper didn't answer and let him continue.

"The politicians, the ones that have been in Congress for decades, are bleeding this country dry!" Brookes said angrily. "A third of Congress is over the age of 70 and they're making millions from insider trading while the average American pays almost thirty percent of their income in fucking taxes! The politicians distract the masses by diverting their attention to social issues, pitting black versus white, straight versus gay, and the left versus the right!"

"Last time, I checked the president wasn't a member of Congress!" Harper countered.

Brookes chuckled. "Very observant! She's just as much to blame, she's a puppet and she doesn't even realize it! She reinforces their rhetoric and spouts more bread and circus for the masses! It's only a matter of time before this country collapses just like the USSR did and when that happens, the fucking Chinese will take over as the world superpower!"

Harper remained silent.

"Come on, Harper! Do you really think the government cares about you? Look at Iraq and Afghanistan, wars that never should have been all in the name of greed and poor policies by incompetent leaders! How many friends did you lose over there? How many nineteen-year-olds did you see bleed out in front of you?"

That struck a chord with him.

Harper wasn't naïve or oblivious to the nation's blunders over the Global War On Terrorism. He had seen many good men die in at least half a dozen countries his politicians had sent him to, many of them his friends.

"You and I both took an oath! You remember that?" Harper argued. "That's the fucking job we both signed up for! It doesn't matter what the orders are, we follow them! You think *this* is the right way to resolve all that? To storm in here and murder the president!"

"Have you forgotten how this country was founded?" Brookes asked. "When in the course of human events, it becomes necessary for one people to dissolve the political bands which have connected them with another, and to assume among the powers of the earth, the separate and equal station to which the Laws of Nature and of Nature's God entitle them, a decent respect to the opinions of mankind requires that they should declare the causes which impel them to the separation. Sound familiar?"

Harper recognized it has the beginning of the US Declaration of Independence.

"It's written in our founding document!" Brookes said. "It couldn't be any clearer! Now is the time to say enough is enough and take a stand! So, what's it going to be, you with us or against us?"

Harper remained silent and Veronica waited tensely, unsure what his response was going to be.

"Look!" Harper called out. "I've had *one hell of a day*! Why don't we reschedule this whole thing for another time, uh? I'll come visit you in prison or something!"

"I'm disappointed, Harper, I figured you to be a true American. Enough games!" Brookes snapped. "Come out slowly with hands raised or I shoot the president."

Harper peeked around the corner. Brookes stood in the center of conference room with the president at gunpoint in front of him. The remaining Cutthroat man stood off to the left in front of the hostages, keeping an eye on them.

Harper searched for a way out of the situation that swung in his favor, but there wasn't any.

Find a way to win.

He took another glance at the office supplies on the desk and then paused. Raising an eyebrow in thought, an idea occurred to him.

"That can't work, can it?" he said quietly to himself. "Fuck it, let's try it."

"What's it going to be, Jake!"

A minute later, Harper tossed out the MP5. "Alright, I'm coming out!"

"Nice and slow!" Brookes reminded him.

Harper slowly stood and walked out of the cubicle; hands raised by his head. Veronica was shocked to see a man she had never met so beat up and willing to give himself up.

He was covered in black soot and his disheveled hair was filled with sand. Blood dripped down from a gash over his eye, down his face, and onto his shirt. More blood seeped from a wound in his hip and a cut across the back his leg. His shirt was charred in several spots and the sleeves were cuffed.

Brookes relaxed. "That wasn't so hard, was it?"

Harper favored his good leg as he limped forward toward the steps, waves of pain from his hip and leg shooting through him.

"You should've stayed home," Brookes said. "This whole thing is beyond you."

Harper eyed Brookes and the man by the hostages. All their attention was on him as he approached the steps and gauged the distance to be twenty feet.

Harper sniffed a laugh and hoppled up the first step. "You're right, Brookes, I should've stayed home."

He took a pause as he stepped up onto the next step.

"I've been shot *several* times today and shot *at* about a million fucking times."

Another pause to take the next step.

"I've blown up a couple dozen things, swam through a damned hurricane, been in *two* helicopter crashes, been dodging rockets all day, raced against airstrikes and vacuum bombs. I even fired a missile out of a *fucking submarine!*"

He came to the top, placed one foot on the final step, and laughed. "I should *definitely have* stayed home!"

Brookes smiled and then looked at his comrade. "Precisely, any last words?"

The man slowly pointed his rifle in Harper's direction, intent on firing at his target from the hip who was fifteen feet away.

Harper braced himself firmly on the balls of his feet. He continued his fit of laughter and paused to ask, "Any way I can get a raincheck for today?"

Harper continued to laugh deeply, laughing louder and louder. He moved his hands slowly inboard, closer to his head, praying he could keep them steady enough. He could hear his heart beating drums he was so nervous, his stomach tightening in anticipation and a bead of sweat rolling down his temple.

Veronica glanced nervously around, not sure what was going on.

Seemingly amused by an act of a man who was about to die, Brookes grinned and began to chuckle. The man by the hostages even smiled until Brookes gave him a nod and said, "So long, Harper."

Harper's laugh and smile instantly disappeared.

"Madam President, down!"

Harper moved fast.

His hand gripped the pistol that was taped to his back above his shoulder blade and he thrusted it forward!

Veronica was throwing herself to the floor as the man by the hostages went to pull the trigger.

Harper quickly took aim.

The man fired three rounds before Harper pulled the trigger in rapid succession, his first round missing.

Three bullets whizzed past Harper's head and he felt a searing flash of pain from his temple.

Harper's second bullet hit the man in the forehead, head snapping back in a spray of red.

Realizing he was still alive, Harper pivoted his shoulders and brought his pistol's sight onto Brookes, who was fighting against Veronica's movement and slow to bring up his weapon.

Harper looked down the pistol's slide and matched the sights on Brookes' head.

He calmly pulled the trigger.

The round passed over Veronica as she hit the floor.

Brooke's right eye was blown open as the round penetrated his skull. It exploded out of the back of his head, a spray of blood with bits of brain and skull fragments. His body went rigid, and his remaining eye rolled into the back of his head. After a second, he slowly toppled over and hit the floor, dead.

Harper let out a breath that he felt like he had been holding forever and reached up to touch the side of his head. A three-inch cut went across his temple and into his hairline from one of the bullets that had sailed dangerously close by.

With the Glock's slide locked to the rear and without looking, he brought the weapon up and coolly blew the whisp of smoke drifting out of the barrel. "*So long*, dickhead."

He looked at Veronica and the other hostages. They stared at him, amazed at what he had just done.

All Harper could do was give them an awkward slight nod.

34

A FEW HOURS LATER, TWILIGHT SPILLED OVER THE HORIZON. HURRI-
cane Taylor was long gone and only a few clouds in the sky remained.

Fasswater stood beside Natalie as she laid in a gurney behind an
ambulance getting ready to take her to the hospital. She had been diag-
nosed with a mild concussion, a dislocated shoulder, and two broken
ribs. With a fractured ulna bone, Fasswater had his arm in a sling. Lisa
had already been air-lifted to Georgetown University Hospital and was
now in stable condition.

"I'll come see you in the hospital when I can," Fasswater promised.

Natalie smiled. "I'd like that."

He paused, working up the courage. "And maybe, once you're out of
the hospital, we could, uh, maybe hang out or something like that? If
you want?"

"Are you asking me out on a date?" Natalie asked.

"I, umm . . . "

Before Fasswater could stammer out a response, Natalie grabbed his
hand. "Yes, I'd love to."

Fasswater exhaled a sigh of relief and smiled.

Crisis adverted.

Natalie was loaded into the ambulance and took off, leaving Fasswater alone. He walked away and took a long look around the compound, eyeing the damage and plethora of activity that was going on

Camp David was an absolute mess.

Burned and collapsed buildings, crashed helicopters and police cruisers, and the ground lay littered with debris and dead bodies.

Reinforcements had arrived shortly after the president exited the destroyed Aspen lodge and was whisked away to a secret location. More Secret Service agents and Marines arrived to secure the site. Detachments from the FBI, NCIS, and even the CIA showed up to begin the massive investigation that lay before them.

Firetrucks had come to put out the burning fires at multiple locations. Local police and country sheriffs secured the main road and assisted the paramedics, both civilian and military, with the casualties. Several had to be air-lifted from the golf course and several more were put in ambulances on the way to the hospital. The civilian contract companies went to work on restoring power to the camp.

Harper sat on the backsteps of an ambulance parked in between Aspen and their destroyed helicopter they had flown in on. A paramedic was stitching up the bullet graze on his thigh after already stitching the cut on his temple and re-stitching the wound on his hip.

"Looks like it hurts," Madi said from the side.

She had a blanket draped over her shoulders after being soaked in the rain earlier.

Harper smiled.

The paramedic wrapped up his work. "Should be good."

"Thanks."

Madi stepped forward as the paramedic left and stared at Harper, grinning.

Harper smiled and scooted over so Madi could take a seat next to him. She threw the blanket over him and two looked out over Camp David.

"That was close," she finally said.

Harper exhaled deeply and touched the bullet graze on his temple. "You can say that again. *I honestly* do not know how we're still alive."

The two broke out into laughter.

Harper leaned over and went to kiss her when a voice called out, "Ah, look at you two lovebirds!"

Harper closed his eyes in frustration. Madi giggled.

Catipon and Kate walked over.

"You're timing is impeccable," Harper said sarcastically.

Catipon smiled from ear to ear, hands out to the side. "That's what I'm known for."

The sound of an approaching Osprey thundered overhead and began to descend to the golf course in front of them. Turning their faces away from the rotor wash, Marines and sailors from the *Iwo Jima* exited the bird carrying medical supplies to assist in the casualty care. Henderson was the last to exit, spotted The Team members, and headed toward them.

Harper saw Fasswater walking around and called him over.

"What's up?" he asked.

Harper reached into his cargo pocket and handed him a satellite phone. "Got that off the guy leading things on the island, the one that got that call. See if you can find out who made it."

"You don't think it was Cutthroat?" Madi asked him.

"Just want to be sure."

"I'm on it," Fasswater said and walked off toward Birch.

"Quite some mess y'all made here," Henderson boomed as he neared.

They just nodded and shrugged, smiling devilishly.

Henderson took out a cigar, lit it, and took a puff. "Y'all did good here, your nation can't thank you enough and all that other bullshit."

The group laughed at his candidness.

Fasswater stepped into the shot-out lodge missing a wall and was relieved to see that the power had finally been restored. He found his equipment had been saved from extensive damage and plugged the satellite phone into the computer. With it in his possession, he was able to run a reverse trace on the last call he had received, a much faster and accurate process than what he was doing earlier.

Using the hundreds of cellphone towers on the East Coast, he nearly jumped out of his seat when the call's origin was pinpointed.

His jaw dropped. "Oh, shit!"

Fasswater transferred the data to a tablet and sprinted out of the lodge.

Elsewhere in the mass confusion of nearly a dozen agencies conducting site clean-up, a figure walked through the crowd with a set destination in mind.

"So, you're telling me you taped a gun to your back and it *worked!*" Catipon exclaimed.

Harper nodded and laughed. "Yep, sure did."

"You copied *Die Hard!*"

"Don't know what you're talking about," Harper lied, eyes wide as saucers.

"What's *Die Hard?*" Kate asked innocently.

Harper and Catipon turned their heads and glared at her.

"You're kidding me, right?" Catipon said.

Madi chimed in. "It's a band, right?"

Harper groaned and held his head in his hands, leaning playfully against her. "Not you too, you're killing me."

"Come on," Catipon said disapprovingly, shaking his head.

"Guys!" Fasswater interrupted them as run up out of breath.

Harper looked up, concerned. "What is it?"

"The call," Fasswater paused to catch his breath, "I just pinpointed the origin. It's here! It's here moving on Camp David!"

Harper jumped up. "Where?"

Catipon began scanning the crowd around them.

"Forty meters and moving this direction from the east."

Catipon and Kate fanned out, moving in that direction. Harper stood next to Fasswater and looked at his tablet.

"Thirty meters."

Catipon and Kate slowly stepped forward, looking at the mix of paramedics, cops, military personnel, and federal law enforcement agents. There were at least eighty individuals that they could see.

"I'm gonna need more than that!" Catipon called out.

"Can you call the phone?" Harper asked.

"Wait one," Fasswater replied and swiped at his tablet.

"See anything?" Catipon asked Kate.

"I don't see shit!" Kate jumped onto the hood of a police car and looked around.

"Should be ringing!" Fasswater announced. "Twenty meters!"

Harper's eyes darted through the crowd, scanning rapidly. Madi stood next to him and did the same.

Still, they couldn't hear the phone or spot the perpetrator.

"Come on, you son of a bitch," Catipon breathed.

"Ten meters."

Kate cocked her head. She spotted a man wearing a suit walking toward the ambulance pull his phone out. She heard it ringing.

"There!" she shouted and pointed.

The man was caught off guard, he dropped his phone and went for the gun in his waistband. He pulled it out and aimed it at Harper.

A look of confusion crossed Fasswater's voice. He knew him.

It was the president's chief of staff, Oliver Stokes.

Harper was frozen in place. He was defenseless and an easy target at this range. He shoved Fasswater to the side and threw his body in front of Madi's, falling to the ground.

"You ruined everything Jake Harper! True patriots will rise!"

Stokes went to pull the trigger when Catipon came in sprinting from the side!

Catipon thrust his arm out and struck the chief of staff with tremendous force in the throat. Stokes flipped backwards where he stood and landed on his stomach.

The gun clattered away and Catipon had him pinned to the ground with a knee in his back within seconds.

Rolling over, Harper opened his eyes and looked back.

"Don't say I never did anything for ya," Catipon said with a smirk.

Henderson flagged down a pair of FBI agents. "Arrest this man immediately for conspiring to kill the President of the United States."

Stokes was immediately detained and taken away, glaring at The Team members. "This is far from over! The revolution has just begun!"

Henderson followed the FBI agents to discuss further what had happened.

Still laying on the ground with a hand over his face, Harper waved him away and then gave him the finger. Madi propped herself up on an elbow and looked down at him. "You gonna stay down here all day?"

Harper looked at her with one eye open through his fingers. "I'm thinking about it."

Fasswater sat up and looked around, amazed by the events of the last day. "Wow."

Catipon walked over, looking down at Harper. They locked eyes and laughed. Harper held up his fist and Catipon gave him a quick fist bump.

"You guys are too cute," Kate kidded as she leaned on the bumper of a cop car nearby.

"I need a drink!" Catipon declared and walked toward Kate.

"Amen to that!" Harper agreed, pointing at him.

"I know a good place down in DC," Kate offered.

Harper looked up at Madi and wrapped his arms around her. "But first . . . "

He pulled her close and they locked lips. They continued to kiss as onlookers cast a glance of shock.

"Nothing to see here," Catipon said, waving the people on. "Keep on moving."

They kept kissing on the ground.

"Alright," Catipon said and grimaced. "Come on . . . I think you're good."

Kate leaned in close to Catipon. "So, about that date?"

Catipon flashed a grin. "What're you doing tomorrow night?"

Playing coy, she responded with, "Going on a date with this guy I know. What about the following day?"

Catipon ran with it. "Ah, can't, I'm busy. Got a date with this girl I know."

The two laughed.

Pulling back from her kiss, Madi looked down into Harper's piercing green eyes.

"Madison Oakley," he said with a smirk.

She grinned. "Jake Harper, can't wait to see what kind of trouble we find ourselves in next."

IN A PUBLIC CEREMONY IN THE WEST WING OF THE WHITE HOUSE, cameras flashed as Veronica had just finished awarding Cunningham, wearing his Dress Blues, the Bronze Star for heroic gallantry for his actions on Rose Island. She had just finished presenting the same award posthumously to Corporal Michaels for saving Cunningham at the expense of his own life, his family in attendance to receive it.

The military personnel who had been killed in action on Rose Island and Camp David had been given a full military burial at Arlington National Cemetery the previous week. The president had been in attendance, her first public appearance since the attack on Camp David. Harper and several other Team members watched from a distance and paid their respects.

The rogue Recon Unit 16 had been reported killed in a training exercise while with the 26th MEU in the Atlantic.

The clean-up of Rose Island had finished, the bodies of fallen Marines recovered and the island finding itself alone once again.

Intelligence agencies were hard at work trying to piece together what happened on the island and at Camp David and a month later, they had more questions than answers. Kate was assigned to coordinate with other agencies as the representative from The Team, although *they* didn't know that.

The attack on Camp David was severely downplayed in the press. It was reported that a small group of unidentified individuals acting as suicide bombers had infiltrated the compound and detonated explosives in multiple locations, accounting for the extreme damage and heavy loss of life.

White House Chief of Staff Oliver Stokes was said to have been arrested for selling government secrets to foreign nations and was quickly forgotten by the public. He now sat in a military prison while being interrogated by a horde of government agencies. So far, he had remained silent. It was theorized that he had orchestrated the attack on Camp David by Recon Unit 16.

The Rose Island story was spun as an uninhabited island, location unidentified, in the Atlantic Ocean in which foreign adversaries had occupied in order to plan attacks on America and other targets. A group of Marines from the 26th MEU had stumbled upon the island and were attacked. It was close to the truth, with only a few details reconstructed just how The Team liked to operate.

While The Team members were sworn to secrecy about what had happened on Rose Island and at Camp David, Cunningham, his Marines, and Sally were not. They had to attend several classified debriefings with multiple government agencies and signed numerous Non-Disclosure Agreements.

For their troubles, Sally received back pay of over twenty years as a cargo pilot and Cunningham was offered any posting he desired within the Marine Corps but elected to stay with his current unit.

After the awards ceremony, Veronica and Cunningham adjoined to the Oval Office for a private gathering where no press, presidential aids, or Secret Service agents were present.

Harper and his team, along with Henderson, Lisa, Fasswater, Natalie, and Sally, waited for them; all dressed formally in jackets and slacks for the men and dresses for the women.

Veronica gave a quick speech of thanks and gratitude to them and then chatted for about ten minutes before she had to attend to other duties. Fasswater couldn't stop repeating "This is so cool" as he stood gawking at the Oval Office.

Harper went over to Cunningham, shaking his head. "Congratulations, I know a medal doesn't change what happened, but I'm grateful for everything you did. I know we wouldn't have made it off that island without you and your Marines."

"I appreciate it," Cunningham said.

"Look," Harper continued. "If you're thinking of a career change, you just let me know. It'd be an honor to have you with us."

"And what exactly is *us*?" Cunningham asked with a smirk.

Harper grinned. "You'd have to find out for yourself."

Cunningham laughed. "Thanks man, I'll think about it."

On her way out, Veronica approached Harper. "I just want to personally thank you for saving my life. And if I'm being honest, Captain Brookes made some compelling arguments, and I wasn't sure if you would come to his side of viewing things."

"Like I said then, Madam President, we took an oath."

Veronica nodded. "An oath I also take very seriously, it's an honor to have men and women like you serving this country."

She departed and they were escorted by Secret Service agents to their vehicles in the building's underground parking garage. Lisa and Henderson walked with Harper as he threw his jacket over his shoulder.

"That plane you saw depart the island turned up in a vacant hangar in Nicaragua," Henderson said. "Serial numbers were removed and not a single trace of evidence has been found."

"We'll continue to look into O'Neal's known accomplices and grill Stokes," Lisa stated.

"We're missing something here," Harper said. "These guys had two separate objectives on the island and O'Neal had no idea about the other."

They came to their two SUV convoy and climbed in. Lisa turned before she got in and said to Harper, "By the way, I've been getting some troubling reports from our African office."

"Oh?"

"Sudan is up to something funny, so be prepared for a call."

Harper gave a quick salute and smiled. "Looking forward to it, ma'am."

The convoy left the garage as did several other Team members.

Fasswater and Natalie, now dating, went back to work at The Team's DC office, going through intelligence and looking for more wrongdoing in the world. Bexley joined them, since he was posted there as well.

Washington returned to his home office of Atlanta to continue planning his wedding with his fiancé. Stevens, still recovering from his wounds and undergoing physical therapy, would stay in the DC area until he was fit for duty. Chambers and Rider had been assigned to the Los Angeles office for the time being.

Cunningham was due back at Camp Lejeune where he was to catch a flight and join his battalion, currently located in the Mediterranean. Sally was going to travel out West, buy some land, and requalify for her pilot's license.

Harper watched them all go and walked over to his car to see Madi leaning against the hood, heels in hand and waiting for him.

"I suppose you wouldn't mind any updates I find during my investigation," Kate asked as she walked up behind him.

"I would love it," Harper said. "Think this thing is over?"

After it was all said and done, Harper had read the preliminary report compiled from all of those on the island. Strange lightning storms, GPSs and compass' not working, Fasswater's finding of the newspaper article claiming the island to haunted, Sally's mention of the man inside of concrete, the heavily decomposed body of the Marine, Martinez, Fasswater's and Natalie's meeting with a former KGB agent claiming teleportation experiments having taken place on the island, Henderson's account of what happened on Grenada in the 80's which the KGB agent seemingly verified, and the crazed pack of crocodiles acting like no other crocodiles on Earth.

None of it made a lick of sense to him, and he couldn't truly believe parts of it.

Kate shook her head. "Not a chance, I'm sure we'll see Rose Island pop up again."

Catipon pulled up next to them in his truck. The two had been going on several dates, but had yet to make anything official. She climbed in and Catipon gave Harper a wave. "Until time next, brother."

"See ya, guys," Harper smiled and waved.

Catipon drove away and out of the parking garage leaving only Harper and Madi left.

Forgetting Rose Island and loosening his tie as he approached, Harper was embraced by Madi and gave her a quick kiss. "Where to now?" she asked.

"I wanna show you this little beach town I know, just over the Chesapeake," he replied with a smile.

"I'm in."

Madi walked to the passenger side as Harper threw his jacket in the back then took a step back and admired his newly acquired car, a 1968 Ford Mustang. He had pulled a few strings and had it shipped back to the states from the island. Harper had had it completely restored and now ran perfectly, topped off with a coat of matte black paint.

Harper rolled his sleeves up, showing his tattoos, got in, and started it up. The engine purred and echoed loudly through the garage.

He looked over at Madi and grinned, "I drive, you get us there."

Madi beamed and Harper pulled out of the White House garage and onto Pennsylvania Avenue. Harper flipped through the radio as he drove alongside the National Mall, approaching the Lincoln Memorial while leaving the Washington Monument behind them.

He came to "You Might Think" by The Cars and turned the volume up as they headed out over the Potomac River.

Madi began to hum along and strum her fingers on the door.

Casting a glance over at her, Harper found himself smiling and tapped to the beat on the steering wheel.

The two started to sing along with the next verse.

Harper slapped the steering wheel and Madi danced around in her seat.

They burst out laughing at their attempts to sing and Harper thought to himself,

No place I'd rather be right now.

EPILOGUE

HUNTER CARLYLE STROLLED LEISURELY THROUGH A BUSY COLUMBIAN market square sporting a pair of sunglasses and dressed comfortable in slacks and a button-down shirt.

It had been a couple months since he had left Rose Island and now the black hair dye was gone to reveal blonde hair, the brown contact lenses removed to reveal blue eyes, and his beard was shaved off.

Stopping at an apple vendor, he asked in fluent Spanish, "How much?"

"Eight thousand pesos."

Carlyle pulled out the money and handed it to the lady, smiling. "Thank you."

He walked away, whistling a tune, and took a bite. Making his way down a set of stone steps, Carlyle pulled out a disposable flip phone and made a call.

"It's me," he began. "The survey of the island went as planned, I managed to confirm all of the grid coordinates you gave me. And besides Stokes, anyone who knew O'Neal has been taken care of."

Carlyle listened as he made his way through a park.

"Yes, I understand. I foresee our timetable being pushed to the right significantly due to *unforeseen* complications."

Taking another bite, Carlyle responded to a question. "I don't know what happened on the island . . . yes, he should've died. I believe the answer to that enigma lies with you, you hired me remember?"

Carlyle sidestepped a pair playful children running down the sidewalk. "Yes, everything else is falling into place as planned and I have trusted contacts making the necessary arrangements. Do you want me to take care of our *little* discrepancy then?"

"Ah, I see," Carlyle said as he approached a crosswalk. "Very well, it's your call."

The call ended and Carlyle finished eating his apple as he waited to cross the road. "Guess we haven't seen the last of you, Jake Harper."

Carlyle tossed the apple in a nearby trash can and crossed the road with the crowd, quickly disappearing.

www.ingramcontent.com/pod-product-compliance
Lightning Source LLC
Chambersburg PA
CBHW060427030726
47495CB00003B/771